"A fine genre-bender mixing sf, fant
New Age elements into a heady brew."

— Locus

THE CHRONICLES OF GALEN SWORD
BOOK THREE

"My clan wishes to hire you," the shifter growled.

"Whom do you wish me to capture?" the hunter asked.

"Orion. Clan Isis."

That confirmed it for the hunter. She had already met the vampire who was to be her prey, and at least two of his companions.

The worlds in which she hunted had finally come full circle. First at Delphi, then New York. Now, once again, she was on a collision course with someone whom she had tried all her life to avoid and forget.

Someone who could destroy her, and with her, the Ark.

The one warrior she always knew she would be forced one day to battle.

Galen Sword.

" ... an intellectual feast ... *Shifter* is a real page turner ... the suspense is heartstopping ... memorable and overpowering ... "
— *Science Fiction Research Association Newsletter*

"[*Shifter* is] one of the best fantasy novels of 1990."
— *Science Fiction Chronicle*

DARK HUNTER

THE CHRONICLES OF GALEN SWORD BOOK THREE

Also by Judith & Garfield Reeves-Stevens

Freefall (coming in 2004 from Pocket Books)
Quicksilver
Icefire

THE CHRONICLES OF GALEN SWORD
Book I: Shifter
Book II: Nightfeeder
Book III: Dark Hunter

STAR TREK
DEEP SPACE NINE: MILLENNIUM
Book I: The Fall of Terok Nor
Book II: The War of the Prophets
Book III: Inferno

Federation
Prime Directive
Memory Prime

ALIEN NATION
The Day of Descent

with William Shatner

STAR TREK: ODYSSEY
Book I: The Ashes of Eden
Book II: The Return
Book III: Avenger

STAR TREK: THE MIRROR UNIVERSE SAGA
Book I: Spectre
Book II: Dark Victory
Book III: Preserver

STAR TREK: TOTALITY
Book I: Captain's Peril
Book II: Captain's Blood

NON-FICTION
The Making of Star Trek: Deep Space Nine
The Art of Star Trek
Star Trek Phase II: The Lost Series
The Continuing Mission: A Tenth Anniversary Tribute to Star Trek: The Next Generation

BY GARFIELD REEVES-STEVENS
Dark Matter
Nighteyes
Children of the Shroud
Dreamland
Bloodshift

DARK HUNTER

THE CHRONICLES OF GALEN SWORD BOOK THREE

JUDITH & GARFIELD REEVES-STEVENS

BABBAGE PRESS • 2003

This is a work of fiction. All of the characters and events portrayed are either products of the authors' imaginations or are used fictitiously.

THE CHRONICLES OF GALEN SWORD #3: DARK HUNTER

Copyright ©1991 by Judith Reeves-Stevens and Garfield Reeves-Stevens.
New Material copyright©2003 by Softwind, Inc. All rights reserved.

Without limiting the rights under copyright reserved above, no part of this publication may be reproduced, stored into or introduced into a retrieval system, or transmitted, in any form or by any means (electronic, mechanical, photocopying, recording, or any other means now known or yet to be invented), without the prior written permission of both the copyright holder and the publisher.

Cover art, illustrations, and design copyright©2003 by Lydia C. Marano

ISBN: 1-930235-20-8
October, 2003

Babbage Press
8740 Penfield Avenue
Northridge, California 91324

www.babbagepress.com

Printed in the United States of America

*For everyone who wrote, phoned, e-mailed, or spoke to us over
the years, letting us know that Galen was not forgotten.*

*And for Lydia and Arthur
who brought him back.*

THE RETURN OF GALEN SWORD:
INTRODUCTION TO THE BABBAGE PRESS EDITIONS
OF THE FIRST THREE CHRONICLES

Over the years, we got used to it. The phone messages that would turn up on our answering service, left by people we'd never met, from British Columbia, or California, or Alaska, once even from Italy. The e-mails that came to us through addresses for other projects and books. The earnest inquiries made at conventions and signings, even at the United States Naval Academy. Always the same thing.

When's #3 coming out?

Over the years, our answer was always the same thing, too.

No idea.

We weren't stumped. No writers' block for us. We knew the very last line of the very last Galen book (#9) before we wrote the first line of the first Galen book, *Shifter*.

In fact, we had written the complete manuscript for the third Galen book, *Dark Hunter*, before the second, *Nightfeeder*, hit the stands. We got editorial notes for the third book, made a few tweaks and polishes, turned in a revised manuscript, and got paid in full by our publisher.

Then, just like every other Galen fan out there, we waited for *Dark*

i

Hunter's publication.

And we waited. And ...

Well, twelve years later, here we are.

What happened?

Life.

Sometime after Galen #2 was published, the science-fiction/fantasy market was deemed to go "soft." Our original publisher cut its list in half. And despite Galen #1 having sold reasonably well, and Galen #2 having sold better than #1, and foreign rights being sold to the U.K. and Italy, Galen #3, was on the wrong side of that 50/50 dividing line.

But we'd been paid for our *Dark Hunter* manuscript, so the publisher retained the right to publish it at some unspecified time in the future. Until then, it was theirs, not ours. They held the reprint rights to *Shifter* and *Nightfeeder*, too. End of story. Or, at least, of that particular chapter.

We moved on to other publishing projects, wrote many books and scripts, but never forgot Galen. About as frequently as we were asked by readers about when Galen #3 was coming out, we asked our literary agent when we could recover the rights to our series.

As it turned out, we were only two of many other writers whose rights to unpublished manuscripts had been similarly affected by the publisher's downsizing of its list. Our agent's answer to our question was a friendly, if world-weary, "Get in line."

So we did, and as the seasons passed and the universe unfolded, eventually we made it to the front of that line and many years after we had written *Dark Hunter*, its publication rights finally reverted to us, along with the reprint rights to the first two Galen books.

Which meant we were free to take all three books to another publisher.

Which meant, of course, that it was time for another complication to arise, one of our own making.

By this time, we were with a new publisher with whom we'd published *Star Trek* fiction and nonfiction, and we had written a new novel for them: *Icefire*. The book was different from anything we had written before — a military-themed technothriller — and it became a *Los Angeles Times* bestseller. Stephen King, whom we do not know

INTRODUCTION

personally but to whom we do light candles of thanks on a regular basis, called it, "The best suspense novel of its kind since *The Hunt for Red October.*" A year later, we wrote another novel in the same vein: *Quicksilver.* It was a *New York Times* bestseller. *Publishers Weekly* said the book "ensured our entry into the technothriller elite."

All that was the good news.

The bad news was that because of the success of our technothrillers, our new publisher no longer considered us science-fiction writers.

We said, Tell that to William Shatner and a couple of hundred thousand *Star Trek* fans.

Our new publisher said, Doesn't matter, your future is "mainstream" now; science fiction is in your past. However, we would like you to write these three *Deep Space Nine* novels for us ... We still haven't figured that one out.

The last delay in Galen's resurfacing arose in our other world — script writing — specifically on a television series we joined in its second season and continued with in its third: *Sir Arthur Conan Doyle's The Lost World*, an Indiana-Jones like adventure set in the 1920s on a lost plateau in South America. (Note: There's a special prize for whoever is first to find the Galen reference we planted in one of the *Lost World* episodes we scripted.) But finally, by Spring 2003, we had turned in all three Galen manuscripts to Galen's knight in shining armor: Babbage Press.

Which brings us to the new editions of the first two Chronicles of Galen Sword — *Shifter* and *Nightfeeder* — and the long-awaited first edition of the third — *Dark Hunter.*

Is *Dark Hunter* exactly the book we wrote twelve years ago? Mostly yes, a little bit no. The story is exactly the same. Same number of chapters. Virtually identical last chapter — and please don't read it until the end. But we do admit to cleaning up the language a bit, tweaking the action scenes, adding some details that could prove useful for the future Chronicles. (Future Chronicles?! See the Afterword in *Dark Hunter.*)

We undertook the same type of minor editing for the new editions of *Shifter* and *Nightfeeder* as well, but there are no major changes, and very few minor ones. For those who know the original editions by heart, we updated a few cultural references for new readers. Example:

iii

Ja'Nette now watches *South Park* instead of *Arsenio*. Rest assured, though, that Martin still remains a fan of Hulk Hogan because, after all, some things are timeless.

Oh, and we also corrected one tiny continuity error in the out-of-print version of *Nightfeeder* that no one but us seems to have noticed. (Happy hunting!)

So that's it.

No more delays.

The wait is over.

For everyone who's never heard of us or Galen, we hope this is the first of many times our paths will cross.

For everyone who's read our other work, and who's trying out Galen for the first time, we think you'll recognize our favorite themes, despite the presence of werewolves and vampires in the place of Navy pilots and Klingons.

And for those of you who shared Galen's first two adventures and have been anticipating his third for many years, welcome back.

We've missed Galen as much as you have.

And this time, we think, he's here to stay.

J&G
Toronto – Los Angeles
1988 – 2003

ONE

That's the problem with Hong Kong these days, the hunter thought, *too many humans.*

She had not expected the population of the city to have changed so greatly in the four years since she had last visited. Everywhere she looked she saw humans. Nothing but humans. Their presence in such numbers depressed her and made her long for the days when the crowded and twisted streets of the city had been filled with the life of both worlds, the First and the Second combined.

But the treaties had changed that intermingling of worlds. The British had agreed to turn over the colony at the end of their ninety-nine-year lease. The People's Republic of China had agreed to make Hong Kong a special economic zone to encourage international business and banking to remain. And, in exchange for continued and unrestricted access to Macao, the Clans Seyshen and Akhenaten had agreed to begin sealing the layer, to forever sever the Second World's Hong Kong from the First World's Western Isles. At word of that agreement, the adepts had begun to abandon the city, leaving it to humans. Only humans.

The hunter sighed, too long without sleep on her journey, jarred back and forth by the lurching of the rattling cab she rode in this early morning, and hemmed in by the crowded wooden buildings and signs that appeared to have grown in place rather than have been built. She longed for the tall trees and cool mists of Deep Forest. And the Ark.

She ran her fingers idly across the sleek surface of the black leather attaché case at her side, feeling the subtle power of the trollstone resonate within. *Soon,* she thought, *soon. When the transfer is complete I shall go home.* There was peace at home in the desert jungles of Australia. And, she hoped, answers for what she had seen two nights earlier in a refuse-strewn back alley in New York: a shifter halfling, a vampire, and —

The cab shuddered to a sudden stop with the metallic squeal of worn brake pads. A bright-red plastic banner proclaiming the year of the dragon swung violently from the rearview mirror. The driver rolled down his window halfway and launched a breathless verbal assault against the ancestors of the old woman who had stepped in front of his vehicle.

The hunter listened carefully, making sure that no signals or codewords concerning his foreign passenger were hidden in the driver's tirade. When she had hired him, well away from the limousines and immaculate cabs of the Mandarin Oriental Hotel, she had placed his Cantonese as coming from the northern regions, across the border. She had sought a driver without friends among the Second World police, or appetites that could be satisfied only by suppliers from the First World. A dark hunter could not risk exposure so close to the layer as yet not sealed.

The old woman whom the driver had insulted to the fifth generation trembled with indignant anger, the faded turquoise garment wrapped around her thin body fluttering, as if caught in a wind. She slammed her bony hand against the dull yellow hood of the cab, bouncing the metal panel against the loops of wire that held it in place. She screamed back at the driver in a hoarse, tobacco-thickened voice, cursing the animals from which he and his ancestors had sprung. All around the cab, interested passersby stopped to watch the altercation. Some eyes came to rest on the foreigner in the cab's back seat, their gaze, the hunter knew, drawn as much by the uncommon color of her red-gold hair as by the strangeness of her green-adapted eyes.

DARK HUNTER

The hunter leaned forward, placing her hand on the driver's shoulder, and said in Cantonese, "Do not attract attention. Let her pass."

The driver started like a frightened hare; his thin black moustache betrayed a nervous twitch. But his shock at his passenger's touch and accent lasted only an instant. The hunter could see he didn't care if he did attract attention. He didn't intend to let the old woman pass. He would lose too much face.

The driver tried to explain that to her. "The witch has cursed us both. She must learn her lesson and — " He shuddered and fell silent as the hunter touched his shoulder.

Despite the driver's protestations, the hunter knew the old woman was not a witch adept — she had no aura of substance. And if there were any lessons to be learned here, it would be the driver who would become the student.

Through the open window, the flow of the old woman's invective had not ceased or slowed. The hunter abandoned the voice of the familiar and the northern human accent no longer encased her words. "Drive on," she said, this time in the voice of the hunt.

She felt the driver's innate resistance ripple through the muscles of his shoulder. She was commanding him to go against a lifetime of social conditioning. The hunter was forced to speak a second time, rare when dealing with a human who was not in combat.

"Drive on," she repeated in the voice that had lured tigers to cages, shifters to silver, and nightfeeders to dawn.

Like them, the driver had no real choice. He jerked the taxi forward, ignoring the old woman's triumphant cackle.

The hunter settled back in the cab, one hand returning to the black case beside her, as the driver proceeded more slowly, reluctant to face additional humiliation if another confrontation with a pedestrian should take place. His cab crept cautiously through the shifting walls of humans that clogged the complex warren of narrow streets near what was left of the Walled City. He turned according to the hunter's directions until even he seemed confused and lost in a section of the ancient metropolis for which maps had never existed.

"Here," the hunter said at last.

3

The cab stopped instantly. The driver hunched over his steering wheel, peering into the darkly shadowed and twisting street for some clue to his location. Eventually, he became aware of the hunter's hand beside him, offering a thick roll of Hong Kong dollars.

The driver took the money from the hunter, avoiding direct contact with her hand. Even before counting it, he began to complain that it was not enough. But the hunter recognized the well-worn pattern to the words he spoke. She simply stared at him with the eyes of the forest until his voice died away and he looked down at the cash in his hands. The money was more than enough. It was also coated with an unnoticeable dusting of a First World dried resin to ensure that two hours from now he would no longer remember from whom he had received it.

The hunter stepped from the cab, one hand firmly locked on the handle of her attaché case, the other quickly adjusting the fitted jacket and trousers of her custom linen suit. She scanned the immediate area with the speed and exactness of a machine. There were twenty-two individuals watching her at this moment: eighteen on the street, one from an inset doorway seventeen feet away, and three from windows overhead. The hunter returned her attention to the man who hid in the doorway. His eyes were locked on the single strand of South Sea pearls she wore at the neck of the silk shirt concealing the dark fabric of her shadowsuit. The man's interest in her pearls was a typical human response, nothing to worry about.

The hunter stepped back from the cab and lowered her left arm with a small sideways twist, as if adjusting the cuff of her shirt sleeve. The handle of the sandcutter fell perfectly into her waiting fingers. She turned her back on the man in the doorway and began walking to the meeting place. Behind her, the cab slowly rolled off along a roadway that gave it only two feet of clearance on either side. When the cab had turned its first corner, the hunter heard the footsteps of the man from the doorway as he began to follow her.

In case the cab driver were to be questioned before the clouding effect of the resin took hold, the hunter had directed him to let her off a half-mile from her actual destination. In this part of the city, that half-mile could encompass a thousand different meeting points and a month of searching. Thus she did not expect to be followed because of anything the driver might do. But the man who had stared so fixedly at her necklace was another matter.

The hunter came to a passageway formed by the overhanging second floors of two buildings that had gradually come to lean against each other over decades of settling on their foundations. She glanced round again. Fourteen individuals were now watching her with limited degrees of interest. She stepped into the shadows of the passageway so that none of those observers could continue to see her.

She listened carefully, filtering out the sounds of market haggling and children crying, of an old truck's erratic engine and radios tuned to a dozen stations, to catch the footsteps of the man from the doorway as he quickened his pace. Seconds after she had, he stepped into the passageway, pausing in surprise, unable to see his prey against the small portal of sunlight at the passageway's end.

The hunter waited in pure stillness less than four feet away. When dealing with humans, her own skills were such that her shadowsuit and other weapons of deception were seldom needed.

"To your left," she said.

The man wheeled to his left. He was no more than twenty, wiry, edgy, and the loose white shirt he wore over loose dark trousers was stained with circles of sweat. He squinted nervously in the direction the hunter's voice had come from. One hand reached behind his back and, just as it reappeared with a knife in place, the hunter lifted her sandcutter. Its projecting blade was shaped like that of a hand adze — a flared petal of unpolished iron the size of a child's fist. But unlike an adze, designed to cut, the sandcutter's blade was thick and perforated with a thousand fine holes. The hunter squeezed the weapon's iron handle, feeling the wizard's script engraved there.

The man's knife clattered to the rough cobbled floor of the passageway and he sank to his knees, moaning in shock as he pressed both hands against the suddenly abraded skin of his face.

In a fluid move, the hunter bent down to scoop up the man's knife, then deftly tossed it so it was embedded in a wooden beam ten feet overhead, lost in darkness.

The man peered up at her through his bloody fingers and the hunter was able to judge the effectiveness of her aim. *Good,* she thought, *his eyes are untouched.* Then she walked calmly from the passageway and this time no one watched or followed her.

She arrived at the meeting place ten minutes later — a large abandoned building, blackened with age, which had once been a warehouse for a trading company that had dealt in First World artifacts. As such, it was far removed from the harbor and the transport lines that served the rest of the city. The shipments of the goods it had handled in its day would have passed through fardoors or the layer itself, making it a secure locale for the coming transfer.

The main entrance door was unlocked and the hunter pushed it open. Its window panes were plastered over with thick grime and the tatters of old posters. Inside the building, the musty air was heavy with a hundred years of stale incense ineffectively masking the sweat of generations of humans and adepts alike. Ahead, a wide hallway punctuated by closed doors caked with thick green paint was unlit and undisturbed. The hunter studied the patterns in the dust on the worn wooden floorboards. Then she walked forward, sandcutter held out, though she sensed no threat.

At the end of the hallway was a set of double doors. She pushed on them with her case and the two large panels swung so smoothly and silently open that the hunter knew there had been working crystals somewhere in the making of their hinges. The double doors closed just as quietly behind her.

"Welcome, Diandra."

Eric Hong waited for her, two hundred feet away, next to a large, silver car parked in the center of a cavernous, three-story space ringed by a wide balcony, ten feet up the unfinished walls. The hunter paused, waiting for her eyes to adjust to the room's odd lighting: broad shafts of thin, cold sunlight pierced the gloom in patterns determined by gaping cracks in the exposed ceiling rafters. Alternating slashes of light and dark painted the room's worn wooden floorboards. The dust-filled air glowed where the weak sunlight swam through it.

The hunter was wary. Her vision at two hundred feet was easily as sharp as any Second World hawk's, but even she could not see what or

DARK HUNTER

who might be waiting in the farthest corners or observing from the encircling balcony.

"We are quite secure," Hong called out to her, his voice echoing in the vast volume of empty space. He stepped forward into the shaft of light that cut across the lustrous hood of his Bentley. The hunter frowned. She never understood how Hong could believe he could travel inconspicuously through this part of the city in such a vehicle. His father had always chosen nondescript Korean sedans, old, dented, unwashed.

"Show your companions," the hunter said. Unlike Hong's, her voice did not reverberate. Indeed, with the voice she had chosen she knew Hong had heard her question as a mere rustle in his ear, like a leaf in the wind.

Hong raised his hand in a clumsy wave. Two figures moved forward from either side of the Bentley. One was a man, older than Hong, though not his father. He was dressed as Hong was, in a conservative dark suit with pale pinstriping. His hair was white, his face extravagantly lined, and despite the suit's exquisite construction, the hunter could see the irregular shape of a shoulder holster beneath his left arm.

The second figure was a woman, much younger, wearing a dark-blue windbreaker and jeans. There was no attempt to hide her purpose at the meeting. She carried an H&K, held ready. Her eyes were not on the hunter; they scanned the room ceaselessly.

The hunter felt reassured. Three humans and two Second World firearms would not be a problem. She walked to Hong and his car. She stopped by the Bentley's gleaming grill.

Hong smiled broadly at her. His teeth were the color of the pearls she wore, in striking contrast to the rich blackness of his hair, carelessly brushed over his forehead like a child's bangs. "In case you are wondering, I have another car outside the back entrance. Two cousins, both armed."

The hunter nodded; she had expected no less.

"And you?" Hong asked foolishly, as if he expected her to reveal the nature of her own defenses and backups. It was a question his father never would have asked. She was a hunter. She needed no backups. And as for defenses ...

7

Ignoring his question, the hunter held up her attaché case. Though not as cautious as his father had been, Hong *was* as single-minded. His avid eyes went to it instantly and he nodded excitedly to the white-haired man beside him. As he did so, the hunter saw the slight tremble that developed in one corner of his thin-lipped mouth and the sudden sheen of sweat that beaded his forehead. The hunter sighed imperceptibly. Hong's negotiations with her had been a lie — he had none of his father's sense of wonder in the treasures of the First World. He was not to be a middleman in the transaction nor did he have any other buyer waiting for the trollstone. Unlike the elder Hong who had confined himself to the role of dealer, the younger Hong was a user of his own goods.

Hong's white-haired companion slipped off his jacket, revealing the stark black straps of his shoulder holster against the white of his shirt. The gun he kept there was a long-barrelled Magnum, obviously chosen more for show than for the subtle use the nature of his employment demanded. The hunter was not impressed.

The man spread out his jacket on the hood of the Bentley. Then he stepped back to the rear passenger door and removed a second black-leather case, identical to the hunter's.

Hong gestured to the shimmering red silk lining of the jacket on the car. "So we don't scratch the paint," he explained.

The hunter placed her case on the jacket. The white-haired man laid the second case beside hers. The hunter waited. Hong nodded quickly at the man. As the older man's hands went to the case's combination lock and spun the wheels, the hunter saw that the nail of his right index finger was painted red. It was not a sign with which she was familiar. She studied his wrists, looking for a telltale mark of his Tong, but saw nothing.

The hunter glanced at Hong, wondering why he had decided to bring this man into his family's organization. Hong met her gaze but couldn't hold it. His face betrayed too much impatience. She sensed the rapid lessening of his control. His desire for what was in her case was threatening to overpower him. She doubted if they would have many more dealings with one another.

DARK HUNTER

With a crisp snap of both latches, the white-haired man opened the second case, revealing neatly banded stacks of American hundred-dollar bills. Hong nodded jerkily at the hunter's case. The hunter suddenly felt the need to count the money, though she had never encountered any significant irregularity within the Hong organization before. She read the truth in Hong's restless eyes — the money *was* short.

She considered her next action. To check the money in front of Hong would cause him to lose face. And if, as she suspected, the full 1.4 million dollars was not here, Hong's loss of honor would be intolerable. He would have no choice but to order his companions to kill her.

Without betraying her emotions or her conclusions, the hunter reached for her own case and swiftly thumbed the dials of its combination lock. Like Hong's case, the first combination disarmed the detonator for the thin sheets of plastic explosive sewn beneath the fine black-leather covering. By the time she had spun through to the second combination, which would release the latches, the hunter had already choreographed the actions she would take to neutralize the threat of Hong's two companions.

The hunter lifted the lid of her case and stepped back. The case held a block of dense, black foam plastic in whose center, tightly embedded in a diagonal cut-out section, rested a narrow metal cannister, a foot long, and four inches in diameter. To the right of the cannister, embedded in a much smaller depression, an irregularly-shaped yellow waiting crystal pulsed gently with inner light.

"Get rid of the crystal," Hong said nervously.

The hunter plucked the yellow crystal from the foam plastic, automatically feeling its heat to estimate how many uses still remained in it. Two customs officials had decided to look into her case this trip and the yellow crystal had faded rapidly under the strain of clouding their vision of what was inside.

Hong was already reaching for the cannister as the hunter slipped her hand inside her jacket and through the fold of her shirt to drop the yellow crystal into a pouch on her shadowsuit. In case she had to abandon her street clothes in the next few minutes, the crystal would remain with her. She heard the sharp intake of breath in both of Hong's

9

companions as her hand disappeared beneath her jacket. She heard the two begin to breathe again when her hand returned into view, empty of weapons. The hunter gave no indication she was aware their reaction was too extreme for what was, after all, a simple transfer between parties who had dealt together many times in the past. The hunter's own concentration increased.

But Hong had missed the moment of tension altogether. The hunter was appalled at how little attention he was paying to his surroundings. Instead, he was holding the cannister with trembling hands, struggling to twist off its lid.

"It's very fresh," the hunter cautioned, wondering why even an addict would risk exposing the trollstone to air when he had no chance of using it right away.

"How long ago?" Hong asked breathlessly.

The hunter had no need to check the Second World watch she wore only as decoration. "Forty-six hours." That was when she had been in the alley in New York, tracking a chittering, scuttling cadre of Close trolls outfitted in full green-black living armor as they surrounded their prey. But their three doomed victims had escaped because the Close trolls themselves had become her prey. Seconds after launching her attack, she had neutralized every troll and netted and gutted the cadre's focus leader to relieve it of its stone of influence. It would have been a routine hunt, except for the Close trolls' intended prey.

Of the trolls' three victims, the halfling had been the easiest to deal with. He had been no more than a child and, to him, the appearance of a dark hunter was as if a human infant suddenly faced a true monster crawling out from beneath a bed. But the young halfling had not been alone. There had been a nightfeeder as well.

A nightfeeder and a shifter halfling in common purpose! The hunter still could not comprehend how such a thing could be possible. It was as if the tigers and gazelles of the Ark consorted in Deep Forest, instead of living their eternal dance of predator and prey. Nor had the nightfeeder and the halfling been alone. They had been accompanied by another adept, late of Clan Pendragon — Galen Sword. Little Galen.

The hunter stepped back as Hong wrested the lid from the cannister and it clattered onto the warehouse floor, rolling off into the bands of light and shadow.

She watched in dismay as Hong eagerly tipped the cannister so that the thick clear sludge of the preserving fluid oozed out and stretched to the ground in a slow tendril. He held his shaking fingers under the solid flow of it, waiting for what must also emerge.

The thick preservation liquid congealed on the floor of the warehouse. A wrinkled brown shape resembling a swollen peach pit slipped from the mouth of the cannister into Hong's outstretched hand.

Hong seemed not to hear the soft wet noise the cannister made as it fell to the floor, landing with a dull thud in the puddled mound of preserving fluid. He moaned as he brought his hands together against the shape he held. He shivered as he tore at the thin, liquid-soaked paper that encased what lay within.

"The air will make it fade," the hunter warned. "In an hour, it will be worthless."

But Hong was beyond hearing her. Sighing greedily, he shook thin slivers of the wet wrapping paper from his fingers until the trollstone was revealed: a deep, translucent, red-black jelly-like organ that glowed with its own pale light.

Even if Hong were planning to use it himself, the hunter could not envisage how he could manage it. The stone of a Close troll — unlike the harder-to-obtain stone of a Far troll — could be used only once, and was worth nothing without the matching organ from a Far troll. So unless Hong had been reckless enough to bring a Far troll's sending stone here in his car, and unless one of his two companions was also his lover, the dripping trollstone he now clenched was useless.

The eyes of Hong's companions were rivetted on their employer and on the glistening object in his fist. The hunter doubted that the two humans had ever seen such a thing before. She doubted that they had ever worked for Eric Hong before. She wondered what could have driven him to abandon the others who had served his father so well and so long. Though, perhaps, the others had seen what he was becoming and it was they who had abandoned him.

The hunter no longer felt safe in the warehouse. The last few minutes were evidence the Hong organization was in disarray, led by an out-of-control addict. There would be opportunities for enemies to penetrate its defenses. She moved closer to the car and the case with the American currency. "You must get that to your buyer within minutes," she said, playing the false game that there was a buyer for the stone.

"There is no buyer," Hong muttered almost incoherently as he staggered toward the hunter. The hunter recognized the signs of imminent trollstone intoxication.

"Then you are wasting it." The hunter reached for the second case, on the alert for any sudden movement from either of Hong's two trans-fixed companions.

"No," Hong gasped. "I have a Far troll sending stone." His hand grasped the hunter's arm. She could feel the cold wetness of the preservation liquid soak into the sleeve of her jacket. "Use it with me, Diandra. Now."

The hunter stared into Hong's glittering eyes, glimpsing the coming insanity just beneath the surface, on the brink of breaking through. With two quick moves, she could shatter his arm. But for Hong's father's sake, if for no one else's, she felt she owed him one last chance for dignity.

"Release my arm."

"If you've not experienced love with a trollstone, you've not lived," Hong whispered. "The things we could share. Our thoughts, our hearts, our ... " He dared brush a finger along the hunter's cheek and a moment later, his shriek filled the warehouse as he stumbled back, clutching his broken arm to his chest. The glimmering trollstone pulsed on the filthy floor, half-coated with dust where it had fallen.

Hong's companions broke out of their stupor. The woman's rifle and the white-haired man's pistol both pointed at the hunter. They looked to their employer for direction.

"The transaction is over," she said. She remained unmoving.

"Not until you've swallowed this," Hong croaked, his face contorting with pain and frustration, reaching inside his jacket with his good hand to withdraw a narrow, finger-sized, green-black trollstone. "Not until you've shared the stones with me ... "

DARK HUNTER

It was apparent then to the hunter that Eric Hong had somehow learned what a few in the Second World had known for a long time: If two lovers each ingested the stone of influence from a Close cadre's focus leader and the sending stone from a Far troll, then the psychic link and mental empathy brought about would — for an unbearably exquisite few hours — artificially transcend all known human limits of bonding. One use of the paired organs was enough to forever understand that human senses were too primitive to see the true wonder of existence. Two, perhaps three uses, and the over-extended human mind would be irrevocably enslaved.

Hong lurched toward her again, his eyes clouded with the madness of a human in thrall to the byproducts of the First World ecology.

The hunter heard the two Second World firearms lock on her. Reassessed her options. Concluded nothing could save the three humans — she had been given no other choice. Felt the cool mist of Deep Forest pass through her and ground her in the serenity of her home. Prepared to withdraw her windblade and —

A single dot of red light appeared on Hong's forehead. For an instant, the hunter hesitated, wondering if it was a working-crystal implanted beneath his skin and what that would mean, what powers it might give Hong. Then three more dots appeared on his chest. The white-haired man and the woman whirled to face the shadows as red dots danced on them.

The hunter looked down at her own body. Saw more red dots. Realized what had happened even as an enormously-amplified voice blared through the warehouse.

"Hong Kong Police!" the voice boomed in a mainland dialect. "Put down your weapons. Do not touch the drugs or the money. Raise your hands. You are all under arrest."

Aiming lasers, the hunter thought with disgust. Not First World crystals but second-rate Second World trickery. She stepped back from the car and lifted her hands in the air. She felt the old wooden floorboards shake with the rumble of advancing police officers running through the warehouse. She heard the crash of the main doors behind her as more officers rushed into the huge room.

13

JUDITH & GARFIELD REEVES-STEVENS

That's the trouble with Hong Kong these days, she thought coolly as she readied herself to dispense with the unsuspecting police.

Too many humans.

TWO

Galen Sword, you have the right to remain silent ...

Sword rapped his bare fist against the bars of the holding cell, deep in the basement of a precinct building on the upper west side of Manhattan. He wasn't sure which precinct he was in. He had been transferred five times since his arrest for no reason that he could understand. But the words Detective Trank had said to him two days ago kept replaying endlessly in his mind.

If ya desire an attorney and cannot afford one ...

Sword had reacted badly when his old friend had delivered his regulation warning. Despite the two uniformed officers who had held Sword against the side of a police van outside the towering skyscraper of World Plaza, despite the handcuffs, the wailing sirens, the ripping away of the equipment from his vest, and the look of unbridled triumph on Melody Ko's face as the police had pounced on him, Sword still hadn't been able to keep himself from shouting out, "Can't afford one? Get real, Trank. You know I'm worth more than two hun — "

With that, one of the cops had slammed him face first against the side of the van. Even then Sword had still believed that Trank was a realist, that the detective understood that the words he was reading were a farce. That official rules and procedures didn't apply to people like Sword. Never had and never would.

Do y'unnerstand these rights as I have explained them to ya?

By this time, Sword, tasting blood in his mouth, had turned his head against the cool metal of the van's side, thinking, *Good thing Orion's not here, the temptation might be too much for him.* The last Sword had seen of the nightfeeder — the sole surviving vampire adept of Clan Isis — he had disappeared down an access shaft conveniently concealed within one of the massive support columns of World Plaza's main tower. For all Sword knew, most of New York's major buildings probably held similar secret passageways, constructed so the adepts of the First World could move through the Second World of humans without attracting attention.

Do ya unnerstand these rights, Galen?

Sword remembered blinking each time the spinning red light from a nearby fire truck swept across him, making it hard for him to see the rumpled form of the pudgy detective, let alone focus on him. The morning sun had still been low on the horizon, casting dark shadows in the canyons of the streets bordering Hell's Kitchen.

C'mon, kid. Don't make this any harder than it awreddy is, y'know?

"What exactly am I being arrested for?" Sword had finally managed to ask. He had waited impatiently for Trank to tell him that he was being arrested for the destruction of private property — or whatever it was that had been constructed beneath the glass pyramid that crowned the top floor of the World Plaza tower — though Sword didn't know how the police would have been able to so quickly link him to the monstrous explosion that had taken out that pyramid less than an hour ago, just as the sun had been rising. After all, they hadn't connected him with the events at the American Museum of Natural History, and that was almost two weeks —

Yer unner arrest for th' murder of Ja'Nette Conroy, a minor.

The exhaustion Sword had been trying to deny finally over-whelmed him. *Of course,* he thought, sagging against the van. Less than two hours before the World Plaza explosion, as he and Martin and Ko and Orion had moved up the hidden access-passage inside the Hell's Kitchen skyscraper, Forsyte had radioed them from the van: The Loft's security monitors showed Trank and Dr. Leah Bernstein had

DARK HUNTER

found the twelve-year-old's bloodied nylon jacket in one of the Sword Foundation vans.

At the time, fearing even the memory of what had happened to the youngest member of his team, Sword's thoughts had been focused on the other disaster for which he was also responsible — Kendall Marsh's being captured and spirited away by the vampires of Clan Tepesh and the shifters of Clan Arkady. While he could do nothing to bring Ja'Nette back, there was a possibility that Kennie was still alive, being held somewhere nearby.

Telling Ko and the others that he would deal with Bernstein and Trank and the police 'later,' Sword had concentrated on the task at hand: destroying the World Plaza mission-control set-up that had been constructed by wizards and shifters and vampires combining First World crystals and magic with Second World computers and technology.

But, inevitably, 'later' had arrived.

With a final *"Sorry, kid, y'know?,"* Trank had turned his back on Sword and walked over to join two female officers who were questioning Ko and Martin by an ambulance. The two cops at Sword's side had then grabbed him by his elbows and pushed him into the back of a patrol car. That had been the last that Sword had seen of both his reluctant assistant and the shifter halfling; his and their arraignments had been held separately.

For more than an hour, Sword had sat slumped in the back of the patrol car, not caring that he was easy prey for the blinding stream of *paparazzi* intent on capturing the tabloids' front pages. Neither ducking nor turning away from the flaring camera flashes, he had instead watched a motorcade of ambulances cautiously retrieving eight gore-smeared police officers and firefighters whose bodies were tangled up in thin, unbreakable threads of something resembling glistening spun glass that cut through whatever touched it. *Splinter wire,* Orion had called it. *Full of 'glitter'* — the adept term for anything made with the magic of crystals. Splinter wire was a First World defense that had been laid in place on the tower's topmost floor. Sword suspected the mysterious wire would dematerialize before suspicious Second World investigators could examine it. Like so much other evidence that could betray the First World's existence.

17

Wondering what other inexplicable artifacts had been left behind in the tower as First World creatures had fled via their teleportation portals called fardoors, Sword tightened his fingers around the bars of his holding cell and dreamed of his own escape. This world of humans was not his, either. No matter that he had been exiled from the First World at five years of age, stripped of his memories and his heritage. No matter that he had been raised as a human, impersonally and expensively brought up by hired and ever-changing strangers as the supposed orphan of a wealthy couple. No matter that those who had abandoned him had attempted to ease his lonely life with an enormous trust fund. The truth, as he had traumatically learned three years ago, was that he had his own identity. He was an adept of the First World, born first in his line, and consequently heir to the Victor of the Greater Clan Pendragon. The truth was that he had his own destiny: He must fight, first for his clan, and then ... and then ... Sword pressed his forehead against the cool metal bars. The truth was he didn't know. There was so much that he didn't know, so much that still was held back from him.

But he would know. Of that he was certain.

As far as the injustice of the past was concerned, he had made himself one vow he knew he would keep. Even if by some miracle, the elemental adept responsible for Sword's exile — Tomas Roth — and Roth's shifter consort — Morgana LaVey, the Victor of the Clan Arkady, had survived the World Plaza explosion after using the fardoor to reach the tower's glass pyramid, neither would find sanctuary in any world: the First World, the Second World, or the Shadow World that lay between them.

But for the present, he had already begun the long road back to reclaim what had been stolen from him and he would prevail. The old Sword was gone forever. He was no longer a dilettante investigator of the paranormal who could be manipulated by others. No longer a blind stumbler in the shadows selfishly seeking his own answers at the expense of others' needs that were equally urgent. What mattered to him now was that, less than two weeks ago, his inadvertent actions had decimated the life cycle of one clan. And less than two days ago, his deliberate actions had cost two clans a fardoor that could reach through space *and time.*

"Yo, Mr. Sword? You down here?"

An intermediate door clanged open and Sword looked up to see two sour-looking uniformed officers and a tall figure in a cashmere, camel-colored coat approaching his cell. The lock-up system in the precinct basement was positively medieval; one of the officers was actually juggling a large ring of keys in her hand.

"Mr. Sword," the cashmere-clad youth said, bobbing his head, "Billy Santini." He extended his hand through the bars.

Sword didn't reach out in return. Santini couldn't be much over twenty, yet wore a $2000 coat and two of the fingers on his extended hand flashed gold rings worth even more. Shifter script could be engraved inside one of those rings.

"Scarlatti, Holcroft & Chancellor," Santini said, hand still held out, as if the name would explain everything.

It did. Sword shook the youth's hand. Santini was from the law firm retained by the Sword Foundation. The officer with the key ring in her hand broke off the handshake as she jerked open Sword's cell door.

"You're a hard man to find, Mr. Sword." Santini stepped back, snapping up the collar of his coat, looking like a street hood in an incongruous and less-than-convincing disguise.

"Why did they keep moving me?" Sword asked as he exited his cell. He paid no attention to the two hostile officers. He had learned early on that the police would tell him nothing and he had been able to speak with Angela Scarlatti for only a few moments at his hurried arraignment this morning. The $5,000,000 bond set by the judge had taken even Scarlatti, Holcroft & Chancellor a few hours to arrange.

"Old trick, Mr. Sword. Trying to keep you in custody and away from your lawyers as long as they can so they can come up with more stuff to charge you with. Ms. Scarlatti's all over the D.A. like oil on a beach. She'll probably get a good lawsuit going for their denying you your civil rights in addition to — "

"Hey, wait just a minute." The female officer by the open door clamped her hand on Sword's shoulder as her male partner pushed past, into the holding cell.

"Is there a problem, officer?" Sword asked calmly as he turned around. As he did so, he slipped a hand with bloodied knuckles into a back pocket. Without his belt, his black jeans hung low on his hips. He'd lost more than a few pounds from his already lean frame during the past few frenzied weeks.

In Sword's cell, the male officer roughly shook the flaccid arm of Sword's erstwhile cellmate — a large, beefy individual by the name of 'Chopper,' with five inches and a hundred pounds on Sword. Sprawled on the cell's single metal bench, he lolled against the concrete cell wall, drool dribbling from his mouth, blood darkening the opening to one nostril.

The male officer addressed Sword accusingly. "What happened here?"

"He got tired of bothering me." Sword turned again to Santini. "Is it possible to start a suit for putting me into such a dangerous environment? Perhaps naming specific officers and going after them individually?"

The female officer waved her keyring at her partner who dropped Sword's cellmate's arm with a shrug. "Ah, forget it for now." She stared at Sword. "We'll be here when he comes back."

It took the next forty-five minutes for Sword to be processed for release on bail and to reclaim most of his personal effects. The rest — his shotgun and shells, explosive detonators, Starbrite Viewer, locator band, Mitsubishi transceiver, gas pistol, and miscellaneous other items of his vest equipment — were being held as evidence pending further charges related to the explosion at World Plaza. Sword made no protest. Last week he had signed Ko's purchase orders for new supplies. Even more effective ones, she had promised.

During the entire procedure, Billy Santini ostentatiously took careful notes of each delay and in monotone whispers brought Sword up to date with the disposition of the rest of his team. But Sword's first priority was finding out what had happened to Kendall Marsh, once lead anchor for *LiveEye News*, now — according to Martin, *golem* to the ancient vampire Manes Hel — Victor of Clan Tepesh. Marsh had left World Plaza on a paramedic's stretcher. Even though, mercifully, the blanket wrapped around her had left her face exposed, Sword had been pained to see that the reporter's usually radiant complexion had been

DARK HUNTER

mottled and chalky. The thick white bandage around her neck had concealed the signs of Manes Hel's feeding.

"Kendall Marsh is officially listed in serious but stable condition at Mercy General," Santini informed Sword.

"Has she come out of ... her coma?" There were few people Sword could tell about what had really occurred within the World Plaza pyramid. Not after what had happened to Marsh, after he had told her only part of what he had discovered in the past two weeks. The reporter had thought he was trying to rekindle their romance and had jumped at the chance to investigate what appeared to be a suspect blood bank preying on the poor and homeless. But knowing even that much had led to her seizure by the Tepesh. In the future, Sword was determined not to involve any other innocents. *Not after what had happened to Ja'Nette, and now Kennie.*

"Uh, they're not calling it a coma, Mr. Sword. But it's hard to get a lot of details 'cause her station's paying for the medical stuff."

"She's to have the best," Sword said. "The Foundation — "

Santini raised a hand to interrupt. "Ms. Scarlatti says the Sword Foundation can't make any offer to pay for Ms. Marsh's medical treatment. Could be construed as taking responsibility for whatever happened to her."

"I *am* responsible." Sword had a sudden feeling of *déjà vu*. Had he always been so dangerous to the people closest to him?

Santini shook his head vigorously. "No, no, no, Mr. Sword. That's definitely *not* the sort of thing you should be saying." The youth glanced quickly around the waiting area, checking for eavesdroppers. "And this isn't the place to be saying it anyway."

"What about Martin?" Sword said, moving on to the next of his worries.

Santini rolled his eyes and whistled. "Oh, yeah, that guy."

Sword prepared himself for the worst. Martin was a halfling, at the most sixteen or seventeen years of age, born of a human mother and shifter father with the attributes humans ascribed to werewolves. To make the situation even more precarious, Martin was a peculiarly wild and unpredictable teenager, to all intents and purposes raised by the proverbial wolves, and he was now in Sword's care.

Two days ago, when Sword had walked out of the World Plaza tower with Ko and Martin to see the waiting fire trucks and police cars, he had realized he had only a few seconds to give Martin his orders, and he had done so at once. "Do *exactly* what the police tell you to do, Martin, as if *I* were telling you what to do. Understand?"

Peering up at Sword from beneath improbably heavy-furred brows, Martin had leaned forward, his knuckles scraping the sidewalk. "Galen Sword mindtalk bluesuits?"

As happened far too often, Sword hadn't fully understood what Martin had said, so he had just kept on with his instructions. "Listen, Martin. This is very important. The ... bluesuits out there are going to want to take you away with them."

The tremor that passed through Martin alerted Sword that the halfling's hard-muscled body was tightening for battle. "Martin Galen Sword go home Loft. Martin stay Ja'Nette room. Martin Galen Sword find Martin father Astar powerful shifter." The unusually lengthy speech had been the halfling's direct challenge to Sword to honor the promises he had made.

Astar, a magnificent silver-furred shifter, had been coldblasted and used as a helpless, living generator to power the World Plaza fardoor that reached through space and time. But before Sword's team could complete their destruction of the Tepesh-Arkady installation and free Martin's father, Tepesh vampires and Arkady shifters had carried Astar's coldblasted form through a smaller fardoor to ... anywhere.

Sword's response to Martin's challenge had been swift and heartfelt. "Martin, I swear we'll find your father again."

And then, there on the sidewalk outside the World Plaza tower, Martin had formally held out a tight fist to Sword in the greeting of the First World, to acknowledge his allegiance as a fighter in Sword's cause, growling his name and Sword's clan in a guttural shifter tongue.

"*Myrch'ntin Pendragych.* Martin do what Galen Sword say do."

Almost instinctively, Sword had reached out to accept Martin's ritual offer of fealty. Brushing knuckles with the halfling, he'd kept his own fist less tightly bound.

DARK HUNTER

"Then go with the bluesuits, Martin, do what they tell you to do, don't fight any of them, and *no matter where they put you, don't use your blue power.*"

Martin's eyes had flickered uncertainly at the urgency of Sword's admonishment. "Where bluesuits put Martin?" he had asked suspiciously, but Sword had had no time to answer. Because, striding toward them, pointing directly and victoriously at Sword, Melody Ko chose that time to make her entrance. She was flanked by police officers.

Now, two days later, all too familiar with how plans rarely remained intact around Martin, Sword studied Santini. "Has there been any ... trouble with Martin?"

"Ah, not any real trouble," Santini said. "He, ah, put up a big fuss about being put in a cell and — "

"How big a 'fuss'?"

"He, ah, well, bit one or ... well, four guards. Martin bit four guards down at the Tombs when he was being booked." Santini smiled apologetically.

"How bad were the bites?" Sword wasn't smiling. He had seen Martin in action. The halfling could just as easily have ripped out the guards' throats.

"Scratches, really. Broken skin. A bit of blood. The police department is filing an injunction to get Martin some blood tests so, ah — "

Sword cut him off. "They want to make sure he doesn't have AIDS."

Santini nodded. "Well, that, yeah, but, ah, actually, rabies seemed to be the chief concern."

"Are they going ahead with the blood tests?" Sword asked.

Santini shook his head. "Ms. Scarlatti filed the usual blocking motions." He looked at Sword with interest. "*Would* the blood tests show anything, Mr. Sword?"

Yes, they would, Sword thought. *Too much.* One of the first tests Forsyte had run on the halfling after his capture was blood analysis of his genetic structure. Though Martin's squat and powerful shape was animalistic in nature, his incisors a bit too sharp and his ears a touch too pointed, there was really nothing in his outward appearance to specifically betray the teenager's unusual ancestry. But the results of Forsyte's electrophoresis of Martin's DNA had been clear and unequivocal —

23

whatever Martin was, he wasn't fully human. Sword could not risk another researcher making the same discovery.

"Have Angie withdraw her motions objecting to the blood tests," Sword said briskly. "But you, or someone else from the firm, is to stay with Martin's blood samples from the moment they're taken till the results of the tests are confirmed. Then I want the samples destroyed. And I only want tests done for communicable diseases. Nothing else."

Santini dutifully took more notes but then told Sword that he wasn't hopeful that Angela Scarlatti could arrange it all. The D.A.'s office was preparing to label Martin an indigent youth.

"*Indigent!* How can he be *indigent?* He works for the Sword Foundation. I take full responsibility for him. He's in my care."

Santini looked apologetic again. "But that's part of the problem. You see, Mr. Sword, you've been charged with the murder of a minor who was also in your care. Ms. Scarlatti doesn't think the court's going to *allow* you to take responsibility for another one just now."

Sword bit his lip in frustration, wondering if there was a legal system in the First World. "Where's Martin now?"

"Spofford Center, over in Brooklyn," Santini said. "The Youthful Offender Unit of Legal Aid is taking his case for now. Ms. Scarlatti thought it might be best to set up some, ah, distance between the two of you. Maybe make it easier for Martin to get released early."

Sword reached for Santini's notebook, flipped to a blank page, and then handed it back. "Take this down, Billy. There is to be *no* distance between Martin and me. Whatever the firm did for me I want done for him. Understand? I want him out, bloodtests or no bloodtests. Otherwise, he's liable to do more than just *bite* the next person who tries to make him do something he doesn't want to. Have you got that?"

Head down, Santini rapidly scribbled in his notebook.

"Now, what about Melody?" Sword asked, half-expecting Santini to tell him that Ko had bitten a few of her guards as well. Ever since his assistant had had her mysterious meeting with his brother, Brin, and Brin had used his healing blue power to repair the arm she'd broken in her fight with the vampire Orion, Ko had not been herself.

DARK HUNTER

Santini flipped back a few pages in his notebook. "You were at the arraignment, Mr. Sword. She refused representation by our firm and ... we haven't been able to put together anything on her since then."

"What are you telling me? That she's still being held?"

"Yes, sir," Santini said. "Actually," he added sombrely, "we're not sure if she's still being held as a suspect in the Conroy killing, or if she's agreed to turn State's evidence."

"State's evidence?" Sword repeated, thinking of the impossibility of that.

"Yeah, like the charges against her would be dropped in exchange for her testifying against ... well, the, ah, real killer."

Sword looked at Santini without giving the youth any further response. Even the idea of Melody Ko taking the stand and actually testifying against Ja'Nette's *real* killer was ludicrous. The child had had her throat ripped out by a werewolf, and not even Ko would be able to bring herself to baldly state that fact in a court of law.

"Pardon me for saying so, Mr. Sword, but you don't seem too concerned about what Ms. Ko might be up to." Santini looked concerned enough for the both of them.

"Whoever Ko's planning on testifying against, it won't be me," Sword said. He'd be happy to help her out of whatever hole she was illogically digging for herself, but he'd damned well wait until she asked him this time. "Any word from Adrian?"

"Dr. Forsyte, yeah." Santini didn't need to check his book for this answer. "He's set up in Ms. Ko's apartment in Greenwich, just as you directed. We've got four attendants with him, on shifts, round the clock."

Sword shook his head impatiently. He was already aware Ko had made significant changes in her apartment so that Forsyte and his computer-controlled wheelchair could function there, despite the fact that since his first run-in with adepts of the First World the physicist had been paralyzed, with the tantalizing and maddening exception of his eyes and two fingers of his left hand.

"But is he all right?" Sword demanded. Without the computer-driven technology of the Loft that allowed Forsyte to control his environ-

25

ment through eyeblinks and joystick commands, the brilliant scientist could fall prey to an understandable, yet near-suicidal depression.

"He seems okay for now," Santini said. "But he sure is one cranky guy. Only thing on his mind is getting back to your place in SoHo."

"And the police still have that closed off?"

Santini nodded. "Detective Trank's not letting anyone near it until the courts decide whether or not the search warrants cover the information in your computers."

At least that was one thing Sword knew he didn't need to worry about. True, the Loft's Cray-Hitachi Model II contained the complete record of his infrequent discoveries over the past three years — the werewolf in Greece, the out-of-place artifacts from the Australian outback — as well as the massive amount of new data he and his team had collected about the First World over the past few weeks, including the organization of the clans and the types of adepts who formed them. Fortunately, the workstation at Ko's apartment would give Forsyte more than enough access to the Loft's computer network to allow the scientist to encrypt all of its data to prevent any unauthorized visitors from accessing and reading it. There was a reason Sword had hired Forsyte's genius, even if the man did bear most of the blame for his own crippling predicament.

Sword and Santini had finally arrived at the last processing counter where any property of Sword's not required as evidence was released to him. Sword scooped up the few items which included his belt, which he now threaded quickly through the loops of his loose jeans. "Then that's everyone," he said, carefully sliding a heavy gold ring on his finger as he thought about what his next move should be: Martin's release, certainly. Then a trip to Mercy General to check on Kennie. And then, he fingered the gold ring ... his mind filling with a vivid picture of what he had seen two nights earlier in the alley near World Plaza. *A dark hunter,* Orion had called her. A red-gold-haired woman who wielded unknown, almost supernatural weapons, and whose closely-fit bodysuit camouflaged her against her surroundings. Emblazoned on the bodysuit's shoulder had been the stylized dragon and sword of Sword's clan — an exact copy, in fact, of the symbol engraved on the heavy gold ring his brother Brin had given him; their mother's ring, his brother said.

DARK HUNTER

And then Sword had realized he had seen the dark hunter once before. In Greece. The woman who had looked up at him in the blinding rainstorm that had swirled over the crumbling temple at Delphi, her strange eyes wide with recognition as her dying prey called out Sword's name. The one who had killed the werewolf he had sought for so long.

Martin had cringed and Orion had looked away as the dark hunter had approached Sword in the New York alley. Dripping with the entrails of the last Close troll she had gutted, the dark hunter had held out to him the creature's steaming liver — what Orion later told him was "the gift to the hunt master."

And then she had called him, 'Little Galen.' What his mother, and Tomas Roth, and his childhood friend, the werewolf Seth, had called him.

The questions that tumbled from Sword had been answered with only one word as the dark hunter disappeared into the night as quickly as she had vanished in Greece.

Softwind.

The tavern that was a meeting place between the Worlds.

Sword knew he *had* to return to Softwind, find the dark hunter again, and learn how —

"Ah, how about the cat, Mr. Sword?"

Sword tugged at his belt, tightened and fastened his belt buckle, momentarily confused. "'Bub?" he asked.

"White cat, maybe a Persian, lived at your SoHo place?"

'Bub! Sword thought. *The police have 'Bub!* "What happened to her? Where is she?"

"In the pound," Santini said. "Hasn't been there long enough for them to, ah, think about putting it to sleep or anything. Ms. Scarlatti, she didn't want to try and have it released until you were out and there was someone to look after it, you know."

Sword put both hands on Santini's shoulders and looked him straight in the eye. "This is *extremely* important, Billy. When animals are taken from a crime scene to the pound, do the staff take their personal belongings away from them the way the police do here?"

"Personal belongings? For a *cat*? You mean like ... a catnip mouse or some — "

27

Sword shook him roughly. "The *collar*, Billy. The cat's collar. Would the staff at the pound take her collar off?"

Santini tried to ease out of Sword's grip. "I ... I don't know, Mr. Sword. Jeez, is it valuable or something? Maybe they would if it looked expensive or something, but I don't know." As Sword released him, the youth stepped back and straightened his coat. "Like, I don't think the firm has ever represented a cat that's been arrested before."

Sword quickly pulled on his own coat — a long, black leather trenchcoat with several bad scrapes from the events at World Plaza. Whatever 'Bub was, she certainly wasn't a cat. The police charges against him could be ignored for months if need be. Even Martin could hold on for a few more hours. *As for Kennie* —

Sword pushed through the precinct's main doors, out to the black limousine that waited for them at the curb. "Let's go, Billy."

Right now, those things that belonged in the shadows had to remain in the shadows — until he was ready to pull them screaming and kicking into the full light of day.

Santini fell into step behind him, half running to keep up. "To the hospital, right?"

Sword shook his head grimly. "To the pound."

THREE

In the abandoned warehouse, swarmed by thirty-five members of the Hong Kong Police, fixed in the sights of twelve H&K MP5 submachine guns, ten Beretta pistols, and eight Mossberg automatic shotguns, lit with the crimson dots of aiming lasers, and only seconds away from arrest and exposure, the hunter closed her eyes and sought Deep Forest.

Within her sanctuary, she heard the far-off drumbeat of running feet — the heavy, hard-soled impact of the officers' boots, and the softer, cushioned footfalls of their undercover colleagues' athletic footgear. The overlapping sound formed a three-dimensional image in the hunter's mind, fixing the position and the vectors of the advancing human forces in the confines of the warehouse. She scented the sharp sweat of Second World excitement — and knew that each of her thirty-five adversaries was male. But there was no panic to her knowledge of their numbers, no sense of urgency in response to the swiftness of their approach. For the hunter, the mists of Deep Forest were cool and all-enveloping.

Human voices shouted out commands, but to the hunter it was as if the harsh sounds were muffled by the dense green leaves and twisting vines and thick trunks that surrounded her.

Then, secure in her grounding, the hunter took a perfect breath and the voices slowed, the swift thudding of the running footsteps

JUDITH & GARFIELD REEVES-STEVENS

dulled and became almost leisurely, as if the humans were striding through air thick as water.

She opened her eyes and prepared for the hunt. Eric Hong was a living statue before her, his broken arm clutched to his side. His one good hand still in motion, lifting the redblack dripping trollstone to his opening mouth as his eyes goggled at the presence of police.

Behind him, the white-haired man's right hand was sweeping gracefully, slowly, reaching for the shoulder-holstered Magnum even as the man's body glided in its arc toward the case of money on the hood of the Bentley.

On the long sleek car's other side, Hong's female companion was in the midst of throwing away her rifle in surrender. The weapon hung, suspended in air, as the young woman in the blue jacket and jeans swung her hands slowly up above her head.

The police swept closer, engulfing the silver Bentley like an encircling tide, guns held ready, feet skidding on the wooden floor, their slowly-working open mouths shouting commands to their intended quarry and into the small radios that some of them carried. The hunter listened carefully. But their talk was all of drugs and money. They had no knowledge of what had actually transpired. They had no idea of what they faced.

So with absolute concentration, absolute detachment, the hunter began to count her own heartbeats as she had been trained. All other action would come without conscious thought.

One. She brought her hands together above her head as she dropped forward to the floor, absorbing the impact of it along her right thigh, then hip and side and arm. Rolling once, tucking in her knees, she slid between the front tires of the Bentley and beneath its chassis. From deep in the forest, she heard the hammer of a shotgun fall.

Two. A shotgun shell exploded, and the wind of an angry expanding mass of shot rushed through the space the hunter had occupied a single heartbeat earlier. She heard the the pellets impact and enter the chest of the white-haired man before he had finished unholstering his gun. His grunt of surprise told her he had no time to feel pain. Her hand moved upward, splitting the breakaway seams of her silk shirt and linen jacket.

DARK HUNTER

One finger caught the gleaming strand of South Sea pearls at her throat and she felt the beads scatter, lost in the undergrowth.

Three. The echo of the shotgun blast reverberated through the warehouse. The scent of the white-haired man's blood filled the close air. The hunter's hands moved downward, and her linen trousers fell away, freeing her weapons and revealing her shadowsuit with its distinctive silver clansign on one shoulder.

Four. A white-uniformed officer dropped to his knees by the front of the Bentley and thrust his flashlight and the barrel of his rifle beneath the car, seeking the woman he had seen roll to safety. The flashlight's dust-filled beam reached out toward the hunter's shadowsuit. The hunter touched her clansign. For an instant, the entwined pattern of sword and dragon flared silver, gold, then white.

Five. The officer's eyes widened. The hunter remained motionless, invisible, hidden by the trees and the mysteries of her home. She held her sandcutter ready. The wizard's script that powered it pulsed beneath her fingers.

Six. The officer looked away, uncertain what he had seen, if anything, beneath the car. Unobserved and in a single movement, the hunter rolled out from the shelter of the Bentley, emerging by the fallen body of the white-haired man.

Seven. A police officer stood over the white-haired man, his foot poised to kick the Magnum out of the man's lifeless hand. The hunter stood up, touched the clansign on her shoulder, became visible. The officer jerked in astonishment, his mouth opening to shout for help, too late.

The hunter's windblade sang its freedom as it caressed flesh.

The front of the officer's white tunic fell apart to reveal the red slash of the sandcutter's kiss.

The hunter recognized the officer's long, drawn-out cry as one more of surprise than pain for her windblade had passed barely more than an eighth of an inch through his skin. But the way the human scrambled backward, clutching and clawing at the welling blood on his chest distracted the attention of his colleagues and gave the hunter as much of a diversion as if she had chosen to sever his head from his shoulders.

Eight. The hunter exhaled.

The discordant movements and sounds of the humans returned to normal as the hunter's senses reluctantly left the cool mists and soft songs of her home. She was in a distant corner of the warehouse, safe, her attention on the black case of American currency. Even if the full amount was not there, she would not be leaving without it — the Ark was not yet complete.

Human confusion still swirled around the Bentley. The scent of Second World excitement she had caught only seconds before had now given way to the ammonia-tinged stench of fear.

Several of the officers clustered around their mysteriously-wounded colleague who sat on the floor near the white-man's body, gasping for breath, while others questioned Hong's female companion, their familiar manner telling the hunter that the woman was one of their own — thus, a paid betrayer of Hong. Two other officers leaned over the silver car's sleek hood, ripping apart the hunter's empty case, running small handheld detectors over each surface, still searching for the telltale signature of the drugs they had obviously expected to find in the warehouse, and had not.

Then, if any in the warehouse still remembered that there had been another in their midst — the woman who had disappeared beneath the Bentley — they forgot as they turned, distracted, toward Eric Hong, as the Second World addict began to pay the price of his First World addiction.

The hunter watched from the shadows as four officers, all plainclothes, struggled to hold Hong's thrashing, writhing form against the floor; four officers whose faces were contorted in human fear and disbelief as they beheld one small example of the First World's power.

Hong's mouth frothed with red bubbles. What had once been the whites of his eyes now glowed red as if they were windows into his skull and showed a brain set on fire.

It had been. In his desperation, Hong had swallowed *both* organs, realizing that the police's presence would mean he could not hope to share the trollstones with the hunter or anyone else.

DARK HUNTER

Now, instead of sharing the complete union of two minds, Hong was at the mercy of his own, caught up in a loop of unrelenting feedback that could not end.

His body shuddered as if it shaken by a giant hand. Whatever hidden fears Hong's mind had repressed, they were now released, amplified hideously. Secret nightmares, festering doubts, all increasing exponentially at such a rate that —

Red light blazed from Hong's bulging eyes in what only the hunter knew was a grotesque parody of the fighting eyes of First World warrior adepts. His screams hit a note and a volume that none could imagine issuing from a human throat. The four officers fighting to hold Hong down relinquished their grip and clasped their hands to their ears.

Suddenly, Hong's horrific cries were silenced as a thick gout of acid bile choked him. The trollstones were merging in his gut.

For one terrible moment, Hong's spine arched inhumanly before his body collapsed, limp, to the floor. As soon as his Hong's back connected with the worn wooden floorboards, red light shone through his shirt at the level of his stomach. With cries of fear, the officers fell back.

Flames shot from Hong's torso and black oily smoke roiled upward, toward the pierced roof, blotting out the shafts of sunlight.

The hunter acted quickly as all human eyes fixed on Hong's pyre. Withdrawing the small grappling claw of her silver snare from her weapons' harness, she spoke to the claw in shiftertongue, the hidden-language of those who had constructed it.

No larger than a hawk's talons, the snare leapt from the hunter's hand and sped through the air toward the Bentley, trailing the fine silver mesh of its woven rope behind it like an afterimage of lightning. Obeying its wielder's commands, the snare swept around two officers who stood between it and its objective, then homed in on the officer who held the case with the hunter's money. Faster than the officer's human senses could follow, the snare sliced at his cheek enough to startle but not to scar. The grappling claw snatched the handle of the relinquished case before the case hit the floor and brought it back to the shadows and to the hunter.

33

By the time the police rushed to the corner of the warehouse into which they had seen the attaché case fly, there was no one and nothing there for them to find.

The hunter and the case were gone.

The hunt, for now, was over.

On the roof of a building directly next to the warehouse, the hunter moved easily through the shadows cast by the roof's wooden barricades, thinking as she often did that Second World architecture made little sense. The building's flimsy wooden structure, decades old, was obviously but a poor attempt to make the building look taller than it actually was.

She chose a corner relatively free from the shafts of direct sun that stabbed through cracks in the overhead, weathered barricades and crouched in it, certain of her shadowsuit's ability to mask her presence from any police who might think to check adjacent roofs.

For a moment she paused to listen to the sounds the winds brought to her, confirming that no one pursued her. In the foreground, she heard the police still milling in the warehouse, speaking into their radios. In the background, she heard the distinctive rise and fall of Hong Kong police-car sirens blending with the long deep wails of an ambulance and one — no, two — fire trucks. But the hunter was confident that human investigators would find the flame that had consumed Hong no match for the typical Second-World exothermic chemical reaction. Other than charring a small section of the wood beneath Hong's body, nothing else of Second World origin not in direct contact with the human would be damaged.

Reassured that the agitated humans below no longer pursued her, the hunter opened Hong's case of Second World currency. As she had suspected, several of the bundles that were to have been American hundred-dollar bills throughout actually contained twenties and even tens and fives in their inner sections. Instead of the $1.4 million dollars she had been promised, there was only eight hundred thousand and change.

With somewhat less of the serenity with which she had just escaped from thirty-five armed Hong Kong police, the hunter stowed seventy

DARK HUNTER

wrapped bundles of bills in the compression pockets of her shadowsuit. She would still feel the money's mass as she moved, but at least the awkward volume of it would be reduced to two dimensions.

With her money secured, the hunter closed Hong's now-empty case and wiped its outside surfaces free of any fingerprints. Then she used the singing edge of her windblade to peel back the case's black-leather covering and reveal the thin, putty-gray sheets of C4 explosive sandwiched in layers of clear crinkly plastic. First snapping the trigger wires leading from the combination lock, the hunter then wedged the flayed case into a gap in the overhead barricade where rain and sun would corrode the explosive in a matter of weeks. As an extra precaution, to ensure that no human would notice the case, she tucked beside it the yellow waiting crystal she had used to cloud the vision of the customs officials. By the time the yellow crystal's charge was finally expended, Hong's case would no longer be dangerous to anyone who might happen upon it. Though the hunter did not think much of humans, she knew they were more than Close trolls. Though not by much.

There was nothing more for her to do. Without indication of pursuit, there were many choices open to her. She could remain until nightfall when the chameleon weave of her shadowsuit would let her walk unseen and unheard through any cordon the police might erect around the warehouse. Or, she could leave now, in daylight, keeping to the roofs and shadowed passages of city buildings and streets until she arrived back at her hotel and a change of clothes. Or she could locate suitable garments in a nearby apartment and —

In frustration, the hunter snapped her windblade out to a brick topping a chimney flue forty feet distant. The corner of the gray-white stone slipped off like ice melting from a leaf and the blade swept back to its hilt before that falling corner struck the roof only two feet beneath it. The hunter hated choices. Life was so much simpler when an objective was clear and the path direct.

When word had reached her that Close trolls had been seen meeting with Tepesh vampires in Softwind, she had acted immediately since any Close-troll activity in the North Shore was fair game for a Dark Hunt. But she had not counted on being cheated by the human

35

dealer to whom she sold the stone. And now she was faced with a bill of her own that would come due in less than a cycle.

Sighing, she stood up, placed the windblade back against her hip where it fused to her leg like a sword-shaped sliver of silver. For a moment, the weapon wavered, losing definition, and then it disappeared, absorbed by the influence of her shadowsuit's fabric.

My main objective is *clear*, the hunter told herself. It always had been. The Ark above all. True, she was now short of the purchase price she had negotiated for the breeding colony of bonobo chimpanzees, but the eight hundred thousand she did have should be enough to keep her bid open. The Zaire poacher would be unlikely to know another buyer of endangered species who could smuggle herds of animals through fardoors.

The realization that she had not completely lost her chimps calmed the hunter. The remaining six hundred thousand dollars would not be an insurmountable obstacle. Another hunt, perhaps two, would suffice.

The proper choice was obvious. She must return to the Mandarin Oriental as quickly as possible and contact her service. And the fastest way back to the hotel was ...

The hunter remembered what Eric Hong had told her: He had two cousins waiting at the back entrance to the warehouse — they would have a car. And since the "back entrance" was the well-concealed end of a maze of tunnels running beneath the warehouse, there was a good chance that Hong's two cousins would still be there and that the police would not yet have found them. Human police, in her experience, had yet to learn how to conduct a proper hunt.

It was still early enough in the morning that the sun's shadows were long. Noiselessly and without disturbing the path of reflected light, the hunter kept to those shadows as she crossed from the rooftop of the building next to the warehouse to those of a pair of decaying buildings a quarter mile from the warehouse. Looking down between the buildings she detected a blind alley where a small white Nissan with Hong Kong plates was parked, its dented hood pointed toward the alley's entrance for quick leave-taking. The battered car was streaked with dirt and its left rear side-window was a sheet of clear plastic held in place by wide curling strips of thick silver tape. The hunter regarded the car and its disguise with approval. Apparently, Eric Hong had not replaced all those who had once served his father.

Silently, the hunter slid twenty feet to the alley's floor along the thin cord of her climbing wire, then twisted her hand so the climbing wire released its grip on the roof above and coiled back into place in the slender catapult tube she held.

She touched the clansign at her shoulder to change the weave of her shadowsuit, to release her from its influence.

Then, using her own trained stealth, she approached the car from behind. Two, unmoving silhouettes — Eric Hong's cousins — were visible through the car's filthy back window. The instant the hunter reached the driver's side of the car, she smelled blood but by then it was too late. There was movement behind her.

The hunter's reaction preceded thought. Though she preferred not to, she was prepared to kill humans if her safety and freedom demanded. She threw herself in front of the car, landing in a half-twist crouch, facing back toward her attacker. In the instant before landing, she withdrew her windblade from her leg and held the shimmering edge of it ready.

"Wrong choice of weapons," her attacker taunted her.

He had leapt to the roof of the car even as the hunter had propelled herself away from the vehicle, and now he perched there, above the front windshield, his grinning red-smeared face explaining both the scent of fresh blood and the lack of movement in the car's two occupants. The two women were dead, their throats mangled, glistening.

The breeze in the alley confirmed what the hunter already knew. Despite his appearance, the figure she faced was not human. It was in humanform. A shifter.

She was too close to her target. Her windblade would not be able to stretch out to the molecular-thinness that gave the blade its impossibly-sharp cutting edge.

The hunter released her blade anyway, counting on at least damaging the adept's molecularly-compressed flesh.

But her blade never touched the adept. Instead it wrapped itself once around an invisible sphere of influence that sprang up around the shifter, then retracted even faster than she had sent it forth. The hunter's hand and arm were struck by an explosive feedback charge from the interference between the blade's edge and the protective barrier.

The hunter dropped the windblade and it shattered like thin crystal on the alley cobblestones. Still on the car roof, the shifter held out one fist, opening it to reveal a large red working crystal and its shielding red sphere of influence.

"Wind against crystal?" the shifter said mockingly. "A traitor with your reputation should know better."

The hunter did know better, but she had brought no substanceless silver with her and nothing else would stop a shifter. The hunter scanned her surroundings, scented the air, listened for sounds, detected no others nearby. She touched the clansign on her shadowsuit.

"Don't leave yet," the shifter said quickly, as if reading her mind. "I'm not like you. I don't work for the humans."

The hunter ignored the insult. She didn't work for humans either. If anything, they worked for her. Or, at least, she used them. "Then what are you doing here?"

"I have been looking for you," the shifter said, licking the blood from his face with an overlong tongue. "Why not give the suit a rest? I only want to talk." He sat down on the car's roof, casually dangling his legs over the windshield; his hairy feet were bare.

The hunter paused for a moment. Any escape route she might take from the alley would involve moving into sunlight so her suit's chameleon fabric wouldn't offer sufficient protection from a shifter in pursuit. She decided to save its charge.

The shifter yawned, revealing too many sharp white teeth, as the hunter's shadowsuit lost its influence over her.

"What is your clan?" the hunter asked. The adept's humanform was small for a shifter, perhaps five-and-half-feet tall. But with his enormous barrel chest, thick beard and bushy hair, the hunter could see him shifting into something on the order of a *Selenarctos thibetanus*, or some related species of bear. In humanform, he wore nondescript brown slacks and a gray sweatshirt. If he had been wearing shoes, he might have passed unremarked amongst human on the streets of Hong Kong.

"Arkady," the shifter said. "My open name is Saul Calder."

The hunter's growing curiosity was replacing her desire to leave. "I am —"

"I know," the shifter interrupted. "Diandra, adept of no clan. Dark hunter." He rolled the working red crystal in his fingers, as if to remind her that he still possessed defenses against the weapons she carried. "I told you, I've been looking for you."

He stopped speaking then, daring her to ask questions. But knowing his purpose, the hunter would not comply.

Saul Calder stopped rolling the crystal. "Don't you want to know why?"

"If you want me to know, then you will tell me." As far as the hunter was concerned, there was only one reason why a shifter from Arkady would come looking for her: The incident at Delphi. Revenge for what she had done to them and to their chances of victory over the Seyshen. She only wondered why it had taken them so long to seek her out.

It had taken the hunter only one week after killing the shifter at the ruins of the ancient Greek temple to realize that her Dark Hunt had been set up by the Seyshen. And it had been her investigations into why Little Galen had been at the same temple at the same time — searching for the same shifter — that had eventually led her to the conspiracy to bring Sword back into the affairs of the First World again.

"My clan wishes to hire you," the shifter said.

The hunter said nothing, puzzled.

"Well?" the shifter demanded, when the hunter did not respond as required by her calling.

"This is irregular," the hunter said. She had never been employed by a *Greater* Clan for the purposes of destroying another adept. At least, not until Delphi. And she had not then known the Seyshen were behind her assignment. "You must know that a Dark Hunt requires that —"

The shifter cut her off again.

"No, *you* misunderstand. This is not to be a Dark Hunt. We want you to *capture* someone of the Second World, not destroy him."

The hunter suddenly wondered if Arkady did *not* know who was responsible for what had happened at Delphi, if Saul Calder was about to ask her to capture herself for Arkady. "Who?" she asked, thinking again of the missing six hundred thousand Second World dollars, "and on which side of the layer?"

But the shifter wasn't about to give out free information. "Are you ... available?"

The hunter nodded and began the customary negotiations. "The softwind says that Arkady has fallen on hard times in just the past cycle." She didn't bother to add that the softwind also said it was because of Little Galen that Arkady had been devastated before the long-awaited war with Clan Seyshen had even begun.

"Arkady has many friends," the shifter said firmly.

"Perhaps the Clan Tepesh?"

"Perhaps."

"The softwind says that Tepesh, too, has had recent setbacks."

"A slight tactical inconvenience on the North Shore," the shifter retorted. "Manes Hel remains Victor. Her clan retains considerable resources elsewhere."

"Then why ask me to capture a human for them? Surely vampires have many advantages in the Second World."

Calder closed his fist around his working red crystal. "You misunderstand again. We do not want you to capture a human for us, we want you to capture an adept."

"All the more reason for me to ask how Arkady intends to pay me. To capture an adept will take even more effort and resources than to capture a human, to say nothing of — "

"Six thousand whole," the shifter said, "plus an additional six thousand in three."

The hunter was too startled to respond.

"And," the shifter added, "we'll throw in a new windblade." He glanced at the metallic fragments still evaporating on the alley cobblestones. "Clan Skye construction, was it not?"

The hunter's mind reeled at the thought of the First World fortune that Saul Calder had just offered her. A *single* working crystal with a *six thousand* charge. That was larger than the Crystal of the Change Arkady that powered the clan's controlled shapeshifting. *And* an additional three crystals totalling six thousand more charges. That meant that at worst she would get three separate two thousands. *And* a new windblade.

The hunter whistled soundlessly. "Who do you want me to capture? The Tarl David himself?"

The shifter's face darkened at the mention of his clan's first Victor. "No sacrilege, clanless traitor," he growled warningly. "That is Arkady's offer. Do you accept?"

"Who is it?," the hunter asked again.

"Do you accept?"

The hunter could only see one pitfall. "I don't capture Seyshen," she said. "And to kill one would cost even more than your offer." *A great deal more*, she added to herself. As far as she knew, no dark hunter had ever killed a Greater Seyshen and survived.

"An *adept*," Calder said. "Not an oozing blob of primordial slime too stupid to follow the moon. Do you accept?"

"*Plus* six hundred thousand dollars." The hunter had seen her opportunity. "United States currency. Hundreds. Untraceable."

The shifter massaged his thick beard with one short-fingered, powerful hand. "You mean, enchanted bills? Wealth attractors?"

"No glitter. Cash. Second World all the way."

The Arkady shifter blinked a few times. "Six hundred thousand? Nothing more?"

"Plus the crystals and the windblade."

Calder nodded, then rolled forward over the hood of the car and somersaulted to his feet directly in front of the hunter who knew better than to flinch.

"By the moon?" the adept asked, holding out his hairy hand in the loosest fist he could make.

"*Sa leel*," the hunter agreed. She made a tight fist to show that she was a fighter in his cause, then brushed her knuckles against his. The chimpanzees would finally be hers, and she would possess a fortune in crystals for Deep Forest. "Now, whom do you wish me to capture? Of what Clan?"

"Orion," the shifter said. "Clan Isis."

The hunter frowned. "But Isis is dust. Ever since Wormwood."

"Orion is the last of Isis."

It could *be done,* the hunter thought, her mind already alert to the possibilities available to her in capturing a vampire. Though she didn't know why anyone, including a dark hunter, would risk it. *Except for me,* she thought. *Except for the Ark.*

Calder watched her closely. "You *agreed.*"

"Do you know his location?" the hunter asked. The idea of refusing the hunt had never occurred to her.

"The last sighting, he was moving between the layer in the North Shore. He has companions there, in the Second World."

The hunter nodded her head. The odds of the hunt were looking better. She had been in New York only two days ago, she was familiar with it, and hunting a vampire would be much easier in the Second World than the First. "What is the nature of his companions?" she asked. She tried to remember if Orion were the vampire she had heard had worked out some arrangement with the Seyshen, of all beings, for protection.

"His companions are useless," Calder said bitterly. "Nothing more than humans for the most part. Substanceless, cowardly."

The hunter heard the edge in Calder's voice as he spoke of Orion's human companions. She wondered if he had faced them before and somehow lost.

"And the least part?" the hunter asked. "Any adepts among his companions?"

"One," Calder said. "Even more inconsequential."

The hunter watched the shifter expectantly.

"A shifter halfling."

The hunter's body reacted as if her senses had picked up an impending attack before her conscious mind had had time to process their signals. "Active in New York?" she asked.

"The North Shore," the shifter agreed with a nod, "beyond the layer."

"And what about the humans with him? Are they his *golems?*"

"They are nothing." Calder's small eyes were dark with unexplained torment. "A coldblasted male. A shirley of a female, and ... a substanceless adept, no better than a human."

DARK HUNTER

And that confirmed it for the hunter. She had already met the vampire who was to be her prey, and at least two of his companions — the shifter halfling and the substanceless adept — as the three of them had cowered in a New York alley during her hunt of the Close trolls.

The worlds in which she hunted had finally come full circle. First at Delphi, then New York. Now, once again, she was on a collision course with someone whom she had tried all her life to avoid and forget.

Someone who could destroy her, and with her, the Ark.

The one warrior she always knew she would be forced one day to battle.

Her brother.

Galen Sword.

FOUR

As soon as the limousine door opened on his side, Sword heard the howling. Instantly his mind flew back to the Ceremony of the Change Arkady. Just Ko, himself, and Martin confronting five hundred shifters in the throes of transformation into nightmarish creatures he had never seen, could never have imagined .

But this was midtown, midafternoon Manhattan, not the Arkady Pit of the Change, the cave that lay somewhere beneath the American Museum of Natural History. The shifters who roamed New York's surface streets by night, were hidden by day, protected in their enclaves by Keepers. There had to be another reason for the uproar. Unless, of course, he had arrived too late.

"Whoa, sounds like the inmates are rioting." Billy Santini stood beside Sword at the base of the worn stone steps of the City Pound. He snapped up the collar of his coat again and shifted one shoulder forward as if straightening a concealed holster. Sword decided that all Santini needed to complete the stereotypical image he was building was a toothpick in one corner of his mouth and an oversized violin case in one hand.

"Maybe it's dinner time," Sword said. He looked at his watch. Twelve past three in the afternoon. Could be feeding time. But it could just as easily be 'Bub. "Let's go."

Sword could smell the pound even before Santini opened the main door for him. There was a strong disinfectant odor, different from the one in Leah Bernstein's treatment room, but still medicinal, though not strong enough to overpower the chief underlying odors of animals in distress. The smell of the place redoubled as the door swung open and warm damp air rushed out into the autumn chill of the street.

Passing from outside to inside made Sword think of the passage between fardoors. Air pressure, Ko had told him. That's what explained the sensation of stepping through some sort of boundary layer in a fardoor. The different geographical locations linked through the tele-portation portals had different weather systems, different air pressures. Sword remembered the pulsing gusts of hot, foul wind that had coursed through the tunnels beneath the Museum of Natural History. Ko's reasoning was that the fardoors had a pressure threshold: Whenever the threshold for the tunnel's fardoor was exceeded, then a blast of air from the cave would rush through. Then, when the pressure was momentarily equalized, the wind would stop.

In Sword's opinion, his assistant had become obsessed by fardoors, though she remained adamant that they did not work by 'magic' — a particularly obscene word in Ko's pragmatic lexicon. When the vampire Orion had told Ko that fardoors' crystal-energy requirements were proportional to the sizes of the openings and the distances between them, she had claimed that she could probably write equations to completely describe all fardoor operation. Sword, for one, hoped she would someday, and then explain them to him. Assuming that Ko ever spoke to him again. Something was going on with her these days. But what, he wasn't sure.

"Come to adopt?" The attendant behind the high wooden counter beamed hopefully. She was just a kid, maybe sixteen, with tied-back hair, a fresh-scrubbed face, and a much-mended, but brilliantly white smock. The name tag she wore identified her as a student volunteer-worker and gave her name as Cathi with an "i." Cathi, or someone, had carefully drawn and colored in a red heart in place of the dot over the last letter of her name.

"No," Sword said. "My, uh, cat was picked up by the police. They brought it here."

Cathi's smile faltered. To Sword's left, a door labeled ADOPTION AREA carried a tacked-up advertising poster of a bright button-eyed, black-and-white sock-puppet dog kissing a fat orange cat. But Cathi was looking over to the door on Sword's right. It bore no decoration, only two signs: NO ADMITTANCE and STAFF ONLY. It was from behind that door that the sounds of baying could be heard. Something in there was rattling windows at five-second intervals. Sword could also hear a chorus of cats hissing and yowling.

"Oh," Cathi said. "Well, I can go get him if we have him." She turned to a large, vertical filing cabinet behind her. "Do you know when he was brought in?"

"She," Sword corrected. He looked at Santini. "Two days ago?" Santini nodded. Sword gave Cathi the Loft's address and described 'Bub for her. "White — really furry — about twenty pounds." *With her collar on,* Sword thought. "Oh, yeah. And she has orange eyes."

"Copper," Cathi said. "That's what they call orange eyes in cats. Breed?" She turned to consult a set of color-coded hanging files in the floor-to-ceiling metal cabinet behind her.

I don't know, beast from hell? "Ah, looks like a Persian but ... she really isn't."

Cathi flipped quickly through the ragged-edged files. "I know, a Heinz cat, right? That's what all my cats are. One sort of looks like a Siamese, you know, cross-eyed and ... oh." She stopped talking as she pulled out one file; it was noticeably thicker than the others. Sword could see a form with a police crest on it.

"Something wrong?" Sword asked.

Cathi checked the file's topsheet. "Cat's name 'Bub?" Her voice sounded pinched.

"For all the good it does," Sword agreed. "What's wrong?" he asked again, frowning at Santini.

"I better call my supervisor," Cathi said, the cheerful enthusiasm gone from her voice. She reached for the black phone on the desk counter.

But before she could lift it, Santini's hand was on the handset. His other held out his business card. "William Santini. Scarlatti, Holcroft & Chancellor. My client here has been falsely accused of a crime he did not commit. He has been subjected to police brutality, violation of his civil rights, and illegal withholding of his private property. My firm is in the process of launching enough criminal and civil suits against this city and its employees to make my client an even wealthier man than he already is. So if you do not wish to become a party to those lawsuits, Ms. — Cathi, you'd better tell my client what happened to his cat *right now.*"

Santini dropped the card on the desk, then straightened the lapels of his coat. Cathi's face paled, then reddened. She looked from Santini to Sword and back again. "We lost her," she blurted out.

Sword felt as if someone had just punched him in the stomach. "Where? Did the police lose her at the Loft? Did she jump out the window of a police car?"

"She ... she got here all right," Cathi said in a small voice, flinching as another glass-rattling round of barking and screeching shook the NO ADMITTANCE door. "She got her own cage and ... "

"And?" Sword prompted.

"The next morning she just wasn't there!" Moisture began to fill Cathi's round brown eyes as she looked up at Sword. "Oh I'm so sorry. I'm so sorry. I ... " She lifted the file's top sheet to reveal the reason the file was so thick: a bulging brown-paper envelope. "All we found was her collar." She held the envelope out to Sword.

Sword tore it open and dumped its contents on the wooden counter: a scuffed and scratched green-leather collar from which hung a two-inch-long, clear crystal pendant.

"Funny kind of collar," Santini remarked.

"Funny kind of cat," Sword muttered as he picked up the collar and shoved it in the pocket of his leather coat. "Look ... Cathi, all I want to do is find my cat and take her home, okay? Now help me here: Where exactly did you find this collar?"

Cathi stared at Sword with forlorn eyes. "But I ... I didn't find it."

Oh, this is just great, Sword thought. This was as good as a conversation with Ko. He took a breath, reminding himself that this kid didn't work for him. "All right, Cathi, then where did whoever it was who found the collar find it?" Unable to completely control himself, Sword had raised his voice. Cathi sniffled.

JUDITH & GARFIELD REEVES-STEVENS

"It was in the cage. Just in the cage. The cage was locked but the collar was in it and the cat ... the cat just wasn't."

Sword looked over at the NO ADMITTANCE door. Only minor protests came from behind it now, a few yelps, then the sound of a male voice swearing. "A cage in there?" Sword asked.

Cathi nodded, eyes downcast.

Sword headed for the door. After a moment's hesitation, Santini did the same.

"Wait! You can't go in there!" Cathi wailed after him.

Sword didn't even pause as he hit the door and swung it open. No one was going to tell him where he could or couldn't go. Not anymore.

The smell in the room beyond the door was less antiseptic and more animal than in the reception area. The ambiance was much grimmer as well.

For a hundred feet, facing rows of wire cages stretched out before Sword. He strode between them and the few yelps he had heard in the reception room increased to a deafening level as the cages' occupants set up an alarm.

Sword stopped midway into the room, Santini close behind him. To one side, a large cage with a bottom open to the concrete floor held an enormous black dog of indeterminate breed, ceaselessly limping back and forth among tattered shreds of newspaper. The dog halted and began barking at Sword. To the other side, a row of stacked cages held hissing cats who stared at him balefully, ears flattened, backing away from him until they cowered in the farthest corners of their wire enclosures. Sword leaned closer to peer in at one large, almost white cat that spit at him furiously.

"Ah, Mr. Sword." Santini tapped him on the shoulder.

Sword straightened up as he heard shuffling footsteps approaching rapidly. He turned to see a frantic old man in pale-green scrubs hobbling between the cages. The fringe of gray hair around his balding scalp was in wild disarray and he held one hand to his knee.

"Who the Sam Hill are you?" the old man demanded.

Behind him, Sword heard the NO ADMITTANCE door swing open again. "He's come for his cat, Mr. Donahue," Cathi called out over the barking and yipping and yowling. "But it's the one who got lost."

48

DARK HUNTER

"I don't care, I don't care," Donahue said, coming to a stop too close to Sword. "You can't be back here. Go out front."

Sword didn't move. "Show me the cage where you put my cat."

Donahue rubbed his free hand over his face. "Look mister, I got too many other things to worry about right now. If you had kept your cat indoors like you were supposed to then — "

"The police brought my cat here. I want — "

Sword saw the young attendant hurrying up the aisle. "I told him he couldn't come in here, Mr. Donahue. But he said he was going to sue — "

"And my client *will* sue if you don't — "

"SHADDUP!"

For a moment, all the animals fell silent, but it didn't last.

Donahue began coughing violently, then recovered with a snort and grabbed Sword's coat in a fist, ignoring the fact that he barely came up to Sword's shoulders.

Santini made a move toward the old man but Sword waved him off.

"It's too bad you lost your cat, mister. Really. But I got bigger things to worry about here right now." Donahue leaned to the side to catch Cathi's attention as she hovered anxiously beside Sword. "*More* food's gone, missy. *Two* fifty-pound bags of Dog Chow this time. And four more locks smashed. And — *Judas Priest!*"

The old man dropped his grip on Sword's leather coat as a huge metallic crash echoed from a distant corner of the cage room, setting off another peak in the ongoing onslaught of animal noises.

"Look, Mr. Donahue," Sword said, "you just show me the cage where you put my cat and I'll get out of your way." 'Bub wasn't lost, Sword knew. She was in residence. Without her collar but with her appetite. *Though one hundred pounds of Dog Chow in two days would be pushing it even for 'Bub.*

Three more metallic crashes reverberated through the room and Sword distinctly heard the clatter of dog claws on concrete. The old man's face turned the color of coagulated blood. "Aagh, all right, all right. Have it your own way." He limped off between the cages, still clutching at his knee. "This way. Back here."

Sword and Santini and Cathi followed Donahue through a maze of stacked wire-metal cages until they reached an empty cage whose hand-

49

written tag read: BUB KO.

Donahue held his gnarled hands open to the heavens and spoke to the ceiling. "How, Lord? How?"

"How what?" Sword asked. He read the tag, made a mental note to remind Ko who had paid for 'Bub in New Orleans, and wondering if anyone else in this place had noticed the large tooth-holes poked through 'Bub's metal food bowl.

"The dogs," Donahue shouted. "Would somebody tell me how in blue blazes the dogs are opening their cages?"

Sword frowned, remembering how 'Bub sometimes managed to undo the buckle on her collar when she wanted to "go for a walk," as Ko had so quaintly termed it.

Another crash rang out, followed by what sounded to be an all-breeds stampede from the Westminster Dog Show.

"That's it!" Donahue shook a fist at the ceiling. "That's more than it!" The old man lunged off toward the front of the cage room, this time dragging Cathi with him.

Santini shot his cuff, then tweaked the knot of his tie as he looked around. "No wonder this city's going down the dumper, right, Mr. Sword? The quality of city employees is definitely on a downturn. We all done here?"

Sword didn't answer. He was looking at the spring-loaded latch on the cage 'Bub had been placed in. To open it required simultaneous pressure on two separate metal rods in two different directions. He didn't doubt that 'Bub had the strength to overcome the resistance of the springs — especially with her collar off — but he couldn't see how she could have managed to get both paws out in front of the cage and —

"Just a minute," Sword said.

Santini leaned in. "What's that, Mr. Sword? You find a clue or something?"

Sword held up his hand to silence him. *Dogs opening their own cages? One hundred pounds of Dog Chow missing?* He lifted his head up and shouted at the top of his lungs.

"*Marrrrtinnnnn!*"

Santini raised his eyebrows.

"Get down here!" Sword shouted. "Right now!"

"Martin?" Santini asked doubtfully. "He's out in the Bronx, Mr. Sword. He — *yowie!*"

Santini scrambled back in alarm as a large dark shape dropped noiselessly from the ceiling and alighted in front of Sword.

"What did I tell you?" Sword asked sternly.

Martin crouched before Sword and placed a long forearm over his head, hiding his eyes from Sword's.

"Martin?" Sword asked.

Martin mumbled something to the floor.

"I didn't hear you," Sword said.

"Martin know," the shifter halfling finally said, still refusing to look into Sword's eyes. "Martin bad bad bad."

Santini bravely stepped forward. "Hey, he's a big guy for his age, isn't he, Mr. Sword. Hi, Marty. My name's Billy Santini." He held out a hand. Martin saw it and drew back, lips curling away from his teeth.

Santini stepped back again.

"It's all right, Martin," Sword said, trying to be reassuring to both Martin and Santini. "Billy's a friend. He isn't here to hurt you."

Martin quickly glanced at Santini, then ducked his head again.

"Look at me, Martin," Sword said. "Look at me."

Martin looked up reluctantly, dark eyes narrowed as if expecting to be hit.

"You've been opening the cages here, haven't you?"

Martin nodded once.

"And taking the food?"

He nodded twice.

"Did you let 'Bub out?"

"'Bub ask," Martin said. "Martin hear. Martin come let 'Bub out bad cage. Bad bad cage."

"Do you know where 'Bub is now?"

Martin nodded again.

Sword pulled Bub's collar from his pocket and held it out to Martin. "Can you get her to wear this? So we can go back to the Loft?"

Martin's eyes sprang open. "Martin go too? Martin go Ja'Nette's room?" When Sword said, yes, Martin offered a teeth-baring grin that displayed his pointed incisors to full effect, then flipped over backward, grabbing 'Bub's collar with the toes of one foot and somersaulting to a perfect landing from which he bounded off between the cages, howling with glee.

Sword glanced back at Santini. The youth was staring at the empty space Martin had just vacated. His mouth hung open. Seeing Sword's eyes on him, he closed his jaws with a snap.

"Kind of an excitable kid," Sword ventured.

Santini nodded wordlessly.

"The way he talks," Sword said. "English isn't ... isn't his first language."

Santini nodded again.

"And he's crazy about 'Bub. Absolutely ... crazy." *And he's as agile as a gorilla on speed,* Sword added to himself. *His feet might as well be another pair of hands. And if he had any more fur on his body the city might make me get a permit to keep him in a residential area. But other than all that, he's just your typical teenager.*

"Uh, I think we might have a problem here, Mr. Sword."

"You think so?" Sword said with resignation. When he behaved himself, Martin could pass as human fairly easily. But after that little exhibition ...

"Um, last I heard, Martin was an indigent youth locked up at Spofford."

"Go on."

"Um, the city doesn't release kids like that. 'Specially when they might be facing charges as accessory to murder."

"Hmm," Sword said, seeing what Santini was getting at.

"And did you happen to see what he was wearing there for pants, Mr. Sword?"

Sword thought for a moment, trying to recall just what Martin had been wearing this time. The halfling went through clothes — when he actually wore them, that is — like a baby through diapers. "Some kind of dark pants, rolled up at the ankle with ... with ... Oh, hell." Martin's pants had had stripes up the side.

Santini pursed his lips. "And his shirt had epaulets and a crest over here." He touched a finger to his shoulder, right where a police officer wore his squad patch.

Sword grasped for a straw. "The staff at Spofford might have ... loaned him the clothes."

Santini shook his head. "Your friend's quite the little acrobat, Mr. Sword. And Spofford's not high security."

The din seemed to be dying down again as Sword studied the cage room. No wonder adepts lived within the confines of their enclaves. The Second World was far too complicated. "So, the police are going to be looking for Martin?"

"'Fraid so, Mr. Sword."

Far down at the end of the row of cages, Martin reappeared, loping toward them with a furry white bundle under his arm, like a burly linebacker with a football.

"He just wanted his cat," Sword explained.

"Oh, I understand, Mr. Sword. I sure wouldn't want to get between that kid and his cat."

Sword watched with dismay as Martin sped toward him, using his free hand as a third leg

"As I said," Sword said futilely, "Martin's not from around here."

Santini tugged on his lapels again. "Jesus, Mr. Sword. You mean not from around New York? Or not from around this planet?"

Sword opened his mouth to reply to what he hoped was a joke on Santini's part, but a sudden flash of insight stopped him. *Not from this planet*, he thought. It had always been a possibility he had kept in the back of his mind, though it seemed too extreme to even discuss. But still ... the First World, the Second World, the fardoors, all this talk of "passing through the layer" ... perhaps it was more than a wild possibility. Perhaps ... Sword cut off the new train of thought. The idea, no matter how farfetched, was obviously something for discussion only with an expert, and thanks to the Sword Foundation, he had hired the best.

It was time to find Melody Ko.

FIVE

"Lemme put it anudder way, Miz Ko: Whatever it is that Galen's mixed up in *stinks*. It's gotta stop. And you're the one who can help us do it. So whaddaya say, hey, Miz Ko? What's it gonna be?"

Melody Ko gave serious thought to the answer she should give Detective Trank. She detested Galen Sword. Sure, she didn't mind admitting to herself that she might have had feelings for him, in the beginning, when she had understood him to be a single-minded pursuer of truth, no matter how peculiar or unlikely that truth turned out to be. And some of those feelings that she had — in hindsight — forced upon herself then might even have been real, in an immature, hero-worshipping sort of way. But now? Sword had been revealed as a taker and a user many times over. The man owed her so much that he had yet to acknowledge, that he no longer deserved her help or her concern. He hadn't proved himself a pursuer of truth. And he certainly was no hero. The truth was, he was obstinate, selfish, and completely illogical. She wanted nothing more to do with him.

But then a troublesome thought briefly caused her to frown. *Could her indignation and sense of being ignored have anything to do with ... ?* No, of course not. Her? Jealous of Sword? Impossible a thousand times over. She'd only tolerated him because she'd been desperate to believe he could help find whoever had so devastatingly hurt the one man she *did* care for.

"C'mon, Miz Ko. His lawyers tracked 'im down and bailed 'im out an hour ago. He's on the streets again. There's no telling what he's gonna do next."

As Trank reached his rough hands across the stained blotter of his desk in an appeal for her cooperation, it seemed to Ko that the whole floor of homicide detectives beyond the smudged glass windows of the office's door and partition walls came to a sudden pause, as if every police officer in the precinct building waited to hear her answer.

Ko stared at the detective's thick fingers, wondering how he managed to fit even one of them through the trigger guard of his revolver, as she worked on composing a half-believable lie that might serve both her needs and the police department's evident desire to lock up Sword where he no doubt belonged. As she saw it, the real problem was that she knew exactly what Sword was likely to do next: Brin, Sword's own brother, had told her that two nights ago, before the assault on the World Plaza installation, when he had suddenly appeared in Sword's Loft and restored her broken arm with his blue power.

Trank leaned back in his precariously rickety wooden office chair and it creaked as if it were about to collapse beneath his awkwardly overweight mass. He shrugged expansively and looked over to the third person in his cluttered and stale-smelling office. "I don't know what else ta say ta her. I really don't."

Ko heard an irritated cough behind her, then Marion E. Raycheba strode over to Trank's desk and sat firmly on the edge.

"Ms. Ko — or may I call you Melody?" The woman smiled at Ko brightly, obviously trying to build some sort of rapport. Ko didn't think that was likely.

Raycheba — known to everyone as Marion E. — owned and operated one of the city's top-rated independent television stations. She had come up from being a newswriter to running the most nettlesome television news operation in the state and didn't mind letting people know how much she enjoyed the power and financial clout that gave her. Even in his most obnoxious jetset days, Ko knew, not even Sword would have sported close to twenty thousand dollars' worth of clothes;

which is what Ko estimated the flashy Gianni Versace outfit had cost the station owner. And the David Webb ring she wore, resembling an egg-sized broccoli flowerette dipped in gold and dusted with diamonds, was beyond Ko's ability to price. She herself didn't care for fancy outfits or showy gems, even though she could usually identify their makers at a glance.

"Melody ... ?" Marion E. repeated.

Ko answered the falsely-innocent bonding question with a glare.

Marion E. crossed her arms and her eyes narrowed until Ko thought she might be preparing to blast laser beams from them. "All right then, shall I just spell it out for you in simple English?"

Ko shrugged. Dealing with Trank, Ko knew that the detective's actions were limited by a set of clearly defined rules. But Marion E. Raycheba and her station's news bureau were not. Marion E.'s operation had hung so many city politicians out to dry that the station owner no longer played by anyone's rules but her own. As far as Ko was concerned, that made the woman dangerous. Especially when so much of what Ko and Forsyte had uncovered for Sword had to be kept from the public.

"To begin," Marion E. said crisply, counting off the first of her points on the slim fingers of one well-cared-for hand. "The so-called terrorist explosions at the American Museum of Natural History on the night of the Society of St. Linus charity ball."

Ko would not ever forget that night. She and Forsyte had set off loud concussion grenades outside the museum to attract public attention and to disrupt the Clan Arkady as its legions of shifters gathered for their Ceremony of the Change. She herself had seen to the placing of the grenades so the museum itself would not be damaged. Sword would have blown it to dust if they had done it his way.

"What about it?" Ko asked.

"Kennie Marsh was first on the scene," Marion E. said accusingly. "She told me she had received an *anonymous* tip."

"She works for you," Ko said. "Why would she lie?" Forsyte had been the one to call Marsh at Sword's suggestion, hoping Marsh's *LiveEye News* van and crew might add to the confusion at the museum.

DARK HUNTER

Marion E. ignored Ko's sarcasm. She counted off a second finger. "Two nights ago. More explosions. The top of the World Plaza tower completely demolished." She leaned closer to Ko and her lustrous brown eyes flashed even brighter. "And Kennie Marsh is among the injured. Apparently in disguise. Apparently working undercover."

Ko glanced over at Trank. The big man sat comfortably with folded hands, like a statue of a smiling Buddha waiting for his belly to be rubbed. But Trank wasn't smiling. He also appeared to have no intention of interrupting.

"So being a reporter is dangerous work," Ko said.

Marion E. shook her head. "Oh, no. I look after my people. I give them everything they need to get the story and stay safe. But I'll tell you what *is* dangerous, Ms. Ko. Being Galen Sword's friend."

Now that *I can agree with*, Ko thought, though she said nothing and kept her face free of expression.

"Galen Sword was at the St. Linus ball," Marion E. continued. "He talked to Kennie there. I've got witnesses. And Sword, I hardly need add, was arrested at World Plaza."

"So was I. So what?"

Trank shook his head. "Miz Ko, c'mon. We're trying to give ya a way out here."

"Ever hear of coincidence?" Ko muttered, still busily trying to think up some way of extricating herself from this latest of Sword's many entanglements. No matter how open Trank appeared to be, she simply wouldn't and couldn't risk telling him anything anywhere near the truth.

"It couldn't have been a coincidence this time," Marion E. retorted.

The implication caught Ko by surprise. "What do you mean, 'this time'?"

Marion E. pressed home her advantage. "Didn't Sword ever tell you about that accident he had about three years ago? When he wrapped his car around the light pole? Almost died?"

Only ad nauseum, Ko thought. For the first year she had worked for him, that was all he *ever* talked about. *I have a destiny*, he said. *I have to fight*, he said. *I'm heir to the Victor of Pendragon.* On and on, blah blah

57

blah. Ko had stopped listening to him talk about his so-called destiny long ago.

"Yeah, he mentioned it once or twice."

"Did he ever tell you what happened about a week later?"

"Why don't you tell me," Ko said unhelpfully.

Ko knew that after he had been discharged from the hospital, Sword had gone to Marcus Askwith, one of the elite lawyers who had set up his original trust fund. He had planned to confront the lawyer with the memories that his brother Brin's healing blue power had restored to him in the hospital. Askwith, apparently, had told Sword he would try to get permission from someone or something to tell the whole truth, but later that night the lawyer had mysteriously burned to death at his home.

Sword's latest theory was that Dmitri, the walking blue-eyed skeleton that had attacked him in the Softwind bar and then again at the Museum of Natural History before the shifters' Ceremony of the Change, had somehow killed Askwith by spontaneous human combustion. But it was a sure thing that Marion E. Raycheba wasn't aware of any of *those* details.

"You must know his lawyer died under ... let's just say, 'unusual' circumstances." Marion E. widened her eyes as if she had said enough to convince even Ko of the veracity of her argument.

"Yeah, yeah, that's right," Trank added. "The guy was burnt like last night's barbecue, right in the middle of his kitchen. An' Galen was there that morning. It's when I met him for the first time, matter a fact."

"That's where Kennie first met him, too," Marion E. said, not taking her eyes from Ko. "And that's where Kennie got suspicious."

"About what?" Ko asked wearily.

"About Sword." Marion E. leaned forward again. "Three years ago, the Sword Foundation had a net worth of two hundred million dollars. Sword's income derived from just some of the interest. Oh, he could apply for one-time disbursements for major acquisitions like his condo, the jet, whatever, but he couldn't *control* the full fund. However, the lawyers who set it up, Marjoribanks and Askwith, *could!*"

DARK HUNTER

Ko didn't get it. She didn't care about money, not like some others she knew. Money was only a tool to be used, nothing to be sought after or hoarded for its own sake. So what was Marion E. trying to tell her?

"Think it through, Melody. Two hundred million dollars. Sword wants control of it. Marjoribanks and Askwith want control of it. Sword has a near-fatal car accident. A single-vehicle accident. He — "

"Sword admitted he'd been drinking," Ko said, cutting the woman off, impatient with the direction this conversation had suddenly taken. At least Sword had been upfront about his drinking — and worse — that night. But she knew he hadn't touched anything stronger than coffee since he had walked out of that hospital. Maybe she could admire him just a little bit for that.

"Uh uh. There was nothin' in the medical files about drivin' under the influence," Trank said. "Tests showed nothin' in his blood that shouldn't a been there. He was clean, no matter what he told ya."

"Moreover, we found out that all his other medical records mysteriously disappeared," Marion E. said, as if this were an important clue.

But Ko knew even more than the detective and station owner. She knew Sword's blood had tested clean because Brin had cleansed it. And that Sword himself had arranged for the records of his treatment at the hospital to go missing.

According to Sword, the emergency surgeons had watched, dumbfounded, as his lacerated heart tissue had grown back together before their eyes, as crushed ribs had knit in minutes, and his torn flesh healed without scars. Of the five surgeons and nurses who had been in the O.R. that night, Ko knew four of them were currently in Hawaii, Key West, and the south of France drawing long-term medical-research grants from the Sword Foundation. The fifth had retired to a small farm in Connecticut, leased for a dollar a year from the Sword Real Estate Holding Corporation.

"Sword never said a thing to me about it being anything other than an accident," Ko stated flatly, and that *was* the truth. He had had two women in his fire-red Testarossa that night. Two supermodels. A cab came out of nowhere and Sword's addled reflexes couldn't cope. Disaster. One woman dead, the other with a ruined face. A typical night on the town with Galen Sword, decadent and dissipated playboy of the

59

western world. Until Brin had appeared in the emergency room after the doctors had written his brother off. Until Brin had healed him. Body and mind together.

"It wasn't any accident, Melody. Oh, eyewitnesses got the licence plate on the cab that cut off Sword's car. But that cab, that licence number, didn't exist. We believe it was a murder attempt." Marion E.'s voice deepened dramatically with these last words.

"What?"

"And one week later Sword torched the man who had tried to kill him — Marcus Askwith."

"You're joking. Sword's not that — " But Ko faltered. There had been a lot of killing in the past few weeks. While it hadn't been humans who had been killed, intelligent beings were dying. And Sword had taken part in the carnage. Done his part very well. A flood of images came back from what she had seen of Sword just recently. He had given up on the shock guns and sedative darts he had spent so much money on. Switched to explosives and shotguns instead. Sprayed silver-halide solutions on shapeshifters to burn their flesh like acid. Collapsed a fardoor to cut a living werewolf in half.

"That's right," Marion E. said in self-satisfied triumph as Ko fell silent. "You work for him. You know him. You know what he's capable of, don't you?"

Ko looked sourly at the woman but said nothing.

Marion E. pushed on. "So, Sword killed Marcus Askwith. No one doubts he's capable of that. He had motive — revenge and control of his trust fund. He had opportunity — Sword was the last person to see Askwith at his office on the day he died. Askwith's secretary said the two of them had quite an argument. Her boss was pale and visibly upset when he left that day. The only thing Detective Trank wasn't able to figure out was exactly how Sword managed it."

"Poison," Trank said.

Ko screwed up her face. Sword's personal motivations were a black hole as far as she knew or cared to know. But biochemistry was one of *her* domains. "Poison doesn't make a human body catch fire," she said scornfully.

"No, no, of course not," Marion E. said. "When Sword met with

Askwith at his office, he slipped the old guy something. Maybe in a drink. Maybe a contact poison. Something exotic, no doubt. Something your employer picked up on one of his many trips up the Amazon or into the Outback. Askwith became queasy, lost color, went home sick. A few hours later he's unconscious. Sword breaks in. He'd been a guest at Askwith's house many times since he was a kid so the security system wouldn't have been a surprise. Then he douses Askwith with something flammable, and torches him. A week later, the trust fund passes over to Scarlatti, Holcroft & Chancellor and comes under Sword's complete control. A slick operation."

"Who the bloody hell came up with that one?" Ko asked, trying to sound belligerent, while her mind swiftly correlated the data she held, searching for confirmation.

Marion E.'s scenario didn't make sense to Ko. *Unless* Sword had killed Askwith not for the trust fund but because the old man refused to divulge details of Sword's past. Could that be possible?

"I'll tell you who came up with it," Marion E. said. "Kennie."

That airhead? Ko thought. "And just when did she do that?"

"When control of the trust fund moved to the new law firm. Technically, there was no need for the switch. Marjoribanks had been gone since ninety-five, but Askwith had other partners. Kennie became suspicious."

Ko put her fingers to her temples and stared down at the floor. Something didn't follow. "But ... Kennie and Sword started dating each other then, didn't they?"

Marion E. snorted. "Dating. What a quaint word. But yes, you're correct. Kennie started seeing quite a bit of Sword then. After all, that was her assignment."

"Her assignment?" Ko repeated. She turned to Trank. "Were you in on this, too?"

"Not, ah, officially or nothin'," Trank said.

"How come? If you suspected all this, why didn't you go after Sword yourself?"

"Aaah, no proof. We looked into it. Couldn't get nothin' from the autopsy on Askwith's hand." Trank stuck out his bottom lip for a moment. "That was sorta all that was left a him, y'know. And we didn't have nothin' else ta go on. Nothin' concrete at least. So I figured, yeah, why not? Let Marion E. take the ball an' run with it a while. If she gets inta trouble with high and mighty Galen Sword, she gets great ratings. Me, I'da lost my job." He looked over at Marion E. appraisingly. "Made a lotta sense to me, anyway."

Marion E. focused intently on Ko. "And how about you? Make sense to you?"

"Can't say," Ko answered truthfully. It seemed ludicrous, but then, so much about Galen Sword was always that way.

Marion E. shook her head, rejecting Ko's answer. "I don't buy that. I think you do. A few seconds ago you were about to tell me that Sword wasn't capable of murder, but something made you stop, didn't it? Something you've seen, something you've learned about Sword in the time you've been with him."

"Did Galen kill Ja'Nette Conroy?" Trank asked suddenly.

"No," Ko said, startled by the blunt question.

Marion E. shifted to a subtler approach. "But she *is* dead, isn't she?"

Unwanted tears stung Ko's eyes. Had Sword been lying to her all this time? Had she really been working for a murderer? One she looked to for help? "I ... yes, yes, Ja'Nette is dead." The day they had gone to the museum, the child had had Martin butcher her hair to a short razor-bristle so she could look just like Ko. And a handful of hours later the twelve-year-old had died violently as a werewolf ripped out her throat.

"And ... ?" Marion E. said. "*Did* Sword contribute to her death in any way?"

Ko nodded, fighting the powerful urge to sob. She hadn't wept for Ja'Nette when the child had died and now she knew why. Tears weren't enough. The loss she felt, the guilt and the pain, none of it came close enough, or was nearly hurtful enough, to make up for the over-whelming emptiness that now swept through her. Ja'Nette had looked up to her. Ja'Nette had trusted her. And Ko had, in return, abandoned Ja'Nette to Sword.

"Yes," Ko said. She felt hot liquid snake down her cheeks. "We ... we all did."

Trank began looking through his desk drawers but stopped when Marion E. produced a white-linen handkerchief from her soft-sided leather case.

"You feel all of you were responsible?" Marion E. asked as Ko wiped angrily at her face.

Ko nodded briefly again. She knew she still needed release. She thought of the forgiveness she craved. She felt the growing pressure to talk. To confess.

"How?" Trank asked. He kept his voice low and undemanding, as if following Marion E.'s lead.

"An ... an accident."

"At the museum?" Marion E. asked.

Ko meticulously folded the handkerchief to a dry side, and nodded again.

Trank picked up a pen and opened a large black notepad bound like a hardcover book. "How'd it happen, Miz Ko?"

But Marion E. suddenly stood up and protectively put her hand on Ko's shoulder. "No, Detective, I don't think she should say anything more."

"Aaah, c'mon. Just a statement and — "

Marion E. patted Ko. "No, no. Let's do this right. We've waited long enough to get Sword. We can wait a few more hours. First thing we have to do is get this woman a lawyer." She looked down at Ko. "And don't worry, my station will cover all your legal fees." Back to Trank. "We lay the whole deal out on the table for her and her lawyer, and *then* we ask for her statement." To Ko. "Does that sound fine to you, Melody?"

Ko blinked at the woman. "What ... what deal?"

"Aaah, nothin' to get excited about, Miz Ko, sorta like state's evidence," Trank said. "You know, you tell us everything ya know about Galen an' what he's been up to, an', ah, we don't press charges. Like, immunity."

"But I don't know anything about Askwith. Sword never said anything. And Ja'Nette, Ja'Nette was an accident." Ko looked from one to the other. *How could I have been so stupid?* What had she gotten herself into? All because of Galen Sword. Again.

"But what about Kennie? Was Kennie an accident, too?" Marion E.'s voice rose as she spoke her missing reporter's name and Ko sensed the almost feral protectiveness the station owner felt for her underlings.

"I don't understand what you're talking about," Ko said, buying more time to collect herself.

Marion E.'s words matched the intensity of her expression. "There are simply too many 'accidents' around Sword. Kennie looked into him a few years ago and couldn't find anything she could run with. She ends the investigation. Breaks up with Sword. Sword keeps his nose clean. Some sort of State Department trouble in Greece, but that's about it. Then Sword hooks up with Kennie again and the Museum of Natural History almost goes up in a fireball. Kennie hooks back up with Sword, trying to find out if there's something new he's involved in. Sword figures out that Kennie is getting close to something so he brings her into whatever he had going up on the top of World Plaza. You *must* understand what this all means."

"You think Sword was trying to kill Kennie?"

Marion E. sat back on the desk and folded her arms again. She nodded at Trank. "See, I told you. She understands just fine."

Trank put down his pen as he scratched at something, squinting in thought. "I still don't think she knows anythin'."

Marion E. stared at Ko, as if she were a specimen under glass. "But she'll find out for us, won't you, Melody?"

Ko couldn't believe her predicament. On the surface, the three of them were in complete agreement. Galen Sword was a menace. He needed to be taken out of her life and off the streets. But the reasons on which she and they had based their shared conclusion were totally different.

Ko knew that Sword actually *did* have a destiny. Brin had explained it completely to her when he came to heal her, as he had his brother, earlier. Sword's destiny was to bring both the First and Second Worlds into an uncontrolled and cataclysmic confrontation that could destroy both — unless someone stopped him. But she couldn't possibly explain *that* to Detective Trank or Marion E. Raycheba. Anymore than she could she go along with what they wanted her to do without enraging Sword and driving him to fulfill his bloody destiny.

"Maybe we should outline the deal a bit more clearly for you,"

Marion E. said pointedly, as if she could read the confusion in Ko's mind. "If you go along with us, as I said, my station picks up the tab. Legal fees, living expenses, whatever you need. Plus, Trank will see to it that all charges against you are dropped. Simple and straightforward, don't you agree? But, on the other hand," Marion E. paused, though not long enough to give Ko a change to reply, "if you turn us down, then you're on the line for anything we can charge Sword with, plus charges of obstructing justice, criminal conspiracy, and whatever else the D.A. is having a sale on today. And no money. The Sword Foundation disbursements to any and all of the conspirators will be attached and completely cut off."

Ko responded to the threat in Marion E.'s voice with a kneejerk response. "I don't care about money."

"Fair enough," Marion E. said. "But how will your partner feel about being cut off?"

"My partner?"

"Dr. Adrian Forsyte, I believe. You're young and only a few credits shy of a good degree. You can get by without the Sword Foundation's funding. But what happens to Dr. Forsyte? There are what, four shifts of attendants caring for him now? All paid for by the Foundation, I believe? And how about his wheelchairs, the computers, the voice synthesizer? Those are all Foundation property. In drawn-out criminal proceedings those could be confiscated. The doctor wouldn't have any income. Most likely be ... institutionalized. What do you think, Detective? Some hospital upstate? Ten to a ward? Maybe a volunteer could read him the *Times's* science pages once a week. You think he'd like that?"

Ko's hands balled into fists at her sides. She felt the muscles tense in her neck as her body prepared to hurl itself out of the chair at the station executive. Ko had wrestled and killed a fur-tentacled-something called a *tagonii* for Forsyte. She had faced what this world called were-wolves and vampires with the same guns and explosives that Sword made use of. And she would do it all again, and more, unhesitatingly, to restore Adrian Forsyte to what he had been.

But before Ko could clamp her fingers around Marion E.'s neck, Trank noisily dragged himself to his feet. "I know you'll do the right thing, Miz Ko. And I'm sure Marion E. didn't mean nothin' personal."

Ko snapped back to reality. She was in the Second World now, not the First. Things were done differently here.

"I mean, about you and the doc, or anythin' else. I mean, alla that stuff, it's in the files an' all."

"Just what *is* in the files?" Ko asked angrily. *How had Sword had managed to mess her up again when she hadn't even seen him for two days?* She took a deep breath. Forsyte was the important one here. Everything else that existed had to be subservient to her goal to restore him to what he was, before he was maimed by the power of the First World. Everything. Including Detective Trank and Marion E. Raycheba. "I said, what's in the files?"

Ko saw Trank shoot a worried glance at the station executive before he answered her. "Galen, and the Foundation, an', ah, all his crazy escapades the last little while, well, they're all under investigation. Kinda."

"And I'm in the files, and so is Adrian," Ko said.

"And what you both, let us say, mean to each other is in there, too," Marion E. said as she unexpectedly cracked her knuckles. Ko understood the executive didn't expect any more hesitation or emotional outbursts from her. The full extent of the "deal" had been laid out for her and by adding Forsyte to the equation, the whole thing was nothing short of blackmail.

But there would be no kneejerk reaction from her to Marion E.'s threats this time. Ko felt complete control return to her mind *and* body. Trank and Marion E. thought they had created a trap for her and she would not dissuade them from their conclusion.

"Call the lawyer," Ko said. "Then we'll talk about my statement."

Ko saw Trank and Marion E. exchange quick, triumphant smiles, but didn't care. She was already formulating her next step. And there would be a next step that neither the detective nor the station owner could ever imagine.

She'd learned a few new lessons in the past few weeks, when so much had happened that was beyond imagination, and almost beyond science.

Traps were just like equations, Ko thought to herself. *They worked both ways.*

SIX

In his dream, he rides a horse. It is magnificent, ebony black, with a sheen that captures the lightning that blazes all around him. The thunder of steel-shod hooves blends with the thunder of the heavens and of his anger. The horse gallops in time to his racing heart and the movement of its pounding legs and heaving sides is but a reflection of his own exertions as he races for his goal.

In his dream, his enemies are arrayed before him, waiting for him, powerless before him.

He catches lightning in his hands and wields it as an avenging blade. He roars his challenge with a voice that drowns the thunder. His muscles ripple, impossibly perfect in form and motion. He swings the blade like molten light and his enemies fall back, bodies sliced asunder.

The two fliers are first — shrieking harpies with static-filled hair sparking in their effort to leave the ground and escape his righteous rage. But they are not fast enough, they are not strong enough, and their bodies become fluttering ribbons tossed in the storm of his vengeance.

Their blood coats him in torrential waves and he revels in it, tasting victory.

He rides on. His lungs ache but the pain gives him pleasure. His muscles move faster and more powerfully than they have ever served him before and in their exhaustion he finds new strength. The horse beneath him moves in such a way that mount and rider are no longer separate. In his dream, he becomes the horse. He becomes motion and energy and attacks his final enemy, his greatest enemy, his most hated enemy.

In his dream, he swings his blade against Galen Sword.

But it does not connect.

The blade sweeps through empty space and the whistle of its passage is eclipsed by Sword's scornful laughter. The black horse stumbles in shock, legs failing, and the jolt splits the two of them, sending the rider forward, sundered from motion and energy, to fall and fall and ...

In his dream, the stars pass by him, remaining out of reach as he tumbles past them into black unknowingness. He hears the crackle of the fliers reborn as they hover around him, mocking him, laughing as he fails in his efforts to fly, as he fails in what they have been able to do from birth.

He looks down. He sees he wears a parachute. The ripcord handle glows fluorescent orange. All he has to do to save himself is pull the handle. All he has to do is grab the handle. All he has to do ... In his dream, he cannot move his arm. He cannot move his hand. He cannot move at all.

In his dream, he is helpless. He can only fall. He can only be swallowed by darkness while his enemies survive and taunt him.

He can do nothing. He is nothing. He falls he tumbles he cannot even cry out for help in his dream.

Then he wakes.

And then Adrian Forsyte, a physicist once of MIT, remembers, and in the loneliness of his affliction and the prison of his narrow bed, the only movement about him is the slow passage of the tears that trail from his wide and staring eyes.

It is an hour before someone comes for him, and each long and waiting second drains him, bit by bit, of whatever sanity he has left.

The door to Forsyte's bedroom opened a crack and a dazzling swath of light fell upon his face. The brilliance of the afternoon sunlight striking his dark-adapted eyes was almost physical. He tried to jerk away but, of course, remained inert. All he could do was close his eyelids and wait for the afterimage of the silhouette in the doorway to fade.

"Are we awake?" the nurse asked breezily. "Or just pretending to be asleep?"

A terrible flood of obscenities rushed from Forsyte's mind to his tongue, but in the nerve paths they followed was a blockade erected by First World ... magic. All that issued from his throat was a pathetic gurgle. His eyes flashed open.

"Oh, good," the nurse said, throwing open the door to its widest, effectively blinding him altogether. "It's time for our feeding."

Whatever it was that had beset the physicist, he was denied even the ability to shake with rage. Instead, he lay still, sightless eyes open, ignoring the springy footfalls of the young woman in the white pantsuit uniform as she crossed the room toward him. He tried to find a focus for the day, for the hour. Something to drive him forward from one moment to the next. Something to hate. At this moment, it was a toss-up between the nurse and the word magic.

The nurse was an affront to his body and to his sanctity as an individual, and he shut his eyes tightly — as close as he could get to protesting her invasion — as she cranked the bed up too quickly, awkwardly bunching his pillow beneath his head. Magic was an affront to his intellect and everything he had studied for and believed in since he had been a child.

Dimly, he felt cool air rush over him and he opened his eyes to see that the nurse had pulled away the sheet that had covered his body. "Let's just see how we're doing down here."

Doesn't she care? Forsyte thought. *Doesn't she know how demeaning this is? How humiliating?*

He watched her face as she went about her work, trying to detect some hint of intelligence or compassion in her. But he found nothing. She was barely into her twenties, more curvaceous than Ko, shorter than Martin, filled with a vacuous, childish energy. And adding to his bitterness was the knowledge that when he had been enshrined at MIT as a quantum physicist on the Nobel track, he had had a dozen just like her in his bed whenever he had wanted them.

JUDITH & GARFIELD REEVES-STEVENS

He closed his eyes as the nurse peeled off his diaper and efficiently checked the sleeve and connection of his catheter. While his eyes were closed, he felt her plastic gloved hands faintly, like the fleeting caress of a ghostly memory. When he opened his eyes, he felt nothing.

"We'll just get you ready for feeding," the nurse said as she reached beneath Forsyte's hips and rolled him on his side, wedging his arm uncomfortably behind him. In disbelief, Forsyte then heard her walk out of the room, leaving him twisted, cold, and exposed.

Sword's probably done this to me on purpose, Forsyte thought bitterly. *He's got all the money in the world. He could have had the best in here to help me. But he's hired novices. On purpose. To insult me. To remind me who's really in charge now.*

Forsyte felt the cold air suck the heat from his body and he couldn't even shiver. *At least Melody understood. At least Melody knew how to deal with me, how to treat me.*

He tried to focus on something more positive. Melody Ko was a good start. Not the best, but good enough. She was responsible for setting up this room in her apartment to house Forsyte and at least some of his support equipment. She had enlarged the doors to accommodate the wheelbase of his computer-driven chair. She had remodelled her bathroom with robotocized platforms so he could actually use the toilet by himself and bathe with minimal help. And at least when she performed all the intimate services that for him were so belittling and embarrassing in the hands of the nurse, Ko acted with a scientist's detachment. When Ko had tended to him, Forsyte had been sure that there was nothing personal in her ministrations and that his useless, naked body represented nothing more to her than another datum of information about the First World, to be assessed dispassionately and without involvement.

Forsyte only wished now that he could forget what Ko had told him a handful of days ago in the privacy of the Loft's meeting room. That she loved him. And always had.

For once his almost-total paralysis had had a positive function. He had been unable to convey his stunned surprise at her admission. Not that he hadn't known about her initial feelings for him. He had, most assuredly, ever since the day he had pulled her from his undergraduate

DARK HUNTER

class to be his lab assistant at MIT. But having young students fall in love with him had been nothing new for him. He had always accepted the routine infatuations as one of the perks of his job, knowing that each would pass in time. In Ko's case, he had responded to the signals she, too, sent out because she was bright. Bright enough to understand and be impressed by the work he was pursuing with his transformable tunneling electron waveguide. And, to be callously honest, because he had never had sex with a Japanese female.

Fortunately or unfortunately, Ko had been more than bright enough to be impressed by his work. She had been brilliant and able to help him with it. During his years of teaching and romancing willing female students, Forsyte had learned that once they discovered that they would never be more just another in a long, unending chain, they invariably fell out of love and left.

With Ko, however, it had been different. With her, since his work was progressing so amazingly well with her assistance, he had never encouraged a sexual relationship, intending to keep her on as long as she was of use to him, or until an even more brilliant student presented herself. Thus nothing had happened between him and Ko, though he'd found she provided him a different form of pleasure when she jealously reacted to the female students he did pursue, even though she naively thought she was keeping her own feelings hidden. Forsyte had found her flatteringly close attention unexpectedly invigorating.

Until the day that close attention had prompted Ko to call in Galen Sword.

Forsyte heard the quick footsteps of the nurse as she returned to swab and rediaper him. In his thoughts, he urged her to hurry. His arm was going numb. The creatures who had cursed him with immobility had seen fit to leave him with residual physical senses, enough so he could feel the agony of his disability a thousand times each day — every time he blinked.

"Here we go," the nurse said and, as if that had been warning enough, heaved him onto his back again with enough force that his breath escaped him with a huff. "All set for lunchies." She walked out briskly, tying a bright red cord around a blue plastic garbage bag stuffed with pads and used towels. Forsyte didn't want 'lunchies.' He wanted the nurse obliterated. And he wanted his chair.

That was another small positive factor in his barren life. He had no idea how much Sword had ended up paying for the high-tech wheelchairs that Ko had built from Forsyte's designs, but whatever the sum had been, Forsyte knew it had been worth it. Some days, the chairs were all that made him want to keep living.

His vision had almost returned to normal and he squinted at the corner of the bedroom, to see that the chair in which he had come to Ko's apartment had not been moved. It was still parked where he had left it, its transformer still implanted in the wall outlet. The indicator LEDs on it glowed green — all batteries fully charged.

To call the device a wheelchair was a misnomer. It bore more resemblance to a small tank. There was a chair section in which he sat, held in place by crossed shoulder harnesses. It had chair arms — the left one containing a keypad and joystick for use by his two movable fingers. But past that, it was to other wheelchairs what a Stealth fighter was to a Piper Cub.

Angling out from the left arm was a high-definition display screen that could present choices for the onboard voice synthesizer, or — combined with the twin laser monitors mounted in his thick-framed glasses that kept track of where he was looking and the commands he sent via coded eyeblinks — the screen could also slave directly to any of the computer systems in the SoHo Loft or the Sword Foundation vans.

On either side of the chair arms were equipment pods which could be outfitted with a variety of special gadgets, and which usually contained at least one taser shock gun with twin darts, and halogen headlights. A third pod was fitted to the back of the chair and held, among other devices, a series of gear-driven plastic rods which could swing out to adjust Forsyte's glasses and even scratch his nose.

Instead of being suspended between two large wheels as on a traditional wheelchair, the chair section was attached by a central stalk to a powerful base propelled by twin rubber treads. The stalk could pivot to hold him level so the base was free to climb stairs and to negotiate bumpy terrain. A sleek, fiberglass canopy encased the drive mechanisms and batteries as well as the onboard computers and radio and cellular-phone systems.

It wasn't his wheelchair. It was his legs, his voice, his eyes, and his ears. To be away from it was to be no more than the pitiful heap that had been left on the floor of his MIT lab because of Sword's interference.

The nurse returned with a wheeled tray. Forsyte could smell chopped egg. He wanted to vomit. *Didn't she even read the instructions Ko left for them? Doesn't she care? Don't* any *of them care anymore?* The nurse was typical of all four of the attendants who now took care of him around the clock. Forsyte decided it wouldn't be enough for one nurse to self-destruct. He wanted them *all* dead.

The nurse tucked a large white napkin under his chin and wheeled the tray up as if she were prepping him for surgery.

Forsyte blinked his eyes twice for no. *No.* But the nurse cheerfully sat on a stool by the bed and made a show of inspecting the food and tepid coffee on the tray. "Mmmm, this looks scrumptious." She had cut the sandwich twice on the diagonal and held a triangle of it up to brush his lips. "Mmm, mmm, mmm."

Forsyte stopped blinking. He just stared at her. He loathed chopped-egg sandwiches. He knew Ko had filled her freezer with quart containers of the chili he did like, cooked according to his own recipe. *Just put me back in my chair,* he wanted to scream at the nurse. But all he could do was stare into her vacant eyes and keep his mouth closed.

"Now, now, now," the nurse chided him as she realized what he was up to. "That's not being a good boy, is it?"

Die, moron, die, Forsyte beamed at her. If magic worked for adepts, why couldn't it work for him? Just once.

"Do we want some juice?" the nurse asked, changing tactics.

We want to see you burst into flames. Sword said such things were possible. Why couldn't it be possible now?

"No?"

Forsyte blinked twice. *Please understand! Please!*

The nurse leaned closer. Her breath smelled like strong mint mouthwash. "We have to eat to keep up our strength." She spoke too slowly, too loudly, saying each word extra carefully as if she were talking to a two-year-old.

Forsyte closed his eyes in despair. He had an I.Q. of one hundred and seventy. He could visualize four-dimensional spacetime. He had an intuitive understanding of the wave/particle dichotomy central to quantum physics. And he was at the mercy of someone who thought his mind was as devastated as his body. *Help me. Somebody please help me.*

In the living room, the phone rang.

Forsyte snapped open his eyes. The nurse looked annoyed, then got up from the stool. She shook a finger at him as the phone rang again. "I'll be right back. Don't you do anything naughty now."

Forsyte stared up at the patterned plaster of the ceiling and strained to hear what the nurse might say to whoever it was who had called. It was probably just her service, but then, it had been almost two days since he had last spoken with Ko outside the World Plaza complex. She had come to get him from the van where he had been monitoring the attack on the skyscraper's fardoor installation and the NYPD's search of the Loft. She had told him that she had convinced the police to take him to her apartment and that she would have the Foundation arrange for a nursing staff to meet him there. She had said she would be in touch as soon as possible and then the police had taken her away. He had heard nothing from her since. He had also heard nothing from Sword, though that was to be expected.

The nurse answered the phone but she spoke so indistinctly Forsyte couldn't tell to whom she was talking. He began to compose wiring diagrams in his mind, creating circuitry that would register changes in his brainwave activity to send radio commands to a small robot. *It could be done,* he decided. *I'd have to make sure that the computer controlling the robot could call on a large library of preprogrammed functions, but in theory it should be no more difficult than sending a two-key initiation sequence to the speech synthesizer to have it speak a prerecorded message.* He groaned softly. He *had* to talk to Ko soon. To *anyone* with a functioning brain.

He heard the phone clatter as the nurse hung up. He looked over to the door, waiting for her to appear and tell him that her service had called and that she would be on triple shifts with him for yet another week. But she surprised him.

DARK HUNTER

"Well, aren't we lucky?" she said with a little clap of her hands. "We're going for a ride!" She slipped back onto the stool and reached for the sandwich again. "But first ... we're going to have to eat our lunchies."

Forsyte bit into the vile concoction. Even if he could have spoken to ask her a question, he wouldn't have. He didn't care who was coming to get him. He didn't care where he was going to be taken. All he wanted to do was leave this nightmare and this imbecile.

"Num num num," the nurse said as her dutiful patient swallowed.

It was exactly how Forsyte felt.

JUDITH & GARFIELD REEVES-STEVENS

SEVEN

Billy Santini flipped up the collar of his coat and glanced furtively up and down the SoHo street in front of the converted warehouse that was Galen Sword's headquarters and, most of the time, home.

A few truck-loading bays were in use at the smaller warehouses across the street, and a handful of storefronts near the far intersection were covered up by steel shutters erratically painted with multi-hued graffiti. But the yellow bands of plastic that sealed the main entrance of the Loft and its wide metal garage door made the brightest splash of color on the street. Printed in endless succession on the bands were the words: POLICE BARRICADE DO NOT CROSS.

"Y'know, Mr. Sword," Santini said under his breath. "If I was your lawyer I'd have to tell you that this isn't the sort of thing you should be doing now." He peered anxiously at two people walking down the street, near the small store on the corner. The sun was close to setting and it was difficult to see if the people wore uniforms. Specifically, police uniforms.

"Don't worry," Sword said, shutting out everyone and everything. "You're not my lawyer. And I own this building." He tore the plastic ribbons away from the Loft's main entrance, then stepped into the shallow alcove and punched a security code into the entry keypad. But

DARK HUNTER

the green light above the keypad didn't flicker on. Instead, the red light burned steadily.

"The code's been changed." Sword turned accusingly to Santini.

"The police have the right to do that, Mr. Sword. This building is sealed pending the outcome of the investigation."

"This is *my* building." As far as Sword was concerned, that was all that mattered. He stalked back to the limousine parked by the curb. He nodded his head in the direction of the warehouse.

Martin got out of the backseat, toting 'Bub under his arm.

Sword could see that 'Bub's carrier was still on the limousine's backseat, but Martin had informed Sword that the cat never wanted to ride in a carrier again. "Carry cage bad bad," was Martin's sole repeated argument and Sword had finally acquiesced, provided Martin gave his word to keep hold of 'Bub at all times when they were away from the Loft. Martin had grabbed 'Bub then and the cat hadn't complained, so Sword had assumed that somehow the two of them had made a deal with each other.

During the limousine ride from the pound, Martin had peeled off the uniform shirt he had been wearing, and Sword had noticed that Santini still seemed fascinated by the amount of body hair — fur, really — that covered the halfling's chest and shoulders. Maybe that at least meant that Santini would stop studying Martin's huge feet and the all-too-agile toes that worked suspiciously like thumbs and fingers.

"Martin go room sleep Ja'Nette room?" Martin asked when he and 'Bub had joined Santini in the entrance alcove.

"The door won't open," Sword said.

Martin wrinkled his heavy brow and made a show of sniffing the air. "Magic?" he asked. "Red crystal?"

Sword ignored Santini's puzzled reaction. "Not this time."

Martin grinned. He thrust 'Bub into Sword's arms. "Galen Sword keep 'Bub. Martin open door blue power."

"Red crystal? Blue power?" Santini repeated tentatively.

Sword said nothing, hoping the youth wouldn't start to ask questions now, and held 'Bub's squirming form away from him. 'Bub yowled, hissed, and swept a paw at him with claws fully extended.

Sword waved 'Bub in front of Santini. "Ah, Billy, could you ... ?"

77

JUDITH & GARFIELD REEVES-STEVENS

Santini reached out gingerly but the large white cat settled without protest in his arms, keeping her unwinking copper eyes firmly on Sword.

"Thanks," Sword said gratefully, then stood to block Santini's view of Martin at the locked door.

The halfling ran two extended fingers down either side of the door, then cupped both enormous hands around the doorknob. Behind him, Sword heard Santini mutter something unintelligible as a sudden flash of blue light sparked out from between Martin's thick fingers. Martin turned back to Sword and Santini, smiled proudly with teeth a bit too pointed, and pushed the door open with one finger.

"Second World locks," the halfling said, then grunted with what Sword guessed was supposed to be laughter.

Suddenly 'Bub scrabbled in Santini's grip, leapt free, and tore into the Loft. Martin, still grunting, scampered after her, hands scraping the ground in almost a four-legged gait. Sword gestured to Santini to follow him in, but Santini didn't move. He just stared after Martin, as the halfling's vocalizations echoed out to the street from inside the Loft.

"Where exactly is that guy from?" Santini asked.

At least that's better than asking what *exactly Martin is,* Sword thought. Then he remembered what Dr. Leah Bernstein had concluded when she misunderstood Martin and thought that his last name was Arkady. "Ah, Russia," Sword said. "Small farming village. Not used to, ah, the ways of the big city."

"Or shoes," Santini said. His expression showed he wasn't completely convinced.

Sword grinned in what he hoped would look like camaraderie. "Hey, I have enough trouble just getting the kid to wear clothes." Then he entered the Loft without giving Santini a chance to ask anything else.

At the end of a short entry hall, the main floor of the Loft opened into the parking garage. Sword palmed five large rocker switches and the standard-spectrum garage lights hummed into life, leaving the other, more specialized light fixtures dark. He swore viciously when he saw what waited for him — nothing.

Usually, the Loft's garage held his Porsche 928 S4, two or three Sword Foundation vans, his Harleys, and an old yellow cab that had proved to be most useful for conducting surveillance in the city. But none of those vehicles was here now.

Instead, the concrete floor was criss-crossed by a gridwork of tape, punctuated by chalked circles indicating — as far as Sword could tell — spots of leaked oil or transmission fluid.

"Wow, they really did a number on you," Santini said as he surveyed the huge garage.

"Who did?" Sword asked grimly.

"Police forensic team." Santini pointed to the gridwork and the circles. "They must have gone over this place with tweezers, looking for bloodstains, hair, anything to use against you. To link you with that little girl's death."

Sword felt the grip of a cold fist of apprehension, then saw that Santini was watching him.

"You think they might have found something, Mr. Sword?"

"To link me with Ja'Nette's ... death? No. Not at all." Sword shook his head decisively, though he knew that when a forensics team analyzed the various stains and debris left on the garage floor, they would find the blood of Saul Calder — the shapeshifter adept who had fought almost to the death here. And they couldn't help but find hair or fur from Martin. What would happen when they tried to identify it, and it proved neither human or animal? Sword felt control slipping through his fingers. Was it possible that his secrets were too big to be kept? Would he always be so vulnerable to outside interference?

"Then you've got nothing to worry about, Mr. Sword." But Sword could tell that Santini didn't fully believe his own reassurance, even as he uttered it.

Suddenly Martin's voice filled the garage. "Stink stink stink!"

Sword looked up past the metal staircase leading to the Loft's upper levels and open grillwork metal floors. "What is it, Martin?"

Martin appeared at the second-floor railing and hung precariously forward over it. "Big mess. Bad stink. Lights come steal many things."

But Sword shook his head at him. "Not Lights, Martin. Bluesuits."

Martin rocked forward and Sword saw Santini step back. "Martin make bluesuits give back Galen Sword things?"

"No, that's all right, Martin. They'll give them back eventually. You feed 'Bub, okay?"

"Food food food," Martin burbled happily at the new command, then did a backflip off the railing and gamboled toward the kitchen off the main lab.

"Was he ever with the Moscow Circus or anything?" Santini asked as his eyes tracked Martin's unlikely gait. Then added quickly: "You know, like an acrobat or something, not like a ... you know."

Good idea, Sword thought with an inner smile. "Almost right. His father was a famous circus acrobat in Russia. Martin's picked it all up since he was a kid."

"On the farm," Santini said dubiously.

"Guess so. So, when can I have my car back?"

Santini seemed as anxious as Sword to change the subject. "Ah, when the police are finished with it. Ms. Scarlatti can file a motion to have it returned. I guess she'll be filing a lot of motions after she's had a chance to talk with you."

"We've already talked." Sword began to pace back and forth on the garage floor. He had just remembered that whatever the forensics people might find was nothing compared to what the police were going to discover in his vans and his car. Ko had told him that a lot of the specialized equipment he had had her install needed permits or was just plain illegal. The police-band scanners, the taser guns, the anti-personnel gas wired to the vans' alarm systems. He supposed that they'd also find the hidden panels in the vans where he kept his shotguns and Berrettas as well. Weariness swept over him.

Sword felt Santini's hand go to his arm. "Are you okay, Mr. Sword? You're looking kind of pale."

Sword shook him off. "No, I'm fine. Just tired."

Santini nodded knowingly. "Anyway, you and Ms. Scarlatti have got to talk again real soon. Not like the way you talked when you were arraigned," he added. "A couple of minutes just doesn't cut it."

Sword stopped pacing and stared at Santini. He didn't know what the youth was getting at.

"I'm talking about the kid, Mr. Sword. You've got to tell Ms. Scarlatti exactly what happened. Where, when, stuff like that. And you got to get out of here, too. It won't look good if they catch you interfering with evidence."

Suddenly Sword didn't want to listen to anything more. He placed a hand on Santini's shoulder. "Listen, kid, it's all right. You've done your duty. You've warned me, told me what to watch out for. So now it's up to me, okay?"

Surprisingly, Santini stood his ground. "Uh uh, Mr. Sword. It's up to Ms. Scarlatti now. She's the only one who can help you once you get to court. And if she's going to be able to help you the best that she can, you really are going to have to talk with her. And tell her everything. You have to."

Why does it always have to be so complicated? Sword thought resentfully. "Do you want to know what happened? What *really* happened?" As if that would make any sense. What would a police forensics team say to a werewolf? How would the coroner respond upon hearing that a swarm of Lights had transformed Ja'Nette's body into floating sparks and transported her back to the First World?

"That's, uh, not my job, Mr. Sword."

But Sword persisted, keeping his grip on Santini's shoulders. "Do you want to know where Martin's really from? What 'Bub is? Do you think any of that is going to help anyone?"

Santini tried unsuccessfully to break free of Sword's grip. "Look, you're tired, Mr. Sword. Maybe you should just go check into the Plaza, get some sleep, call up the office in the morning and — "

"I can't. The sun's almost down." *And I have to find a vampire to help me figure out what to do with Kendall Marsh and meet a dark hunter in a tavern that exists on the other side of a teleportation portal.*

Sword released Santini, wondering how the kid would react if he did hear the truth, the whole truth and nothing but the truth. Santini seemed fairly level-headed and ordinary, Sword decided. Maybe it was time he had someone like this working for him. No more geniuses, no more techno-wizards. Just someone to deal with the ordinary world, with the awful and mind-numbing complexities of the truly mundane.

"Billy," Sword began, "I want you to listen carefully to what I'm going to tell you. All right? It's about me, and Martin, and what really happened to Ja'Nette."

For the first time that day, Santini began to look nervous. "Uh, I guess so. If you say so, Mr. Sword."

Sword took a breath. "Right. First the girl. Do you remember a few weeks back when the terrorists attacked the Museum of Natural History?" He waited for Santini's apprehensive nod. "Well, it wasn't terrorists. It was — "

With the sudden thunder of an arriving train, the triple-width garage door began to grind open and the strain of its motors and the creaking of its drive chains shook the Loft.

Sword wheeled, his hand instinctively going to an empty pocket of the equipment vest beneath his leather coat, grabbing for the handle of his gas pistol. But he was weaponless. Powerless. He glanced over to the light-switch control panel to judge the distance he'd have to cover to reach the second tier of lights he had had installed in the garage — lights that had stopped Orion. But through the widening gap of the opening door, Sword saw daylight. It couldn't be vampires. But it still might be shifters.

Then he recognized the vehicles that had rolled up to within inches of the garage door and knew that it was something worse than shifters.

It was Melody Ko. And the police were with her.

Santini moved in front of Sword. "Let me do the talking here, Mr. Sword. You don't need any more heat."

At the precise moment the garage's specially-armored and Kevlar-reinforced door had lifted just high enough to clear the Sword Foundation van, the black vehicle squealed forward, followed by an unmarked brown Taurus flashing a portable cherry light. Behind the black van's tinted windshield, Sword saw Ko's pale, determined face. At the wheel of the brown Taurus, Sword recognized Detective Trank and beside him, Dr. Leah Bernstein.

Bernstein's presence was no surprise to Sword. When the physician had treated him and Martin for the wounds they'd received during the shifters' Ceremony of the Change, she had clearly doubted his story of being mugged and had become very concerned about Ja'Nette's where-abouts and well-being. Sword had promised to call her again to reassure her about what he was involved in and, of course, he never had.

Obviously Bernstein had tired of waiting and had taken her suspicions to the police and then the police had found Ja'Nette's torn and bloodied jacket in one of the Sword Foundation vans.

But what was Ko doing with Trank and Bernstein? And what —

Sword saw a flashily-dressed woman step out of the back seat of the unmarked police car: Marion E. Raycheba, Kendall Marsh's boss.

Then the black van's back doors popped open and Sword heard the familiar hum of the lift plate that moved Dr. Adrian Forsyte's chair into and out of the back compartment. He saw Ko walk around from the side of the van to check the lift plate lowering the scientist and his chair to the floor of the garage. With that, everything fell into place for Sword. He stepped out from behind Santini, ready to speak for himself.

Of course, he thought, *Melody would do anything to be able to stay with Adrian and keep him supplied with the equipment he needs to stay active.* So Ko had finally sold him out. He had always known she was capable of doing so. It had never been a question of *if,* only *when.*

Trank, Bernstein, and Marion E. stood beside the brown police car. The trio stared at Sword. Trank was the first to break the silence.

"Galen, didn't yer little pal tell ya that ya can be arrested all over again just by bein' in here?"

Sword slipped his hands into the pockets of his black-leather duster. "Mr. Santini quite properly pointed out to me that a police seal on the premises must not be violated. But there was no indication of a police seal when we arrived. And without that indication — "

"Ahh, ferget it, Galen. You got bigger things ta worry about anyway." Trank turned to watch Forsyte successfully disengage his chair from the lift plate and roll forward to join the group confronting Sword.

Sword greeted Ko and Forsyte coolly. "Hello, Melody. Adrian."

Ko said nothing. Forsyte's onboard speech synthesizer crackled into life. "HELLO, GALEN. I AM GLAD TO SEE YOU ARE WELL."

Sword glanced at Bernstein and Marion E., taking note of the hard expressions on the two women's faces. "For the time being, at least," he replied. "So, Trank, what's this about?"

Trank rubbed the heel of one hand against a jowl and stared up to the garage lights high above his head. "Ahh, Galen, Galen, it's about a lot of things. A whole lot of things." The detective's voice sounded tired but when he brought his eyes down, they bore into Sword's. "Mostly about the girl, though. Where is she?"

Santini spoke up automatically. "Detective, my firm's client is under no obligation to answer your questions without the presence of his attorney. Mr. Sword, you don't have to — "

But Trank didn't let him finish. "Can it, kid." He walked over to Sword, put a hand on his arm, and drew him aside, speaking in a low, confidential manner. "Look, Galen, I always thought that you 'n' me sorta had an unnerstanding. I mean, you go off on your ghostbustin' tangents and all, but you and me had the same bottomline, ya know? What's right, what's wrong. And if somethin' bad has happened to that little girl, then I *know* that you know that that's wrong. And we gotta do somethin' about it."

Sword looked over at Ko. "I agree one hundred percent. Someone has to do something about it."

Santini made an attempt to step between the two of them. "Uh, Mr. Sword. Can't we at least wait until I can call one of the partners?"

"No, Billy, the detective's right." Sword waved him off, as he reassessed his options. He had been prepared to bring Santini into his morass of secret knowledge. Perhaps it was also time to share what he knew with Trank. Maybe the police didn't have to be a complication. Perhaps they could even be of help. From what he read in Ko's expression, he knew she had to have told Trank and the others *something* about what was going on. Perhaps his best move was to follow her lead.

"What has Melody told you?"

"Sorry, Galen, I'd rather hear it from you." Trank eyed him, patient.

"Why not," Sword said with a shrug as he heard Santini moan behind him, "Ms. Scarlatti's going to fire me, Mr. Sword. She's absolutely going to fire me for this."

"Everything goes back to about three years ago. When I had that accident."

Marion E. stalked over to Trank to poke a finger into his well-padded side, making him wince. "The accident! I knew it. I *knew* it. It was all about control of that trust fund, wasn't it, Sword?"

Sword frowned at her. "No. The accident had nothing at all to do with that."

DARK HUNTER

But Marion E. swept on. "Because Kennie told me that that was when you switched control of the trust fund from Askwith and Marjoribanks to — "

"What's Kennie got to do with this? What are you talking about?" *And what was Kendall Marsh doing discussing my finances with her boss?*

"The whole point of her undercover investigation, Mr. Sword." Marion E. crossed her arms and gave Sword a tightlipped look.

"What undercover investigation? When?"

"Three years ago. When you and Kennie were getting so close, remember?"

Trank scrunched up his face and shook his head. "Ahh, Marion, how about letting Galen get on with his story. We can go over all that other stuff later. Galen ... you were saying? About the accident?"

Sword felt as if he had been sucker-punched. *He* was the one who was always being accused of using people, and now to find out that the only person ... He opened his mouth and a chest-shaking yowl filled the garage.

Bernstein, Marion E., and Forsyte fixed their eyes on Sword's mouth in amazement. But Trank, Ko, and Sword immediately looked up to the true source of the bloodcurdling scream — a dark shape hurtling down the Loft's metal staircase. Trank's hand was already inside his jacket, going for his gun. But Sword knew the halfling better now. Martin was simply being happy. While nearly naked, of course. Wearing only an extremely brief pair of lurid, purple satin World Wrestling Federation shorts.

Martin touched the stairs only twice as he vaulted downward like a somersaulting rocket, hitting the landing on all fours, then rebounding into the air like an enormous rubber ball to slam to a stop on the garage floor at the side of Forsyte's chair. The halfling's lips pulled back from his teeth and he screeched deafeningly. He slapped his right hand against the concrete floor with explosive force. At the same time he lifted the back of his huge left hand to Forsyte's face and stroked the scientist's cheek gently.

By this time, both Trank and Marion E. were gaping at Martin. Dr. Leah Bernstein looked less surprised.

85

JUDITH & GARFIELD REEVES-STEVENS

Sword walked over to Martin while Santini begin to babble ineffectual explanations at Trank and the others. "Ah, apparently his dad was an acrobat with the Moscow Circus. Raised on a farm, small town, out in Siberia or something. He's, ah, he's not from around here."

Sword patted Martin's densely-muscled shoulder. "Did you feed 'Bub?" he asked.

Martin nodded enthusiastically. "'Bub eat Martin eat. Big stink bad bluesuits take no food steal steal bad. Eat lots." He turned to Sword, grinned again, and burped. Sword grimaced as the putrid smell of partially digested cat food wafted over him.

"Good, Martin, very good. Now, we're having an important talk here so it would be even better if you went back upstairs to look after 'Bub, all right?"

Martin twisted to stare at Ko as if he hadn't seen her for years. "'Bub okay. 'Bub go for walk."

Sword groaned inwardly. The damned cat's collar was off again. "Where, Martin? Where?"

"Upstairs up up. Had to go." Sword relaxed somewhat. At least if 'Bub was prowling around upstairs, she wouldn't be interfering in what he had to say to Trank. Though an invisible housecat might be all it would take to convince the detective about the truth of the story he was about to hear.

"You can stay then," Sword said to the halfling, "but you have to be very quiet."

Martin nodded. He kissed Forsyte's hand and Sword saw the physicist lightly brush the edge of Martin's cheek with one of his operative fingers. "Martin quiet like on hunt."

"Good." Sword turned back to Trank. "Where were we?"

Trank answered slowly, not taking his eyes from Martin as the halfling squatted by Forsyte's side. "The accident. You were going to tell us what happened to the girl."

Sword nodded. Now it was time.

The sound of Michael Jackson singing suddenly sprang up. The sound came from the Loft's upper level and everyone looked up and then questioningly back at Sword. Martin gave a small moan.

DARK HUNTER

Sword's chest felt tight. He and Ko had always scolded Ja'Nette for playing MTV too loudly. Now it sounded as if the television set in her room was on.

"Just the cat," Sword began to explain. "She's always walking over the remote controls and — "

The metal staircase shook with a volley of rhythmic clangs.

" — turns on all the ... " Sword's voice died away. Martin's moan became louder.

In Ko's wide, apprehensive eyes, Sword saw the confirmation of what he and Martin had heard. The clanging footsteps shared the same rolling pattern produced by Ja'Nette every time she'd raced down the stairs from her fourth-level bedroom. How often had he and Ko told her not to run on the stairs?

"Someone else up there ya haven't tole me about?" Trank asked suspiciously.

Sword shook his head but said nothing. The ringing sounds quieted for a moment, as if whoever was making them was crossing the third floor to the next staircase. Then they began again.

Martin's moaning changed to a distressed *ooo*-ing sound from deep in the back of his throat. Ko was clutching the back of Forsyte's chair. "Sword ... ?" she began to ask, almost in a whisper.

"That doesn't sound like a cat to me," Dr. Bernstein said as the familiar rhythm faded once more and then began again .

But the time for explanation had come and gone.

Through the open metal slats of the walkway above, Sword stared at the small figure that raced to the top of the final staircase and then jumped down the stairs into the garage's bright lights.

It was Ja'Nette.

EIGHT

It had been a long time since Melody Ko had felt anything remotely akin to real fear, but she was feeling it now.

Ja'Nette was undeniably dead. Ko had watched as a werewolf had lifted the screaming twelve-year-old to his muzzle and ripped the throat and the life from her forever.

Yet, here and now, Ja'Nette was also undeniably alive and her eyes shone with alertness and childish enthusiasm as she half-ran, half-skipped toward Martin.

All present were silent and the only sensation of which Ko was aware was an inner cascade of arctic icewater, numbing her, taking strength from her knees, and the breath from her lungs.

"Hiya, Martin." The little girl waited expectantly at the halfling's side, a broad and friendly smile transforming her face so that, even with her once-elaborately braided hair now cut as severely short as Ko's, what she appeared to be was a sweet child. But what she was, was a walking corpse.

Martin did not return the smile. He turned away and gripped Forsyte's hand in his.

The child didn't seem to notice. She turned to face all the others. "Hiya, everybody. Hi, Melody. Hi, Sword. Hi, Adrian." She bounced once or twice in her unlaced Reeboks, then slipped her hands into the

DARK HUNTER

back pockets of her ripped-knee jeans the way Sword often did. "What's up?"

Dr. Bernstein spoke first. "What's your name, child?"

Ja'Nette made a funny frown and looked up at the ceiling. The werewolf's jaws had almost severed Ja'Nette's head from her body but now Ko saw that not a single mark blemished the smooth dark skin of the child's neck. Ko's heartbeat thundered in her ears. She wondered if the others could hear its clamor.

"You know who I am, Dr. Bernstein. I'm Ja'Nette." She smiled at Trank. "Right, Detective Trank?"

Trank nodded slowly, his tongue making a bulge in his cheek. "That's right, Ja'Nette. How ya doin'?"

"I'm doin' okay." The girl looked around the garage and her smile faded. "Hey, Sword, where's your cars?"

Ko saw in Sword the same incomprehension that she was experiencing. There could be no doubt that Ja'Nette was dead. There could be no doubt that they had both seen her body taken by the Lights somewhere in a part of Central Park that Ko had never known existed. Whatever this apparition was before them, it could not be Ja'Nette. It could not be real. It must not be.

Then Ko felt Trank's cutting gaze on her. "Miz Ko, I think we had better have a talk." His voice sounded harsh, but not from fear. From anger.

And why not? Ko thought. Just an hour ago I told him that Ja'Nette was dead. *I told him that Sword was involved. I promised to deliver Sword to him in exchange for immunity for Adrian and me.*

"What's everybody starin' at?" the Ja'Nette apparition asked.

Dr. Leah Bernstein went over to the girl. "We were worried about you, child."

"Me?"

Bernstein laid the back of her hand against Ja'Nette's forehead. Transfixed with ghastly fascination, Ko half-expected to see the hand pass through the girl as if she were nothing more than mist. But whatever the apparition was composed of, from Bernstein's reaction, it obviously felt just like the flesh of a living human child.

89

"We were worried you might have been hurt," Bernstein continued. She took Ja'Nette's hand in hers, quickly checked the girl's fingernails, then touched two fingers to Ja'Nette's wrist and counted off seconds on her watch.

"Get outta town," Ja'Nette protested laughingly. "I wasn't hurt. It was Sword and Martin who got jumped."

"Let me look in your mouth, dear." Bernstein reached up and angled Ja'Nette's head so the overhead lights shone into her mouth. "Say ahhh."

Ja'Nette stuck her tongue out and ahhhed for the doctor.

"How did Martin and Mr. Sword get ... jumped?"

Ja'Nette frowned at Sword as soon as the doctor released her. "Hey, I thought you said you went to her office to get fixed up," she said accusingly. "You always yell at me when I say I don't want to go to the doctor's."

Bernstein bent down in a half-crouch to bring herself to eye-level with Ja'Nette. "Why did Mr. Sword need to be fixed up?"

Ja'Nette looked as exasperated as only a twelve-year-old could be. Ko remained an awestruck witness to the terrible realism of whatever illusion was being perpetrated.

"I told ya, Sword and Martin got jumped by the bad guys."

"What bad guys, dear?"

Ja'Nette sighed noisily as though she realized that she was the only one who could put things right. "We were driving around and we went to Häagen-Daz for ice cream, and so we were all walking by the Park, right? And these two guys came out from one of those big stone walls, okay? And they were pretty scary and everything and wanted Sword's watch and our money but Melody sort of grabbed me and took off with Adrian and the bad guys jumped Sword and Martin. Course, Sword and Martin beat up the bad guys, right? But they got sort of bashed up themselves and they said they were going to see you and that you'd fix them up." Ja'Nette peered into Bernstein's eyes. "*Didn't* they go see you? They said they would."

The doctor straightened up, shooting a glance at Trank who in turn stared hard at Ko. The detective's building temper was given away by the crimson flush spreading across his meaty cheeks.

"Oh, they saw me all right," Bernstein said. "Told me they had been mugged. And that you were fine."

"Well, I am," Ja'Nette said brightly, then repeated, "So, what's up?"

"Not a whole lot now," Trank said. "Ya didn't get hurt in the mugging, did ya?"

"No way," the child said earnestly.

"Ya sure now?" Trank stressed. "We found your jacket, you know. Had a lot of blood on it."

Ja'Nette made an exaggerated frown. "Eww, yeah, that was pretty gross, wasn't it? Martin sorta used it like a bandage."

Billy Santini now moved in to confront Trank. "Detective, I suppose I don't have to tell you what all this information does to your charges against my firm's client?"

Trank held up a thick finger. "Not so fast, Skeezix." He looked down at the little girl. "So, Ja'Nette, where ya been the past few days?"

"With my momma."

A sudden nightmarish image replayed itself before Ko's eyes — Ja'Nette's mother, an adept of the Clan Marratin, materializing as a ghost on the night that Ja'Nette 'went home.' A black-skinned woman with obsidian eyes twice the size of any human's.

"Your momma still around?"

Ja'Nette nodded. "Sure. Ya wanna meet her?"

Trank nodded back and Ja'Nette skipped back over to the staircase, leaned against the railing, and yelled up to the next level. "Mommmaa! Some people wanta meetcha!"

Ja'Nette skipped back to the knot of adults. "I think she's in the bathroom."

Trank spoke to Ko, trying to keep his voice low so Ja'Nette wouldn't hear, but it crackled with menace anyway. "I don't know what kinda scam you wuz trying ta pull here, but after I drop the charges against Galen I'm gonna see what kinda charges we can get goin' against you for ... for ... I don't know what for. But it'll be somethin'!"

Since Ko couldn't offer any defense other than the Ja'Nette-thing wasn't of this world, she remained silent.

Then the metal staircase clanged with a new set of footsteps, moving slowly this time.

Oh, no, Ko thought. *Not again, no more.* With all her heart she wished for the past, three months earlier, when her life had been normal and she'd been able to believe that the First World and its adepts were nothing more than Sword's delusions. But the time was the present and it *was* Ja'Nette's mother who appeared on the staircase, clad in a colorful kaftan, her unseen hair wrapped in a matching turban. She descended the stairs slowly because 'Bub slinked in and out of her feet, purring so loudly that Ko could hear the animal even fifteen feet from the stairs.

The next few minutes were as disjointed and unnatural as any nightmare half-remembered. The woman on the stairs had normal eyes and a gracious smile, and greeted everyone whom Ja'Nette introduced to her, with a gentle handshake. She was from Kenya, she explained, originally. But with the troubles there and her university work precarious at best she had thought it prudent to leave Ja'Nette somewhere safe, with old family friends. Yes, Sword's parents and her parents had been close acquaintances, and yes, Ja'Nette was thrilled to spend time in New York, so exciting for a young girl, but she'd be going to London next, joining her mother for a year at least, and what a pleasure to meet Galen's friends and the people whom Ja'Nette had spoken so much about.

Ko felt faint. She felt the Loft waver around her like something seen through intense heat, just as it had when she had been influenced by the yellow waiting crystal, when Brin had appeared to her in this same place. *Is this a reaction to First World trickery?* Ko thought, in a last effort to make some sense out of senselessness. *Is this feeling a side effect? Does anyone else notice? Does anyone else care?*

Apparently, no one else did. The small talk with Ja'Nette's mother hit a lull and Trank gruffly announced that it was time to leave.

Santini intercepted the detective again as he headed for his car. "My firm's client will be expecting immediate and full restitution of his illegally-seized property, as well as — " Trank's fierce glower made the young man change tactics. "Um, anyway, I'm sure Ms. Scarlatti will be talking to you in the morning." Santini got out of Trank's way.

Marion E. was already in the unmarked police car, impatient to leave, but Bernstein held back. Ko could see the gray-haired doctor peering at Martin's bare chest. *Of course,* she thought. *Dr. Bernstein treated Martin's wounds after the Arkady Ceremony of the Change. But those wounds are gone. There aren't even scars.*

Bernstein walked over to Sword next, as if he were no more than an experimental animal, brusquely took his chin in hand and turned his head so she could see the triangular scar on his left cheek. *At least,* Ko thought, *that scar is still there.*

Bernstein let go of Sword. "Something stinks here, Galen. You told me the girl had already gone home to her mother."

Sword's grim face was pale. "I told you that she was *going* home."

The doctor shook her head. "You can't lie to me, Galen. Never have been able to, never will be able to." She glanced back over at Martin. "Something *really* stinks here." Then she nodded good-bye to Ja'Nette's mother and got into Trank's unmarked police car.

No one except Ja'Nette waved as the brown Taurus backed out onto the street and drove off. The sun had set and the street outside the Loft was dark.

After an awkward pause, Sword went over to the garage-door control panel and hit the release control. The rattling clamor of the descending door ended only when the door had closed entirely. As soon as the outside world was safely cut off, Martin's howl of despair filled the Loft. He still had not let go of Forsyte's hand.

In the presence of the truly unfathomable, Ko said and did nothing.

She heard Sword address Santini who was still staring at Martin. The halfling's lament had not sounded in the least human. "Maybe you could wait in the limousine for a few minutes, Billy." It wasn't a question. "I'll be out in a little while."

"Uh, you still going to need it tonight, Mr. Sword?" Santini managed to mumble.

Sword shook his head, as if the motion could clear his mind. "I let too many things slide the past few days. And I can't afford to let anything slide again."

Santini nodded and left by the main door at the end of the entrance alcove.

Sword waited until he heard the door lock click shut, then he went to the woman who claimed to be Ja'Nette's mother. "Who are you?"

JUDITH & GARFIELD REEVES-STEVENS

The woman bowed her head, though not in greeting, Ko thought. When she lifted it again, her eyes had become gleaming black orbs that seemed to wrap around her head, glittering beneath the garage's overhead lights. "I am Sial, keeper to the Clan Marratin."

Ko decided that Sword must really have become used to the sights and experiences of the past few weeks because she could detect no change in him in response to the woman's dramatic transformation. "*Are* you Ja'Nette's mother?"

The woman's right arm flashed upwards and her fingers danced in a pattern that reminded Ko of Tomas Roth and the gestures he used to call forth magic. "There is no Ja'Nette," the keeper said.

Ko turned to look at the child —

— in time to see her unravel like tattered strings tossed by the winds, melting like the memory of a dream.

Martin howled again and buried his face in Forsyte's lap. The halfling's anguish was a mirror for Ko's own.

Ko drew some comfort from Sword's rare state of discomfiture as he addressed the black-eyed figure. "I'm ... sorry."

But the keeper of Marratin did not acknowledge Sword's apology. Instead, she went to Martin, 'Bub still trailing at her side, tail lashing. "The Victor of Marratin gives thanks to the warrior of Arkady who fought for its child and called for the Lights to take her home." The turbaned woman extended a long finger to Martin's face and touched him lightly at a point between his eyes. "Look to the center to find us at your side."

Martin's tear-filled eyes were wide and his mouth half open, but he kept silent.

Then the keeper came for Ko. Ko forced herself to stare deep into the glistening black eyes, to discover if any rational structure for sight existed within them. But she saw nothing, or, rather, nothing she could recognize. She could not even read emotion in Sial's fathomless eyes.

"The Victor of Marratin gives thanks to the human of the Second World who cared for its child." The keeper paused for a long moment, then gestured again with both hands. "You are released from your enchantment."

94

Ko doubled over, breathless, as a searing wave of pain crashed through her arm and her ribs collapsed inward. Moaning, she slipped to her knees, cradling her arm, her aching chest. Dizzy, nauseated, she slumped forward until her forehead touched the cool cement floor of the garage.

Then Sial strode away toward Sword. *What enchantment?* Ko thought in a daze. *There is no such thing.* Her arm felt just as it had when Orion had broken it. But after Brin had healed her, her broken arm hadn't hurt at all. Neither had her ribs — the ones the werewolf Seth had cracked.

Ko's vision clouded and the coolness of the concrete beneath her forehead called to her. She longed to sleep, to escape the unwanted pain and confusion. But she couldn't. She had to hear what Sial said to Sword. She had to know. She had to know everything. Forsyte always said her desire to know, no matter what the cost, was her greatest flaw.

But Sial said nothing to Sword. Not at first.

Instead the tall, turbaned woman struck Sword a two-handed blow in the face. Though Sword staggered back, he managed to stay standing, but only just. *Good,* Ko thought. *Hit him again.* Her vision was blurring in time to the pulses of pain that accompanied her gasps for air, but Ko wasn't about to miss the sight of Sword being given what he deserved. She struggled to stay conscious.

Behind Sial, Martin growled low, but in unmistakable warning. But the keeper frowned at the halfling. "Such misplaced devotion does you no honor. You know what he is responsible for. A warrior cannot interfere in such matters."

Martin did not reply but he began to rock back and forth on his haunches. When the keeper turned back at Sword, Ko saw Martin duck his head as if he did not want to see what happened next.

But Sial did not strike a second time. She spoke to Sword instead. "The Victor of Marratin says that these illusions were not cast to keep you or aid you because you are not worthy of such actions. As all clans have duties to maintain the layer between the Worlds, so the layer has been maintained this day."

"If you show me how," Sword said, "I can maintain the layer — "

Sial raised her hand again, long fingers arched like claws. "Do not speak to me, betrayer of the Worlds. You have no substance. You have no honor."

"They were stolen from me!"

Sial struck again.

A faint smile came to Ko's face as she heard the keeper's voice hiss like the spitting of a monstrous snake. "You know *nothing*. You have *nothing*. You are *nothing*."

"I — "

Ko's eyes closed then opened as she heard another blow impact Sword.

"And you took my child."

Ko squinted uncertainly. She wasn't sure but it looked like blue fire blazed from the keeper's eyes, the same color of fire that she seen emanate from Martin's hands when he opened locks and doors.

Sword was holding his hand to his mouth and Ko saw the brilliance of fresh blood seep from beneath his fingers. His bottom lip was split.

The Marratin keeper waited, as if daring Sword to speak again. But he didn't, having apparently for once learned his lesson.

"Marratin has done its duty here," Sial intoned. "But be warned that if you ever pass through the layer again, we will be free of all restraints and exclusions.

"This is your only world now, betrayer. See that you keep to it as the substanceless pretender that you are."

Slowly, Sial turned her back on Sword with all the deliberateness of a ritual gesture. 'Bub stretched up on her hind legs, mewing softly and lightly tapping against the keeper's kaftan with her paws.

Ko saw the keeper's severe face soften as she looked down at the cat. "We are sorry, soft one, but it is not our decision." 'Bub dropped to all fours but her copper eyes stayed fixed on the woman.

Then Sial looked again at Martin, said, "You could do better, warrior of Arkady," and turned around again. And again. Until the vibrant colors of her kaftan glowed like luminous jets of gas and she dissolved into a shimmering tower of near-blinding light.

Near-blinding light that disappeared without leaving an afterimage in Ko's eyes.

Not electromagnetic radiation then, Ko thought woozily, stomach churning. *But what else is there?* She threw up on the floor. *Can't be particle-based. Otherwise we'd all be cooked by the radiation.* She gave up the fight and stretched out on the floor with a sigh. The keeper was gone and Ko decided it was time to close her eyes and organize her thoughts, despite feeling as if her body were spinning uncontrollably through space.

Let's see, if we postulate the existence of a separate spectrum of discrete energy, perhaps polarized from the E.M. spectrum that we know about ... She became aware of someone large standing over her and half-opened her eyes. It was Martin. She tried to smile up at him but the pain in her arm and her ribs somehow made it difficult to move any part of her body. But she didn't mind. She had a plan.

Martin can carry me up to one of the guest rooms and I can use a portable terminal to sketch in some Feynman diagrams of a polarized matter-energy spectrum that ... She felt Martin's powerful hands on her, lifting her gently and effortlessly. She discovered with relief that her pain was already so great that the movement added nothing to it.

Of course, polarized matter-energy. Polarized spacetime. Different dimensions. 'Bub's mass discrepancy. Teleportation. One cause, so many different effects. The equations began to swim before her eyes. Despite her delirium, it was all so clear. Almost as if a cloud had been taken from her eyes.

Almost as if a clouding enchantment had been lifted.

Ko looked up at a new face that stared down at her. *I know those eyes.* "Brin," she said weakly, "what did you do to me? Why —"

"It's Galen, Melody. Shhh."

Ko felt both storm-tossed and exhilarated. Brin, Galen, brothers, so much alike. *Except for the blue power.* Passed down through the father according to Martin. She'd have to point that out to Sword. They seemed to be missing something about Brin's blue power.

"Sword ... ?" Martin was carrying her somewhere but Ko couldn't tell where. "Where are ... ?" The world was too confusing for her right now. Too tiring. Too everything. But she had a plan. Didn't she. *I have to have a plan. I have to.* What would her life be worth without a direction?

"It's all right, Melody, we're going to the hospital."

"No, we're not," Ko muttered. "Just need to sleep. That's all." Dimly, she realized that all the fatigue that Brin had taken from her had returned also with her broken arm and cracked ribs. "I don't need to go to the hospital."

"I have to see Kennie," Sword said. "She's my responsibility."

Figures, Ko thought resentfully. *We're going to the hospital for* his reasons, *not mine*. "Just let me rest," she mumbled. She felt Martin lay her down carefully and she guessed she was in the backseat of the limousine she had seen parked out front of the Loft. That Billy Santini guy must be nearby.

"No time to rest," Sword said, and it was as if his determined voice echoed from another room. "Whatever happened in there ... for whatever reason, I've been given a second chance."

Ko felt herself spiralling down into blackness and her instincts kicked in. She fought her way back up to the light. And Sword. "Bloody ... hell. You? For what?"

"To get back in." Sword's voice began to fade again. "To find my home. To go back to where I belong, through the layer, to the First World."

"She warned ... you ... not to."

"It's not her decision to make. It can only be mine, now."

"She'll ... kill ... you."

"I'm not afraid. Not anymore."

Tendrils of night wove their web tightly around Ko. She knew she had to give up, let go. But she'd be damned to hell before she'd ever willingly let Sword have the last word.

"I ... hate ... you ... Sword."

Oblivion swallowed her before Sword could reply and Ko's last fleeting thoughts were of victory.

And Brin.

DARK HUNTER

NINE

Sword stepped from the elevator, stared down the surprisingly long hospital corridor, and for a moment felt as if he were somehow back in Martin's 'other streets,' deep beneath the city.

It was the lighting, he decided. The hospital was old and the corridor fixtures created pools of light on the gleaming polished-aggregate floor. The adepts' passageways constructed under New York City — and who knew how many other cities? — also had light fixtures too few and far apart. Some had been powered by electricity. Others by strange, floating facets of the ubiquitous power source in the technology of the First World — glowing red crystals. Sword closed his eyes for a moment to remember what it had felt like to brush his fingers against a working red crystal and see its light suddenly falter, as if his touch alone was somehow able to sap its energy supply.

"Coming' through," someone called out.

Sword opened his eyes with a start and stepped out of the way as an orderly pushed an empty gurney into the still open elevator behind him.

"You okay, mac?" the orderly asked suspiciously.

"Yeah, fine," Sword said, though he didn't sound convincing even to himself. "Do you know which way to room — "

The elevator doors slid shut while the orderly inside the elevator car continued to stare intently at him.

"Crystals," Sword murmured out loud, trying to recapture the train of thought he had been following.

"I beg your pardon?" A woman in a white lab coat had arrived to press the elevator call button.

"What did you say?" Sword asked. He scanned the hall again, struck by the fact that all the hospital staff he could see looked skittish and tense. The sound of a phone ringing at a nurse's station caught his ear and he realized it had been ringing unanswered since he had stepped out onto the floor. The noise was unbelievably irritating.

The woman glanced over her shoulder, looking in the same direction Sword just had. "You said something first."

"Is everything all right around here?" Sword asked. Five minutes ago in Emergency, as he had helped Ko check in, the hospital had seemed normal. Was there something unusual about this particular floor? Had something just happened here?

"What do you mean by that?" the woman demanded.

"Sorry, nurse, I was—"

The woman's lips pursed. "That's *doctor*."

"Doctor," Sword said quickly. The elevator arrival bell chimed. "Sorry. I was just looking for room — "

"Then read the signs on the walls," the woman snapped and pushed her way onto a crowded elevator heading down. Visiting hours were just ending.

The doors of the second elevator closed tight. The phone at the nurse's station was still ringing, its noisy summons still unanswered.

Sword ran his fingers over his close-cropped hair. Then he turned around, looking for the room signs on a nearby wall. In a few seconds, he deciphered the colored bar directional signs, his success in no small part due to his university training in reading ancient hieroglyphics, and finally set off for Kendall Marsh's room.

Everyone he passed along the way seemed jumpy and Sword increasingly felt as if he were on those 'other streets,' for more than just the similarity in lighting. Years ago, before he had begun to investigate claims of the paranormal in an attempt to uncover his origins, he knew he would have jokingly attributed the charged feeling on the hospital floor to it being the time of the full moon, even though the moon was only half full this night. But his subsequent, exhaustive studies had failed to turn up a single scientific experiment to confirm the linking of the phases of the moon to people's moods or accident rates. And, as he knew now from direct personal experience, it didn't require a full moon to change a human into a beast. The trigger for that particular transformation was First World red crystal.

Sword snapped his fingers. *That's* what he had been thinking about when he had arrived on this floor. Red crystals and his ability to somehow nullify whatever power they contained.

He remembered that there had once been a time when it had been very difficult for him to even speculate about such things — crystals, the paranormal, shapeshifters, and worse. But after the accident, consideration of these and other related topics had suddenly become easier. Lately, he'd been wondering if the memory-blocking liquid the wizard had made him drink as a child had been so overwhelming that it somehow had acted to prevent him from even *thinking* about the paranormal in general, even as it had hidden and still hid specific details of his past life from his conscious mind.

I have Brin to thank for the little I have been able to recover, Sword thought. *Odd that my brother was able to restore my health completely, but not my memories.*

He came to what he hoped was the turn in the seemingly endless corridor. The state of his childhood memories would have to remain as but one more question in a long list of questions to be answered someday. His memories, red crystals, yellow crystals, blue powers, dark hunt —

As Sword rounded the corner, a blue-uniformed security guard was suddenly before him, hand on a businesslike revolver in an open holster.

"Visiting hours are over and this corridor is off limits, sir." The guard was young, no older than twenty-five, and he was obviously struggling to make his voice rough and intimidating. *Inexperienced. Probably his first time out,* Sword thought. *Not the usual choice for this kind of job, either.* The man's haircut seemed expensive for what a first-time guard could earn.

Sword tried to look friendly. He hadn't had much practice doing so. Being wealthy, he'd never lacked for people who wanted to be his friend, without his having to do anything to encourage them.

He glanced at the guard's name tag: KEITH FRANKLIN. "Nothing to be concerned about, Keith. I'm an old friend of Kennie's. I understand they — "

"There's no 'Kennie' here. You'll have to leave now."

Sword hesitated, stalling for time. Keith had obviously been hired by Marsh's television station to make sure that no one — either the purported terrorists or Galen Sword — could get close to the reporter while she remained in a coma.

"If you don't leave, sir, I'll have to — "

"Why don't you check your list of people who *are* allowed in," Sword said pleasantly. If he could persuade Keith to consult the list, then he might be able to spot just one of the names on it and come back when a different guard was on duty.

The security guard looked uncertain.

"C'mon, make a call or whatever you have to do, but you can trust me. Kennie's an old friend. I'm probably on the list." Sword waited a moment, then added, "And I wouldn't want you to get in trouble over this. This being your first assignment and all."

Keith made no attempt to hide his surprise. "How'd you know this was my first assignment?"

"You don't look much like a security guard," Sword asked, hoping he didn't sound too condescending.

Apparently he hadn't been. Keith became talkative. "I'm not," the young security guard said wonderingly, looking about him as if it was only now that he realized he was in a hospital corridor. "I'm a bank teller ... "

Maybe there's an oxygen leak somewhere, Sword thought. Everyone on this floor was in a strange state. *Well, then,* he thought, *might as well go for broke.*

"Keith, my name is Galen Sword and I wouldn't — "

DARK HUNTER

"Oh! Mr. Sword. Sorry. Yes, please, go right ahead." Keith almost jumped out of Sword's path. "I was told to expect you."

Now that was just too easy, Sword thought. He didn't move. "Who told you to expect me?"

Keith looked puzzled. "Why, my ... I ... I can't remember, actually. But I do know that we're expecting you."

"Who's 'we'?"

Keith looked down the short corridor toward the only room door that Sword could see. The door was closed.

"Paula," Keith said. "My girlfriend. Partner. She's in Kennie's room now. We share the shift."

A bank teller named Keith and his girlfriend named Paula, Sword thought. *What kind of a security agency came up with these two?*

"And who did you say you're working for?"

Keith thought for a moment. "Um, the client's name is ... Marion E. Raycheba. You know, from that television station."

"Yeah, I know her," Sword said. Something — even if he didn't know what it was — was definitely wrong here. So it was only prudent to prepare for the worst. In the past few weeks, Sword's definition of 'the worst' had expanded exponentially.

Sword casually glanced over his shoulder to see if anyone else had come around the turn in the corridor. For the moment, no one had. "So, I guess I'll just go in there, shall I?" He pointed at the closed door ten feet away.

Keith nodded. "Yes, please. You — "

Keith's breath left him in a sudden whoosh as Sword drove his fist deep into the young guard's stomach. Before Keith could even try to draw in a new breath, Sword was behind him, one hand twisting the young guard's left arm up his back. Sword's other hand captured Keith's gun.

"My arm, my arm," Keith gasped as Sword pushed him up against the wall.

Sword eased up on Keith's left arm, but only after first checking to see that they were still alone in this branch of the corridor.

A small circle of red stained the blue shirt fabric caught in the bend of Keith's elbow.

103

"Sorry," Sword said, surprised to have damaged the elbow at all, wondering if he'd caused a compound fracture. Ko had taught him the defensive move. She hadn't told him it would break bones.

Then he quickly but carefully guided the unprotesting security guard toward the door to Marsh's hospital room. With his gun hand, Sword reached around Keith and pushed the door open, immediately shoving the young guard through to draw the first attack of whoever — or whatever — kind of accomplice waited in Marsh's room. An instant later, Sword burst into the dimly-lit room, crouching low and holding the gun out before him. His eyes seeking the enemy in each corner.

Nothing moved within the room.

Standing by the room's tall window, wearing the same blue uniform as Keith, Sword saw a young woman with long brown hair holding a hand to her open mouth in surprise, ignoring the revolver in her own holster.

On the narrow hospital bed directly in front of Sword lay the silent, sheet-draped form of Kendall Marsh, alive only because the heart monitor above the bed and the bubbling oxygen feed said she was.

Other than Keith's moaning and the rhythmic beep of the cardiac monitor, there was no other sound in the room.

Sword caught the scent of the second guard's perfume — sandalwood and musk. *New and yet still somehow ... no, not the perfume,* Sword thought, as he slowly rose to his full height, keeping his gun trained on the brown-haired woman. He let Keith flop to the floor, still clutching at and babbling about his wounded arm. *There's something else in here that's familiar. Something other than perfume, something other than lighting, something ...*

"Good evening, Mr. Sword."

The voice — sure, resonant, and familiar — came from a corner Sword had stared directly into just moments earlier.

Where he had seen nothing.

Sword lowered his gun. He knew his weapon would be useless.

Orion, last vampire adept of the Clan Isis unfolded his tall frame from the shadowed corner, extended his hand in greeting, and smiled, the handsomely-sculpted planes of his mobile face serene. Most impor-

DARK HUNTER

tantly to Sword, the smile did not reveal the vampire's feeding fangs to be in place.

Sword dropped Keith's gun into his coat pocket, then took the vampire's hand.

"I didn't think I'd see you so soon," he said, surprised at the relief he felt at encountering Orion again. Vampire adepts, like so much of the First World, were both the same and far greater than any of the legends told about them in the Second World of humans.

True, Orion had fangs which slipped out of hidden sockets behind his other, more normal-appearing teeth, and true he used those fangs to draw the blood of his prey, but with his own eyes Sword had seen that what a vampire took from his prey was not just blood, and not just life, but *everything* that defined another intelligent being.

Minutes after the attack of the Close trolls in the Hell's Kitchen alley near the Tepesh enclave, Sword had watched Orion battle and defeat a seven-foot-tall, gray-furred Right wolf in full shifterform. The creature's musculature had been enormous — although Orion had thrown a car on top of her, the creature had tossed it off just as quickly and as easily. But the whole conflict, from the shifter's first appearance to her final defeat, had lasted, by Sword's reckoning, just under fifteen seconds.

Immediately afterward, Sword, accompanied by Martin, had been witness to what a First World vampire was truly capable of. As Orion had sunk his fangs into the shifter's neck to drink in her blood, he had taken on her attributes. His chest had swelled with the growth of new muscles. His eyes had changed from human normal to the shifter's phosphorescent green. New-grown fur had sprouted from his body and a muzzle had begun to jut out from his face.

And then Sword had seen and heard evidence of the most incredible ability of all.

The vampire had captured the shifter's mind.

In a voice that was not his own, Orion shared with Martin all the memories and the knowledge of the shifter whose blood he had consumed, and Sword had learned that for a vampire's prey there was no final death, only the terrible limbo of absorption.

Martin later told him that the knowledge and the personality of that shifter would become a part of Orion for all time, together with all the thousands of others the vampire had taken in his uncounted centuries of life.

It wasn't at all clear to Sword how Orion could sustain his sanity. Or how Orion could keep even the concept of an independent identity. But now Sword knew how one vampire could turn the tide of an entire First World war — simply by absorbing the knowledge and personality of a rival clan's Victor.

I'm glad you're safe, Orion," Sword said, and meant it. "And in one piece."

The vampire looked down at Sword, taller by a hand. His wavy brown hair was drawn into a loose ponytail as he had worn it when Sword had seen him last. "And I am glad that you have escaped the dungeon you were taken to."

Orion's choice of words made Sword smile. "I wouldn't call a police holding cell a dungeon."

"I would," the vampire said as he moved to help Keith to his feet.

"Keith, I'm really sorry about your arm," Sword said to the young guard. "I didn't know what to expect in here."

But Keith didn't appear to have even heard Sword's apology. He was staring up into Orion's eyes. Expectantly, devotedly.

"Will he be all right?" Sword asked Orion.

Across the room, Paula had lost her surprised look and, as she walked around Marsh's bed to join Keith, she also stared at Orion with an almost sexual anticipation.

Orion lightly traced a finger over the blood stain on Keith's blue shirt. "He will be fine, Mr. Sword." The vampire rolled up Keith's sleeve and Sword saw that the blood was seeping from a thick bandage that had been applied to the young guard's inner elbow, as if he had just given —

"Oh," Sword said as he realized what the connection was between Keith and Paula and Orion.

Orion adjusted Keith's bandage, then looked at Sword. "'Oh,' indeed, Mr. Sword. Do you find this distasteful?"

Sword wasn't sure what he felt. "That depends. What happens to them?"

"Only what they want to have happen to them." Orion patted Keith's shoulder as a human would pat a dog's, then continued to talk about Keith and Paula as if they weren't there, or as if they couldn't understand. "I am a predator, and I am not in my ... preferred environment, as you can no doubt tell from the reaction of the humans out there on this floor." The vampire adept waved dismissively at the closed door behind Sword.

"Those people know that you're in here?" Sword found that hard to believe.

"Not in any actionable way, Mr. Sword. But somewhere beneath their levels of conscious awareness, where their more primitive skills and senses have been relegated by generations of civilization, they know what's near." Orion gently pushed Keith and Paula to one side. "They will dream about me tonight. And in their dreams they will know what they have been spared." The vampire smiled. "Or am I being too romantic? Does it all sound too mystical to one such as you who has lived his life bound by science and technology?"

"Doesn't sound mystical at all," Sword answered truthfully. "Sounds like pheromones."

Orion shook his head in amusement. "Pah. Second World ignorance."

Sword didn't feel the need to debate Orion's dismissal of science and mentally tabled the discussion to pass on to Ko. Instead, he went to Marsh's side.

The reporter had been cleaned up since he had seen her being carried to the ambulance, but there was still no vitality to her skin. A slender green-tinged tube ended in twin outlets beneath her nose. An I.V. drip had been taped to her arm. Her cheeks were hollow and her eyes were motionless behind closed lids.

Sword touched her hand and it was like touching a dead thing. All that he could think of was the day only a week ago when she had returned to his secret refuge, his Trump Tower condominium — the luxurious apartment he still owned even though everyone else thought he had sold it after his accident. But Kendall Marsh had not been fooled.

She had kissed him. She had given him back her trust and her love. Then she had shown him the way he could take control of the events that conspired against him. And this was how he had repaid her.

He'd sent her unprepared into a den of Tepesh vampires. Or, if Marion E. Raycheba could be believed, the star reporter had been using him as a lead into another story about his background, and her fate was the result of her own act of betrayal.

Sword didn't know which scenario was correct. He didn't care. Kendall Marsh had come back into his life partly by accident, partly by design, but mostly because he had wanted her to.

He reached out for her hand as if his touch could warm her cold flesh, then stopped, knowing it could not.

Orion placed his hand lightly on his shoulder, this time as one friend to another.

"How is she?" Sword heard the unsteady huskiness of his own voice, cleared his throat.

"She lives," Orion answered.

"That's not enough."

"Manes Hel has fed on her, Mr. Sword. Manes Hel has made this woman her *golem*."

"But you've ... fed on Keith and Paula. And they're not like this."

Sword turned to look at the young couple who attended Orion. They stood together on the other side of the room, attuned to Orion's every move.

"But they are, Mr. Sword. It is just that the guidance I give them is different from that which Manes Hel has given your friend."

Sword didn't understand. Keith and Paula were alive. Kendall Marsh was next to lifeless. How could they be the same? "What sort of 'guidance'?"

"The instructions I give them. The nourishment of mind and body I provide. I have taken from these two and so I must give back to them. Manes Hel has taken from this woman and has yet to complete the promise made between predator and prey. Until that pact is sealed, your friend will remain in this state."

Sword saw a chance for hope. "Could she be released? If the 'pact' were sealed?"

Orion studied Marsh's still form. "Perhaps . . ."

"But?" Sword finished for him. "*How* is the pact sealed?"

"By blood, Mr. Sword. Manes Hel must return to her *golem* to complete the transaction half done."

Now Sword thought he understood. "When Manes Hel fed on Kennie, she was interrupted."

"You blew up the fardoor installation, Mr. Sword. 'Interruption' is an understatement."

"And now Manes Hel has to return to Kennie to finish what she has begun?"

"That is correct."

"You're certain?"

Orion looked impatient. "Mr. Sword, the Victor of Tepesh has imprinted on this human as I have imprinted on those two." He gestured to Keith and Paula. "There is no choice involved. Prey and predator cannot remain apart after imprinting has taken hold. And since your friend has no ability to go to Manes Hel, then Manes Hel *must* return to her. It might take days, even months, but not even I could resist the lure of a hunt half-finished."

Sword felt the muscles of his chest relax as he reached the first positive conclusion of this day. There *was* hope. "So you had your ... *golems* join the security agency working for Kennie's employer — so they could be here in the daytime when you can't be — and all you have to do now is wait for Manes Hel to appear. This is an ambush."

But his view was too simplistic for Orion. "No, Mr. Sword. This is justice."

"For you, yes." Manes Hel was responsible for the destruction of Orion's entire clan and Orion had been cheated of the chance to face the Tepesh Victor in matched battle at the World Plaza. "But you must realize that for me your presence means that Kennie is safe."

"She is not safe, Mr. Sword. Not while the Victor of Tepesh lives."

"Then safer than she'd be if I were the only one at her side," Sword qualified.

Orion nodded. "Yes, much safer." He thought a moment. "A thousand times safer. Perhaps safer than — "

"Okay, okay," Sword interrupted. "I just want to help."

Orion bowed his head graciously. "I appreciate your offer. However, I believe you will have other, more pressing matters to attend to."

Sword touched the thin sheet enshrouding Marsh. "No. I don't think so."

"The police took you captive, Mr. Sword. They will be looking for you. Eventually they will come here."

"The police have been dealt with. They have no reason to hold me."

Orion lifted a skeptical eyebrow.

"Orion, what do you know of the Clan Marratin?" Sword asked by way of explanation.

"Ahh, interesting" the vampire adept said, his dark eyes looking intrigued. "Illusionists, manipulators of distant influences. I presume you are telling me the police have been shown that whatever crime they thought had been committed did not, in fact, occur?"

"Something like that."

"You know Arkady and the Tepesh will still come after you. Are you not afraid, Mr. Sword?"

Sword didn't even have to think about his answer. "On the contrary. They should be afraid that now *I'm* coming after *them*. Whatever lies ahead is not dependent on Arkady and the Tepesh. They've had their chance, and they've failed. Now, everything depends on me, on what *I* decide to do next, and I don't plan on failing. Ever."

Orion laughed softly, in appreciation, not derision. "Well said. I suspect that neither clan knows what they face in you."

"And what do they face in me, Orion?"

The nightfeeder looked away. "As I once told you, Mr. Sword, I am a vampire. I do not believe in legends." Then he tilted his head back and opened his lips as if to taste the air. "And I cannot remain here much longer. My presence is too disruptive to the normal function of this place."

"Don't leave yet," Sword said. "I still want to help you."

As if he were granting Sword a favor of immense forbearance, the vampire adept paused, waiting.

Sword looked around the small hospital room. "First of all, is this the best place to take on Manes Hel when she comes? *Does* Kennie have

DARK HUNTER

to be kept here?"

The vampire frowned at the cardiac monitor, the I.V. drip, and the oxygen tube bubbling in its bedside bottle of water. "I will admit there is a certain utility to these contrivances, but it is surely no replacement for even the least blue of a wizard's liquid."

Though he had no way of evaluating Orion's complaint, nonetheless Sword recognized the conclusion. "Then let's move her. I can arrange for that. We can get her into a more private place. With more room for more guards. I can have UV lights installed to help with the am — "

Orion's hand flashed out and grabbed the collar of Sword's coat. "Do not impugn my honor."

"All right. I won't have UV lights installed," Sword continued without breaking the flow of his words. "But I can still ensure privacy. Without risk of exposure like there was at World Plaza."

Orion considered Sword's words before relinquishing his grip. "And we could arrange for a wizard to treat your friend? Instead of this childish quackery?"

"Certainly," Sword agreed. "Whatever will be best for Kennie." Marsh was suffering from a First World affliction. Perhaps she would do better with First World treatment as well.

Orion tapped at the bouncing green trace on the cardiac monitor's display screen, mechanically recording what little life remained in the the reporter's body. "Trust me, Mr. Sword. Almost *anything* would be better for her than being treated in this manner. As nothing more than a machine herself."

"Fine, fine," Sword said, relieved to be taking action again, making plans. "I'll take care of the arrangements. How can I contact you?"

Orion moved away from Marsh's bed, over to the room's single window. On the chair beside the bed was his coat — long and dark like Sword's, but not leather. "No offense, Mr. Sword, but you cannot contact me. Living as long as I have has led to the development of several bad habits. Guarding my privacy, I'm afraid, is chief among them."

111

"How long *have* you lived?" Sword asked suddenly. The human legends said centuries and he wondered what First World reality lay behind those legends.

But Orion brushed the question aside. Instead he spoke authoritatively to his *golems*, still waiting patiently across the room. "Your instructions remain the same. I shall be nearby until sunrise and then I will join you at the usual time."

Keith and Paula nodded confirmation.

"Will you contact me?" Sword asked Orion. *He's going to leave by the window*, he thought. *How theatrical.*

"I shall, Mr. Sword. Your offer of assistance makes much sense."

Then, with impossible-to-follow swiftness, the vampire blurred into motion, opening the old hospital window in a flurry of flying paint chips, leaning halfway out through its opening, and then pulling back into the room with a large dark struggling —

"Martin?" Sword stared in amazement as Orion dropped Martin's kicking, squealing, and naked form to the floor.

Martin realized where he was, then leapt over the bed to crouch at Sword's side.

The halfling brushed at his upper arms where Sword could see the livid handprints of the vampire's grip even through Martin's thick furlike hair. "Nightfeeder bad bad," Martin grumbled. Then muttered a few more words in shiftertongue beneath his breath.

"The small one had been hanging there for the past five minutes," Orion explained. "Knowing his lack of enthusiasm for clothes, I was afraid he might grow cold. And attract attention." He returned Martin's fierce gaze. "I suggest a doctor's coat. And perhaps one of those masks they seem so attached to. It could only improve this one's appearance."

Sword pushed down on Martin's shoulder as the halfling began to rise out of his crouch. "I'll take care of it," Sword said.

Orion moved gracefully to the door leading to the corridor and saw Sword's look of surprise. The vampire glanced back at the open window. "Me? Leave through there? You've spent too long in this rough place, Mr. Sword, and not enough in your true home."

"Wherever that is," Sword said. "I wouldn't know."

DARK HUNTER

Orion paused at the door. His face softened. "No, I don't suppose you would." He opened the door and quickly tasted the air. "Good night, Mr. Sword. Make your arrangements, but don't try to move her until I contact you."

"Do you know when?" Sword asked.

"Yes," Orion said, "I do." Then he was gone before Sword could reformulate his question in more specific terms.

Martin sniffed the air several times and stared at Keith and Paula. "*Golems*," the halfling whispered, as if telling Sword a secret.

"I know, Martin," Sword said. "But they're working for Orion. They're on our side. Protecting Kennie."

Martin apprehensively tapped a finger against Marsh's arm, and shook his head sadly. Then he went on to another subject as if Marsh had ceased to exist. "Melody sleep downstairs arm all white big."

"That's a cast," Sword explained. "To make her arm better."

Martin rolled his eyes as if he thought Sword had made a joke. "No wizards," he said. "Not make arm better. Make arm all white big." Then Martin eyed Sword with concern. "Nightfeeder hurt Galen Sword?"

"No. Orion is my friend. He's your friend now, too."

Martin scowled darkly at the thought, but tapped Sword's hand with the back of his own. "Maybe nightfeeder Martin friend. Maybe. Still no good bad stink."

Sword decided to let that comment pass and leaned down to smooth the sheets that covered Marsh. Across the room, Keith and Paula adjusted their uniforms. Sword straightened up and reached into his coat pocket to bring out Keith's revolver. "You'll want this back," he said.

As Keith came over for his weapon, Sword checked — as Ko had taught him — that the gun's safety was on. As he did so, he saw that the bullets visible in the cylinder had an odd shine to them.

Sword swung the cylinder open and shook the cartridges out.

"*Silver* bullets?" he asked Keith.

"Are they?" Keith asked in return.

It was unlikely, Sword decided after a moment, that the young bank teller had any real knowledge of what he was involved in. He was only a soldier for Orion, doing all that he was told, without thought or question. He reloaded the gun and gave it to Keith. "I guess your boss just wants you to be prepared for anything."

Keith nodded and left the room without saying anything to Paula, who, in turn, returned to her post by the window to resume her watch.

Sword took off his leather coat and held it out for Martin. "C'mon, Martin, let's go see if Billy's up to another ride in the limo with you."

Martin took the coat and peered into one of its sleeve openings. "Where we go limo Billy?"

"To the Loft," Sword said as he tried to guide Martin's arm instead of his foot into the sleeve, then gave up and let Martin figure out the problem for himself.

"Martin Galen Sword go home?" Martin asked as he wrestled with the coat.

"It's not as simple as that," Sword said, "but I guess you could say so. Yeah, I guess so. For the time being."

He leaned against the door frame and took the opportunity to massage his temples. *Right on time. Just as always.*

"Everything good all right?" Martin asked from the depths of Sword's coat.

Small black stars began to flicker at the edges of Sword's vision. "Yes," he lied, accepting the inevitable with the first signs of his migraine. The incapacitating headaches had been with him forever. Whenever he finished a period of intense activity or concentration, whenever he came to a point where it was all right to rest, the migraines came, too.

"For true?" Martin asked, patting Sword's temple as if to show he understood Sword was hurting in the head.

"For true," Sword said, but this time he *was* telling the truth. His situation was much clearer for him now than it had ever been. He knew who all the players were now and that he was one of them. His interruption of the Arkady shifters' Ceremony of the Change that had trapped the clan's Victor halfway through her transformation had been costly to the shifters. They had lost both invaluable red crystal and many warriors in their fight to save their leader and her consort, Tomas Roth — resources they needed badly in the war they were preparing to fight with Clan

DARK HUNTER

Seyshen. Now, because of his action, Arkady had been forced to ally itself with the vampire clan Tepesh, whose victor, Manes Hel, was Orion's sworn enemy, the one responsible for the destruction of Orion's entire clan. Sword knew he had gained in the last vampire of Clan Isis, a powerful ally — if only temporarily — in his own fight against Tomas Roth, the adept who had exiled him from his true home.

Sword's eyes met Martin's. "Trust me, Martin, for the first time since the night that you and I met, I do understand exactly what we're up against."

Martin rolled up his eyes to the ceiling again, as if Sword were trying to make a joke again, and a bad one at that.

"Martin keep Galen Sword safe. Galen Sword still not know anything."

TEN

Three hours out from Alice Springs, the hunter told her driver to stop.

Billows of fine, red-brown dust enveloped the Land Rover as it braked on the scorched desert. In the still dry air of midday, the particles seemed to hang as if caught in time, just like the flat barren land that surrounded them.

The driver slipped the gear lever into neutral, then used a balled-up red handkerchief to wipe at the sweat on his forehead. His skin was the baked brown leather of someone who had spent too much time in an environment for which he had not been designed.

He turned to his passenger. "You're sure, are you?" He looked behind the Rover in the direction they had come. The only road across the Outback was the one marked by the Rover's tire tracks.

"Quite sure," the hunter said. She reached down and pulled her sand-colored knapsack from the floor to her lap. She put her hand on the door latch.

"Each time, it's different," the driver said.

The hunter waited for him to continue. They had had this conversation before.

"Almost ten years now," he said. "Who knows how long you'd been coming before that, too." The dust had wafted away from the vehicle, and the blazing sun and the achingly blue sky were without filters. The

DARK HUNTER

only sound was the smooth idle of the Rover's engine. "You come to the Alice three, four times a year, you hire me to take you out here, and each time you have me take you someplace different."

The hunter was noncommittal. "It's a big country. Lots to see."

The driver, as always, did not believe her. "What are you looking for out here?"

"Perhaps I am not looking for anything. Perhaps I just enjoy the Outback."

The driver laughed. "Only thing on God's green earth enjoys the Outback is the dingoes that gnaw on the bones of foolish Yanks like yourself — no disrespect — and the Abbos."

The driver's casual, hurtful term for his own country's aboriginal peoples reminded the hunter it was time she left the disturbing world of humans. She opened the door, momentarily struck by the intensity of the sunlight on her bare leg below the cuff of her hiking shorts. It was fortunate she would not be out unprotected in the sun for long.

"I trust you will come back for me before the dingoes come to gnaw my bones." The hunter stepped from the Rover and swung her knapsack onto her back.

"Right you are, Ms. Forrest," the driver said. "Twenty-four hours and I'll be back. Same as always."

"Same as always."

The driver saluted her, then put the Rover back in gear. "Good luck finding whatever you're after." Then the Rover drove off, slowly enough that the hunter was not overcome by the dust, to pull around in a tight circle. Then the Rover's engine revved rapidly as the vehicle accelerated and disappeared in a red brown cloud, retracing the tire tracks that stretched back to some semblance of Second World civilization.

The hunter waited until the sound of the departing vehicle was swallowed by the desert's immensity and the black dot of its decreasing image melted into the heat ripples distorting the horizon. Then she turned to face the sun.

For long moments, she attuned herself to the Second World desert. Her knapsack's straps weighed light on her shoulders. She had no need of food or water this close to her home. She carried only her shadowsuit, insubstantial in mass, and three compact computer data disks for the Ark's mainframe. She had no gifts this visit. Her only need was for information.

The hunter stood beneath the sun and inhaled the dry air of the desert, of the Outback, of the basaltic dust from Precambrian sediments undisturbed since before the time of the Tarls. Then she exhaled with the breath of the forest, calling it to her.

She lifted her First World eyes to the sun, ignoring its coarse spectrum as she had been taught. Against the searing blue of the sky, the sun turned black, blocked by her search for other energies.

Slowly, she tracked her eyes ninety degrees north, along the ecliptic, letting her gaze slip out of focus to better locate the marker that she sought.

At the edges of her vision, the dark cross was indistinct, rare and difficult to find in air so sere, but it was there, as it always had been. And it marked the path she must follow to her home.

She fixed her sight on the cross's center until the cross vanished beneath her direct scrutiny. Then she closed her eyes and inhaled deeply of the dust and the sun and the true history of the place she stood in and —

Even before she exhaled again, she felt the temperature drop and heard the whisper of gentle wind moving leaves in high treetops. Whispers like secrets.

— exhaled with the breath of the forest, the moisture of her life pulled from her lungs, grabbed by the greedy dryness of the air around her and —

There was a river nearby. She heard it gurgling against smooth stones, lapping against mossy banks and old logs, and knew that coins of sunlight flashed on it like silver with a purity the Second World desert had never known. The purity of home.

— took in the last of the barren land around her, the barren world of humans and their cruelty, and with a final thought and a final subtle change in her orientation, as she had been taught, she took one step forward —

Through the layer.

— and was in Deep Forest.

DARK HUNTER

The next time the hunter inhaled, her lungs were renewed with the life and scents and humidity of the First World.

She opened her eyes.

Ginnwaru was waiting for her.

The hunter smiled at her friend, knowing 'friend' was a human term and one the Clan of Deep Forest would not use. The Clan would understand it, though, as they understood everything, and she felt justified in her own use of it.

"Hello, my friend." Except for the one word of English, she spoke in the forest-tongue and her voice sounded richer in the midst of her home's tall trees and vibrant greenery. Dappled light played with the smooth brown soil of the ground in the sparkling patterns of a school of fish. Everything was alive here in a way no human could understand. Except, of course, for those the driver said "enjoyed" the Outback.

Ginnwaru did not reply directly to her. He made no effort to look in her direction nor even change his position of repose. He remained motionless, a lithe dark-skinned figure poised with one hand on a wanderstick, with one foot resting on a locked and straightened knee.

The hunter looked to Ginnwaru for news of the forest since her last visit and found it in what little she could read in the elaborate patterns of chalk-white dots and lines cut into her friend's ancient skin: There was no cause for alarm or concern. The forest continued. That was enough.

"It is good to be back," the hunter said. She slipped her knapsack from her shoulders and laid it on the ground without looking. It would find its way to her no matter where she wandered now. In Deep Forest, there were many friends to the Clan.

"Is Dajara free from the keeping?" she asked. "I have questions for her."

Ginnwaru rocked for almost a minute as the hunter's inquiry raced from him through the path of the trees. The hunter was not surprised by the delay. Even after more than three hundred cycles, the Clan of Deep Forest still had not become totally used to dealing with the adopted elemental in their midst. She grinned as finally, Ginnwaru admitted defeat.

119

The old one's narrow chest expanded with a thorough breath and he opened his eyes, blinked twice, then turned to look at the hunter. His mouth spread in the heartfelt smile of his humanform, splitting the thin silver bristle of his sparse beard. "Diandra," he said. "You are home."

"Yes, Ginnwaru, as are you."

The two friends embraced happily and the leaves above them echoed the motions of their greeting. All was alive.

"Diandra comes to the village," Ginnwaru said.

The hunter nodded her head in acknowledgment, knowing that her actions were more easily interpreted than her words.

Ginnwaru smiled again and motioned with his wanderstick — a six-foot length of a thin, barkless tree branch — inviting the hunter to follow at his side. And she did. She did not glance back at her knapsack because she knew it would already be gone.

The hunter smelled the communal cookfire of the village before she and Ginnwaru came to the clearing. She heard the laughter of the children playing, the crying of a baby, and the splashing of the river where its banks widened at the village's edge.

Each sound, each scent, opened doorways for the hunter. These were not her clan, she was not of their descent group, but they were her family and this was her home.

The children came to her first, swift and in overlapping shades of brown and black. They called her name and danced about her like the froth on waves. They hugged her legs and swung on her hands and she laughed with them, remembering when she had been their age and the arrival of a traveling cousin had been a time of wonder and excitement. The hunter counted twelve of them and rejoiced to find the clan so strong.

Ginnwaru shook his wanderstick at the giggling horde, but the children knew him too well to believe in his false annoyance and danced around him as well. When he at last joined in their simple chants the excitement was too much and three children collapsed on the ground in helpless fits of laughter.

The hunter picked up two of the younger children and Ginnwaru, one, and they entered the village where all the others waited.

DARK HUNTER

The hunter felt tears spring into her eyes. Everything was as she had last left it. Surrounded by forest, bisected by the long Core River, the village clearing glowed incandescent in the brilliant light of the afternoon sun. Only the broad smiles of welcome and the large, untroubled eyes of the clan shone brighter.

Over and over they chanted their greetings in the language of the trees. "Diandra comes to the village. Diandra is home." They came from the leaf bowers where they slept and loved, and from the river where they played and washed, to welcome the elemental who had been taken in as their own.

The hunter let the children slip from her arms and they bounded off to join their parents. The leaves all around joined in the sounds of celebration.

It was as if she had never left. And in the way that the clan reckoned time's passage, she never had.

"Diandra is home," Ginnwaru said.

The hunter reached out to touch those who surrounded her. "You are home, you are home," she said to each in turn, repeating the welcome. And as always, alone among them, she was the only one who knew that soon she would have to leave again.

With night the stars came like a shower of diamonds — each with a distinct color, a special pattern to the way it flashed in the clear air. And for each pulsing star, a forest leaf fluttered in matching rhythm. Here, everything was intertwined.

The hunter stood off from the fire where the old ones told their tales to the children. She knew each word of each story, each song of the Lights, each deep-throated growl of the Tarls, and she smiled at the simple memories they brought back to her.

But her childhood had been an easier time, bounded by the leaves and the water and the roots. She was older now and there were things beyond the forest that affected her.

The hunter turned away from the fire toward the stars, caught by the magenta glory directly beneath Orion's belt. In the Second World, she knew she would need a telescope or binoculars to see the nebula as clearly as it appeared tonight.

She heard the pad of bare feet on firm earth behind her and in this place, at this time, even her hunt-honed instincts did not make her turn in challenge. It was Ginnwaru, his wanderstick tapping the ground beside him as he made his way to her.

When he reached her side, he looked up into the night sky as well and each pinpoint of light above reflected clearly in his eyes.

"The leaves of heaven," Ginnwaru said in a roughened voice. Acting out the children's favorite story of the Fall of Tarl Gabriel and the Sundering of the Layer — growls and all — had left him hoarse.

"The light of the forest," the hunter replied. The ancient words were part of an ancient responsive written in the Rings.

Ginnwaru whistled softly into the night, sending forth his fluted breath to the leaves above and around him. "Diandra talks with Dajara," he said, then turned and walked off, away from the firelight and into the forest.

The hunter followed openly, having no need for stealth.

Lit only by the pale, pure light of the stars, Ginnwaru led the hunter to a keeper's circle almost an hour's walk from the village clearing. The circle was one hundred feet across, empty of trees, with a small mound in its center as if Lights had once gathered here. The hunter closed her eyes and peered into the blackness but saw no residual glow of magic. Whatever clan had once used the circle before those of Deep Forest, their influence had faded thousands of cycles ago.

"Dajara walks the circle," Ginnwaru said. He placed a foot upon his knee and assumed a pose of rest, balanced with his wanderstick. "Diandra talks with Dajara."

Ginnwaru closed his eyes, took a deep breath, then froze in place, as solid as the trees around the circle.

The hunter waited.

Leaves rustled with the passage of starlight through them. Animals flowed swiftly along branches, quick shadows among deeper black. Then the hunter felt the green pulse of the forest deepen as Dajara drew near. Dajara had been her parent, her teacher, and her home. The hunter could recognize the presence of Dajara anywhere.

Dajara approached from the direction of the Keep of the Rings and from the length and sure sweep of her strides, the hunter knew that she was in her purest manifestation, and not in her humanform. The hunter was surprised because she had not known that a Ceremony of the Change Deep Forest had been held since her last visit.

The hunter raised her line of sight by five feet, waiting for the appearance of Dajara as she really was. The leaves announced her coming. The branches parted with the creaking of their bark. The hunter felt the heat of fast growth, the shivering of shoots, and knew that Dajara had entered the circle, even though she had not yet made her physicality known.

Then one shadow moved among a dozen others and rippled as if the growth of tender seedlings had been speeded up a thousandfold.

The hunter watched as her parent's form took on physical aspects before her, knowing that she was witnessing the transformational camouflage of which her own shadowsuit was but a pale reflection.

Then Dajara herself quickened, abandoning the cloak of the forest, and was full and complete in the circle where the hunter waited. In the humantongues, the hunter's parent was a dryad, austerely slender, almost human in shape, but ten feet tall and made in the interlinked textures of all that was green and growing.

The hunter stepped closer, eager to make her greeting, and Dajara swept forward in kind — the bark of her skin sliding easily over the wood of her muscles — to meet her pupil and her adopted child. The hunter reached up to feel the caress of Dajara's branches. "Dajara is home," she said.

The dryad's voice was woven of leaves and the faint rush of the forest wind. "*My child is home.*"

"I had not expected to find you in greenform," the hunter said.

"*Expectations.*" Dajara's sigh was like effortless laughter. She took the hunter's hand in her grasping leaves, a parent escorting a beloved child. "*Diandra and Dajara sit on the fairy mound.*" The hunter followed, content with her parent's wishes.

The mound had been worked with crystal so that every spot on it was comfortable and yielding. The hunter sat and hugged her knees and leaned against Dajara as she would against a tree. She heard the whisper of Dajara's roots as they slithered into the soil beneath them.

"*Moonrise,*" the dryad said.

The hunter could see the first signs of moonglow brighten the edges of the surrounding forest's black silhouette. The optical peculiarity of First World skies had invariably caused problems whenever she had brought over builders for the Ark, although she had been careful never to bring through the layer any Second Worlder who possessed the slightest background in astronomy. If the moon as it appeared here was ever seen in anything but its crescent phase by a human with a practised eye, then it would be even more of a revelation of the First World's true nature than the ultraclarity of its stars.

Nor, the hunter knew, had any of the Ark's builders ever detected the layer they passed through. *Not that it would matter much longer,* she thought.

"*Diandra hunts,*" Dajara said. It was a statement of supposition which was as close as the forest-tongue of the dryads could come to asking a question.

"Soon," the hunter answered, hearing Dajara's leaves flicker with annoyance at her use of the English word invoking a period of time that was not the present. The hunter was aware that she was breaking the pattern of the clan's orderly functioning by stating a future intention, but she also knew her parent would understand. They both had learned from each other in the hunter's cycles among the clan. "My prey is a vampire adept."

Dajara composed another statement. "*Diandra hunts Orion, last child of Isis.*"

The hunter was not surprised. She had rarely found any limits to the knowledge held by the clan's old ones. Where that knowledge came from, she couldn't be sure. Certainly, she had never seen any of the clan in commerce with the wizards who claimed to tell the future, as if such a thing were possible by magic or technology. But there was often help to be found in what her parent could tell her. The trick was in knowing which questions to ask of a race that did not believe in questions any more than they believed in the past or the future.

"I am not to kill him," the hunter said.

"Arkady wants the last child of Isis."

The hunter was pleased. Somehow, Dajara was already aware of the offer that had been made to her by the shifter Saul Calder in the alley in Hong Kong. If she had been talking with anyone or anything else, her next words would have been a question asking why Arkady wanted Orion in the first place, but that was not how things worked in Deep Forest.

"Arkady gains much by taking Orion captive," the hunter said instead, then waited for Dajara to expand on her supposition.

But the dryad didn't expand. She disagreed. *"Arkady gains little. Tepesh gains much."*

The hunter was electrified by the logic of Dajara's statement. *Such perfect sense*, she thought. *Arkady has no use for Orion* except *to give him to the Clan Tepesh as ... as ...* "Arkady makes payment to Tepesh for Tepesh support in the North Shore," she said.

Dajara's reply rustled forth almost instantly. *"Arkady is finished. Tepesh is finished. Isis is finished. Orion continues."*

The hunter wondered how Clan Isis could be considered to be finished if at least one member of the clan still survived. But, more important to her, to the Ark, was that Dajara had just stated that Orion would continue to survive. That would increase the odds that her hunt would be successful. Unless ...

"Diandra continues," the hunter said said, wanting to know if the vampire's survival in any way conflicted with her own.

She felt Dajara's leaves brush affectionately through her hair. *"Diandra continues. Orion continues. Worlds are finished."*

The hunter leaned away from Dajara's trunk and in her shock spoke in English. "All Worlds?" She had always known that the Second World was doomed. That was why she had created the Ark. That was why she even bothered following the political machinations of the clans. But the First World was eternal. It had to be. "When are the *Worlds* finished?"

Dajara took long moments to respond, and when she did she painstakingly replied in the tense-bound language her child used in the Second World. *"The Worlds have always been finished. Since they have been formed, they have been finished. Since they have been formed, Diandra continues, Orion continues."*

The hunter rubbed her palms against her temples. She felt the way she had when, as a student, she had been faced with the apparent

125

contradictions and complex arguments contained in the Rings of the First Clan. So many adepts now rejected the Rings as the superstitions of an earlier time. But no matter whether all that the Rings contained was timeless poetry or ancient historical fact, the study of their verses had honed the hunter's mind as surely as the forest had honed her physical prowess. If there were hidden knowledge in Dajara's words, then the hunter was determined to find it. But did the word "finished" mean an ending as in "destruction" or an ending as in "completion"? And why did Dajara seem to stress that she and the last of Clan Isis would continue together?

"The Worlds are destroyed," the hunter said in the forest-tongue.

Dajara said nothing.

The hunter tried again. "The Worlds are completed."

"Diandra is troubled," the dryad whispered. She moved a branch to coax the hunter into leaning against her once more. Still disturbed, the hunter allowed herself to be settled back into position. The moon was clearing the black shadows of the forest horizon. The light it cast, even though only half was illuminated, was dazzling.

"Yes," the hunter agreed slowly. Troubled was a good way to put it. "The vampire is somehow involved with Little Galen."

The hunter felt her parent stroke her hair. She closed her eyes, trying to recall her childhood when the embrace of her parent's branches was her whole world. Again she spoke in English, her words couched in tenses. "That makes twice that our paths have crossed, and both times Arkady has been involved."

The dryad's shift in position coincided with her child's renewed use of the Second World language. *"Diandra's path crosses only once with her brother's."*

The hunter apologetically touched the branch resting on her shoulder. She was too tired to keep thinking in the eternal now of the forest-tongue. She kept with English. "But I have seen him twice, Dajara. Once at Delphi where the Seyshen set me up to kill the Arkady shifter. And once, last week, in a New York alley when I hunted the Close trolls."

"No matter how many times you see or do not see, from the first day of birth, both paths are the same."

DARK HUNTER

Our paths are the same? The hunter thought that over. She sat up, her fatigue forgotten. "Then seeing Little Galen wasn't an accident? Or a coincidence?"

The hunter felt Dajara's roots twist in discomfort in the soil of the fairy mound.

"Clan Arkady and Clan Seyshen are apart in Council," Dajara sighed.

The hunter was puzzled. The softwind had been predicting an all-out war between Arkady and the Seyshen for scores of cycles. In fact, if not for Little Galen's disruption of the last Arkady Change, then the war would probably have already been joined and — the hunter gasped. She twisted around to confront her parent.

"Dajara, is my brother part of the Seyshen-Arkady war? On purpose?"

Dajara's leaves swayed with the wind and the sparkling starlight. *"Orion fights for the Seyshen,"* she whispered.

Then the softwind was true, the hunter thought. The Seyshen *had* made a pact with a nightfeeder when war with Arkady had seemed inevitable. In her mind, she quickly counted out the cycles since the last Grand Gathering of the Council had collapsed amidst the bitter conflict between the two greater clans: *Almost forty.* That would be three years ago, just when she was set up by the Seyshen.

Beneath her, the hunter felt the vibration of the dryad's roots withdrawing from the soil. She realized she had only moments before Dajara would leave her. She stood and looked up into Dajara's branches.

"Then for whom does Little Galen fight?"

The hunter heard the smallest filaments of Dajara's roots ripping away from the runners that spread from her trunk as the dryad rose to her true height.

"Dajara, please," the hunter said, reaching up to the dryad who had kept an elemental as her own. "Does my brother fight for Seyshen or Arkady?"

She could accept that Orion fought for the Seyshen while she fought for Arkady. It would complicate her hunt more than she had anticipated, but the problem was her brother. He was fighting for someone. And he was involved with Orion. When the moment of choice came, she needed to know on whose side he would fight — on the vampire's or his sister's?

The hunter's stomach knotted as she reconsidered what Dajara had told her. *If my meeting with Little Galen at Delphi and in New York was not a coincidence ... if our paths are the same ... then —*

"Not Pendragon," the hunter said as Dajara gracefully released her branches from her child's grasp until the hunter's hand closed only on a single leaf, easily shed. "My brother cannot be fighting for Pendragon."

She felt the dryad trail a small branch through her hair in a gesture of parting.

The hunter implored her parent. "Dajara, please please listen to me. Clan Pendragon is ended. Let the other clans fight for the spoils. I want no more of it. I will not go back. I cannot go back."

But the dryad was already moving surely and steadily down the gentle slope of the fairy mound, one shadow among many, returning to the cloak of the forest and the Keep of the Rings.

The hunter called after her. "I am of *your* clan, Dajara. Diandra Sword, Clan of Deep Forest. Not Pendragon! *Never* Pendragon! No matter what my brother does."

From deep within the forest, the rustle of the dryad's words came from everywhere, from nowhere, to reach her flame-haired child who stood alone on the fairy mound, silhouetted against the rising half-moon light. "*Diandra Sword of no clan. Not Pendragon. Never Deep Forest.*"

"No," the hunter protested. The forest was all she lived for. "Deep Forest is my home."

"*Diandra is home.*"

"But I do not understand! How can I be home and not home?"

Whisper. "*Diandra continues. Orion continues.*"

"But what about my *brother*? For whom does *he* fight?"

The hunter's cry arced through the trees and the night and at once the hunter knew that she had gone too far. Daring to question Dajara for the whole forest to hear could not go unnoticed or unpunished.

She steeled herself for the journey back through the village without Ginnwaru's protection. Wary, she stepped down from the fairy mound.

DARK HUNTER

And then, as it always did, the forest surprised her.

Far off, from someplace hidden, like the telling of a secret, she heard her name among the leaves. And then her answer.

"*Diandra ... Little Galen fights for Brin.*"

ELEVEN

Despite her ear protectors, Ko flinched as the gunshot boomed through the Loft's first basement, echoing with a sharp metallic ring from the old brick walls.

Then she tugged off the hard-shelled earmuffs so they hung around her neck like old-fashioned stereo headphones. She waved her good arm over the barrel of the shotgun clamped in the firing vise. As the gunsmoke cleared away, she squinted through the thick lenses of her safety goggles to check the spread of the buckshot pattern on the silhouette target thirty feet away.

She grimaced. *Another failure.* The pattern left by her custom-poured buckshot was asymmetrical, bulging too far off to the right. If the silhouetted torso had been an attacking shifter — and not a vampire as Martin had tried to indicate by using chalk to draw in two crude white fangs — she guessed she might have been able to blow off one of its arms, but she definitely wouldn't have stopped it. The trouble with shifters was that some had more than two arms. Saul Calder's mate, for instance.

Ko awkwardly fumbled in her overalls' pocket for a pen so she could mark the chart on her clipboard, guiltily impatient for her cast to come off, aware that Forsyte, working above her in his lab, faced

DARK HUNTER

every day as if his whole body were encased in plaster wrap. *Only two more weeks.*

She checked off the boxes for 'asymmetrical,' 'right bulge,' and 'clumped spread' on her chart, then prepared herself to go through the bother of loading the next shell. With the price of silver comparatively low, Sword had told her to buy fifty pounds of the metal for her buckshot experiments. That amount allowed for a lot of different shell, shot, and powder combinations. She found herself grumpily wishing that shifters could only be killed by platinum. Her workload would have been considerably lighter — even Sword would have thought twice about buying fifty pounds of platinum.

"Naw, probably not," Ko muttered. Sword had seemed different in the past three weeks since his release from police custody and the dropping of murder charges against him. He hadn't actually been as demanding, or as scattered, or even as rude, Ko had noticed, and he had even had some success with one of his characteristically-convoluted plans — this time, moving Kendall Marsh to a more easily-defended location.

Within a week of Sword's making contact with Orion again, the Sword Foundation had purchased a private, eight-room sanitarium in rural Connecticut, and Sword had had Marsh transferred, safely and legally. Marion E. and her television station's lawyers were caught offguard when Marsh's cousin emerged from nowhere to take custody of the comatose reporter. Sword had even managed to keep his tracks covered effectively. Neither Marion E. nor the police were aware that Sword had hired a detective agency to locate Marsh's nearest relative in Florida, and that Sword had then entered into a contract with the cousin to gain power of attorney over Marsh's disposition and care in exchange for an annuity. Given that Sword was involved, the complex scheme had gone surprisingly smoothly — despite some trouble at the private convalescent hospital Sword had originally considered. Of course, Ko thought, the detective agency had been recommended by Orion. So Sword wasn't totally responsible for the plan's success.

However, Ko admitted, if only to herself, all of Sword's team's legal problems did appear to be less threatening than they'd seemed three weeks ago. After some huffing and puffing, the state prosecutor's office

131

had finally decided not to consider Forsyte's chair an unlicensed motor vehicle. And as part of a complex series of plea bargains, Martin's 'escape' from the Spofford juvenile facility was officially being overlooked — though Sword still had to make restitution for a guard's stolen uniform and several hundred pounds of dry dog and cat food.

And even though an overzealous city clerk, while doing the paperwork to clear Martin's record, had discovered that Martin, supposedly an employee of the Sword Foundation, had no Social Security number, it looked like Sword would get lucky there, too. Working on the assumption that Martin *was* from one of the former Soviet republics — as Billy Santini had helpfully suggested during a meeting with Detective Trank — the city's agencies were currently involved in what would have to be an unsuccessful attempt to find Martin's birth certificate and the documentation giving him permission to be in the United States. But Sword, as usual, had simply thrown money at the problem, telling his law firm Scarlatti, Holcroft & Chancellor that he was willing to pay whatever it cost to keep Martin in the country, even if it meant buying a summer home for a citizenship judge, and then he'd signed over another breathtaking retainer check to Angela Scarlatti. Ko's sympathies were with the lawyer who'd held her hands to her ears and sworn at Sword with a few choice Sicilian curses for even thinking that such a thing might be possible or that her firm would countenance it. Later, Sword had told Ko that as far as he was concerned, if it ever came down to Martin being threatened with deportation, he was going to tell Martin to tell the INS — in his own words — just where he really did come from.

And best of all, Trank had reluctantly halted his investigative attempts to link Sword with the explosions at World Plaza because the NYPD's forensic specialists hadn't been able to figure out what kind of explosion *had* taken place. Through friends at a scientific supply house, Ko had heard that there was so much contamination of the crime scene by bizarre chemical compounds that some outside experts were suggesting everything from the detonation of a low-yield atomic device to the impact of a comet had been responsible for the destruction of the glass pyramid crowning World Plaza tower.

DARK HUNTER

But some charges hadn't been dropped. Weapons charges, mostly. Ko had made some ... improper modifications on a number of firearms which Sword had then hidden illegally in his vehicles. There was also the matter of the unlicensed demolition charges and the anti-personnel gas cylinders hooked up to the Sword Foundation van's burglar alarms. Although Scarlatti was confident she could keep the state's charges down to simple misdemeanors for which Sword could pay fines, the lawyer had told Sword that the anti-personnel gas might come under federal jurisdiction. So, in the meantime, Ko had been instructed by Sword to use only cash for all questionable equipment and chemicals.

That suited both Sword and Ko perfectly. But not, she knew, for the same reasons. However reformed, Sword still assumed that the laws didn't apply to people who were as financially empowered as he was. He still thought nothing of circumvention whenever he felt he had a good reason. Ko, on the other hand, knew she was above such arrogance. Laws were to be obeyed. Except, of course, by professionals with the intellect — *not* merely the wealth — to understand that the intent of the law was not to rule out actions required for reasons lay people could never understand — such as those actions required to conduct complex scientific research. Confident that she was in no danger of ever succumbing to Sword's brand of presumption, Ko was now making good use of all manner of informal supply routes that had not been open to her in the days when Sword had insisted on purchase orders and payment by check, with the result that the Loft's arsenal was steadily becoming even more impressive.

Still working with one good hand and what little assistance the fingers of the hand in the cast could provide her — *about as useful as a mitt full of tube worms* — Ko managed to eject the spent shell from the shotgun and reload it with cartridge number twenty-seven. The chart on the clipboard had room for forty shell descriptions. It was going to be a long afternoon.

She toggled the switch that would advance the overhead conveyor to bring a new target into position, then tugged the ear protectors in position again. She fired number twenty-seven, recoiled again at the blast and the echo, and when she took off the protectors once more, she heard a new sound: the intercom buzzer.

133

Ko made a quick check of the spread on the target — for some reason Martin had drawn *three* fangs on this one — then went to the back wall and the Loft's intercom panel.

"Ko here."

Forsyte's voice synthesizer answered. "COURIER AT THE DOOR."

Ko closed her eyes. Did she have to do everything here? "Where's Sword?"

"NEW JOISEY."

Ko couldn't help grinning at the inflection Forsyte had programmed into his voder. Sword had been making a lot of runs into Jersey recently, mostly to pick up certain supplies Ko had ordered that technically couldn't be shipped into New York state. "Be right up."

Cautiously, she slipped her cast into its sling for the hike upstairs to the garage, then left the long room that she had converted into the Loft's shooting range. As she headed for the stairs, she glanced into the room where Sword had had holding cells installed after he had returned from Greece. The one that had once held Saul Calder remained unrepaired. She was still waiting to hear back from the metallurgical lab where she had sent the ends of the bars that had been broken apart. To her eye, the bars had looked as if they had been cut and polished by something almost inconceivably sharp having been forced through them, though the actual verdict would have to wait until she and Forsyte could examine electron-microscope photos of the severed edges. But whatever had broken through those bars, she was certain that it hadn't been Saul Calder. Or else why hadn't the shifter used that capability on them during the fight in the garage?

But Ko put aside thinking of that investigation as she ran up the stairway, rattling the metal stair railings with each step. That made her think of Ja'Nette instead.

When she reached the garage level, she walked over to the entry hallway leading to the main door. Sword had ordered many changes to the Loft in the past few weeks, including this.

She checked the new security panel by the short hallway. A color video display showed a wide-angle view of the street area around the outside entry alcove. *What's Adrian thinking about?* Ko wondered with a flash of annoyance. *That's not a courier, that's a police officer.*

She pressed the Talk button. "What can I do for you, officer?"

"Lady! I've been freezin' my butt off out here for the past ten minutes talking to some freaky computer! I got your stuff for ya!" The cop held up a large yellow plastic pouch to the camera. It was too big for the armored drop-off slot that couriers were required to use. The pouch was clearly labeled: PERSONAL PROPERTY.

Ko had the security feed shunted from the main door and the armored blast plate swung to the side in ten seconds. She had been waiting three weeks for this.

As the cop walked into the entry hall, Ko held out her good hand and greeted him by saying, "You took your bloody time about it."

The cop curled his lip as if to stop himself from saying something he might regret. "Lady, you're lucky to be gettin' it back at all, never mind late."

Ko grabbed the evidence pouch out of the cop's grip and he instantly rubbed both hands together and blew over his fingers. For the past ten days, the city had been hit with an early taste of winter temperatures. Ko had actually begun to wear the few sleeved pullovers she still owned.

She slipped the pouch under her cast and put her hand on her hip, waiting impatiently for the cop to leave. But he just stared at her, still warming his hands.

"Well," she said, "are you waiting for me to thank you or something?"

The cop scowled, shoved a hand into the outside pocket of his blue nylon-covered winter jacket. "Heaven forbid you should thank me, lady. But you do hafta sign for it. If it's not too much trouble for you, that is."

Ko thrust out her hand. The cop held out a folded wad of papers. Ko could see her own signature in one corner, where she had signed to acknowledge the items taken from her when she had been taken into custody.

"You got a pen, lady? I seem to have lost mine."

Ko knew what he was doing. She knew he could see the pen in her overalls pocket, just as easily as he could see the cast on her arm. But there was no way she was going to let him grab the pen for himself.

She pulled the pen out, kept the cap in her mouth, then wiggled the fingers on her plaster-wrapped arm. The cop smirked as he wedged the papers into her immobilized hand and said, "In triplicate."

When Ko was signing the second sheet against the wall, the slippery pouch slipped out from underneath her cast and she instinctively jerked back, knowing what she had been carrying that night. But the plastic pouch hit the floor without blowing up. *Of course,* Ko thought, *they would have kept all the explosives until the final charges are dealt with.* The cop didn't offer to pick up the pouch and Ko didn't bother to ask. She held the three signed forms out to him. He took the white and the yellow and left her with the pink.

"You have a nice day, okay?" he sneered.

Ko went back to the security panel and tried to have the blast door swing shut against him before he could get completely out the door. Unfortunately, the double-door system had an interlock to prevent exactly that. Ko decided she'd have to think about wiring in an override.

Only when the panel showed that the Loft was secure again did Ko jog upstairs to Forsyte's second-level lab. She found the physicist parked in front of a large workstation screen. The screen was displaying a colored street map of Manhattan and Ko saw red crosshairs for every location in the city where Sword and she had made some sort of contact with the First World.

There was the alley — one of remarkably few in New York City — off the sidestreet south of Canal, where Martin had first taken Sword to Softwind. Then the cul-de-sac five blocks directly south, where Sword and Martin had reappeared after their visit to Softwind and their fight with the Softwind bouncer, Dmitri. At first, Ko hadn't believed Sword when he had insisted that he had left Softwind through the same door he had entered, only to find himself in another location. But now that she had seen fardoors in operation for herself, she had reluctantly concluded that perhaps the entrance to Softwind was a teleportation portal after all.

Farther north on the map, more crosshairs marked the beginning of the tunnel-like passages beneath the Museum of Natural History, and the path she and Sword had followed to the enormous cavern housing the Arkady Pit of the Change, and then the condominium building — now deserted and slated for extensive renovation by its untraceable offshore owners — where she and Sword and Martin had emerged to meet Brin.

Interestingly enough, two of the crosshairs came fairly close to each other — the location of the Pit, and the place in Central Park where Martin had taken them the night that the Lights had come for Ja'Nette's body. Guesswork had placed both locations in the vicinity of the Croton Reservoir. It made Ko uncomfortable to admit that she could not say for sure that either site was actually in or under Central Park. Because ... she shuddered. *A thing either is or isn't,* she told herself firmly. *When there is absolute proof, then I'll decide what I'll accept as the truth, and not before.*

She stood in the doorway to the lab and hefted the pouch in her good hand, thinking: *The police never bothered to check all the pockets in my equipment harness. Maybe there's a little bit of the truth still in here.*

"Wasn't a courier, Adrian. It was the police. They finally found my stuff."

The treads on Forsyte's chair squeaked against the rubber Pirelli flooring of the lab as they moved in opposite directions to turn him around in place. To Ko's familiar eye, the barest flicker of a smile fought to appear on the physicist's thin face. Two of his fingers tapped at the small keyboard on the left arm of his chair. "THOUGHT IT WAS LOST FOR GOOD," his speech synthesizer said.

"So did I." Ko went to a large metal desk and pulled an X-Acto knife from a black Sword Foundation coffee mug bristling with pens and pencils. "They have no idea about organization in the police. I tried to explain it to the ones who were booking me. You know, give them some pointers for a more efficient system, but ... " She slit open the end of the pouch and glanced at Forsyte. He still seemed to be smiling but she didn't know at what. "No organization," she concluded, leaving the subject behind.

Instead of emptying the pouch across the desk, Ko then methodically pulled items from it one at a time and placed each one in an orderly series of rows.

Forsyte rolled over to watch the unveiling. "EVERYTHING THERE?" his voder asked.

"None of the weapons," Ko said. She sat on the edge of the desk and held the pouch wedged beneath her cast and peered into it, feeling like a child searching for the prize in a box of cereal. Beside her on the desk was a keychain with the keys to Sword's Harley-Davidson Softail which Ko had ridden to the World Plaza; a small, hard plastic case that held a notebook and pen; a miniflashlight; the sending unit of her transceiver — with no connecting wire, earpiece, or VOX mike; her locator band — which the police had obviously thought was a piece of jewellery and not a communications device; and a butane lighter. Next, Ko removed a long billfold and opened it by pressing it against her chin.

"Hey, all the money's there." She grimaced. "*And* all the credit cards I cancelled." She laid the billfold down on the desk. The next item out was her equipment harness, folded tightly and tied up with one of its own loops. "Damn."

"WHAT'S MISSING?" the voder asked.

"All the good stuff." Ko let the pouch slip down to lie on the edge of the desk, then leaned forward to place her cast against the harness so she could untie it with her other hand.

"ALL THE CUSTOM EQUIPMENT IS BEING REPLACED," Forsyte's mechanical voice reminded her.

Ko was rapidly checking all the empty pouches on the black canvas harness. "I don't care about the equipment, Adrian. Losing it was a good excuse to get Sword to spring for a new generation. But there were some other — aha!"

Ko withdrew a wadded-up ball of Kleenex, no larger than a pebble. "Guess they didn't know what to do with you," she said. She set it aside with the other objects. Her hand went back into the same pouch and she brought out a second, larger Kleenex-wrapped item. She stood up and placed it on a clear spot on the desk and began to pick away at the tissue. "There wasn't any of this left on the sidewalk or the street when I went back that weekend."

"DON'T KNOW WHAT YOU'RE TALKING ABOUT," the voder said.

"This," Ko answered. She held up a triangular shard resembling smoked glass, about three inches long with a base less than an inch wide. "Bloody hell!" She suddenly dropped it and placed her cut finger in her mouth.

"CRYSTAL?" the voder asked.

Ko saw the interest in Forsyte's intelligent gray eyes. "That's what we're going to find out," she said. Then she checked the cut on her finger. The shard had been sharper than she had anticipated. She picked it up again, this time using the tissue as protective padding.

"This is part of the glass, or whatever it was, the World Plaza pyramid was made of. There were hundreds of panes of this stuff."

"WHY DON'T YOU THINK IT IS GLASS?" the voder asked.

Ko held the shard up to one eye and sighted through it. "In the actual pyramid, the panes seemed to have some sort of weird optical effect. When we were running around up there, just before dawn ... I don't know. At first I thought that the panes were angled to magnify whatever was outside. Got a good close-up view of the surrounding skyscrapers. But I went back later. There weren't any tall buildings nearby."

Ko squinted at Forsyte through the shard. It was like looking through a car windshield with heavy sun tinting — everything was clear, but dark. And not at all magnified. Ko held the shard away from her eye, then brought it back.

"SEE ANYTHING DIFFERENT?" the voder asked.

Ko shook her head, then swore as this time she sliced into the bridge of her nose. "That's worse than razor blades!" She dropped the shard onto her equipment harness which still lay on the desk, then dabbed at her nose with the Kleenex.

Forsyte rolled closer to her and she bent down so he could have a close look at her wound. His fingers tapped on the keyboard. "NOT DEEP." Then he pressed the replay button. "SEE ANYTHING DIFFERENT?"

Ko held the tissue out and frowned at the blood on it. "Nothing," she said. "Up on the tower, the effect disappeared when the sun got brighter. But just at dawn, when it was darker ... " Ko studied Forsyte's face so she could precisely judge his reaction to what she was going to say next. "Adrian, I think I was able to see buildings that, well, that weren't really there."

Ko saw neither support nor criticism in his eyes. Only thoughtfulness.

JUDITH & GARFIELD REEVES-STEVENS

At least he didn't press the laughtrack button on his synthesizer, she thought.

Then Forsyte's two fingers began to peck slowly at his keyboard as he built a sentence that wasn't already stored in his synthesizer's memory of standard sentence fragments. "DO YOU BELIEVE THE SHARD ENABLES YOU TO SEE THROUGH THE LAYER?"

Ko sighed in pleasure. He understood perfectly. But then, why wouldn't he? He was a scientist, he was a genius, and as unscientific as it seemed, in some way she and Forsyte were linked. If not by their minds, then by their hearts. They had been through enough together.

"I was afraid to say it out loud," Ko admitted. "But yes, I think that might be a possibility. Just one problem, though. I don't have the slightest bloody idea what the 'layer' is."

Forsyte tapped at his keys. "THAT'S ALL RIGHT," his voder said. "I DO."

TWELVE

Martin howled as Sword's Porsche pulled into the Loft's garage. The halfling liked the way his deep voice reverberated in the large open space. He could hear things rattle. That was good.

Sword had not let him howl as they had driven through the streets of the city today. Bad.

But Sword *had* let him ride with his head out the window on their way out of the city. Better than good.

The sensation of having air rush across his face faster than he could ever dream of running had overwhelmed Martin. His nose and taste-buds had taken up new scents at a rate beyond his ability to isolate and understand them, and all the hair on his body had bristled with the dizzy waves of excitement that swept through him. His yips of delight had made even Sword happy because Sword had begun to drive faster and faster.

Herbivores, predators, machines, dung, green growing, dark dying, shifters, Lights, old magic, burgers, children, humans, sundancers, fairies — all the life and existence of the Worlds had exploded in Martin's brain at the same time.

Until the bluesuit chased them and made Sword stop and show a wizard's mirror with his face trapped in it.

While Sword and the bluesuit talked, Martin had amused himself by repeatedly pressing the silver wizard's stone that made the side windows go up and down.

Then, as soon as the bluesuit was on his way back to his own car, he had asked Sword a reasonable question. "Why Galen Sword not kill bluesuit?" According to Sword's scent, Martin knew Sword *felt* like killing the bluesuit.

"That's not how the rules work in this world," Sword had growled.

"Stupid rules," Martin had said sympathetically. Feeling and not doing was hard. But Arkady shifters didn't have a problem killing bluesuits. He decided to ask Sword if Clan Pendragon and the bluesuits had a treaty beast somewhere to keep the peace between them. But later, when Sword was in a better mood.

Sword had started the car moving again then, but too slowly, even though Martin had strongly urged him to go faster faster. And then when Sword didn't, Martin had offered to drive. Having watched Sword closely enough, he was sure he could drive the car faster and aim it better, too. But Sword had refused.

Life with Galen Sword was interesting, but very confusing. Sword just didn't understand how things were supposed to be. Maybe when Sword kept his promise and found Astar, Martin's father would show Sword how to feel better by thinking and acting the right way.

But until then, Martin decided, the next best thing was for Martin to feel better. And that was easy.

Sword's Porsche came to a stop in the garage.

Martin took a deep breath, ready to rattle *everything* in the Loft. Just as Sword's hand landed on his shoulder. "I think that's enough howling for today, Martin."

Martin let the air whoosh out of him. Sometimes life with Sword was worse than confusing. How could there *ever* be enough howling?

Sword, as always, got out of the car by opening his door .

Martin decided to show off how much he was learning. He carefully opened his door and stepped out. Dropping out the window was better, but Sword liked it when he did things the slow way.

While Sword took the packages out of the back seat, Martin draped himself over the Porsche's passenger door, looking down to make faces

DARK HUNTER

in the gleaming black surface that reminded him of the eye of a Marratin witch. He hoped it was Sword himself who was responsible for capturing the bluebound adept responsible for the car's swiftness, and for trapping it inside the car with a punishment chant. He wondered why Sword had not also worked out an arrangement to protect the car's lustrous finish. Sword was always warning Martin not to scratch the paint.

Martin hung head down, staring at his image in the side of the Porsche. He had not liked the visit of Ja'Nette's mother, nor the substanceless reflection of Ja'Nette that the witch had called forth. He could still smell the stink of reflected magic in the Loft, even though almost a full cycle had passed.

He noticed a spot on his cheek and had just lifted a finger to scratch it when he heard Sword shut the car door over on his side. Sticking out his tongue out for the benefit of the bluebound adept inside the car, Martin vaulted backwards over the car door and landed neatly on the garage's concrete floor. Then he walked around the car to Sword who praised him for not scratching the paint.

Martin nodded. Paint was all Sword talked about when he got near the car.

"Great," Sword said, "let's go show Melody and Adrian the new clothes you got." He started up the metal staircase.

Martin sighed. In addition to paint, Sword also had a fixation on clothes. Martin didn't understand why Sword and Ko kept insisting that he get more. He had thought they would be pleased when he had picked out the World Wrestling Federation sweatshirt he wore now. It had a full-body wizard's mirror of the most powerful wrestling warrior ever, even better than the Hulkster.

True, the Lights in the television set said that Stone Cold Steve Austin might be turning bad, but Martin couldn't believe that any being who could wrestle *while* he was coldblasted — even if he *was* only a human — could ever follow the reflected path. So Martin was proud to wear his new sweatshirt. And he hadn't taken it off for at least as many days as he had fingers on one hand.

So why were they still insisting that he get more clothes? It was as senseless as Ko's and Sword's insistence that he run water over himself

143

every day. *Water.* All over him. Everyday. Martin shivered at the thought of the gilled ones. Sometimes he thought that Ko and Sword just didn't understand *anything.*

With that, he gave a little howl of thanks for not having gills, and leapt up the stairs after Sword.

In the second-floor conference room that doubled as the Loft's kitchen, Forsyte waited patiently for Sword to reply to Ko's question.

As if I have a choice, the physicist thought, though he knew he didn't feel as anxious or as powerless as he might have even a month ago. Back then, he hadn't known if the three of them would stay together or not. Ko couldn't stand Sword and her aversion had made her obsessed with him. Sword, being obsessed with himself, ignored Ko altogether, and that just made Ko all the worse. Forsyte was sick to death of the two of them and would have left long ago if he didn't need them so badly. Without Ko's technical help and Sword's unique resources, he knew he'd never find the adepts who'd paralyzed him.

So he'd become the linchpin. He'd deflected Ko's desire to leave by telling her that he *wouldn't* leave with her. And then he had reigned in the harebrained behavior that had threatened to drive everyone away — even Martin — by telling Sword that he *would* leave if he weren't put in charge of all of them.

Sword had bought the bluff. He'd acquiesced and surrendered control of their activities. To him.

Of course, Forsyte thought, *then he had gone off and done exactly what he wanted to, anyway.* But at least Sword had acknowledged that the three of them were better off together than apart.

And if Sword had had any doubts remaining about the truth of that, then Forsyte was confident that the present fate of Kendall Marsh would keep Sword from initiating any more First World investigations without informing the rest of his team.

Good word, that, Forsyte thought. *Team. That's what the past weeks have brought us. Our trials by fire: Finding Martin. Breaking up the shifters' Ceremony of the Change. Taking on the Tepesh vampires.*

He and Ko and Sword — and Martin — had discovered that they could work together, succeed together. And, most crucial of all, that they had to remain together if any of them were to survive what lay ahead.

Though neither Sword nor Ko had stated any of this explicitly, Forsyte was certain that both had come to the same realization that he had. Since the apparition of Ja'Nette had freed them of most of the legal complications of the child's death, Ko had spoken no more of leaving, and Sword had talked over every plan he felt they should undertake. Naturally, whatever Sword did, whatever Sword suggested, Martin now supported him without question or equivocation.

For his part, Forsyte had not overtly challenged Sword's authority. Curbing Sword was as good as controlling him.

So they were a team and they had a mission. And now it appeared that by working together they would at last have a workable plan — for *real* action.

"Okay, let's try again from that perspective. I'll ask him." Sword got up from the long black conference table and walked to the far end of the table where Martin sat working with his chalks and papers, oblivious to the conversation that had gone on around him.

Sword stood beside the halfling and looked down at the image he was creating. Forsyte couldn't see what it was this time but guessed it was another clansign from the appreciative way Sword whistled. "Wow, what's that one?"

Martin looked up with a delighted smile and lifted his drawing so that Ko and Forsyte could see it as well. Forsyte wanted to whistle, too. The design Martin had created on the rough paper was remarkable. Once again it was the work of a skilled artist.

"Clan Sahda," Martin said. "Lesser clan. Rocktwiners. Bite always biting."

The symbol of Clan Sahda was in the shape of an ancient scroll, worked through with an elaborate woven pattern that might represent the twisting of a fine twine, assuming that the term 'rocktwiners' bore some relation to the standard concept of twine. Attached to the scroll, in a place suggestive of a wax seal, was a simple line representation of a beetle's carapace. Martin had expertly shaded the curve of the scroll and even added specular highlights to define the dark blue scarab shape.

"Clan Sahda," Sword repeated as he carefully took the chalk drawing from Martin so he could study it more closely. He looked over at Forsyte. "What's this now, thirty-one?"

Forsyte blinked once. Martin had reproduced the clansigns for thirty-one First World clans so far. The halfling might even have drawn more but it had taken a few days for Forsyte and the others to realize what Martin was doing with the art supplies Ko had purchased for him. The fact that Martin had actually been drawing images in addition to chewing on the pastels and painting himself with acrylics had taken them all by surprise.

Fortunately, Martin didn't like the taste of drawing chalks and when he finished each of those pictures, he wasn't inspired to lick the paper as he did with other apparently better-tasting media. The halfling had built up quite a collection of clansigns in Ja'Nette's old room by the time Sword had thought to take a look through the sheaf of drawings.

Ko had been the first to realize that, when Martin had told them he didn't know how to read or write, he had been referring to a specific set of First World languages, and not the general skills of recognizing and drawing symbols, of which he apparently knew hundreds. She had been talking with Billy Santini a few days after returning from the hospital when Santini had asked to autograph her cast. Martin had been entranced by what Santini had done and had pestered Ko to let him do the same. To Ko's surprise, Martin had then inscribed her cast with a beautifully ornate device that Martin said was his namesign. Though the halfling had insisted the design he had drawn wasn't writing because it didn't show "where real things were and were not," he did maintain that the design 'said' "*Myrch'ntin*" — his name as it was pronounced in his shiftertongue.

"That's excellent," Sword told the halfling as he handed back the Sahda clansign.

"Not rocktwiners," Martin said gravely, and shook his head slowly and emphatically, as if he were communicating with a group of particularly slow learners. *Which, to his frame of reference, we probably are,* Forsyte decided.

He watched as Sword then sat down on the edge of the table and smiled affably at Martin. The halfling's resigned look told Forsyte that

Martin, at least, wasn't a slow learner when it came to understanding Sword. Forsyte saw a smile play over Ko's face.

"Martin, what's the layer?"

"Already ask Martin that." Martin's hands began to open and close rapidly. "This many times."

"But you still haven't given us an answer we can understand."

Martin slapped his hand on the table. Obviously, the halfling didn't feel that was *his* problem.

Sword tried again. "Okay then, if you can't tell us what the layer is, then can you tell us what it *looks* like?" He glanced back at Ko as if to confirm he had chosen the correct new approach. Forsyte saw Ko incline her head. Slightly.

Martin curled his bottom lip. "Looks like layer."

"So you *can* see it?" Sword asked.

Martin shifted restlessly in his chair. Forsyte felt sympathy for the halfling — he knew what it was like to have to communicate with idiots. But he also shared the excitement present in the quick glance Sword directed at him and at Ko. If Martin could see the boundary dividing the Second World from the First, then there was a chance the halfling could teach them to see it, too.

"*Where* do you see it, Martin?"

Martin shrugged, looked around the room. "All over."

Sword squatted down beside Martin. "Can you see it in this room?"

The halfling poked a finger in his ear and twirled it vigorously, without looking at Sword, or responding to his question.

"Well, then, could you see it outside? Like in the street?"

"Sometimes." Martin's voice was hesitant, reluctant.

"Do you see it above you? Below you? In any particular direction?"

"Why?"

"Martin," — Forsyte saw Sword check again with Ko — "I want you to think about the times we passed through the layer. When we went to Softwind, and the Pit of the Change, and when we took — "

"Martin not go." The halfling began to rock his chair from side to side.

Sword tapped himself on his chest. "Okay, but what about me? Could I go through the layer by myself?"

Martin nodded, rocking even harder.

Sword put a hand on the back of Martin's chair to still it. "What about Melody? Or Adrian?"

"Maybe. Don't know," Martin huffed.

But Sword pressed on. "What if I wanted to go through the layer by myself, how would I find it?"

"Find *what?*"

To his credit, Forsyte noted, Sword remained calm. "The layer, Martin. How can I find it?"

"Layer *everywhere*," Martin exclaimed with obvious frustration. "Galen Sword look. Galen Sword find. How find air? How find day? Look everywhere. Find everywhere."

Forsyte heard Sword sigh as he straightened up, thanked the halfling for his drawing again, and then suggested that Martin might like to go play in the garage.

With an enviably swift roll, Martin was out his chair and out of the kitchen. The metal walkway outside the main lab shook with the halfling's bounding footfalls, and the enormous metal groan that followed announced Martin's launch from the railing. Then Forsyte heard the rhythmic creaking that meant Martin was swinging, hand over hand, along the overhead pipes twenty feet above the garage floor.

Damnation, the physicist thought, *I envy* everyone *their physical abilities.*

"Did that tell us anything?" Sword asked.

"LAYER CAN BE SEEN," Forsyte had his voder say.

"And it doesn't seem to be location-dependent," Ko said thoughtfully. "That means it could be a moving boundary."

From out in the Loft's central areas, they heard Martin howl with the distinctive warbling quality that meant he was now doing loop-the-loops around the metal beam that Ko had reinforced for him.

Sword poured himself a mug of coffee. Forsyte even envied Sword's being able to complete that simple movement unaided. "So we can forget about trying to find a pattern on the map to track the layer's appearance in the city?"

"I wouldn't give up on that too fast, Sword." Forsyte watched as Ko walked over to join Sword at the kitchen counter, beside the coffeemaker. She reached for the pot of coffee, holding up the pot to him, to offer him some. Something Sword hadn't bothered to do.

But coffee through a straw had long ago lost its appeal for Forsyte. He blinked twice.

"If passing through the layer into — into the First World, I presume — was something that was available at almost anytime, almost everywhere, then the adepts we saw in World Plaza wouldn't have needed the second fardoor to escape their installation. No," Ko said, frowning as she continued to think it through, "there has to be some type of limitation on passing through it. Either by location in time or by location in space."

Forsyte couldn't resist. "HOW EINSTEINIAN," he punched out on his voder.

Ko gave him a quick grin as she poured herself a mug of coffee, but Sword merely continued to study the ceiling with a faraway look. "You know," he said, "Tomas Roth already told me that. In the museum that night. He and Morgana were talking about fardoors. 'The portals can be aligned in time,' he said. At the time, I didn't understand the significance of what he meant."

Then Sword abruptly brought his attention back to present-day realities. "So — what should we do next?"

Ko sipped at her coffee. "I'd suggest waiting until Martin's cooled off a bit, then ask him to take us through the layer."

"CAMERAS," Forsyte had his voder say.

"Right, Adrian," Ko said with a nod. "This time when we go through, we won't be chasing shifters or vampires. We'll take cameras, sampling jars, maybe some astrosurvey equipment to try and get a fix on where we've ended up."

"Do we have astrosurvey equipment?" Sword sounded surprised.

Ko took another sip of her coffee. "Yep, you bought some last year."

"Why?"

"Why not?"

"I'll have to start reading all those papers you have me sign," Sword said lightly, then grew serious again. "What do you think the equipment will tell us?"

"Three possibilities," Ko said. "One: the layer acts like a fardoor and we'll find ourselves some place else on earth."

"You think that's likely?" Sword asked.

"You mean do I think instantaneous teleportation is bloody likely?" Ko said. "Something happens, Sword, but 'likely' has nothing to do with it."

She set her mug down on the black-laminate counter. "Anyway, two bits of data could support the theory."

Forsyte listened intently. Despite her weak self-esteem, he'd never doubted the strength of Ko's intellect. His former student was a first-rate thinker.

"The first piece of data is that we could still see the moon on the night Martin called the Lights for Ja'Nette's body — and that was after we had passed through the layer. I didn't get a chance to check its coordinates precisely, but it seemed to be in about the right place at about the right time."

True, Forsyte thought, *though at the time I remember thinking that the moon was too bright.*

"That suggests," Ko continued, "that wherever we were, we weren't too far from New York. In a geographical sense, that is. Also, the ambient temperature didn't appear to be noticeably different."

Forsyte saw Sword frown. "But what about the temperature, Melody? It was completely different in the Arkady Pit of the Change. Don't you remember how hot and humid it was?"

"What about what we saw outside the cavern's mouth?" Ko countered. "When the helicopters landed with the Seyshen?"

Almost more than anything else, Forsyte wished he had been with them in the cavern. They'd told him they'd seen waves of helicopters carrying Seyshen warriors and uniformed human soldiers into battle with half a thousand shifters. Alone, in the privacy of his own mind, Forsyte admitted to himself that it was the sheer violence of the scene that he found enthralling.

"I remember the sun being really bright — "

"That's what I mean," Ko interrupted impatiently. "The sun was just rising. In fact, it was the first rays from the dawn that triggered the

Crystal of the Change. And as soon our eyes had adjusted to the daylight outside, we saw all that vege — "

"Lush, green plants," Sword agreed. "They looked almost prehistoric."

Ko shook her head. "Back up, Sword."

"Well, tropical, then."

"Try rain forest. Anyway, the point is, with the kind of vegetation we saw, there's a possibility we were somewhere within Brazil."

Sword looked skeptical.

"I'm serious." Ko looked at Forsyte. "Adrian, the sun rose while we were there, but when we came back out in New York, dawn was still about an hour off." She turned back to Sword. "I even told you that at the time."

"You told me a lot of things then," Sword said, clearly referring to Ko's walkout, when she'd sworn never to return.

But Ko wasn't interested in her earlier decision. Once she had made up her mind to remain part of the team, she'd moved on. Despite her unchanged feelings about Sword.

"What I'm trying to tell you now, Sword, is that when we passed through the layer beneath Central Park, we could have been 'teleported' " — Ko grimaced as she used the term — "about one or two time zones farther east. Brazil."

Sword looked at Forsyte for his comment. Forsyte tapped at his keys. "GIVEN THE CIRCUMSTANCES," the voder said, "THAT SOUNDS REASONABLE."

"So what're the other two possibilities?" Sword asked.

Ko rubbed at the razor-cut bristle of her spiky black hair. "The second possibility is the one I already told you about."

"That the First World exists in a ... parallel dimension? But Martin has already told us the First World and the Second World aren't two different places — just different parts of the same place."

"Forget 'parallel dimension.' That's your description, not mine." Ko nodded her head in Forsyte's direction. "Adrian calls it a spacetime continuum that's somehow polarized in relation to the one we live in."

"I know enough physics to know that *light* is polarized, Melody, not things," Sword argued.

151

"Light can be a wave phenomenon," Ko countered. "So can matter. And if a light wave can be polarized in three-dimensional space, then maybe matter waves can be polarized in four-dimensional spacetime. It's either that or we have to consider the possibility that passing through the layer sends us light-years away — to another planet around another star in our own continuum — in complete defiance of relativity. And that's just plain nuts."

Sword looked to Forsyte. "You really agree with this, Adrian?"

Sword and Ko waited patiently while Forsyte composed his reply.

"MY WORK WITH JA'NETTE INDICATED HER ABILITY TO TRANSLOCATE PHYSICAL OBJECTS MIGHT BE RESULT OF SIXTH-DIMENSIONAL GRAVITATIONAL DISTORTIONS THROUGH SUPERSPACE."

Forsyte saw the blank look in Sword's eyes and hit the 'kill' button, cancelling the rest of the statement he had just programmed into the synthesizer. He typed in a new, shorter explanation. "MUCH IN PHYSICS RULES OUT POSSIBILITY OF TRAVEL FASTER THAN SPEED OF LIGHT IN VACUUM. HOWEVER, NOTHING IN PHYSICS EXPRESSLY RULES OUT WHAT MELODY SUGGESTS ABOUT CO-EXISTING DIMENSIONS."

"'And that which is not expressly prohibited is mandatory,'" Sword said, waving his coffee mug in a mock salute to Ko, ceding the victory to her.

"So what's the third possibility?" he asked.

Forsyte already knew the answer to that one. His eyes met Ko's.

"The third is something we can't even imagine," Ko said.

THIRTEEN

In spite of the cloudless sky and the brilliant afternoon sun, the early winter wind cutting through the outdoor observation deck of the Empire State Building was bitterly cold.

Melody Ko suppressed the urge to shiver, rationally aware that her body was warm enough in her black down-filled parka to last at least thirty minutes outside. She was determined to take her landscape pictures before the sun set so she could develop them before tomorrow morning. That was when Martin was scheduled to take them all through the layer on a leisurely — for once — sampling run in the First World. The excursion was Sword's idea, and Ko had to admit Sword wasn't quite as hard to work for now that he was planning activities properly. Thanks to Forsyte's ultimatum, the team's operations were finally approaching a semblance of normalcy.

Right, normal, Ko thought. *I'm up on the Empire State Building to photograph buildings in another dimension with the one hand I have that hasn't been wrecked by supernatural creatures.* She walked around to the north side of the open-air deck, where she could look uptown and see the distant green swath of Central Park. Since the Park had been a common element in two passages through the layer, she planned to concentrate her photography on that section of the city. It was fortunate

JUDITH & GARFIELD REEVES-STEVENS

the harsh wind was keeping most of the tourists and school groups inside. She had the deck almost to herself.

Ko let her camera case slip off her shoulder, and with her one good hand in its thin black-wool glove, gently lowered the case to the deck. The move was not too difficult since she had removed all the good equipment and the case was much lighter than usual. All that was in it was ten disposable cameras loaded with color-print film she'd picked up on the cab ride from SoHo. Rather than make a lens mount for the World Plaza pyramid glass shard because it was too small to cover her Nikons' lenses, she'd decided to simply tape the fragment over the disposable cameras' smaller lenses, settling for quantity of data over quality. Besides, after that long kitchen session with Sword and Forsyte and Martin, she hadn't wanted to waste what little daylight remained to her.

When she'd told Forsyte what she planned to do, the physicist had reminded her that she'd survived her first two semesters at MIT on quick and dirty lab work and that he was pleased to see that she still knew how to carry on the noble student tradition.

Her student days, Ko thought. Before the flier adepts had come to investigate Forsyte's work with transformable electron tunneling, when he had still been whole, when she'd believed she and Forsyte might even ...

No, she told herself, *thoughts like that are as useless a distraction as pointless shivering.* She would not indulge herself in mind or body.

Ko concentrated once more on the job at hand.

Before leaving the Loft, she'd used a microscope to compare the edges of the shard against those of another broken piece of common glass, expecting to find differences — perhaps hidden razor-thin ridges — that would account for the shard's unusual and dangerous keenness. Finding nothing, she had still been careful to wrap the edges of the shard in several layers of black insulating tape so she could handle it without risking another surprise cut.

Ko bent down and placed the tape-edged shard on the open lid of the camera case and pulled out the first of her disposable cameras, together with several prepared squares of wide, silver tape. Working quickly, she used the sections of silver tape to fix the shard to the front of the small, boxy camera, checked to make certain that none of the tape overlapped the lens, then stood up to take her first set of photographs.

The sun was low in the sky and cast strong sharp shadows across the city below her.

What am I doing? Ko suddenly thought in disgust. *I have to visually check the view through the shard first.* The inexpensive cameras didn't allow her to look directly through their lenses. Unless she removed the shard and looked through it first, she wouldn't know what she was getting on film

Must be the cold, she scolded herself. *I don't usually make mistakes like this. Except when ...*

Ko stiffened as she remembered under what conditions she was most likely to make mistakes, most likely to forget to complete important thoughts, most likely to —

She whirled around. The camera slipped from her gloved hand.

And Brin caught it, deftly, easily, as if he had been expecting her to drop it just when she did.

"Hello, Melody," he said. His fine blond hair caught in the wind and his clear blue eyes — so much like Sword's in all but color — flashed in the stark, obliquely-angled sunlight.

"You lied to me," Ko said. It was the first thing she thought, the first thing she felt.

Brin looked amused. "Did I?" He held out the camera for her and she snatched it from his hand.

"And you ... you did something to me." That's what Ja'Nette's mother had implied and that assessment still seemed reasonable. Though Ko remembered little else of what happened after her collapse on the garage floor that night, she knew her last thoughts had been of Brin.

She saw Brin glance down at the white edge of cast showing between the stretched cuff of her black parka and her half-pulled-on glove. "Not a very useful enchantment, it seems." He reached out his hand to her.

But Ko pulled back. "Don't touch me."

"But that must be uncomfortable, Melody. And awkward. And your ribs must be sore. You must feel exhausted."

"I feel fine."

Brin slipped both his hands into the pockets of his long gray coat. The fabric looked much too thin to Ko to offer much protection against the wind and cold, but Brin seemed unaffected. "As you wish," he said.

"That's exactly what I wish. What are you doing here anyway?"

"I enjoyed our last talk. I thought it might be time for another." He nodded at the camera in her hand. "You must have more questions you wish to ask me. Perhaps about the glass you have."

"Funny thing," Ko said suspiciously, "but the last time we 'talked,' I don't remember asking you a lot of questions. Much less getting any answers."

"Melody, how can you say that? All those questions about Adrian Forsyte ... the fliers ... my brother. And I answered all of them. You don't remember that?"

"No," Ko said, but her tone was less certain. After Brin had left her that night — the night the team confronted the vampires of Tepesh in the World Plaza tower pyramid — she did recall wondering why she hadn't asked Sword's brother even the simplest question about the First World.

You know that's not true, Melody.

Ko started. Brin hadn't spoken.

Oh, but I did.

"I don't believe in telepathy," Ko said even as Brin's voice continued in her mind.

How else would I know the memories given to you by the waiting crystal? How else would I know about your needless pity for Dr. Forsyte, whose misfortune is solely his own?

"Adrian counted on me and I held back when I could have helped," Ko said bluntly. "He trusted me."

The doctor used you, Melody. He does not honor what you feel for him. Not the way I do.

Ko's face felt hot, flushed, and she knew its cause was not the wind. "What?"

This time, Brin spoke aloud. "You are refusing to acknowledge the truth."

DARK HUNTER

"How about you?" Ko challenged in return. "How about *you* telling *me* the truth about the way this glass — "

"My brother," Brin said. "I've told you all you need to know about him. About the danger he represents to the Worlds."

That stopped Ko in midsentence, the glass shard forgotten. "I thought that was over."

"My brother is still as dangerous as he has always been, Melody. There was exceptional risk the night that he recklessly attacked the Tepesh installation. And it is only by the concerted efforts of the keepers of a dozen clans that the evidence of that night has slowly been disappearing from the files and the storage lockers of the investigators of the Second World."

Ko saw Brin scan the almost deserted observation deck, but they were completely alone.

"That night my brother almost did what some say he is destined to do — expose the First World to the Second in such an uncontrolled and violent manner that only war can result. The final war. Do you remember all this now, Melody?"

Ko found herself agreeing, though it still didn't make a lot of sense to her. Not complete sense at least. "Yes, but — "

"And you accept its truth?"

Ko struggled to complete her question. " — if Sword's so dangerous, why did you send me off to help him that night? Why did — "

"I knew your skills could get him in and out quickly, without disturbance. That you could help keep his activities secret."

"But — three years ago — when he had his accident, why did you save his life then? Why didn't you just let the danger die with him?"

"Whatever else he might be or become, he is still my brother."

"Yet he can destroy the Worlds?" Ko said as she hugged her cast-bound arm to her chest, aware that Brin's presence, so near, was once more affecting her ability to think and reason clearly.

"Only if he is allowed to remain *uncontrolled*," Brin emphasized. "It's important to me that you understand, Melody. *That's* why my brother was exiled from his home and his kind, and why we took his memories of his heritage from him. But since we are not barbarians who would murder a child simply for what it *might* do, we also

157

protected him to prevent the stories of destruction told about him from ever coming to pass. I assure you, we all wanted him to keep his life."

"So what went wrong?"

"The accident." Brin's hand took hers and Ko experienced what he felt as if his feelings as well as his words could also be transmitted directly to her. "My brother was not abandoned in your world. He was given wealth. He was always watched over, guided, shielded. And I was one of those whose duty it was to be near him."

Ko felt the warmth of Brin's hand spread throughout her body. She made no move to withdraw her hand from his, nor did she question her lack of need to do so. Somewhere, deep within, a part of her knew Brin was somehow enchanting her again. But that part was not in control now.

"I was near him on the night of his accident, Melody. I felt the life draining from him. Felt him falling into endless darkness. I could not stand by while I had the power to prevent that fall. But in doing so, I interfered with the wizard's potion that had clouded my brother's memories."

Ko saw Brin color slightly as he looked down at her. "Two accidents happened that night. One was my brother's fault. The other was mine. And I have spent the past three years attempting to make amends."

"Why don't you talk to him directly?" Ko asked, though she understood why he couldn't, anymore than she could to Forsyte.

Still holding her hand securely in his, Brin looked toward the sun, low on the horizon. "I can't. They won't let me."

"They?"

"Do you have any knowledge of the ... politics of the First World?"

Ko felt she had none, but she could guess. "I know of the war that's been building between the Clan Arkady and the Clan Seyshen."

"One war among dozens, among hundreds," Brin said. "The clans are ancient. Their animosities toward each other older still. Reaching back before any time any one of us can remember. Even the night-feeders."

"Like a force of nature," Ko said, not sure where the words had come from.

DARK HUNTER

"I knew you'd understand, Melody," Brin said. "Like a force of nature. Wild, complex, unrestrained."

Ko no longer remembered or cared about the point of their conversation. She felt in tune with Brin, mentally *and* physically at ease with him. *I've never felt this way even with Adrian,* she thought. *Certainly never with Sword. How could two brothers be so different?* "But why does any of this keep you from talking to Sword" — she hesitated, realizing that the last name would apply to both — "to Galen, directly?"

"There are those who say it was no accident that I restored my brother's memories when I did."

"But the car crash," Ko said. "You had no choice."

"There are those who say that my brother's accident was no accident. That I was somehow responsible for that as well."

"They think you'd try to kill your own brother?"

"No, not kill him. They think I might have arranged the accident so that I would have an opportunity — an excuse — to use my power to restore his memories while claiming that I was only trying to save his life. Which was my duty after all."

Ko felt the chill of the wind again as Brin released her hand and gathered his coat closely around himself. "If it becomes known that I am trying to contact my brother directly, then there are those who will point to those actions as proof of my treachery."

The part deep within Ko that still remained rational surfaced suddenly, searching for the elusive logic beneath Brin's words. "Why would bringing back Galen's memories be considered treachery? And who would say that?"

"The Victor of Arkady, for one."

"Morgana?" Ko asked.

Brin nodded. "And the Victor of Seyshen, among others."

"And Morgana's consort? Tomas Roth?" Ko asked. "Is he involved as well?"

"Yes, but not as a victor. He is only regent to the Victor of Pendragon."

Ko touched her forehead, trying to remember what Sword was always going on about. "And that's Sword — Galen, right?"

159

A shadow darkened Brin's face. "Not since he was five years old and the decision was made for his exile. Despite what he may think, my brother is no longer in line."

Ko stared at him. "So *you* are the heir to the Victor."

Brin looked off to the horizon again. The crimson setting sun reddened his fair hair.

Ko went on, completing the puzzle.

"And the other clans think that you brought Galen back into play to cause confusion ... to bring the threat of a catastrophic war to the front of everyone's concern ... and draw attention from yourself and from other conflicts." Now it was obvious to Ko why Brin would have enemies in the First World. Why they would hate him and think that he was capable of risking the Worlds for the sake of his own power. But Brin's enemies were wrong.

"They think you're trying to overthrow Roth's regency and take control of Pendragon."

Brin reached for her hand again. "And Arkady, and Seyshen, and ... It's all a lie, Melody."

But Ko was barely listening. She felt jolted by the elation and relief she felt at the renewed pressure of Brin's hand around hers. This time, even through her glove, it was as if their bodies and minds had joined as well.

"And what is the truth?" she asked breathlessly. "What *do* you want?"

Do you have to ask?

Ko trembled. But whether from anticipation or apprehension, she didn't know.

What can I do for you, Melody? How can I help you?

Ko stared up at him. Her mind empty. She had no questions left. It was as if Brin were somehow relieving her of the necessity of rational thought at all, and she was responding to him on a more vulnerable, instinctual level.

"The glass?" Brin asked her gently. "Did you not have a question about the shard?"

The glass. She had forgotten about the glass. She had dropped the disposable camera on the deck floor without noticing that she had done so. Thin slivers of the shard were still attached to the camera's body by tape, but the rest of the shard had shattered.

"Bloody hell," Ko whispered, forgetting that she had seen Brin catch the camera.

Brin let go of her hand, knelt down, and collected the shard's fragments without Ko once thinking it was remarkable that he didn't cut himself. He straightened up, the fragments in the palm of one hand.

"Here," he said, holding out one dime-sized piece, "while the sun is still at the proper angle. Look through this."

Without a thought for the sharp edges of the fragment, Ko took the small fragment and held it up to her eye, gazing out at the city as Brin had instructed. She felt the warmth of him against her body as he stood close behind her, one hand on her shoulder, one hand pointing out to the Park, now completely in the shadows of the buildings to its west. "There, Melody. Look. Tell me what you see."

Ko looked. Then gasped. She saw narrow towers outlined in thousands of lights. She saw broad thoroughfares lined with tall trees. She saw an ocean's edge as far to the north as she could see. She saw movement on the streets below. But it was not New York that she saw.

"What ... what is it?"

"The North Shore," Brin said, the soft puff of his warm breath against her cheek incredibly distracting.

"But how ... ?" The strange city wavered as the angle of the light that fell upon it changed. Beyond the city, Ko saw something else — like a double exposure. The buildings of Manhattan — coming back into view. "No," she said.

"Do you want to see more?"

Ko nodded, caught up in her discovery, but still intensely aware of Brin. She tilted the glass in her hand, trying different angles. She thought she might have caught a glimpse of something in the sky, a dark shadow with trailing arms like a giant X shape, but it disappeared the moment she focused on it.

"That wasn't a good glass to begin with," Brin said as he took the shard fragment from her fingers. "Poor quality. There are better makes."

Ko looked at her blood-soaked shredded glove with curiosity. Her exposed fingertips covered with bloody scabs formed by coagulation and frozen blood.

She turned back to Brin. "Where can I get more of it?" she asked eagerly.

Brin looked thoughtful. "Well, now that you ask, there is a well-stocked shop on Forty-seventh. In the diamond district." As he spoke, Ko felt the light caress of his hand on her cheek.

It took her a moment to register what Brin had said. "I can go there and ... and *buy* more of this kind of glass ? Seriously?"

"Oh, no. Not 'glass.' " Ko heard the way he said the word — dismissively. "What you had was a trick of the Second World. A poor imitation of what exists in the First World by nature."

"But there's a shop that sells something that will show me the North Shore?"

"Much more clearly," Brin said. "And at a broader range of angles."

"But not glass. Something else?"

Ko felt the touch of Brin's hands on her shoulders. "The shop will be open tomorrow morning. Ask for First World crystals. First World micas and tourmalines. There is a special room in back. You must be most insistent, Melody."

Ko felt dizzy. Was looking into the First World really going to be as simple as this?

Yes, as simple as this.

Ko felt Brin's touch become an embrace and she did not resist, did not think of resisting, did not want to resist.

As Brin's lips sought hers.

DARK HUNTER

FOURTEEN

There was only one legal street parking space unoccupied within two blocks of the Happy Thought Gold and Diamond Exchange, and Sword gunned the van for it, swinging around a stopped cab, nearly missing a slow-moving garbage truck, until —

"Damn!" Sword braked the van with a lurch as an even swifter Honda Civic slipped into the space before him. "Where the hell did that come from?"

"Just go around the block," Ko said. "There's a garage back at the corner."

Sword glared at the Civic as he rolled past it but the driver kept her head down. "And look at that!" Sword complained as he saw that the two parking spaces in front of the Civic were being taken up by a black Rolls Royce Silver Cloud I, its exhausts swirling with vapor despite the no-idling laws.

Ko waved her hand in front of Sword's face as he stared past her at the Rolls. "Just give it a rest, Sword. Drive around the block."

"Fast fast fast," Martin urged from the back of the van. Yesterday's excursion to New Jersey had been so exciting for the halfling that as soon as Martin had understood that there would be another outing this morning, he had put on his clothes without being told and raced down to the garage. Sword had told Martin that there would be no

163

howling and no head out the window, but Martin had said he didn't care. The words 'going for a drive' had come to exert a powerful new force on him.

"Maybe we should hire a full-time driver." Sword accelerated again, ignoring the blaring horn of the cab he had passed, which was now trying to pass him.

"What's wrong with the car service?" Ko said. "Turn right here."

"Do *you* want to drive?" Provocatively, he deliberately drove past the street corner Ko had indicated.

But Ko didn't rise to the bait. "As if you'd let me," she said.

From the back of the van, Martin said hopefully, "Martin drive. Fast fast fast."

Before Sword could reject Martin's offer, the cab that had run the red light behind the van suddenly cut in front and stopped violently. Sword stomped on the van's brakes and leaned on the horn. The cab began to move forward again, but only at a few miles an hour.

"We could definitely use a driver," Sword said again, continuing to tap at the horn. He couldn't be sure but he thought he saw the cab driver waving his hand with one finger extended. "A driver would be a lot more convenient than the car service. And we wouldn't have to wait around when it was raining."

He turned on the highbeams and the cab slowed again. Ko's voice rose.

"Will you forget the cab? Turn right *right here!*"

Again, he hit the brakes, then cut right, heading into a narrow laneway lined with delivery trucks, all with parking lights flashing amber and red. "Where's this supposed to take us again?"

"The next street over," Ko snapped.

Sword grinned. He'd finally gotten to her.

"So you can go around the block, Sword, and *park.*"

Obediently this time, he drove along the laneway until it ended at the next street, just as Ko had said it would. He waited half over the pedestrian-crossing lines, blinker on, watching for an opening in traffic so he could turn right again.

In the back of the van, Martin rocked from side to side in his seat, staring out the back window with curled lips and making soft car-engine noises to himself.

When Sword pulled out onto the street again, Ko said, "Remember to go *two* lights down before you turn."

"Your wish is my command," he teased in a voice pitched deliberately too low for Ko to hear clearly.

"What?"

"I said, Billy Santini. He seems like a level-headed kid. Pretty sharp."

"Yeah, so what?" Ko asked, holding tightly to her harness as he braked for another red light.

"We could hire him as a driver."

"Yeah, right. 'Say, Billy, mind taking the limo up to the Royalton and picking up our friend, Orion? You can't miss him, he's the one with the fangs. Oh, and be sure to watch out for those darn shapeshifters, Billy.'" Ko shook her head disparagingly. "I don't think so, Sword."

Sword felt his good humor and intentions begin to dissipate. Yesterday afternoon, Brin had put in a sudden reappearance but only to talk with Ko. And now, somehow for reasons he still did not quite understand, that reappearance had delayed the Sword Foundation plan — *his* plan — for a methodical gathering of samples and information from the layer's other side. To honor the commitment he had made to the members of his team, he had reluctantly accepted Ko's and Forsyte's voting to buy the First World crystals *before* going through the layer.

All he had said to Ko was, "It *can't* be that easy."

But Ko had insisted that Brin's explanation was logical. She'd argued that it was only reasonable to assume that First World adepts would have businesses in the Second World. And then she'd reminded him that when he and Martin had gone to Softwind to negotiate having 'Bub's enchantment lifted, they'd learned that the economy of the First World was partially based on crystals.

Moreover, she'd reasoned, the installation on the World Plaza tower — and the hidden passages in the columns — had to have involved real-world construction and labor costs. Since no one could buy a New York construction crew for a handful of red crystals, Ko told him it made perfect sense to her that there was some sort of currency exchange procedure between the First World and the Second.

After all, Ko added, how else was the Arkady enclave by Central Park able to handle its property taxes? Or pay ConEd? How did Saul Calder buy his townhouse? On and on she had continued until Sword had managed to get a word in.

"Okay, okay, okay," he had conceded. "I give up. I'll accept that there are shops in the city, run for adepts, where First World goods can be obtained. But why did Brin decide to tell you about them?"

"To help us, of course."

At that moment, Forsyte had cast his vote with Ko, and Sword's objections had become moot.

The light changed and Sword pulled forward, putting on the van's blinker for the turn at the next light. Behind him, Martin tapped his fingers against his window in a remarkably unrhythmical pattern. Beside him, Ko leaned forward as if that would make it easier to see around the corner. She started to say something but Sword cut her off with, "I'm turning, Melody. I know where I'm going."

He decided it was useless to argue with her anymore about the car service. He'd go along with this crazy idea of buying First World crystals. He wouldn't say 'I told you so' when they were laughed out of the store. And after they got back from going through the layer, he'd phone up Angela Scarlatti and see about hiring Billy Santini as a driver. Ko could just deal with it after the fact. It would be a lot less tedious than trying to convince her through logic. *In fact, for someone who calls herself a scientist,* Sword thought, *Ko doesn't know the first thing about logic.*

The van creaked as Sword made a hard right and was back on the block where Brin had told Ko she would find the First World shop. *The so-called First World shop,* Sword corrected himself. He decided that he'd feel better about this venture if he thought that Ko had told him everything that Brin had told her. Ko's explanation for Brin's not contacting him directly still seemed unconvincing.

Or else, he thought suddenly, remembering Ja'Nette's mother's mention of lifting an enchantment from Ko, *Melody really* doesn't *remember everything Brin said to her and she's merely re —*

"Sword! You're going to miss it again!" Ko blared.

DARK HUNTER

Sword gritted his teeth and skidded into a spot by the curb in front of the entrance to the parking garage. He could see the red neon of the Happy Thought Exchange's sign a half block up. He could also still see the billow of exhaust coming from the Rolls that had taken up two parking spots farther along.

"Aren't you going into the garage?" Ko asked.

Sword put the van in park and jammed down the emergency brake pedal. "We'll be okay here."

"This is a tow-away," Ko warned. "By the time you get back here, you're going to have a ticket. The garage is just over there."

"It's not about money," Sword said firmly. "It's more convenient to leave the van out here." He shifted around in his seat. "Martin, Melody and I are going into a store up the street. I want you to sit here and if a bluesuit comes by and wants to talk to you, you call me on the locator band, all right?"

Martin nodded eagerly and fumbled with his seatbelt release. Then he patted the locator band he wore around his wrist. Like the new ones Sword and Ko wore, the Forsyte-designed device resembled a modernistic bracelet of anodized black aluminum, about two inches wide and a quarter-inch thick. But beneath its metal skin and the four glowing LEDS on its outer surface was a sensitive radio mechanism that could be used to track and communicate with whoever wore it — either by voice or by a surreptitious vibrating pad on the inner surface.

For a fully-equipped excursion, the miniature Mitsubishi transceivers and VOX microphones, powered by full-size batteries that were carried on the equipment harnesses, were more convenient and had a longer range. But for those instances when Sword did not want to attract attention yet still be prepared, the locator bands were much preferable.

When Ko had assembled improved replacements for the bands that had been recently lost or damaged, she had constructed several with an extra-large circumference so that Martin also could now wear his on his wrist, instead of pinning it to a shirt that most likely wouldn't stay on him for more than a half hour at a time. The flush-mounted signal buttons were also larger on Martin's bands to allow for his larger fingers.

"Press top button for Galen Sword," Martin said proudly as he began to climb over the seat back. He had been learning his lessons well during his time at the Loft.

Sword checked the outside mirror, got out of the van, then leaned back in to invitingly pat the driver's seat for Martin.

At once, the halfling scooted into the driver's seat, then sat on his hands. "Martin learn lessons. Not touch anything."

Ko sighed heavily as she pushed her door open, and jumped out of the van.

"Except for the radio," Sword said, checking his coat pocket to make sure he had the keys so that when Martin inevitably did start fiddling with the van's controls nothing too serious could happen.

"Radio!" Martin exclaimed. Both hands flew out from beneath him and he began flipping every switch on the central radio above the van's computer station. "Top forty!"

Sword made sure the computer keyboard was folded out of Martin's way, then closed the door and pulled on a pair of leather gloves. The early winter cold snap was continuing. He joined Ko on the sidewalk.

"You have 'Bub's pendant?" Ko asked as they headed up the street toward the Happy Thought.

Sword pointed to the inside pocket of his coat. "For the tenth time, yes."

"This is a good opportunity for us, Sword. I don't want you screwing it up."

"Me screw it up? Hey, who got us out of the Pit of the Change by threatening the Arkady Crystal?"

"Who told you to threaten to touch the bloody crystal in the first place?"

"Who had the UV lights installed in the Loft so Orion didn't rip us to shreds?"

"Who didn't tell anyone else that he was bloody well dealing with a vampire until the vampire tried to kill us? And who let Roth and Morgana come back through the Tepesh fardoor? They were dead, Sword. Finished. But you wouldn't press the detonator fast enough. You let them come back."

DARK HUNTER

Sword halted on the sidewalk outside an unprepossessing store-front whose small, broken-lettered sign proclaimed it to be the HAPPY HO G GO D & DIAMOND EXCHANGE. "Who saved Martin's father's life?" *That'll stop her,* he thought. And it did.

Ko turned her attention to open the door of the shop. It was locked. Peering through the battered silver-metal grill that covered the shop's glass door, she waved to a figure inside the shop. The doorlock buzzed open. "Well, I just hope you didn't end up putting our lives back on the block," she said, then stepped inside before Sword could reply.

You're not getting the last word this time, Sword thought. *I'm going to remember exactly where you left off so we can continue this discussion as soon as we're ordered out of this place.* Then, knowing it was a complete waste of the Sword Foundation's time, Sword followed Ko into the small shop.

The layout of the Happy Thought Gold and Diamond Exchange was typical for the area — long and narrow with a counter that ran the length of the garishly overlit front room. Looking up, Sword saw flaking fluorescent panels that seemed to be in the process of falling out of the buckled acoustic tiles of the ceiling.

Ko marched directly to the counter and sat down on one of four beat-up, red vinyl-covered, chrome-legged counter stools, not one of which was level. On the glassed-in shelves beneath the counter, Sword could see old, mismatched, velour-covered display boxes: rings mostly, hundreds of gold rings, some with stones, some without.

"We're interested in crystal," Ko said to the sole occupant of the shop, an old woman clad in a white balloon-sleeved shirt tucked into an old-fashioned high-waisted black skirt. Though the old woman was frail and stooped with hands gnarled by age and arthritis, she had an youthfully luxuriant shock of blindingly white hair sweeping back from her face in a cartoon caricature of a fifties' duckbill.

The old woman's hair was so stiff it didn't shift position as she nodded to Ko. And when she spoke, her voice was deep and rough, as if it belonged more properly in someone a hundred pounds heavier who smoked three packs a day. "I have cousin in Bronx who handles estate goods. Baccarat, Steuben. You'll love very much." She puckered her lips and made a kissing sound. "I get you his card."

169

JUDITH & GARFIELD REEVES-STEVENS

Sword groaned. He had barely survived driving uptown with Ko. How was he going to stand a trip to the Bronx?

The old woman began to paw through an ancient cigar box resting precariously on a wooden stool behind the counter. The shallow box was filled with torn-up pieces of paper, matchbooks, business cards, and — Sword leaned forward to see more closely — *loose teeth?*

Ko shook her head at Sword warningly. "Not that kind of crystal. First World crystal."

The old woman gave no reaction to show that Ko's words held any special, secret meaning. Her twisted fingers continued to flip through the box.

"Micas and tourmalines," Ko said.

The woman stopped searching and looked up at Ko. She closed one eye. For the first time, Sword noticed she had no eyebrows.

"Micas and tourmalines?" the woman repeated.

Last night, Ko had explained to Sword and Forsyte what she thought was the significance of Brin's specifying those particular minerals. Both were natural polarizers of light, and if Second World micas and tourmalines could polarize Second World light, Ko thought that perhaps their First World analogues would respond similarly to First World light.

He'd told Ko she was reaching but Ko had pointed out that sunlight, which was unpolarized, became polarized by its passage through the atmosphere. "On a clear day," she'd said, "if you look through a polarizing filter at a spot in the sky directly opposite the sun, you'll see an X-shaped pattern. And when the sun's setting in the west, you'll see the same effect in the east, one hundred and eighty degrees from the sun's position. It's how bees navigate and — "

"What does this have to do with *anything*?" Sword had protested.

"How about — when I looked through the glass fragment from the shard, I thought I saw an X-pattern due north, Sword. Either the glass had a strange flaw that created an illusion only under unbelievably precise and coincidental conditions, *or else it was polarizing something other than the light from our sun.*"

"So what other source of light is there, Melody?"

170

"The light of the First World's sun, you idiot!" Ko had almost shouted at him. "The light from another, co-existing dimension! A dimension that is polarized to ours in four-dimensional spacetime, which interacts with ours at particular times, at particular frequencies, and — oh, I don't know — it's not like I'm saying I have all the answers, Sword. But your brother has at least given us a direction to go in and we'd be fools not to follow up on what he said."

Forsyte had ended that part of their altercation by pointing out that the semi-precious gemstone, tourmaline, though more often found in pinkish shades, was also known to occasionally occur in decidedly red forms. And as Martin had told them more than once, whatever the First World's red crystals were, they weren't rubies. And Martin was still insisting, repeatedly, that he did know the difference between Second world gems and crystals of *real* worth.

"That's right," Ko said to the proprietor. "We're looking for micas and tourmalines — crystals — that come from the First World."

The old woman nodded gravely. "Is gold and diamond only here. Some emerald, some ruby, not so much. What you want is" — she turned her head to Sword, but closed both eyes tight — "hobby store. Baby stones. I have cousin in Queens with — "

Ko turned to Sword and held out her hand. "Give me 'Bub's pendant."

Sword pulled a small brown envelope from his coat and placed it in Ko's waiting hand. He could only hope that Martin had been right when the halfling had guaranteed that 'Bub would stay in Ja'Nette's room while the collar was off. Two weeks ago, Sword had found a small pile of twisted metal and plastic pieces hidden behind the bookshelf in Martin's room. It had taken him a good minute to realize he had finally found 'Bub's carrier. Martin claimed the Lights had stolen it. Or the bluesuits. Sword got the message: As long as Martin was around, 'Bub was never going to be inside a cat carrier again.

Ko held the brown envelope upside down and 'Bub's green leather collar fell out on the counter. When the clear crystal pendant attached to it hit the glass, it chimed like fine metal.

In an move almost too swift for Sword to follow, both the old woman's hands flashed forward to hover over the collar and pendant as if she were warming her hands about a fire. "Ahh, clear crystal bond," she crooned. She bared her teeth at Ko and winked with one eye, then another. "With this here is little reptile at home, is not?"

With a triumphant glance at Sword, Ko leaned forward, thunking her cast against the glass. The old woman's eyes sprang open at the sound and she regarded Ko with even more interest.

"This is the type of crystal we're interested in."

But the old woman pursed her lips and made a liquid 'tsk-tsk' noise.

"No, no. You say micas and tourmalines. Seeking facets. Viewing planes. This binding crystal. Glitterful binding chant." The old woman swayed closer to Ko. "Two different things. Two different crystals."

Suddenly, the old woman grabbed for Ko's hands and began to roll Ko's fingers through hers, as if searching for something. "Where you get bond?"

Sword reacted instantly, pulling the old woman's hands away from Ko's. Undeterred, and with considerably more strength than it seemed she should have, the old woman began to manipulate his fingers instead.

He was only able to pull away when the old woman's fingers touched the outline of his clan ring beneath his glove.

"Woman have no ring. You have ring."

The old woman smirked horribly. "Making the halflings, no?"

"No," Sword said emphatically, understanding the implication. "What about this clear crystal bond? Do you recognize it?"

"Is not yours?" she asked, surprised.

"It came with my cat," Sword said.

"Saber-tooth?"

"Housecat." This was turning into a replay of his conversation with Tantoo. Did saber-toothed tigers still exist in the First World?

"Housecat?"

The old woman's eyes widened. "And only want viewing planes? Sure not need calling stones? Firespitters?" Her eyes darted to Ko and back again, then she whispered suggestively, "Darkmakers, yes?"

"Sword, will you *please* tell me what's — "

DARK HUNTER

Sword put one hand over Ko's mouth. "I might be interested in a few of those," he said. "Depends on how much glitter you're charging."

Ko swore into Sword's glove as she tried to pull away.

The old woman winked lewdly. "Humans, hmm? Always quack, moo, oink."

Sword returned the smile as if he knew exactly what the old woman meant. Then he took his hand away from Ko and gave her a look that told her that under no circumstances was she to speak until he said so.

Ko's jaw tightened, but she didn't say a word. Sword knew he'd pay for it later but right now Ko understood that he was in charge.

The old woman reached out to pat Sword's hand. "We go back room. No shirley stones." She shook her head disdainfully at the goods in the counter displays. "Have water. Talk. See what have. Maybe deal. Maybe buy sell." She made her liquid kissing sounds again.

Sword suddenly realized that haggling was expected and played his role to the fullest. "I'd like to talk and see what you have. But I don't think I want to buy anything today."

The old woman's eyes sparkled. Clearly, he had adopted the right tone. "Not sure have anything to sell today, anyway. Very busy since Arkady. But maybe. Never know."

"Maybe," Sword agreed.

For a few seconds, no one said anything. Sword glanced toward the back of the store and made a half gesture indicating that he was ready to go there. But the old woman shook her head. "Other customer. Small room. Pick up order, gone soon. Not long."

Sword nodded. It had taken three years to get this far. He could wait another few minutes.

"Do you do much business with these?" Sword asked, pointing to the rings inside the glass counter. "With the humans?"

The old woman giggled with an odd hiccoughing sound. "No substance, good eating," she snorted.

A few more awkward seconds passed in silence. Sword thought Ko would burst if they had to wait much longer.

"You mentioned Arkady," he said, trying not to sound too interested. "Ever have much trade with the Tepesh?"

173

The proprietor rocked her head from side to side. "A bit yes, a bit no. Not too many times open at night."

Sword nodded. That made sense. Vampires probably did most of their shopping for crystals in the twenty-four-hour jewellery stores of Las Vegas.

The old woman waved her fingers at Sword. "You show me ring?" she said as if it was such a small favor to ask that Sword couldn't possibly say no.

Knowing that he probably didn't have a choice, Sword nodded and began to pull off his right-hand glove. He didn't know what reputation Clan Pendragon still had in the First World and he had no idea what reaction to expect from the old woman.

Sword held his fist out to the proprietor. His mother's heavy gold ring gleamed in the shop's overbright lighting.

"Ohhh," the old woman breathed as her body appeared to stretch over the counter top to get closer. "Lights' finest." Her face was only a foot away from the ring. A long pink tongue shot from her mouth and the pencil-thin tip of it lightly licked Sword's ring, tracing its carved clansign of sword and dragon entwined.

Ko said nothing but her face paled with the effort. Sword controlled his deep instinct to jump away from what was probably normal behavior for the old woman's species of adept. *I must act as if I know that. As if I've seen this a hundred times before.* Though he sincerely hoped he never would again.

The pink tongue slithered back into the old woman's mouth and she returned to her previous stance. "Pendragon," she murmured. She looked at the back of the store again.

"If the other customer needs more time, perhaps I could come back later," Sword said. He didn't want to make it look as if he were trying to get away, but neither did he want to risk the proprietor's somehow sending a message to Arkady or Tepesh that a Pendragon was trapped in the shop.

"Other customer pick up big order. Finish soon. We have water. Talk. Not long now."

DARK HUNTER

"They're probably going to tow the van," Ko abruptly volunteered. The tightness of her voice told Sword that she was ready whenever he was.

"Next time park in garage at corner," the old woman said pleasantly. "We validate."

Sword used the opening Ko had provided. "I'll do that. Next time." He scooped up 'Bub's collar and pendant, then started to move away from the counter. "We should be going now, Melody. We'll be back — "

The old woman's arm whipped over the counter, rapidly elongating until it was at least six feet long and its hand circled around Sword's elbow. "Wait, wait, I give special deal firespitters. One day only."

"No thanks," Sword said. He pushed the hand from his arm and it snapped back to its owner as if on an elastic string. Ko was already at the front door.

"Cost more next time," the old woman said hopefully. "New shipment next time. Price go up."

"Open the door lock, please," Sword said.

The old woman scowled and reached behind the counter, grumbling, "Only one firespitter left. Not know when get new one in."

Ko rattled the handle noisily. "Will you just open this bloody thing!"

Sword heard the buzz of the opener. "Thank you," he said, then turned to follow Ko out.

But Ko couldn't get the door to budge. Too late, Sword realized that the buzzing noise had come from another door — the door at the back of the shop. The door was opening.

"Sorry, sorry," the proprietor said. "Safety. Only one door open at time."

Automatically, Sword's eyes scanned the second doorway's perimeter, looking for the telltale shadow flicker of a fardoor's perimeter. Nothing.

A second old woman, identical to the first, glided through the open door. She also wore a high-waisted long black skirt that reached all the way to the floor.

"Sword," Ko hissed. "I don't think she has legs under that."

175

"Shh," Sword said. Another figure was leaving the back room. A human male, in a navy topcoat and deep-brimmed felt hat. Hunched over with the effort of carrying two large black-leather sample cases, one in each hand.

That's a lot of glitter, Sword thought without knowing why. "We'd like to leave now," he said loudly.

The old woman behind the counter whirled around as easily as Forsyte's chair could turn in place and pushed the back door to start its closing.

"Yes, yes. You go n — "

"*You!*"

The voice electrified Sword's consciousness, summoning a frenzy of half-remembered images.

The dark man of his childhood who had exiled him.

Who sought to wrest control of Pendragon from him forever.

And who had cheated death escaping through a fardoor that reached through space and time.

The regent to Pendragon, Tomas Roth.

FIFTEEN

The hunter walked the streets of Manhattan, feeling comfortable, feeling safe. Although, unlike Hong Kong, not everyone she passed in this city was human, she was secure in her element so near the boundaries of the layer.

Her purpose on these Second World streets was twofold. For any who would ask — and for the gargoyle adepts who closely tracked the comings and goings of those who moved between the Worlds — she was here for a hunt. Her authority was the Clan Arkady. Her prey, the last survivor of Clan Isis, the vampire Orion. It was explanation enough and ensured her unrestricted passage.

But her main objective at this hour was not the nightfeeder. His capture could easily be put off for a cycle or two. She had a different quarry in mind, though the lack of challenge in tracking this one prevented her from thinking of what she did now as a true hunt.

At first, she had thought that finding her brother was going to be as instantaneous as it was simple — Little Galen was actually in the Second World phone book, or at least his Park Avenue organization was. It had been such an obvious way to start her search that the hunter had almost not bothered. But, upon checking into her suite at the sleek hotel on Forty-sixth, preferred by many travelers of her sort, she had found the Sword Foundation listing in the Manhattan directory in her bedside table.

The hunter had called the number but it was the weekend and a recording had informed her of the Foundation's weekday operating hours. There were other Swords listed, but none who could claim kinship with the Clan Pendragon.

In her first attempt to find Little Galen two years earlier — after what the hunter had initially thought of as their accidental meeting in Greece — she traced him to a two-story condominium near the south end of Central Park. At the time, she had worried that his choice of location was so he could view the shifting node of the layer that regularly transected the Park — providing more evidence, like his hunt for the Greek shifter, that her brother did remember his heritage. But when she had learned that his home faced south, away from the Park, she had known that it was simply coincidence that had brought him to that location in New York. In fact, the high-status building he had selected was more proof of the soundness of the wizards' decision to distract her exiled brother with formidable, Second World wealth.

The hunter knew Little Galen's riches had been, in part, compensation for the life that the wizards recognized he would have to live among the humans, but it had also been another way to make sure that he could never truly disappear into dangerous anonymity.

Thus her brother's condominium had been, this morning, the first place in the city to which she had traveled from her hotel. The security guard, resplendent in a uniform any Light would love to either wear or set aflame, had been courteous to her, but had firmly insisted that Mr. Galen Sword had not kept residences in the Tower for at least three years.

The hunter had returned his courtesy in kind, and then asked her question again with the voice of the familiar.

This time, the guard had answered that Mr. Galen Sword made use of his home in the Tower once, perhaps twice, a month, but did not stay there on a full-time basis. When the she had asked if the guard knew where Mr. Sword lived now, or if he knew how Mr. Sword's new home could be found, he had directed her to the car service that often brought her brother to the Tower, and came to take him elsewhere.

DARK HUNTER

The hunter had used her ordinary voice to thank the guard for his time and he had politely expressed regrets that he had been unable to help her in her search.

Midtown, at the car service's dispatch office, it had taken the hunter less than five minutes to obtain a print-out of the Sword Foundation's account summary. More than half the charges attributed to Little Galen personally either began or ended at a specific address in SoHo which, the dispatcher helpfully told her, Mr. Sword often referred to as 'the Loft.'

In all, less than two hours of morning had elapsed since the hunter had stepped from her hotel room, and the street she traveled now was but two blocks' distance from her brother's current home. As her green-adapted eyes automatically sorted the neighborhood buildings and vehicles and people into the forest grid, she thought about Little Galen and wondered what her brother could remember of his *real* home in the First World. He had lived there for a few tens of cycles at least, while Pendragon still held power. The hunter remembered nothing, of course, as the fall of the line had occurred just before her birth. Now she wondered if her brother would remember something from those days that he could tell her. It would be good to hear — and not purchase — a story about the better times which did not come from the impersonal and fact-filled lips of a wizard. Though the hunter herself had learned very early on never to discount the word or the deed of wizards — they could not lie — neither, she knew, did they always reveal the whole truth or purpose of their actions.

Now, only one block from the Loft, the hunter strode briskly along the uneven and crumbling sidewalk. Though clad in the deep green cape-like coat that concealed her shadowsuit and hunt tools, she was aware that her presence still drew the attention of those she moved amongst. Humans glanced at her indirectly, often more than once. The adepts, and there were many in more or less humanform, looked quickly away, fervently hoping that they were not her prey. And, from the shadows, or the roofs, halflings, too, followed her progress intently, studying her to see if she carried a bounty. But so far her luck had held. She herself was not among the hunted. Though the actions she contem-

JUDITH & GARFIELD REEVES-STEVENS

plated undertaking in the next few cycles, if not days, could well earn her that distinction.

At first appearances, the street of the Loft was unremarkable to the hunter. Most of the places of commerce on it were for the transport and storage of items of interest only to the Second World. Besides a few shops, elevated loading docks lined both sides of the street, and pedestrian traffic was concentrated only at the corners. Few humans, it seemed, wanted to walk down this street on their own. That gave the hunter pause.

She stood two storefronts past the corner, near a metal-covered sidewalk elevator opening, and moved her hands through her hair as if to adjust the golden clip pinned there. But the clip was more than a decoration to keep the heavy mass of her hair in place. The clip held a quiver of silver telling threads and she removed one now, catching it against her palm, no more conspicuous than if it were an ordinary sewing needle.

The hunter scanned her surroundings, noting the five humans nearby who were in sight of her. She found it peculiar that she no longer detected any adepts or halflings in the vicinity, as if they, too, chose to avoid this street.

The hunter counted down the building fronts until her eyes rested on her brother's home. Instead of a loading dock, the Loft had a street-level garage door, with horizontal metal panels, and wide enough to admit at least three vehicles abreast. Alone of all the flat surfaces in sight, the steel-gray garage door was free of graffiti.

To the right of the metal-panelled door was an entrance alcove with the building's number written above it. No other mark was evident.

The hunter held the silver telling thread upright, two inches from her eye, and sighted past it, moving it with her line of sight as she looked away from the Loft and back again. The diffraction pattern cast against her eye by the out-of-focus chanted thread clearly rippled as the Loft came within sight.

The hunter's experienced eye read the ripple. Little Galen's Loft had been subjected to a focused enchantment sometime in the past year. But an odd one. Something she hadn't encountered too often. She searched

180

DARK HUNTER

her memory for an explanation. Then she had it. Though it was an answer without meaning.

The silver telling thread had detected the slow pulsations of a residual binding chant. But so weak she wondered why anyone had bothered to cast it in the first place. The chant was barely strong enough to cause a nightfeeder some discomfort if an invitation to cross the threshold of the building were not issued. But it would in no way prevent other, less tradition-bound adepts from freely entering.

She checked the street again for watchers. Only four humans were within range now, but none looked in her direction. Though many areas in the Second World had powerful binding chants, cast in order to keep humans at bay, the hunter knew the magic set upon her brother's Loft was not nearly strong enough for even sensitive humans to notice. Something else had to be affecting them to keep them from travelling this street.

The diffraction pattern hovering around the telling thread began to fade as the silver's charge was expended. The hunter snapped the slender chanted metal in half, then tossed it to the sidewalk where the pieces sublimated in seconds.

The only other reason she could think of to explain the presence of the residual binding chant was that it served as a signal, announcing the Loft's location. But whether that signal was a warning for other adepts to stay clear or an invitation to attack, the hunter was not certain. What she had learned, though, was that she was not the only adept to have found the home of Galen Sword.

The hunter approached the Loft, studied its construction with professional interest. Only the Rings knew if she might find herself with a bounty some day and in need of a fortress of her own.

Surrounding the garage door was a protective, overlapping frame of solid metal to prevent forcible entry. There was no handle, no lock, nor apparent switch for opening the garage door from the outside. Presumably, Little Galen made use of some type of signal mechanism or radio switch or other means of communication with someone left inside. *And it would have to be a someone*, the hunter thought, *not a something*. Unlike the homes of true adepts who chose to live in the

181

Second World, there would be no conscripted Lights, or lares and penates, to guard her substanceless brother's home in his absence.

The pedestrian door in the small alcove beside the garage entrance did have a handle, but no visible lock. Instead, a common electronic keypad embedded in the wall beside the door implied that a numeric combination was needed to enter.

The hunter paused outside the alcove, looking up, noting the false panel attached to the building's front exterior, just above the recessed entryway. No doubt the panel concealed a second door that could drop down and seal in unsuspecting intruders who tried to tamper with the first door.

She looked down at the sidewalk and saw the metal plates at the alcove's threshold that would grip the falling door. *A clever plan*, she thought. The sort of thing the Tepesh would use to protect their enclaves. She wondered if her brother had devised the arrangement himself or if he had seen it somewhere else.

Reasonably assuming that any other safeguards protecting the Loft would not be lethal, the hunter stepped into the alcove and pressed a button on an intercom panel beside the keypad. She saw no name or other identification inscribed on the panel. A few seconds later she heard a faint whir above her head and looked up to a panel of dark glass set into a corner where the alcove's ceiling joined a wall. She stood still for the camera she guessed was there, observing her.

The intercom speaker hissed. "CAN I HELP YOU?"

For a moment, the hunter was surprised. The voice was clearly of mechanical origin, and thus impervious to the effects of magic. Not even the skills of the hunt could affect the functioning of substanceless mechanisms.

After a moment's reflection, she leaned closer to the intercom and spoke in her human voice. It was only natural for Little Galen's household gods to be made of Second World technology, not First World magic, but still she wondered what certain apocalyptic Ring scholars she knew would make of this situation.

"I wish to meet with Galen Sword," she said.

DARK HUNTER

The speaking machine replied more quickly than she had expected. "CALL THE SWORD FOUNDATION," the voice commanded, then gave the number she had already phoned.

"The office does not open again until Monday morning," the hunter said. "I wish to meet with him here, before then." She waited for the device to invite her to leave a message.

"WHAT MAKES YOU THINK YOU CAN MEET HIM HERE?" the voice asked.

The hunter was intrigued, aware that Second World machines could speak but impressed they now had the intelligence to conduct a conversation.

Let's see how smart this machine is, she thought. "I know he lives here. I know he is companion to a halfling and a nightfeeder as well."

She waited but the machine did not reply as quickly as before. *Now it will ask me to leave a message,* she thought.

But when the voice came back, it asked another question. "WHO ARE YOU?"

The hunter looked straight into the lens of the hidden camera. "I am Diandra Sword, Clan of Deep Forest. I am Galen Sword's sister."

Far from being confused, the mechanism showed itself capable of quick decision. The door beside the hunter thrummed with the movement of hidden locks and bolts.

"THE DOOR IS OPEN," the machine voice said.

The invitation having been given, the hunter entered her brother's enclave.

SIXTEEN

There was only one thing to do and Sword did it.

He charged toward Roth. His only thought was to get to the adept before Roth could employ whatever weapons an elemental had at his disposal, whether First World crystals or Second World guns. In Sword's recent experience with the Regent to Pendragon, Roth had used both.

But the second old woman shielded Roth with her body. Her brilliant white hair spread open like a fan as something bulbous, wet, and sparkling rose up within it. Something like a giant eyeball hoisted on a stalk.

Sword ducked his head and drove into her midsection. The old woman's sinewy body bounced away as if rubber, then she toppled over with a sudden wet suction sound. As her black skirt lifted up, Sword saw a single, writhing, slimy footpad pull out of contact with the floor. The sight almost cost him the initiative of his charge.

But not quite.

He slammed into Roth like a black-leather avalanche, smashing the adept against the closed door behind him. Roth's breath exploded from him. It smelled of flowers — the scent of magic — and something deep within Sword cried out in protest that the metabolism of magic within an elemental was a blasphemy against nature.

DARK HUNTER

The regent to Pendragon had dropped his heavy cases as soon as Sword had begun his rush and, as Sword's impact drove him back, his hands disappeared into his navy overcoat.

"*NO!*" Sword yelled in the elemental's face, in an effort to startle him as they grappled and fell. Roth's deep-brimmed hat slipped from his head, revealing the trim fringe of dark hair that haloed his bald scalp. His dark glittering eyes were like jewels in a hard and square face that might have been carved from stone. He hurled an insult as he struggled to free a hand from his coat.

"Gill-breather!"

"Traitor!" Sword gasped back without quite knowing why. He was almost on top of Roth as both of them fought to gain a definitive hold on the other. Behind him, he could hear glass smash in time to Ko's frantic grunts of effort.

A beam of blazing red light struck the wall beside his head. *Crystal or gun?* Sword still had no idea.

Then Roth's knee smashed into his thigh as the powerful elemental jerked his head up to crack his forehead against Sword's nose. Sword's vision smeared with red. But not from blood. A seething nimbus of red energy was flaring, crackling around Roth's freed fist. *Red crystal!* The adept was attacking with a weapon of the First World.

Sword seized Roth's fist and began to pry it open. Sharp forks of crimson lightning shot through Roth's fingers. The adept's free hand swung up to rake Sword's face and gouge at his eyes.

Blood flooded Sword's vision but he still persevered.

Sword forced Roth's fist open, hearing a fingerbone crack as he did so, then pressed his own fingers against whatever lay within and —

— the red nimbus collapsed as Roth's crystal was drained of all energy and —

— Sword swiftly clapped his hands against Roth's ears, stunning the adept with the jarring concussion. The elemental fell back, defeated.

But then something else seized Sword and held him fast. Two long elastic ropes like twin pink anacondas. Sword twisted about just in time to see the second old woman's eyestalk rise up as her floor-anchored body leaned toward him to reel in her arms.

185

"Crush him!" Roth shouted from the floor, where he lay still clutching at his ears.

The old woman faltered and Sword felt her grip loosen.

"But can't kill — "

"CRUSH HIM!" Roth thundered.

The pink coils tightened, then went limp, and Sword was freed as Melody Ko's cast connected with an eyestalk.

Roth was halfway to his feet by the time Sword's foot caught him in midsection and drove him down again.

"Where's the other one — from behind the counter?" Sword yelled at Ko.

Ko's pale face was drenched in sweat. "I got her, too. They *don't* have feet."

"We do," Sword said. He pointed to the cases Roth had been carrying. "Grab those. We're taking them with us."

"No!" Roth was almost on his feet again. "You don't under — "

Time seemed to stop for Sword. Again he saw himself as a young child, terrorized by the dark-eyed elemental who tormented him for his inability to manifest the powers of a true adept. Again he saw Roth whisper to his mother in their enclave's garden. Again he heard Roth's voice echo in his child's mind: *Not like us ... something wrong ... congenital ... a freak ... can no longer stay with us ... can no longer stay ...*

He saw Roth and Morgana gloating over him as he lay bound somewhere deep beneath the Museum of Natural History. Roth claiming that the line of the Victor of Pendragon — Sword's line — was finished.

He saw Roth as Morgana's consort, in the Tarl-scaled robes of the Clan Arkady, standing atop the shifters' sacrificial stone in the Pit of the Change. Giving the title of Victor of Pendragon to the werewolf Seth — Morgana's son — his childhood friend.

And then Sword had disrupted the ceremony, stopped it in mid-Change. The shifters' victor, Morgana, was caught halfway in transformation into her true reptilian shifterform. Her son Seth had died.

"You have no right to be here!" Roth had screamed at him.

"You had no right to send me away!" Sword had cried out in response.

Rage overwhelmed Sword.

DARK HUNTER

He struck at Roth for a lifetime of lies.

For a heritage stolen.

For a destiny denied.

Again, and again, until Ko dragged him away.

"That's enough, Sword! Enough!"

Roth lay on the floor, eyes rolled back in his head, but still alive.

Sword's breath came thickly. "We're taking him with us, too."

Ko pulled on his arm, trying to force him to the front of the shop. "C'mon, Sword. What if he's not here on his own? Just sap his crystals and let's get out of here."

Sword pushed Ko away from him, crouched down beside Roth, and began digging roughly through the adept's coat pockets. He found a handful of small, glowing red crystals, rolled them together in his hands until their fires were extinguished, until they were no more than red-tinged gravel. He took Roth's wallet. Answers could be found in many places.

Ko was beside the front door. "Whatever you decide to do, do it fast!" she urged. "We've got to go!"

Sword stood up, started toward her, then turned back and dragged Roth to his feet by his collar. "You're coming with us."

He jammed his other hand in his coat's pocket. "I have a gun, Roth," he lied, "and so long as I'm touching you, your blue fire won't protect you. Not like it did in the Pit. Don't ask me how I know that, but I know it's true."

The elemental only groaned. His head lolled back. Blood dripped from his slack mouth.

"Sword! Will you hurry it up!"

"If you try to run, if you even try to struggle or call for help, I will kill you. Do you understand?" Sword jerked Roth's head up. "Do you understand?"

The adept nodded almost imperceptibly.

Sword threw Ko the keys to the van. "Get it started. Tell Martin to get ready to hold on to Roth. I'll give you a minute and then I'll follow."

Ko looked quickly back at the counter, where the unconscious body of the proprietor lay, covered in glass from the display cases Ko's cast

187

had shattered. The old woman's snail-like footpad was oozing clear slime onto the floor.

"I'll buzz open the door," Sword said. "Get ready, Ko!"

He pulled Roth forward until he could lean over the old woman's body and press the door buzzer.

The door rattled. Ko yanked it open, wedged a matchbook from the proprietor's cigar box into the lock to keep it from locking again, then rushed out, dragging both of Roth's cases with her. Sword saw her elbow her way awkwardly through a group of strolling browsers, some of whom glanced in through the shop window. Immediately, Sword tried to look as if he and Roth were examining something on the counter.

Sword lifted the adept until he stood almost upright. "Who did you come with?" Sword demanded.

Roth's voice was bitter. His eyes went to Sword's pocket, where Sword had told him he had a gun. "You're no better than your father, Galen. It's over."

"Try telling me that again after you've been coldblasted for a hundred years, asshole."

Roth's dark eyes flickered at mention of the First World punishment.

"That's right," Sword said. ""I'm learning fast."

"You'll die even faster." Roth's head snaked forward and he spit in Sword's face.

Only the vibration of Sword's locator band saved Roth. Ko was signalling the van was ready.

Sword prodded Roth toward the front door of the shop. Roughly. Opened the door.

"To the left," he ordered. They stepped out on to the sidewalk and —

Ko was running toward them, frantically waving her good arm. She no longer had the cases. Sword looked down the street.

The van was gone.

Ko was shouting as she ran. Something about —

Sword turned.

Saul Calder jumped him.

DARK HUNTER

SEVENTEEN

There was still one physical activity which Adrian Forsyte could accomplish as ably as any other person: tap his finger in impatience.

That's what he did as he waited in his chair at the entrance to the Loft's main lab, listening to the light footsteps of the woman ascending the stairs.

If this Diandra Sword *was* Sword's sister, and if like Sword's brother, whom Forsyte had never met, she had connections in the First World, then it was possible she might know something about how to reverse his paralysis.

It was equally possible, Forsyte realized, that he had just admitted a shifter or some other form of noxious adept into the Loft. But after two years of forced inactivity, he was willing, indeed eager, to admit a little risk into his life. It was hateful to always be left behind, even on as inconsequential an excursion as the team's shopping trip to a Manhattan jewellery store.

I'm actually hoping this woman isn't whom she claims to be, he thought. *Because of the challenge it would be to expose and defeat her myself, before Sword's team returns.*

The woman was almost at the top of the stairs.

Forsyte held down the center button on the keypad mounted in his chair's left arm and blinked twice. The chair's onboard computer read

189

the interrupted pattern of reflection from the laser light projected from his thick-framed glasses' fiberoptic emitters, that shone into the corners of his eyes, In response, the computer cycled command priorities from the Loft's mainframe to his chair's systems.

His chair's internal menu of commands set itself in Defensive Mode as he pressed the center button twice more.

Forsyte checked the computer display screen by his left hand. He had only to look at a command option on the screen, blink twice, and his chair would take action. An onscreen gauge indicated that his chair's tasers were fully charged, and that all the other surprises Ko had added in the past few weeks were also standing by.

Forsyte heard the woman pause on the metal walkway.

He tapped the playback key on his synthesizer control to release a preprogrammed sentence. "TO YOUR RIGHT, THROUGH THE WIDE DOORS."

The woman turned, saw him. Forsyte backed into the lab, trying to lure her into following him. If he had to, he could instruct the lab's doors to close, locking her in with him.

The woman hesitated at the doorway to the lab, obviously conducting a visual search. She did not step inside. Forsyte saw her glance in turn at each computer display screen, including the large overhead ones Sword had installed for him. She seemed most caught by the oversized examination chair in the center of the lab, whose bindings were strong enough to restrain a werewolf. Forsyte wondered if the chair's proportions revealed to her its purpose.

Finally the woman turned to look at Forsyte. "Was that your voice?"

"I SPEAK WITH A VOICE SYNTHESIZER," the voder said.

The woman nodded her understanding and the movement swirled her fiery cloud of red-gold hair around her. *Sword certainly isn't that arresting in appearance,* Forsyte thought. *Nor does he convey such ... assurance,* he decided, was the only word that fit.

"It was you I talked with at the door," the woman said.

Reflexively, Forsyte blinked once. Then he realized that Diandra Sword wouldn't know his shorthand signal for 'yes' and moved his finger to the synthesizer's controls.

DARK HUNTER

But she spoke again before he could press the appropriate key. "Was your eyeblink a signal?"

Forsyte was impressed by Diandra's close attention. He blinked once again.

"Is my brother here?"

Forsyte blinked twice.

"Is he expected?"

Once.

"Do you believe that I am Little Galen's sister?"

Forsyte wished he could laugh. Whoever this woman really was, she was refreshingly perceptive. He tapped two fingers on the synthesizer's keys. "DECISION NOT MADE."

She accepted his statement without protest or further statement. Forsyte decided that her reaction could mean that she was who she claimed to be, or that she was as good a poker player as she was an observer.

Diandra still made no move to enter the lab. "Are you aware that this building carries a residual binding chant?"

The hair on the back of Forsyte's neck rose up from his skin. She was familiar with the First World. "DON'T KNOW WHAT THAT IS," his voder said.

"Do you understand the term 'chant'? For enchantment?" When Forsyte blinked once, Diandra continued. "A binding chant establishes a zone of influence, one intended to keep things either within the boundaries established, or without."

"POWER SOURCE?" the voder asked.

Diandra looked at him questioningly. "Magic, of course. What is your name? And your relationship to my brother?"

"DR. ADRIAN FORSYTE. I WORK FOR HIM."

"Medical doctor?"

"PHYSICIST."

Diandra smiled brilliantly with sudden knowledge. "Hence your interest in power sources. I take it you do not believe in magic."

Forsyte's two operative fingers typed rapidly, angrily. "MAGIC PUT ME IN THIS CHAIR."

191

Diandra's smile disappeared instantly. "I'm sorry. I'd assumed ... a disease. Have you contacted a counter?"

"WHY?"

"To cast a second enchantment that will counter the one that afflicts you."

Forsyte's mouth went dry. How long had he waited for someone like Diandra? "CAN IT BE DONE?" the voder asked.

Forstye hit the repeat button. "CAN IT BE DONE?"

Diandra reached up to her hair, to her golden hair clip, withdrawing a thin strand of silver wire, no longer than a needle.

"You know of telling threads?" she asked, then continued when Forsyte blinked twice. "They're sensitive to the influence of magic. Different ... " She paused in thought. "I believe someone of your background would call them 'frequencies.' " She laughed lightly. "Frequencies of magic. Does the concept disturb you?"

Forsyte blinked once, very slowly for emphasis. Diandra was knowledgeable about *many* worlds, it seemed.

"Whatever the reality behind the terms that are used," she continued, "the telling threads can be employed to detect the presence of magic, and the type of magic." She held the metal strand close to her eye. "I shall use it on you."

Forsyte was transfixed, fascinated, partly by the prospect of finally learning what had been used against him, but mostly by Diandra's reference to the concept of magic having frequencies. As a scientist, he did not accept that anything termed supernatural could exist. By such definition, the events and phenomena he had witnessed with his own eyes, and which Ko had described to him, could *not* be supernatural.

Somehow, Forsyte told himself, shapeshifters, Lights, glowing crystals, nightfeeders, and all other First World phenomena *had* to fit into the standard model of the universe that had been painstakingly constructed over hundreds of years of patient scientific investigation and discovery.

The accepted history of science was the ongoing process of creating theories, applying them to observed phenomena, and then refining those theories, whether to encompass the cosmological implications of quantum physics or the gravitational effects of relativity. Or even the

DARK HUNTER

existence of a parallel continuum of spacetime, concurrently removed from our own yet connected to it, with its own worlds, its own inhabitants, its own physics, and its own energy spectrum.

The frequency of magic. The implications of those words fit so perfectly with Ko's and his first attempts to reconcile First World phenomena with Second World physics, that Forsyte was suddenly overcome with the passionate conviction that the direction he had chosen to understand the problem was correct. *Now the only difficulty is going to be proving it,* he thought. Did he at last dare to hope that his work might soon be made simpler by his being freed from his chair?

Diandra moved the telling thread to one side of Forsyte, then back to him again, tracking it with her eye. She did this several times before she lowered her hand.

Forsyte sensed her defeat with profound disappointment.

"It shows me none," she said. "No chant. No magic." She snapped the thread in half and tossed the pieces to the disc-textured rubber flooring of the lab. Forsyte watched the pieces fall but didn't see them hit, almost as if they had evaporated in the air.

Diandra repeated her examination with a second thread, only to achieve the same result. "How was this done to you?" she asked.

Forsyte sighed, despairing. "TOO LONG TO GIVE DETAILS THIS WAY," the voder said. "ASK GALEN. HE WAS THERE."

But amazingly, Diandra did not abandon the subject.

In less than five minutes, she led him through a surprisingly efficient series of questions which he could answer in yes or no eyeblinks and obtained the broad outlines of how he had ended up in his chair.

"I sympathize, Dr. Forsyte, but if I am to have any useful insight about your condition, it will have to wait until I can learn about the event in greater detail. I shall wait for Little Galen to return."

Though Forsyte suspected Diandra was more interested in her brother and his First World interactions, than in his own plight, he agreed with a quick eyeblink. At least he still had hope. He activated his voder again. "PLEASE COME IN. SIT DOWN." He backed farther into the lab by a desk with a chair she could use.

But Diandra still didn't enter the lab. "I assume that you are able to control most of the devices in this building through the mechanisms in

193

JUDITH & GARFIELD REEVES-STEVENS

your chair. I saw the double-door trap at the street entrance." She touched the edge of the lab's doorway. "I presume that these doors can be similarly used."

"DO YOU INTEND TO ATTACK ME?" Forsyte's voder asked.

"Not at present," Diandra answered politely. "Do you intend to trust me?"

Forsyte wanted to, but knew he couldn't yet. Perhaps if she had been able to offer help to him ...

"If not, why not?" Diandra asked.

Forsyte tapped out his answer. "GALEN HAS NEVER MENTIONED YOU."

"That does not surprise me. Little Galen was exiled before I was born. I do not believe he knows he has a sister."

Curious, Forsyte thought. *That would make her younger than Sword. But according to Melody, Brin is also younger.* He tapped out another statement. "GALEN KNOWS ABOUT BRIN."

"That does not surprise me, either." Forsyte noted a new, hostile undercurrent in Diandra's voice. "Have you met Brin? Has he been here?"

"BRIN HAS BEEN HERE ONCE," the voder said. "I HAVE NOT MET HIM."

Diandra's steady gaze fixed on him. With almost a shock, Forsyte noticed something odd about her eyes. They were a strange, shifting shade of gold and he couldn't quite focus on them.

"Then perhaps you are safe," she said. With that, she crossed the threshold and entered the lab, and sat down on the chair by the desk next to Forsyte.

Forsyte had his chair rotate so he could still see her, then began to program a sentence that would ask her what she had meant about him being 'safe'.

But Diandra began to question him again. She hadn't yet realized that a real conversation with him required long stretches of waiting if his synthesizer contained no suitable preprogrammed responses.

"How many others work with Galen? Is the halfling among them?"

Forsyte cleared his previous sentence. "ME. KO. THE HALFLING MARTIN."

DARK HUNTER

"He is a shifter halfling, Dr. Forsyte. His clan name would be *Myrch'ntin* in shiftertongue. Martin is his open name. What about the nightfeeder, Orion? Does he work here, too?"

"DOES NOT WORK FOR GALEN," the voder answered.

"But they communicate with each other?"

Forsyte thought he detected some slight urgency in her now, as if of all the topics they had touched upon, Orion and his connection to Galen Sword was the one she was most concerned about. He blinked once.

Diandra opened her dark-green cape but did not take it off. Forsyte couldn't make out what she wore beneath it. It was as if details of her clothing were obscured by remarkably dense shadow.

"Often?"

Forsyte blinked twice. He estimated that since Kendall Marsh had been moved to the Connecticut sanitarium, Sword and Orion were in contact at least two or three times a week by a phone-message system. Orion never came in person. The vampire followed the Tepesh wherever he could track them and was always on the move, always turning up in unexpected places. Forsyte hesitated to let Diandra know that.

But the way she was looking at him now told him she'd already sensed his lie. "It does not matter, Doctor. I was just curious. I met Little Galen and his two companions in an alley not so many weeks ago. In the midst of some trolls."

Forsyte's fingers jumped to the keypad. "YOU ARE THE DARK HUNTER."

Diandra inclined her head, a formal gesture. "Clan of Deep Forest," she said after a moment, as if adding extra information, even though she had already given her clan name to Forsyte over the Loft's intercom.

"GALEN HAS BEEN PLANNING TO GO TO SOFTWIND TO MEET YOU."

"I'm saving him the trip." Diandra leaned back against the desk. Her elbow brushed against some of the items arranged there, spoiling the neat rows. She glanced back at what she had disturbed. "Part of your work?" she asked.

Forsyte blinked twice. The desk still held several of the items the police had finally returned to Ko. She had added since to the collection

195

the few fragments of shard glass she'd managed to recover from the observation deck on the Empire State Building.

Diandra used a pen from the desk top to poke at the pile of fragments, evidently aware of their viciously-sharp edges. "Are you sure this is not part of your work? It appears to be debris from a viewing plane."

The woman is a treasure trove, Forsyte thought. "MELODY KO'S WORK," the voder said.

"Melody Ko," Diandra mused as she moved the fragments. "Is she a troll?"

"HUMAN," the voder said.

"My brother's friend? Lover?"

Diandra seemed amused by his emphatic double blink.

"Is she yours?"

Forsyte hesitated, blinked twice.

"As I said, I sympathize for your condition and shall try to help you counter it." Diandra turned her attention back to the items on the desk.

"THANK YOU," the mechanical voice offered.

Diandra poked at a small wad of tissue that Forsyte had seen Ko take out of a pocket in her harness. "May I?" she asked, then picked up the tissue and peeled it apart. "This *must* be part of your work." She held out the object nested in the tissue for his inspection.

Forsyte blinked twice. It looked like a broken piece of clear yellow glass, half the size of a child's finger. Some of the flashes of light that came from it, however, were not reflections.

"It is a waiting crystal," Diandra said. She picked it up delicately between thumb and forefinger and held it to her ear. "And it is charged. Do you know where this came from? Have you had commerce with fairies?"

Twice again.

"Do you know how to use it?"

Twice.

"Would you like to?"

"WHAT IS IT?" the voder asked. "FIRST WORLD?"

"Most definitely," Diandra said. "Red stones are working crystals. They carry a charge and, under proper conditions, their energy can be manipulated to produce many different outside influences. But this yellow stone, it's more like a vessel. It accepts energy. Then uses it to produce inner influences."

Forsyte stared at her without comprehension.

"It is a doorway. A light to earlier days." She moved her chair closer to him and placed the crystal on the left arm of his chair by the keypads. *"Put your finger on the stone, Doctor."*

Her voice was suddenly so compelling that Forsyte complied instantly.

"We will travel together," Diandra said. "Look into the crystal. Look into yourself."

Forsyte looked down at the stone and a sudden bloom of honey-gold light sped out of the crystal, to bathe his body.

I can feel it, he marvelled. *And my eyes are open.*

Forsyte closed his eyes but the golden glow still filled his vision. *Impossible.*

All is as it was. Diandra's voice came to him as if she spoke within his mind. *Look into yourself.*

And when Forsyte next opened his eyes, he had a whole new meaning for the word 'impossible'.

Because he was *standing.* In his lab at MIT again.

And he was not alone.

EIGHTEEN

Sword swung Roth around just as Saul Calder slammed into him, and all three combatants were thrown to the sidewalk.

Roth absorbed the worst of Calder's charge and lay stunned, just out of Sword's reach.

Unhurt, Sword scrambled to his feet, even as Ko rushed to his side.

But Calder was up faster, and he hurled himself at Sword again.

Sword braced for impact. Even in humanform Calder was stronger than he was — perhaps even stronger than Martin — wherever he was. Worry for the missing halfling shot through him. *Where* was *Martin? Had Calder already killed him?*

Calder swept into him and Sword seized his one chance at victory. Offering no resistance, Sword fell with the shifter, succeeding in throwing him off balance.

Together, they rolled across the sidewalk, scattering pedestrians, Calder roaring as maniacally as if he had already begun his shift. Sword knew he could not allow *that* to happen. Too many human lives would be threatened.

As the shifter's powerful hands dug for purchase on his throat, Sword wasted no time trying to pull them away. Instead he reached up under the odd jacket Calder wore — some kind of uniform — intent on the leather pouch he knew the shifter wore — the pouch that would

DARK HUNTER

hold the red crystal enabling Calder to change form.

And it wasn't until he had the pouch in his hands that Calder realized what his prey's intentions were.

At once the shifter leapt away but Sword's hold was just strong enough to snap the leather cord holding the pouch around Calder's neck.

Calder staggered, fighting the direction of his momentum, and knocked over two gaping bystanders to the screams of others nearby.

Sword tore at the pouch, ripped it open to reveal a glowing red crystal whose depths seemed to pulsate.

A panicked cry jerked Sword's attention from the crystal to Calder. And then to the hapless bystander who had ventured too close to the shifter, and was now in danger of dismemberment.

Sword thrust out the pouch, the First World stone still shielded in its leather from his own touch. "Stop! Or you know what I'll do!"

Calder dropped his still intact and living victim, took a step toward Sword, then rocked back like an animal kept at bay by a blazing torch.

The sidewalk crowd fell back in fear.

"*Pendragych leel!*" the shifter hissed, furious. "*Pendragych leel ka!*"

What Sword had learned of shiftertongue from Martin told him the shifter had just accused the Clan Pendragon of being moon followers — but the insult's significance escaped him.

Still holding one hand over Calder's small crystal, just as he had with the massive Crystal of the Change Arkady, Sword took a precious moment to assess his situation. At least fifty gawking onlookers, more every second. And in the distance, sirens.

"Melody, you okay?" Sword called out, knowing as long as he and Ko were on foot, they had no hope of escape, let alone keeping Roth captive.

"Roth's got a concussion or something," Ko yelled over the mounting noise of the crowd. "Or he will have if he doesn't stop moving. Any suggestions?"

Sword made a move to touch Calder's crystal, forcing the shifter to jump back farther. As Calder did so, it became more apparent that his uniform was like something a car service driver might wear.

199

The Rolls Royce. Outside the jewelry shop. Calder was Roth's driver. That meant the shifter had seen Sword and Ko go in, and Martin stay behind. "Maybe you could get a cab?" he shouted back to Ko as Calder began to circle him, growling inhumanly.

"What about calling the police?" Ko retorted as Sword heard the thud of what he hoped was Ko's cast on what he hoped was Roth's head.

Calling the police did have its merits, he reasoned rapidly, thinking of the two unconscious slug creatures on the floor of the Happy Thought Gold and Diamond Exchange. He'd love to see Trank wish away that kind of evidence.

"How 'bout it, Sword? Time's running out here."

With the pouch keeping Calder at his distance, Sword glanced at the crowd again. And for the first time, he saw at its edge three cold-eyed individuals who merely watched, watched like — *the old school ... the gargoyles ... watchers ...* The old term made him shiver. And he knew why they were here. To keep him from exposing the First World to the Second. The gargoyles were police, but of a different kind.

"Can't." Sword glanced back to Ko. She was up against the door to the shop. At her feet lay the unconscious elemental. Clumps of white plaster dotted his scalp.

"Only other thing we can do, Sword!" Ko yelled over a frantic series of car horns and squealing brakes.

Sword wheeled. *Now or never,* he thought, knowing he couldn't postpone the inevitable forever.

"Hey, Calder!" he yelled. "You want this?" He shoved his hand inside the leather pouch and swept his finger across the stone's surface until a faint tingle told him he had sapped the crystal's energy.

Even as Calder shrieked out a warning, Sword drew back his arm and lobbed the pouch high into the air. Away from the crowd.

The shifter leapt six feet in the air to intercept the pouch, yet still came short. Landing on all fours, he whirled and took off in the direction Sword had thrown the pouch.

At once, the crowd abandoned Ko and Roth and surged after Calder, as Sword had hoped. He took off in Ko's direction.

But then everything changed once again as the wail of the crowd merged with the screech of rubber resisting pavement — and the

DARK HUNTER

crunch of metal meeting metal — as Saul Calder fell from the air and the curb-side Rolls jerked forward, hit from behind by a long-body black van.

In the Rolls's side window, Sword saw yellow eyes crazed with hatred. Half-human, half-reptile. The Victor of Arkady. Roth's consort. Morgana LaVey.

And in the black van whose side sign read SWORD FOUNDATION, a short, hairy driver who bayed in victory.

"Bloody hell, Sword," Ko said. "It's Martin."

NINETEEN

The last of the waiting crystal's golden glow of energy faded as Melody Ko entered Dr. Adrian Forsyte's cavernous basement lab at MIT.

Forsyte waved to his student assistant, amused as always by her grave nod in reply to his greeting. To Ko, science was a religion, this lab was its church, and her employer was its spiritual leader. Forsyte idly wondered what his young assistant's reaction would be when she experienced the less spiritual side of her favorite professor.

She would be a challenge. He had no doubt about that. He studied the severe way she had pulled back her carbon-black hair in the plainest style possible. The drab, shapeless clothes. The perpetual frown on a face he knew could be beautiful with makeup *and* the necessary adjustment in attitude.

She certainly fit the pattern for deliberate repression: mother dead in childbirth; father a world-class surgeon — make that *the* surgeon, based on the press the man got — who relentlessly pressured his sole offspring to succeed, yet forever withheld from her his parental approval.

Ko had confided to Forsyte that she had quarrelled with her father over her decision not to study medicine at Harvard. Forsyte guessed that 'quarrel' did not begin to cover the conflict that had divided father from daughter, since it had led to the surgeon's abrupt withdrawal of all contact, almost to the point of denying Ko's existence.

DARK HUNTER

I'll loosen her up, Forsyte thought. When it was time for her turn. But that couldn't happen for a while yet. Ko was still too valuable an assistant for him to lose to a casual emotional embroilment, even if there wouldn't be any real repercussions.

Five years as one of his department's fastest-rising stars had taught Forstye it didn't matter how many complaints his female students made to the faculty-review board — as long as he continued to publish and produce as he had. All the world of academe loved a professor on the Nobel track, and the board knew that Forsyte had no intention of disappointing his department or his school in what really mattered: his research.

Besides, Forsyte thought smugly, Sonja and Heidi, the two delightful exchange students from London, were more than keeping him busy for the moment. In fact, his life was so diverting now that he couldn't decide which gave him more pleasure — his new conquests or the expression on Ko's face when she realized that's what they were.

"Melody," Forsyte said teasingly as Ko approached the forty-foot-long test bed she had helped him build. "Would it hurt to smile at me more often?"

Ko looked up at him like a kicked puppy. "Dr. Forsyte, Galen Sword's here to meet you."

Then Galen Sword walked into Forsyte's lab.

Forsyte stared at his assistant. She'd actually done something against his direct orders.

He remembered her insisting to him that, despite the stories in the tabloids, Sword was a rigorous skeptic who relied on the scientific method and controlled experiments in laboratory settings. Then she'd offered as evidence of Sword's skepticism his standing offer of $100,000 for proof of any in a long list of supernatural events and powers he was keen to witness. Not that anyone, of course, had yet taken him up on it.

But Forsyte was a physicist and if there was one great truth in science, he knew it was that a scientist — professional or amateur — was just as capable of self-delusion as any other fool. And he distinctly remembered telling his assistant that he would not have any self-proclaimed investigator of the paranormal set one foot inside his lab.

"Dr. Forsyte," Sword said and held out his hand.

203

Angrily, Forsyte ignored it, disgusted by the implicit rich boy's whine in Sword's voice, feeling an almost visceral dislike for the man. The artless mop of thick, black curls. The diamond-studded Rolex that could fund a year of research. And, worst of all, that famously handsome, dissolute face. It was common knowledge throughout the world that the Sword Foundation had access to a fortune, and judging by its founder's pallid appearance and demeanor, at least some of that money was invested in the fruits of pharmacology.

Amazingly, Ko persisted. "This is the apparatus I described to you," she said, directing Sword to the test bed — a rat's nest of interconnected cooling pipes, laser tubes, yellow and black checked wiring cables, and precision clamps and fittings — the heart of Forsyte's research into transformable electron-tunneling.

"The unit that you built yourselves," Sword said, tentative, as if seeking reassurance that he recalled at least something of whatever it was that Ko had told him.

Her head ducked down, Ko avoided Foryste's stony gaze as she gave Sword a quick runthrough of the set-up, By the end of the briefing, Sword rubbed his fingers against one temple, and briefly closed his eyes, as if this were the fifth TTE device he had seen this week, or as if he were in the throes of a hangover.

I will have to punish Ko for this, Forsyte decided. The thought almost restored his good humor. But then Sword spoke again.

"So, you're basically taking the output of the lasers, concentrating it to provide a rapid fluctuation in temperature in the gas sample chamber, then using the supercooled magnets to direct free electrons to a ... 'probability' path that extends through the twenty-foot-long bubble chamber running between the electron emitter and the, uh, electron detector."

Forsyte amended his last thought. It probably was the twentieth TTE device Sword had seen *today.*

"At the same time sending duplicate streams of electrons along the vacuum channels to the duplicate detectors," Ko added, with a quick glance in Forsyte's direction, for confirmation that she was saying the right things. But Forsyte still stayed silent, and conspicuously turned his attention to his notepad, and away from Sword.

DARK HUNTER

Sword nodded. "So you can measure the difference in the arrival times of the two groups of electrons."

"Precisely," Ko said, sounding relieved that Sword had followed her presentation.

"And ... ? Sword asked. " ... the results, Ms. Ko?"

Ko looked imploringly to Forsyte. "Dr. Forsyte, I think it would be best if you reported on your findings."

Forsyte looked up from his notepad and pointedly checked his watch — a forty-nine-dollar and ninety-five-cent Casio that probably kept more accurate time than the ostentatious crap Ko's playboy wore. Heidi and Sonja were due in the lab in half an hour. With luck, he'd have Sword out of his lab and his life by then.

He walked up to the test bed. "Know how long it takes an electron to cross twenty feet of vacuum, Gary?"

"Galen."

"So do you know?" He didn't wait for Sword to even try to answer. "About one fifty-millionth of a second. A twentieth of a nanosecond. Point zero five times ten to the minus ninth. That kind of time mean anything at all to you?"

"It's fast."

"Understatement. The point is that the speed at which the electrons whip through the vacuum channels is as fast as anything can go. Speed of light in a vacuum. Nothing faster. Absolute barrier. Foundation of relativity and cosmology and any other 'y' you care to name. Any trouble following this?"

Sword shrugged.

Forsyte continued. "By generating the transformable tunneling effect along the probability path in the center of the bubble chamber, you know how long it takes *that* group of electrons to get from one end to the other?"

"Not a clue," Sword said, offhand and diffident, as if the significance of the most important work in the world escaped him completely.

"Well, it's no time at all," Forsyte said, enjoying immensely the sound of that phrase. He made a mental note to remember to use it in his Nobel acceptance speech.

"Sorry, I don't follow," Sword said.

205

"I'm sorry, too," Forsyte said, catching Ko's gaze before she dropped her eyes guiltily. "I thought everybody knew about the speed of light. In a nutshell — Gary — "

"Galen," Sword said again.

" — what we're doing here is causing electrons to move from one position to another at an apparent speed in excess of the speed of light."

Sword's brow furrowed. "So in other words, Professor Forsyte, what you claim to be doing here is impossible, since nothing is supposed to be able to move that fast."

Forsyte wished he had a cigar to reward the boy genius. "Yes, and no. The trick to the whole thing — as my assistant should already have told you — is that we are *not* breaking the speed of light barrier. Because, as we can tell from the absence of any disturbance in the bubble chamber through which the probability path runs, no electron is actually traversing the distance between the emitter and the detector. As far as the electron is concerned, it's not moving, it's just tunneling."

Forsyte paused. "Perhaps I can make that even simpler for you. The electron's making a quantum jump from one location to another. The difference is that most electron quantum jumps are on the order of a hundred-trillionth of an inch, but the ones we create here make a jump of twenty feet."

Sword turned to Ko. "There doesn't appear to be anything supernatural going on here."

Forsyte moved behind his young assistant, and rested his hands on her thin, rigid shoulders. He smiled as he felt Ko begin to tremble. Knowing that such closeness confused and disturbed her only provoked him to take it even further.

He smiled at Sword. "I assure you there is absolutely nothing supernatural about what Melody and I are doing here. In fact, until we figure out a way for those electrons to carry *information* across that twenty-foot space, we're not even in violation of causality."

"Then why'd you want me here?" Sword asked.

"Melody," Forsyte murmured as he rested his chin on the top of her head and slid his hands down to squeeze her arms — hard. "He's all yours to have fun with now. Just get him out of my lab."

DARK HUNTER

But Ko surprised him again. Shaking him off, she appealed passionately to both him and Sword. "Mr. Sword, I know that this is not the kind of thing that you usually investigate, but there *is* a connection. And Dr. Forsyte — please — we need Mr. Sword's expertise because you and I both know we *can't* ask for government help."

To Forsyte's extreme annoyance, Ko's outburst created a distinct change in Sword who looked alert and interested for the first time since entering the lab.

Before Forstye could stop her, Ko hurried on. "Dr. Forsyte has published preliminary work on the design of the TTE device. Three months ago, he was contacted by two post-graduate students in astronomy and physics from the University of London — Sonja and Heidi — who claimed they had made radio-astronomy observations suggesting that transformable electron tunneling might occur during the initial moments of a supernova detonation. This has profound implications for Dr. Forsyte's ability to patent his device when he perfects it, because natural phenomena cannot be patented."

"Therefore," Ko went on in a rush, "Dr. Forsyte invited the two of them to come here and observe his work, and he asked me to demonstrate this equipment for them. When I did so, I overheard discussions between them that indicated they'd already seen more powerful versions of this same equipment in operation."

Ko took a deep breath as if even she were embarrassed by what she had to say next. "Mr. Sword, I believe that Sonja and Heidi have witnessed the transmission of matter by similar devices. And I submit that such a process qualifies for inclusion in the paranormal events that you investigate." She paused to catch her breath.

"Are we talking about ... teleportation?" Sword asked.

Ko nodded quickly.

"Ms. Ko, you mentioned not being able to go to the government. Why do you say that?"

"I thought perhaps Sonja and Heidi were from another lab. One that had developed matter transmission in secret, perhaps for military applications."

Sword continued for her. "And you thought that after having read Dr. Forsyte's preliminary work, they had come here to check up on you and your progress." Sword looked at Forsyte. "Do you go along with that, professor?"

Forsyte shook his head vehemently, plotting Ko's punishment. The only saving grace was that anything the stupid girl had said to someone so patently uncredible would be containable. "They're two *students*, Mr. Sword. Both charming girls. Maybe they've got spurious signals in their observation data of supernova. Maybe they've got the real thing. TTE that is. But they're hardly spies."

Sword shoved his hands into the back pockets of the fashionably styled jeans he wore and leaned back against the testbed. "So — where do we go from here? Looks as if your assistant thinks there's something for me to investigate. Looks as if you don't."

Forsyte felt his temper rapidly slipping out of control. He glared at Ko, willing her into silence and obedience. "This discussion is both pointless and time-consuming. As I have already made clear to my *assistant*, I find it hard to imagine that the Pentagon could get its hooks into the University of London."

He heard Ko mutter something to the floor. Sword asked her to repeat herself.

"They're not *from* the University of London." Ko's cheeks colored. "I checked with the faculty of astronomy there. I paid for the call myself."

She looked down at the floor in obvious distress. "They've lied to you, Dr. Forsyte. We have to find out why. We have to find out where they are from. I know you think I'm wrong, but I'm afraid you might be in danger."

Forsyte barely kept from exploding, only Sword's presence preventing Ko's dismissal on the spot.

"Tell you what," Sword said quickly, "I'm interested in pursuing this on my own. I get paid by my foundation so there's no charge to you, and I don't have to hang around here. How about if I just get some basic information on the girls? If they're not from the university in London, then maybe I can track them down, find out where they really are from. No charge. No hassle. Sound fair?" He looked at Forsyte again. "All right with you, doc?"

DARK HUNTER

Forsyte reached out to Ko and tapped her lightly but threateningly on the chin. He was already thinking ahead to how he could make sure that Ko would be unemployable by anyone in the future. "Yes, fine, *Gary*. Whatever you want. Just stop wasting my time and leave my lab. And, you, take this gentleman up to my office. Give him Sonja and Heidi's correspondence file and send him on his way."

Ko flushed but she obeyed his order. "Yes, Dr. Forsyte," she said. "Right away."

She began to walk toward the door, Sword behind her.

"Oh, and Melody?" Forsyte added just as she was about to leave. Melody Ko's punishment was just beginning.

"Yes?"

"Sonja and Heidi will be joining me here in about ten minutes. See to it that we're not disturbed, will you?"

The flash that appeared in Ko's eyes, followed by a renewed flush of her cheeks, gratified Forsyte immensely.

"And one last thing, Melody." Forsyte was feeling much better now and couldn't resist. The weak always made it so easy.

Ko dared to look back at him. Sword kept going.

"You really *must* smile more often."

Ko and Sword vanished within a glow of golden energy. The yellow waiting crystal pulsed beneath Forsyte's finger.

And trapped helplessly in his chair, trapped helplessly in the memories he shared now with Diandra, watching his past play itself out, Forsyte knew that only eight days more of 'normal' life remained to his former self.

TWENTY

Sword slammed into reverse and floored the accelerator, fishtailing the van into a one-hundred-and-eighty-degree spin.

Beside him in the passenger seat, Ko braced herself.

Behind him, Roth groaned. Martin had the semi-conscious elemental firmly wedged into one of the seats in back. It had been a struggle to get the halfling to relinquish the driver's seat. He had wanted to run over Saul Calder again. And again. But when Sword had asked Martin to help him keep Roth prisoner, the halfling had enthusiastically heaved the adept into the van and then sat on him.

As the van skidded around to face in the opposite direction, Sword pushed the gear lever into drive, then checked the side mirror.

Saul Calder was on his feet and running for the van.

Sword hit the gas again and the van's tires squealed as they spun without catching the road.

Calder's arms were outstretched. In his side mirror, even at this distance, Sword could see bloodrage in the shifter's eyes. Then the tires caught traction, the van bucked forward and sped away, leaving Calder a diminishing figure with no hope of catching his prey. For now.

Ko's head fell back against the passenger headrest. Her eyes were closed and her skin was the same shade as the plaster of her cast. She was finally paying the price for going on the attack with her broken arm.

DARK HUNTER

Sword cracked open his window to listen for sirens, but heard none. "Think we should turn on the police scanner?" he asked Ko, knowing she had re-installed the illegal equipment the police had confiscated. *With luck,* he thought, *by the time the police interview the witnesses at the Happy Thought, I'll have the van back in the Loft's garage and be on the phone to Trank reporting its theft.* That should buy them enough time until he could get in touch with Angela Scarlatti to cover the legal ramifications of what they had just done.

Ko grunted assent and reached down beneath the center portion of the dash, pulled up the onboard computer keyboard, and with one hand typed in the commands that activated the police scanner. A moment later, she was studying the dash's video display, reading the typed communications being sent back and forth over the police bands. "All they're reporting is a disturbance and a possible hit-and-run. Officers are reporting to the scene now. I'd say we've got about five minutes before they put out an alert for a black van." With a sigh, Ko sat back in her seat, cradling her cast.

"All I need," Sword said, picking up speed. The van swayed violently as he drew around a slow limousine by sliding quickly into the oncoming lane. He glanced into the center mirror to see Roth's head bob up and down behind Martin as the van bounced over New York City's potholes. The fact that no alert had yet been given by the police was increasing the odds they'd make it safely back to the Loft after all.

Perhaps, Sword reasoned to himself, the gargoyles functioned in the Second World as they did in the First. In which case, there would be no police pursuit today. That happy thought gave him his first opportunity to consider things other than immediate concerns.

"So, Martin, you were going to tell me how you learned to drive," Sword said. The sudden appearance of the halfling in the SWORD FOUNDATION van had been as unexpected as Roth in the crystal shop and Morgana LaVey in her waiting Rolls.

"Easy. Watch Galen Sword. Push pull spin turn fast fast say bad stinkwords. Galen Sword want Martin drive more?"

"Hold on!" Ko suddenly said. She turned in her seat to look back at Martin. "How'd you *start* the van in the first place?"

211

Sword looked down at the ignition switch. Sure enough, there was no key there. Yet the van was running and the steering wheel was ... unlocked. *Of course,* he thought. *Makes perfect sense.*

"Blue power unlock turn wheel make van go," Martin said proudly, confirming Sword's guess.

Ko put her good hand on the dash. "Sword, is the motor running?"

Sword hit the accelerator again and the roar of the engine was loudly apparent. "I think he means the blue power *started* the van, Melody. But good old gasoline is making it go."

There was still no sign of police in pursuit so Sword risked slowing and stopping for the next red light he came to. The southbound traffic on Ninth looked heavier past the light and he put on the blinker to cut over to Seventh for the rest of their drive to SoHo.

He tapped his hands on the steering wheel as he waited for the cab ahead to turn left. "Melody, you realize that we didn't just stumble across Roth by accident, don't you?"

Ko frowned.

"Brin set us up. He knew when Roth was going to the shop to pick up whatever's in those cases and he came to you just in time to make sure we'd be there when Roth was."

Ko stared out the side window, keeping her face hidden from Sword. "Why would he do that?"

Sword continued thinking out loud, not having solved that one yet. "Well, obviously, Brin wants Roth and me to face each other in some sort of conflict. But I don't know if it's because he wants me to take out Roth or because he wants Roth to take out me."

"There are easier ways to take you out, Sword. Especially for adepts."

Sword had to agree with her. The way Brin could come and go at precisely the right moments indicated that — somehow — he was keeping a close watch on the team's activities. But if his brother just wanted to kill him, Sword knew the brake cables on any of the Loft's vehicles could have been cut long ago, or a hundred other accidents arranged.

He stopped on that word — *accident.*

DARK HUNTER

"There's got to be a pattern here, Melody." Sword pulled around the corner after the cab. "My death or incapacitation can't be the point here. Simply by being exiled, without memories of my real life, I already was incapacitated. So it's not that my brother wants something to *happen* to me. It's that he wants me to *do* something. Something that he can't do."

"That doesn't fit with what Brin told me, Sword. He said he wanted to stop you from ... from fulfilling some family curse or something. From bringing the two Worlds into violent conflict."

Sword thought back to a conversation he had had with Orion, in a van much like this one, just before they had moved on the Tepesh enclave in the World Plaza tower. "Orion told me something about First World legends, too. Something about a warrior who tradition said might be a Sword of Pendragon. But I didn't get any sense that the legend was negative."

"Maybe it depends which side you're on," Ko said wearily. "I'm beginning to think the First World is as screwed up as our own."

"But at least in this world — our — your world — we're able to choose the side we fight for," Sword said with conviction, the depth of which took him by surprise. "What if there's the same choice in the First World? I might only have been brought back to the First World by an accident but — "

Sword nearly lost control of the van as the realization slammed into him.

Ko grabbed for the wheel. "What's wrong now?"

"*It wasn't an accident.*" Sword pushed Ko's hand away, tightening his own grip on the steering wheel until the plastic creaked.

"You're repeating yourself," Ko complained, settling back with an exasperated sigh. "You already said that Brin sent us to the shop so we'd run into Roth and — "

"No! I'm not talking about that anymore. I'm talking about *every-thing*, Melody! I'm talking about the beginning." Cold sweat breaking out all over him, Sword pulled off to the side and stopped by a hydrant. He couldn't drive. Not now.

A conspiracy had consumed his life!

"What beginning? Why are we stopping?"

213

"My car accident," Sword said. "Brin was behind that, too. He *caused* it." He turned to look searchingly into Ko's eyes. Saw the truth in them. "And he told you, didn't he? I can see it in your face. On the Empire State Building, he told you all about my accident."

Ko pulled back defensively. "All he said was that there were some groups in the First World who *thought* that he had caused it. So he would have an excuse to bring back your memories. But he also said that wasn't how things had happened."

The pieces were falling into place for Sword. "Brin lied to you. When he healed your arm, he enchanted you — just as Ja'Nette's mother said. And under that enchantment you believed everything he told you. You had to. You had no choice."

But Ko was unwilling to believe Sword. "Don't forget he healed you, too. Does that mean *you're* enchanted?"

"Maybe," Sword answered. "Maybe that's why I did everything Brin told me to do. Everything he *planned* for me to do."

"What are you talking about?" Ko said. "You've done bloody nothing."

"The war, Melody," Sword said. "That has to be it. Roth and Morgana talked about it. Martin told me about it."

He thumped his hand on the arm of the driver's seat. "Arkady and the Seyshen broke apart in council *three years ago.* The Seyshen hired Orion to be ready to fight in that war *three years ago.* And that's when I had my accident! *Three years ago.* When Brin *caused* my accident, gave me back my memories, and ... and brought me back into the First World ... for the war."

"But if we're to believe all this stuff, you're a *Pendragon,* Sword. You're not Arkady. You're not Seyshen. Just whose bloody side are you supposed to be on?"

Sword's heart thundered with his excitement. For three years — no, for more than twenty, ever since his exile — he had been caught in a trap that he hadn't even known existed. And now he was going to break free. "That doesn't matter anymore," he said.

"What?!"

"Whatever Brin was trying to get me to do, it hasn't worked out the way he planned. And now that I know about him and his lies, I'm not his pawn anymore."

"So whose side are you *supposed* to be on?"

"I don't know, and for right now, that's really not important either. What *is* important is that for good or bad, I will be able to *choose* the side I fight for. In *both* worlds. The First *and* the Second."

"We have so few data on the First World. How will you know which side is which?" Ko shook her head as if the enormity of the whole absurd challenge was too much to be comprehended, let alone accomplished.

Unthinkingly, Sword held his hand to her, fist loose, then pulled it back, remembering Ko was only human. "I hope that I won't have to determine that on my own. I hope to have help from my friends."

Ko stared at him. "Too bad, Sword, you don't have any."

"Maybe I want to change that. Maybe I want a lot of things to change."

Ko regarded him stonily. "Some things can't change."

But Sword wouldn't accept her refusal. "If I'm — if we're — going to survive, if we're going to succeed, some things *have* to change. I need your help, Melody. I know I can't do this on my own."

Ko slumped back in her seat. "The only side you'll ever be on is your own." She closed her eyes again. "We should be getting back to the Loft before the police get a lead on the van."

Sword sat still for a moment, then turned around to Martin, wondering what the halfling would have made of the conversation that had just taken place, wondering if he'd understood any of it.

But Martin had heard enough to understand all that was important. Keeping one hand firmly on Roth, the halfling leaned forward and held out a fist in the greeting of the First World, tightly bound, and spoke in shiftertongue: "*Pendragych*." The meaning was clear. Wherever Sword went, whatever Sword must do, Martin would be at his side. Sword's clan was now Martin's as well.

Sword responded in kind: "*Pendragych*." Martin nodded in satisfaction, and then sat back, Roth still held immobile beneath him.

Sword pulled back into traffic.

JUDITH & GARFIELD REEVES-STEVENS

He was no longer a pawn moving blindly in response to the dark machinations of others unknown. He had his own path to follow. And he knew very well which side he would choose to fight for.

The side he was *born* to fight for.

"Pendragon," he repeated softly. Within that name was the wealth of his heritage and key to his destiny.

And now, he was about to discover the truth of all that had been kept from him.

For as soon as they reached the safety of the Loft, the Regent of Pendragon would surrender all his secrets.

Because the heir to Pendragon would demand it.

TWENTY-ONE

The energy of the yellow crystal flared in time to the rhythms of Adrian Forsyte's machine in the lab at MIT.

In the Loft, in his chair, Forsyte focussed all his awareness into his two operative fingers, to feel the high-frequency whine of the machine's generators that fed the lasers' capacitors, the swift low throb of the machine's vacuum pumps struggling to keep the vacuum channels purged, the hum of the circulating pumps as they bathed the machine's superconducting magnets in liquid nitrogen.

All the power of that doomed lab converged in the machine's creator — the labor and knowledge that it had represented, the energies of known and unknown nature that it had dared to tap. All of it coming to rest now in one man and one moment restored to life by the waiting crystal's golden fire.

In the Loft, Forsyte tried in vain to eject himself from his chair. But he was powerless to move. There was to be no escape from this final playback of the last night of his life the way it had been.

In the lab at MIT, the twin ready lights of the test bed's lasers reflected like two red pupils in the dark glass of Forsyte's safety goggles. He heard the door open behind him. He turned to greet the two women who had changed his life in these past two weeks.

Forsyte took off his glasses, ready to smile. Only then did he see whom he greeted.

"What the hell are you doing here?" he said crossly to Ko. "And you," he barked at Sword. "Where're your goggles? Didn't you see the warning sign on the door?"

The open door beside Sword held a metal frame with a smudged sign that read: CAUTION: LASER LIGHT. Sword closed the door. "Dr. Forstye, I think you should shut it down," he said. "Those girls don't exist."

"What the hell are you talking about?" Forsyte snapped. "Of course they exist." He'd never forget the nights he had spent with them. God, did they exist.

"I've had my people search every database possible, including restricted government computer systems — Social Security, I.R.S., the DMV in fifty states *and* equivalents in Canada *and* Mexico. Even broke into EC citizenship records — "

"What is your *point*, Mr. Sword?" Forsyte saw Ko cringe at his tone, but he didn't care. Not only was Ko's fool useless, he was an interfering fool. *How dare she waste even more of my time with this nonsense?*

"They have no records, Dr. Forsyte. Nowhere. Not by name, not by institution, not by fingerprints. If they entered this country from somewhere else, there is no record of it. If they were born here, there is no record of it."

"Then your people are incompetent, Sword. Now get out!" Forsyte smashed his fist against the test bed, making Ko jump. "I've had enough of you and your 'investigation.' "

Ko stared at him, stricken, seemingly unable to find her voice.

That ineffectiveness made it even easier for Forsyte to direct his anger to his young, so-soon-to-be-ex-assistant. "And as for *you*, you might as well get out with him. I don't want to see — "

Sword stepped between Forsyte and Ko. "You clearly don't understand how money works. With what I shell out, there's no such thing as incompetence. And, as far as I know, there is only one group of people who have the power to so thoroughly wipe records."

"Let me guess," Forsyte said sarcastically, sure he detected Scotch on Sword's breath. "Little gray aliens from a galaxy far, far away."

DARK HUNTER

Sword wasn't amused. "The government, Dr. Forsyte. Probably one of the few institutions that has the ability to pay more for computer services than I can. Your assistant's suspicions were correct. You're under government surveillance by an extremely powerful organization."

"And you're nuts in May. If Melody's dismal little theory is correct, then why are Sonja and Heidi *helping* me with my work? Why are they sharing their research? Why don't they just take a sledgehammer to the thing and be done with it?"

"Ms. Ko doesn't think that Sonja and Heidi *are* trying to help you. She thinks they're trying to hold you back with a more subtle sledge-hammer."

Forsyte could feel the cords of his neck rise. "Who cares what *she* thinks?" He pointed to the test bed. "*I* made that. It's *mine*."

He turned to stare witheringly down at Ko. "And no matter how clever those little fingers of yours are, you'll never begin to appreciate the true importance of my work! Sonja and Heidi are light-years beyond you!"

Incredibly to Forsyte, his mouse of an assistant somehow found the courage to talk back to him.

"Please, Dr. Forsyte. The ... the modifications they've had you put in ... expanding the probability path ... it can't work."

Her impertinence was unbelievable. "You have the gall to tell me science? If it weren't for the bell curve, kiddo, you wouldn't even have made a 'C' in Quantum Mechanics 101!"

"But there will be an energy discharge," Ko squeaked, cringing even as she did so.

Only the look in Sword's eye kept Forstye from striking her. "I've already accounted for that, *Professor* Ko. That's why the new dampeners are installed along the pathway. To absorb it."

"But they won't absorb the discharges. They will — "

A delighted smile on his face, Forstye pushed past Ko on the way to the door to his lab. The change in his mood was so abrupt, others who'd witnessed similar behavior from him had informed him he might qualify as a victim of psychosis. "Sonja! Heidi! Please, come in. I was just getting ready to try a test run of the new modifications."

219

The two platinum-haired creatures in the doorway were like a double projection of the same image, and Forsyte felt a familiar tremor run through him. They were the most beautiful females he had ever seen. Though they had giggled when he had asked if they were twins or sisters, each had the same shimmering, almost metallic pale hair. Their ice-blue eyes, impossibly fair skin, and chiselled features were those of mythic Nordic goddesses.

But their enthusiasm — and energy — were as real as they were divine to Forsyte. For the first time, he'd even let some elements of his work slide, so exhausted was he becoming by the arduous night studies he'd been conducting with them both. Yet still the girls appeared each day in his lab and his office, looking as untouched and perfect as they looked right now.

"We're not disturbing you, are we, Adrian?" Sonja's voice was feather-soft, never demanding.

"Of course not, my dears. Come in, come in." Forsyte ushered the two women into the lab. "These others were just leaving."

Ko started for the door in an almost instinctive reaction to his dismissal. But Sword stayed put. "Actually, we were going to watch the demonstration."

Forstye attempted civility for Sonja's and Heidi's benefit. "Actually, you were going to leave."

Sword drew Forsyte aside and dropped his voice to a confidential whisper. "Simple choice, doc." Forsyte stiffened at the hateful term as Sword continued. "Either your assistant and I are going to stay here, at the back, out of your hair, and watch what happens, or else before you're able to push me out that door, I'll be sure to mention that you gave me their correspondence file and I'll drop the results of my investigation."

Forsyte was sure he could smooth that over, but then Sword added, "Even if they're not government agents, when they hear what I have to say, they might not be so willing to play Doctor again. Do we understand each other?"

Sword had him. Forsyte pointed to the generator cabinet ten feet away from the side of the test bed. "Stand over there, by the generator.

DARK HUNTER

Wear your goggles. Don't touch anything. And don't say another word."

"Hey, doc, like I said, I'm doing this on my own time. C'mon, Ms. Ko." Sword led Forsyte's distraught assistant over to the generator, and Forsyte tossed over two pairs of tinted safety goggles, purposely making sure they fell short. Then he returned to the test bed to prepare for the first run of the modified TTE device.

As if they had trained all their lives on such equipment, Sonja and Heidi breezed easily through the systems check, calling out readings as Forsyte entered the values on the computer workstation that tabulated the results of each run.

With such expert help, it took less than ten minutes to calibrate the TTE device. Forsyte took a final check. The vacuum channels were holding. The gas mix in the sample chamber was superheated. The laser capacitors were fully charged. The atomic clock counted smoothly, providing a benchmark for the local relativistic frame of reference.

The display screen confirmed that the device was ready to fire. Forsyte pulled his goggles up to cover his eyes and, though it wouldn't matter to him if they were blinded, looked to be sure that Ko and Sword were wearing theirs. His department, after all, was very strict about its insurance regulations.

Sword's arrogant form was dead center against the cabinet, as if he had decided to become part of the generating equipment that towered five feet over him, bristling with dials and switches.

Forsyte waved for Sword to stand to the side. "You're too close to the cut-offs. I said *by* the generator, not *on* it."

Sword moved a few feet to the right, well away from the fluorescent orange handle that controlled the emergency shut-off system, and though Ko was nowhere near the shut-off switch, she nervously shifted position with Sword, trying to look anywhere but at Forsyte.

Forsyte studied his assistant with new interest, realizing that now that he'd found her replacements, she was finally eligible for the patented Professor-Forsyte treatment. For all her brilliance when it came to the world of science, Ko clearly was untutored in the finer arts. And he was an expert teacher. He'd apologize oh so eloquently. Disarm her with deception. Overwhelm her with persistence. Then take her on

221

an outing to the facility where he stabled his horses. A ride in the country with a well-staged picnic. She wouldn't stand a chance. She'd be just like all the others.

And then, Forsyte thought with satisfaction, *I'll take my revenge for this Sword she foisted on me.* He could just picture his serious young assistant's face when he told her he was personally going to see to it that she was out — of this lab, this faculty, and this field. And his life.

He looked at his latest student conquests.

God, I love science, Forsyte thought.

Then he pressed the button. Expecting to hear and see what always happened next during the TTE device's normal cycle: a loud bang as the capacitors discharged, accompanied by a brief red flash from the gas sample chamber, a blue flash from the light on the camera mounted ten feet above the bubble chamber, and then, at the same time, four or five screens' worth of numbers spraying across the workstation display, giving the elapsed time measurements as counted out by the computer and the atomic clock, followed by the hum of the generators starting up again as the capacitors recharged.

But that's not what he heard and saw now.

There was no initial bang announcing the beginning of the cycle, only a steadily increasing thrum that didn't sound as if it came from the generator at all. In place of the customary red flash from the gas sample chamber was a curious red glow — extended, continuous. Sonja and Heidi began to back away from the chamber as Forsyte discovered the source of the thrumming sound — the test bed. It was vibrating.

Forsyte looked in consternation at the screen of his workstation. But the numbers rushing by on it blurred the display. He blinked rapidly, trying to freeze the onscreen numbers, to see what it was the computer was recording, but just then the screen cleared, as the computer system reset itself in the overload of data.

The thrum from the test bed was now almost deafening and Forsyte looked up to see Sonja's and Heidi's long fine hair begin to rise up around the two women as if they were caught in a tremendous field of static electricity.

"Get away from the test bed!" he shouted, as he bent down to the workstation computer in a feverish attempt to calculate the source of the electrical leakage.

At least we'll have a record of some of this, Forsyte thought as he typed madly at the workstation to bring the TTE device's computer back online. Vaguely, he heard what sounded like Ko's voice calling out to him above the din just as the lab's overhead lights blew out in explosions of glass.

"Dr. Forsyte, disconnect the dampeners! Disconnect the dampeners!"

In the lab's only light now — the red glow that was almost blinding in intensity and the strobelike flashes of the bubble-chamber camera — Forsyte saw the groaning test bed twist up at its corners as if an incalculably huge mass had come to rest on it. Frothing gouts of liquid nitrogen shot forth in all directions as the supercooled magnet housings cracked, filling the air with haze that collected on the floor in a low-lying fog as the liquid nitrogen warmed into a gaseous state. "What the hell ... ?" Forsyte muttered.

In the fury that now shook the lab, Ko was suddenly at the control panel for the shuddering test bed. Forsyte abandoned his calculations the instant he saw which cables she was trying to dislodge — the dampeners! The only thing keeping the reaction from completely running away. He lunged at his assistant, grabbed her, dragged her back to the workstation.

"You fool!" he screamed over the earsplitting whine that came from somewhere within the glowing test bed. "If you take those out — "

"This is *not* a tunneling reaction! There's something in the dampeners!" Ko flung out an arm, gesturing toward a far corner of the lab. "And they put it there! To destroy your work!"

Forsyte pulled the goggles from his eyes, squinting in the direction Ko was pointing, through the thick air now cut through by red lances of light, and he gasped as he saw with whom he had shared his work and his bed.

Sonja and Heidi, their long hair spread out in twin, aligned spheres of platinum spikes sparking as if with electrical discharges, each holding her arms out before her, waist level, hands palm down.

Sonja looked straight at Forsyte, blew him a kiss, then both she and Heidi rolled their eyes back in their heads, twisted their heads backward at the same grotesque angle, as both their bodies began to shake violently at the same frequency, blurring before Forsyte's astonished gaze like the numbers he'd seen cascading on his screen.

A sphere of red energy rose from the center of the heaving test bed, like a slow-motion explosion, suffusing the lab with its eerie, hellish glow.

The dampeners! Forsyte thought with sudden panic. *Ko was right. Sword was right. I have to disconnect the dampeners. Undo whatever those ... those creatures have done to my machine. My work ...*

He rushed toward the test bed. Heard both Ko and Sword shout at him. Some kind of warning. Something about —

Forsyte collapsed. Halfway between the generator cabinet and the crumbling test bed. His muscles writhing uncontrollably. Every nerveway in his body seared. The red glow was like lava.

Forsyte rolled onto his side. *"Melody!"* he cried, knowing but not caring that his entreaty could endanger her. *"Help me! Hurry!"*

Ko was almost into the red nimbus just as Sword rushed up to yank her back.

Forsyte screamed at Sword. "You bastard, Sword! You bastard! She was coming to save me! And you stopped her!" Then scalding oil swept over him. As the edge of the glow crept toward the generator cabinet.

God, no, Forsyte thought in horror. Whatever else it was, the red sphere was an energy source created by the test bed ... and the generator was designed to feed the test bed ... if the energy source engulfed the generator, then the feedback —

Forsyte called on inner resources of strength that come only to those facing death. He forced the words from his mouth as if they were the last words he would ever speak.

"THE HANDLE, MELODY — PULL THE CUT-OFF HANDLE — FEEDBACK — MELODY — FEEDBACK!"

In those last long, slow moments, Forsyte saw Ko look at the generator cabinet. At the cut-off handle. Orange. Fluorescent. *She couldn't miss it. She knew what to do.*

But she didn't do anything. Even though Sword no longer held her back.

The red glow brushed the edge of the generator.

No! Forsyte screamed in his mind.

Engulfed the generator.

This is your fault, Sword. This is —

Feedback —

Forsyte flew through darkness for the longest time, spinning, twisting, as insubstantial as a ghost, it seemed, barely feeling the rush of air across his body as he fell. *I'll have to open my parachute soon,* he thought. *Or else I'll hit the —*

He hit the ground.

He was still alive. On the floor of his lab.

Weak beams of amber-colored light from battery-powered emergency lights crisscrossed the smoking wreckage of the test bed and the generator. Haze swirled lazily over two fallen bodies: Ko and Sword.

That should make my life simpler, Forsyte thought vengefully. *Now it's just my word about what happened here.*

Two moving figures approached him through the smoke.

Forsyte felt a thrill of disbelief as he saw Sonja and Heidi, hair still in sparking halos from some unseen source of power, glide through the smoke as if with skates, or wings. They stopped beside him.

Heidi's pale blue eyes were inches from his, her face on its side just like his. Though Forsyte hadn't seen her bend or kneel. Then he saw that the woman's entire body was suspended horizontally, floating inches above the floor. Forsyte held his breath, too apprehensive to even try to move.

"So now you know," Heidi said primly, like a teacher completing a difficult lesson.

Incredibly, somehow, Sonja hovered beside her. "But you'll never understand why," the second woman added.

"Never," Heidi repeated pityingly.

Sonja. "Because it's just the way you are."

Heidi. "The way you'll always be."

Forsyte tried to speak. To ask them why he deserved this. To ask why him. But he found he was speechless. The shock, he decided. Besides, he was afraid he already knew the answers.

"Good-bye, Adrian." They spoke in unison in the soft voices that had beguiled him.

Forsyte watched wide-eyed as they floated up, still horizontal, beyond his field of vision. Then he felt a sharp pinch on the index finger of his left hand. And then that hand's middle finger.

"So you'll always know," they said with a giggle. And then they were gone.

Forsyte fell again through darkness, spinning, twisting, as insubstantial as a ghost, it seemed, until he fell out of a glowing, yellow cloud of light. Until he fell out of the memories of the waiting crystal and into his chair, in Sword's Loft, beside the mysterious visitor who had shared these memories with him. And his thoughts.

He looked up to Sword's sister but found no trace of judgment in her gaze. And Forsyte knew why. Judgment had already been given.

Diandra reached out for the crystal beside Forsyte's left hand just as the last of the stone's inner glow faded. She tossed it back to the desk with the rest of Ko's things.

"As I said, Dr. Forsyte. No magic has been used on you. I think you've always known that. Whatever afflicts you is the result of your own making — whether by the power of the energy produced by your equipment or by the power of your own mind."

Forsyte closed his eyes. More than anything, he wished to fall again. To spin. To ... but the waiting crystal's power was gone and there was no place left to fall.

He was where he deserved to be. Where he'd chosen to be.

The sound of the garage-door opening echoed through the Loft.

Forsyte opened his eyes.

"I assume that that will be my brother," Diandra said, standing. "I shall be most interested to learn how he has changed since the events you remembered. If he, too, has changed." She walked to the lab's door, then turned, asked, "Will you have your chair bring you or should I push you? The choice is yours."

DARK HUNTER

Tears blurring his vision, Forsyte heard the fliers' joint voice once more.

"So now you know."

He had his voder ask Diandra to push him.

TWENTY-TWO

As the Loft's garage door rumbled shut, the hunter waited at the foot of the stairs for her brother to see her, unimpressed by the acuity of his senses.

Sword had jumped from a large black van the instant it stopped, noticed the wire-cage elevator bringing Forsyte to the garage level, then sprinted around to the vehicle's sliding side door. All without seeing her.

The hunter had seen her brother twice before: once in Greece, once in New York. But now, with Forsyte's memories from the past so fresh in her mind, she had a more-informed frame of reference that told her Galen Sword had changed dramatically, intriguingly, the past three years.

He was leaner, though not conditioned. The soft curves of his earlier, immoderate consumption had disappeared from his face. His dark eyes were still shadowed, but no longer were puffy. And she could see that his strength and his swiftness had improved.

I wonder if he knows? she thought. *I wonder if even in his dreams he knows his origins, his potential, what he must never become?*

A passenger emerged from the front seat of the van and the hunter saw what had become of Forsyte's young assistant who had chosen not to aid the man she loved.

DARK HUNTER

Melody Ko had aged far more than three years. As if she sought penance, she had cropped her long black hair to a spiky crown of bristles that barely hid her scalp. The seriousness that had marked her before had given way to grim resolve.

The hunter heard Forsyte's chair hum forth from the elevator cage just as her brother wrenched open the van's side door, revealing two more passengers inside the back seat.

She recognized the brutish figure of the immature halfling she had netted in the alley. The one called *Myrch'ntin*, who'd treated her appearance as the coming to life of a childhood nightmare. He was neither human nor beast, without place in any world — not even the Ark. Except, it seemed, in her brother's home in exile.

The second passenger was unknown to her. The spikes and flares of his aura, though, marked him as an adept, not a human. The hunter read the aura. Erratic, barely visible, it carried an unmistakable signature held by her own: Elemental. Injured.

And not in her brother's favor, judging from the rough way Sword's halfling pushed the adept from the van and then began to bind the elemental's hands.

The hunter frowned at the carelessness she witnessed. "Tie his hands behind him, halfling. So he cannot see them when he wakes," she ordered.

Sword jerked around as if struck. Ko turned also, though slowly, her shoulders sagging with exhaustion. From the van, the halfling stared at the hunter, sniffed the air, then whimpered. Unable to catch her scent, he had recognized who she was and what she was. His whimper turned quickly to a rising howl of fear.

The hunter stepped forward, arms open to show she carried no weapons. It took only two steps for her brother to recognize her.

"You ... ," he said in undisguised shock. "From the alley. From Delphi. Who *are* you?" he demanded.

The halfling grabbed at Sword, trying to pull him back into the van. "Dark hunter Galen Sword! Dark hunter!"

Diandra's brother stood his ground. "It's all right, Martin. She's not hunting us, are you?"

229

The hunter shook her head. Prey worthy of a hunt was of higher standard than these two.

With no threat imminent, Ko turned away, walked over to Forsyte, and was soon engaged in a conversation with the chair-bound man that required lengthy pauses. Presumably, telling him how they had caught their captive. The hunter expended no effort to listen. She'd shared enough with the unfortunate human already.

The halfling had retreated half behind the van, growling softly over the bound body of the injured elemental.

"Do you have a name?" Sword asked.

The hunter paused before answering him, trusting she would be able to control the events she might unleash with her next words.

"Diandra. Diandra Sword."

Her brother's eyes grew wide. She knew that for an instant he had stopped breathing even as his heartbeat accelerated.

"Are we related?" he asked, as if sensing the threshold he stood upon.

"Little Galen," the hunter said, "I am your sister. Our mother gave birth to me soon after you ... after you were sent away. After the fall."

"The fall of what?" Sword involuntarily stepped closer to the hunter. Just as she stepped back.

"The Clan Pendragon," the hunter answered. "Our line has ended. Pendragon is no more."

"Our mother?"

"Dead." *Worse than dead*, the hunter thought as her brother staggered back to lean against the van, overwhelmed by her revelations.

"Our father," Sword asked faintly as if he already knew what she must say.

"Dead as well," the hunter said. Then added, out of pity for his bleakness, "You knew more of our mother than I," she added. "I also was sent away."

Sword stared down at the concrete garage floor for a moment, then looked up at the hunter. "But you're different from me," he said. "I have no powers."

Is that why he thinks he was exiled? the hunter thought, then realized that because her brother's aura was completely shielded, that explana-

DARK HUNTER

tion might have the ring of truth to him.

"So why were *you* exiled?" Sword asked the hunter.

"Our line had fallen — ended — so I was to be killed. Not exiled," the hunter said, the old grief welling in her, prompting her next question of her brother. "Do you remember Alexander? Our mother's brother?"

Sword's eyes darted back and forth as he searched whatever First World memories he still possessed. "*Uncle* Alexander?"

"Yes," the hunter said. "He was the one who took me from our enclave in the last days. Brought me to Deep Forest. Or so I'm told. I was too young to know this for myself."

"I remember Alexander telling me something one day," Sword said with a far-off look. "Something that ... that I was never supposed to forget."

Herr Slausen, the hunter thought. She recognized the wizard's handiwork.

"It was ... something in a book. The family book? Is ... was there such a thing?" Sword looked at her, clearly wondering what else she might verify that he had only dreamed might exist.

"*The History of the Greater Clan Pendragon,*" the hunter said. There was a copy in the Keep of the Rings. But Dajara had said Pendragon did not continue, and the hunter had committed her existence to preserving what could and should survive.

"Lysander Sword," her brother said with increasing agitation. "That was it. Lysander Sword, the ... the hero of ... Florence? Does that make any sense to you?" He looked at her hopefully.

"A reference to the Great War with the lesser clans. It took place centuries ago," the hunter said.

"That's what Uncle Alexander told me," Sword said excitedly. "He told me that Lysander was a great hero to the clans, and that Lysander was my ancestor, and that I should never forget that."

The hunter noted how her brother drew strength from even this fragmented and incomplete account. But their uncle had been a powerful warrior and even now, in the words once spoken to a child, Alexander's substance was still manifest. Yet why had he not revealed the destiny that her brother would have had if — *unless Alexander never had the chance to,* the hunter thought. Then, as now, she knew, the wizards were everywhere.

Stuffed in the open side of the van, the injured elemental moaned, breaking the moment.

"Is it your intent to keep this one captive?" the hunter asked.

"Oh, yesss," her brother answered, glaring at the adept with a hatred that took the hunter by surprise. "Don't you know him?"

"By his aura, he is an elemental," the hunter said. "But I have not seen him before."

"He's Tomas Roth," her brother said, and then the hunter heard nothing else beyond that.

In the compressed depths of her shadowsuit beneath her cape, weapons pressed against her as her body converted instantly to the way of the hunt. Her fingers spread, aching with her desire for the feel of the hilt of her new windblade. Saliva sprang into her mouth with her need to see the elemental's blood spilled to the air.

After all this time. The Destroyer of Pendragon. Deceiver of my mother and my father. Self-appointed dealer of my own death.

Never had the hunter's vows been so tested. The prey was still unconscious. She could gut him as easily as a Close troll and no one would know. No one —

— except —

— *Dajara.*

The hunter drew a perfect breath. She closed her eyes and saw cool mists. She grounded herself in Deep Forest. Her parent's voice filled her, soothed her. *The past is the past. Pendragon is fallen. The line does not continue.*

The forest still within her, she opened her eyes to see her brother's wondering gaze.

"You do know Roth," he said.

Continuance lies in keeping the past where it belongs, the hunter reminded herself. She was strong enough to keep it there. As always, the vows of the hunt would release her from the useless desire for revenge. The strength of the forest would give her the wisdom to sustain her vows. But her brother had neither the hunt nor the forest. He had nothing, yet could do so much. For a fleeting instant, the hunter wondered if it would be better to kill him now, at a time of her own choosing, before he could inadvertently set anything further in motion, beyond any world's control.

Diandra continues.

Dajara had told her that her own fate was to survive. That meant there was hope for the Ark.

But does my brother continue? she asked herself. It was a question she had never asked Dajara. What would the forest say for Little Galen?

The instant passed and her brother still lived. As long as Clan Pendragon was not resurrected, the hunter had no quarrel with Little Galen. For all that he had apparently accomplished, he was — at present — in no position to lay claim to the title of Victor of Pendragon. It was not as she had feared after her last meeting with Dajara. She would not have to destroy him. Not, at least, for now.

Relieved, the hunter exhaled and her weapons melted back into two dimensions.

Her response to her brother was in the voice of the familiar so Little Galen would not detect the distress she'd felt.

"He is consort to Morgana LaVey, the Victor of Arkady, is he not?" she asked.

"More important, he's the one who had me exiled," Sword said.

"Truly?" the hunter asked.

Sword looked at her questioningly. "You don't know?"

"There was much chaos in those days, Little Galen." She strengthened the voice. "Little is actually known about what happened and who was responsible." Without perceptible effort, the hunter assessed Roth's condition and the strength of his aura.

Both told her that the elemental was now conscious, though he chose not to reveal it. "Who told you Tomas Roth was responsible for your exile?"

"No one," her brother admitted. "But I remember him challenging my — our mother about me, about my lack of powers. And he was there when the wizard gave me the potion to drink."

And thereby saved your life, the hunter thought.

"And now he's going to answer a lot of questions for me, aren't you, you bastard?" Sword leaned into the van to refasten the adept's ties behind his back, as the hunter had commanded. "You might be interested to hear what he has to say, yourself, Diandra. So you can find out what happened, too."

The hunter saw Roth's eyelids flutter at the mention of her name. It was one thing to be held captive by Galen Sword, quite another to confront a dark hunter.

She stepped back, anticipating the brief moment the elemental's hands would be free. She knew the adept would strike then, and she had already decided it would be best if she did not interfere. This was not her battle, nor could it ever become hers. Her destiny lay with the Ark, and not with a struggle that had begun with the Fall of the Tarls.

But before Roth could make his move, the halfling reached out, took Roth's head in one enormous hand, and smashed it against the inner wall of the van.

The elemental's aura sputtered back into semi-consciousness.

"What did you do that for?" Sword demanded of the growling halfling.

"Tomas Roth wake up. Martin make sleep again."

Observant beast, the hunter thought. *Myrch'ntin must also have noticed the change in Roth's aura. So the halfling's adept half provides him — and my brother — with First World eyes.* That meant he — and Little Galen — could identify most humanform adepts and perhaps even see the layer.

Sword quickly retied Roth's hands behind his back, then hoisted the heavy body into his arms with some effort. "Which would be better?" he asked the hunter. "Keeping him in a holding cell in the basement, or on an examination chair in the lab?"

"The chair upstairs?" the hunter asked. "The one that looks configured to hold a shifterwolf?" Her brother nodded, short of breath.

Once again, the hunter chose the voice of the familiar to conceal a lie. "The chair, most definitely. If it can hold a shifter, it will withstand an elemental."

Sword shifted Roth in his arms. "Martin, you want to take the cases up?"

The halfling rooted through the front of the van, then jumped through the door with two large black leather cases. The hunter recog-

DARK HUNTER

nized the scent that came from one and the almost unnoticeable glow that showed through the cracks in the other.

"Were those Roth's?" she asked, again using the voice of the familiar.

"Yeah," Sword huffed as he carried the elemental to the elevator. "They won't open. Any idea what's in them?"

"None," the hunter said, knowing exactly what the two cases contained: her fee

Now all she had to do was find and capture the nightfeeder.

And then set Roth free.

TWENTY-THREE

Ko knew something was terribly wrong with Forsyte. She'd known it the moment he'd rolled into the garage with reddened eyes and tear tracks on his face. Something terrible that had something to do with Diandra Sword. But for once, Ko wasn't thinking of Forsyte first and hadn't ask him why he was so distressed. Her arm hurt too much. And she couldn't stop thinking of sleep — and Brin. So as Sword had talked with his sister, she had limited her conversation with the physicist to the briefest of descriptions of the excursion to the crystal shop.

It's not enchantment, she told herself as she rode up in the Loft elevator with Forsyte and Sword, who had Roth slung over his shoulder. *And Brin wouldn't have manipulated his own brother. He's not a liar. Sword is.* Maybe after she'd slept off her exhaustion, things would seem clearer. *It's not enchantment!* The words echoed so forcefully in her mind that it was almost as if another were speaking.

Sword's sister had taken the stairs and was already in the main lab. Martin was there, too, standing guard over the cases Roth had been carrying in the Happy Thought. The halfling, though, was staying far back from the lab's examination chair. It was the same chair that Sword and Ko had strapped Martin into when the team had first captured the him. Since then, Martin had kept a careful distance from it.

DARK HUNTER

Ko eased off her black parka, gingerly sliding it over her cracked and crumbling cast. The hard-plaster construction had been an effective weapon to use on the single-legged creature she'd fought in the crystal shop, but her whole arm now felt even worse than it did when Orion had shattered it.

She held the parka in her one good hand, looked over at her equipment locker, at least ten feet away, and decided she couldn't be bothered making the walk to hang the coat up. She dropped it on a lab chair. *Maybe Sword will hang up something for a change*, she thought.

Ko walked slowly over to the examination chair as Forsyte rolled off in another direction, toward Diandra Sword. Ko knew that the physicist's response to her debriefing had not been characteristic. He had merely accepted what she'd related without any demand for additional detail. Of course, usually she elaborated without need of questions, knowing how badly he felt at being left behind on the team excursions. Now she had the feeling that Forsyte was avoiding her, keeping his chair in motion, not meeting her eyes. Even more strangely, she discovered she did not resent his inattention. Nor did she feel the need to know why he might be keeping his distance. At least, not right now.

Sword had finished tightening the restraint straps across Roth, securing the adept's hands at the sides of the chair where they were hidden from his line of sight as Diandra had directed.

Ko looked up to study the so-called dark hunter who stood on the other side of the chair. Diandra seemed to know a great deal about the First World, which meant she, unlike Sword, probably was a real adept. *With powers, whatever that means.* But this sister story ... Ko wasn't convinced. There was some resemblance, but it certainly was not as strong as that between Sword and his brother. *And Brin never mentioned that he and Sword had a sister.*

Sword stepped over to stretch his back against one of the lab workbenches. "Martin, let me know when he starts to wake up again."

Martin slapped a hand against the floor. "Then Martin make sleep again?"

"Not until I say so," Sword said, cracking his back and straightening up with a look of relief.

Martin grunted but nodded obediently.

JUDITH & GARFIELD REEVES-STEVENS

Sword looked over at his supposed sister and from the dopey expression that came over his face, Ko realized that he had accepted her story, although she had offered no proof that Ko had heard about. Diandra had affected more than just Forsyte, it seemed.

"Aren't you hot in that cloak?" Sword asked Diandra.

"No," the woman said. "What do you plan to do with him?"

"Ask him some questions."

"And then?"

Sword shrugged. "What would you suggest?"

"Politically, this adept is very powerful. In the First World, that is. I would release him."

Sword reacted with the disbelief that Ko felt. "After what he did to us?"

"How can you be certain that what you remember Roth doing is what he actually did?"

Ko was struck by the utter reasonableness of Sword's sister's argument, and was sure that all who heard her would agree. But it seemed that Sword still had objections because Diandra held up her hand to forestall his interruption.

"I've heard the softwind, Little Galen. I know how your memories were supposedly restored. But how can you trust them?"

"The memories Brin brought back for me — are you saying they're like Marratin illusions?"

"You've had dealings with Clan Marratin?" Diandra asked, her strange gold eyes alive with interest.

Sword answered cautiously. But Ko was finding Diandra's words very compelling and wondered why Sword could have doubt at all. "I've had dealings with Marratin. But I've had enough other dealings with the First World to know that my memories are real." He paused. "Besides, Brin's power is healing, not illusion."

"Brin's *blue* power is healing, Little Galen. His — "

"Why does everyone from the First World keep calling me *Little* Galen?" Sword asked his sister.

But it was Tomas Roth who answered. "Because it was also your father's name, *Little* Galen."

238

DARK HUNTER

Martin had missed Roth's ascent to consciousness. The halfling jolted forward, growling menacingly at the elemental.

Sword placed his hands on either side of the examination chair and met the adept's dark eyes directly. "It's all right, Martin."

Still growling softly, Martin retreated back to guard Roth's cases.

"What did you do to my father?" Sword asked the adept bound to the chair.

"You know what happened to your father, Little Galen. You were there. You saw him."

"No," Sword said, his voice thin and tense. "I saw nothing."

"The night you went away. The night I saved your worthless life." Roth's arrogance was so pronounced it seemed to Ko as if the elemental could rise from the chair any moment he wished to, and that he was staying put only to humor his captor.

"You're lying. He wasn't there that night. You were always supposed to be with him. But you were alone. There was just the wizard. You. My mother — "

"He was there, boy. In the library! Think!"

"The library ... ? Mother was there — *the old man?* With the cane? That wasn't my father. I'd never seen him before. My father was young. My father was — "

"*A warrior?* What of it? You and your whole damned line — all of you — were warrior adepts. For all the good it did Pendragon."

"Warrior?" Sword repeated. He looked to Diandra. "We're warriors?"

"No longer," Diandra said.

Roth spoke harshly. "Your father saw to that, Little Galen. He let the fighting eyes consume him. Pendragon lost everything."

Sword's hands flexed as he stared at Roth. "And what about me?"

"You? You're not your father, boy. You're nothing!"

Sword's hand became a fist. The hand with his mother's ring.

Roth saw the movement, laughed scornfully. "That won't change anything, *Little* Galen. Little *warrior!*"

Sword's face darkened and he dropped his fist, stepping back as if afraid of unleashing his own rage. "It wasn't supposed to be like this," he said to no one.

239

Diandra spoke to Sword. "Why put yourself through this? What is it you want?"

"Answers!" Sword said fiercely. "I want answers for my life. And *he* can give them to me."

Roth gazed on Sword with disdain. "Where would you like me to start, warrior?"

A languid voice spoke from the entrance to the lab. "Why not with the war between Arkady and Seyshen."

Ko knew that voice without having to look to confirm her suspicion. So much for Sword's fifty thousand dollars' worth of improved security.

The vampire, Orion, strolled into the lab. Even beneath his long coat, wide-brimmed hat, and the fabric mask and dark sunglasses obscuring his face, his voice and walk were unmistakable. "Begin with the roots of that conflict, why don't you, Victor of Arkady." Orion took the mask and glasses from his face revealing golden skin blistered and fissured. *Of course,* Ko thought, *it's still daylight. He's been testing himself in full sun again.* "What's that, Tomas Roth? You say you're not Victor? You have not yet killed your true love, Morgana?"

Then Ko noticed that Orion was gesturing only with one hand. His other hand and arm were held out in a curve from his body, as if he were carrying something very large and heavy and —

'Bub!

Ko knew at once that the vampire had made his entrance through the barred window of Ja'Nette's old bedroom. Where Sword's cat had been — without her collar.

With that, Orion reached up to scratch at empty air just about where 'Bub's head would be. If the white Persian were four times normal size. Which she was, Ko knew. When 'Bub was invisible.

Sword had made the same deduction because he pulled a green-leather collar from the pocket of his coat and held it out wordlessly to Martin who scrambled to take it from him.

Orion released his invisible burden, dropping it to the floor with a surprisingly loud thud, then swept off his hat and opened his coat. As she tracked the movements, Ko suddenly realized that Orion's eyes had been on Diandra the entire time. Though when Diandra looked at Orion, the vampire quickly looked away.

DARK HUNTER

"You know what she is, don't you, Mr. Sword? We saw her in the alley that night."

"She says she's my sister," Sword answered.

"What?" Roth turned to stare at Diandra as if wondering what her reasons were for so deceiving Sword. "You have no sister," the adept said. "You're the last of your line, Little Galen. The very last."

Sword turned back to Roth. "What are you talking about? What about my brother Brin?"

"*Brin!*" Roth's mouth twisted into a cruel smile. "Untie my hands and I'll show you about Brin."

"Don't release him, Mr. Sword," Orion warned.

"Not a chance," Sword agreed. Ko saw him take a long deep breath as if preparing for a plunge into deep water. "Now we're going to take this one step at a time, right from the very beginning." He spoke first to Orion. "What are you doing here in the daytime? I thought you were keeping track of the Tepesh?"

"Ah, but I am," Orion said. "And their spoor leads here."

"To the Loft?" Sword asked.

Ko thought she detected some slight defensive movement fluttering Diandra's green cape-coat. But she herself felt no heightened need for battle preparations. She wondered why, realizing that nothing seemed all that important any more.

"To this area," Orion amended. "But I can only conclude that this is to be their final objective. Once the sun has set."

Roth moved against the straps of the examination chair, as if testing their ability to hold him. "Of course this is their objective," he snapped at Sword. "Did you think Morgana would just let you take me and leave you alone as if nothing had happened? I told you once before, Little Galen. You have no place in the First World. And now you have sealed your fate just as miserably in the Second."

"I think not, Victor of Arkady," Orion said.

Roth's response was a snarl. "*Ory'on s'yshench ka!*"

"Shall I take you now?" Orion moved imperceptibly closer to the adept. "And make all that you are a part of me? Do you think that will please your consort Morgana? And what of Manes Hel when she learns that the last child of Isis has absorbed all the secrets of Arkady and its

241

dealings with the Tepesh? Do you think the Victor of Tepesh will then spare *any* of your line?" Orion opened his mouth and his feeding fangs slid slowly from behind his human-normal teeth. "If you are so eager to join the undead, Mr. Roth, I would be pleased to oblige."

Ko was struck by the sudden and deep silence in the room. She heard only the faint, metallic chime of 'Bub's collar as Martin succeeded in fastening the green-leather band with its clear-crystal pendant around 'Bub's neck and a twenty-pound Persian cat materialized once more in a flurry of bright sparks. But that was all. And, except for Diandra, whose attention had finally moved from Orion to Roth's cases, everyone else seemed frozen, waiting. Ko roused herself with an effort.

"Sword, if the Tepesh are planning on attacking, shouldn't you be doing something?" she asked. She hoped someone was ready to fight vampires again. She certainly wasn't.

Sword shook his head. "We're ready for them, Melody. We have been for weeks." He looked at Roth. "I'm not the child you sent away." Sword turned his back on Roth, clapped his hands. "Okay, everyone, this is how it's going to go down. Diandra?"

Ko stared at Diandra. One of Roth's cases was open before her and Martin had backed off into a corner. *How'd she do that?* Ko recalled her own inability to open those cases. She'd not wanted to force them, but it was as if they'd been super-glued shut. "What are you doing with that?" she asked.

But before Diandra could answer her, a familiar sound jarred them. Ko and Sword gave a half laugh together.

"What is it?" Orion asked.

"The front doorbell." Ko walked over to a security panel. "You think the Tepesh vampires would use it to make their first move on us?"

"As a matter of fact," Orion said seriously, "that might be the first thing they'd do."

DARK HUNTER

TWENTY-FOUR

So I'm not the only one to know about the residual binding chant on this building, the hunter thought as she heard Orion answer Ko. *But a Tepesh battle cadre would not be stopped by such a flimsy enchantment. They can breach this building's threshold at any time. Only a staid and conservative remnant from an earlier time would still be bound by the honor of the chant on this building.*

She looked at Orion, the last of his clan, and felt oddly moved. The first time Orion had entered her brother's Loft, he must have waited for Galen to give him permission and the nightfeeder now mistakenly believed that the Tepesh must do the same.

Orion quickly looked away from her, but not before his intent gaze stirred the hunter's interest. *He looked away from me that night in the alley,* she remembered. *I wonder why? I wonder what disturbs him?*

"A courier," Ko announced with a lethargic sigh. "I'll handle it." The hunter saw the image of a human female on a television screen on the wall near Ko.

"No!" the hunter said. "If there are Tepesh out there — "

"Then they would have come in the same way Orion did." Ko gestured upstairs, using her good hand. "Through the bedroom window on the fourth floor."

243

But Orion shook his head. "They would not come through there, Ko. I myself could not have entered easily if 'Bub had not opened the bars for me. The way across the upper wall is too exposed."

Ko grimaced. "'Bub *opened* the bars for you?"

The entry buzzer rang again.

"I'm coming, I'm coming," Ko said. The hunter saw the nightfeeder take up position next to the entrance to the lab as Ko left and headed down the stairs. Forsyte made no move to follow, staying quietly beside the hunter in his chair, without explanation.

The hunter spoke quickly. "Galen, she must not open the door."

"It's okay, Diandra. She won't have to. We get couriers here five times a day — there's an armored exchange slot they can put the package through. I've tested it with Martin and it's secure."

"And how are you preparing to fight them?" the hunter asked, wondering why her brother did not fear the Tepesh.

Her brother looked over at Roth who had been following everything intently. "It's a surprise," he said. "Now, about that case? How did you open it? Even Martin couldn't open those things."

The hunter held up the lighter of the two cases for her brother to see, displaying its contents — Second World currency. "A simple pressure lock, well-hidden. First World design." What the hunter did not tell her brother was that a living lock could not be opened by mere blue power such as a halfling might possess, and forcing the case could be deadly for the unaware. For such a lock to be detected and its threat neutralized, a contract had to exist between the Light Clans and the one who sought to open it. Fortunately, the hunter had had many dealings with the Lights.

Sword whistled and reached into the black case to pull out a banded stack of American hundred dollar bills. He riffled the stack expertly, then looked back at the case, at its dimensions. "Could be more than half a million in there."

Six hundred thousand to be exact, the hunter thought. *Precisely what we agreed to, precisely what I need.*

"What's this for, Roth?" Sword asked the adept bound to the chair.

But Roth's attention was on the hunter.

DARK HUNTER

The hunter knew she had to let the elemental know what he should expect, so he would be ready when the moment came. "I am Clan of Deep Forest," she said to him. *Your sins of the past are no longer of concern to me,* she thought and tried to believe that she truly felt that. "I have taken the Vow of the Hunt."

Roth's face was a mask, though the hunter knew the adept was now worried that he was her personal prey, their business relationship notwithstanding. Sword's face merely showed puzzlement.

The hunter watched her brother drop the stack of bills back into the first case, and pick up the second, heavier case. "What's the vow of the hunt?" he asked.

"The Congress of the Hunt must remain neutral in the politics of the First World."

"Like Switzerland in World War II?" Sword asked as the hunter heard two sets of footsteps on the metal stairs leading up from the garage below. Next to the doorway, the nightfeeder moved into fighting stance.

Not a precise analogy but close enough, the hunter thought. She nodded in agreement. Then she saw Roth smile as her brother examined the second case, looking for some way to open it. "So where's this hidden lock?" Sword asked.

The hunter took the case from her brother before his ignorance could harm him and ran her finger along its edge, locating the blue-bound catch that would unseal the top fold. The catch dissolved beneath her fingers and a single Light escaped, its flight unnoticed by all but the hunter and Roth. And by the halfling who ooohed softly in his corner.

The hunter handed the open case to her brother who pulled back its top cover to reveal a black-silk-wrapped object resting on crimson-like embers. The hunter was pleased. It seemed Arkady was prepared to live up to the full terms of its contract.

"I advise you not let him touch a thing in that case," Roth warned the hunter sharply.

Why? the hunter wondered. *He can't activate any crystal that is not already primed, not if his powers have been suppressed.* But she erred on the side of caution. "He may be right, Galen," she said, using the voice

245

JUDITH & GARFIELD REEVES-STEVENS

of the familiar to express concern. "It could be dangerous." She held out her hand for the case.

Her brother did not look convinced, yet he gave the case back to her as Ko came back into the lab. She was carrying a brightly colored courier envelope. But, astoundingly, behind her was the courier — the black human female the hunter had seen on the Loft's television screen — listening intently to whatever she was hearing through the bright yellow headphones of her tape player.

Sword's voice was edged with anger. "Melody! What the hell are you doing?"

Ko reacted automatically in kind. "What the bloody hell does it look like I'm doing?" She waved the package. "I got the — "

"Why'd you let the courier in?" Sword asked. "You know — "

"What courier?" Ko answered, turning around to see what everyone was staring at behind her, then jerked in surprise to see the courier, whose head was nodding back and forth in time to unheard music. "Where the hell did you come from?"

Forsyte began to roll forward in his chair, toward Ko, but Sword motioned him back, as if to say that he would handle this. "Have you been here before?" he asked the courier. But the courier did not answer. Her head stopped its rocking motion, steadied, as her eyes suddenly focused on Roth in his chair.

"Untie me!" the adept shouted at her, cursing and struggling in his restraints.

An Arkady lackey come to free Roth? the hunter wondered. *But how had she gained entrance?*

"Yes!" Orion exclaimed. "I remember her. She was there!"

The courier turned her head toward the nightfeeder.

"When I came to this city," Orion said. "On the street corner when the bloodlust came unexpectedly and I imprinted against my will."

The courier brought her hands to her yellow earphones.

"At Rockefeller Center," Sword added. "When I was talking with Kennie. She was there, too!"

The hunter saw her brother and the nightfeeder look at each other in startled comprehension.

"Sword," Ko said slowly. "I swear I didn't — "

246

DARK HUNTER

Enchantment, the hunter thought. Ko had *let* her in. At once, the hunter focused on the courier's neck, searching for the telltale glow of shifter's crystal that would foretell a coming shift. And did not find it.

With an apprehension she had rarely felt, the hunter realized that what Ko had given entrance to was worse than any shifter.

The courier pulled her yellow earphones off, and with them long strands of skin from her scalp and her face. Great stringy webs of tissue, glistening where they lifted from the underlying bone and muscle. Quickly followed by clothes cascading from her body like discarded skin shed by a moulting serpent as the courier turned herself inside out until whatever corporeal shape she retained was spread thick with an oozing, oily darkness — less than solid, more than liquid — and she was before them in her hidden aspect of —

Seyshen.

Even as the nightfeeder blurred across her vision, the hunter drew a perfect breath.

In an instant, Little Galen, the humans, and one half-human stilled, trapped in a realm where the passage of time was measured not by their minds, but by the slowness of their bodies and their limited reflexes. But the three unbound adepts in the room accelerated.

The hunter counted her heartbeats.

One. The Seyshen slid to the floor like a black wave of oil collapsing on a beach, its many feet propelling it forward — toward its target.

Like a bolt of crystal's lightning, the nightfeeder streaked for the Seyshen, before Ko was even able to turn toward a storage locker.

A pair of tethered darts from Forsyte's chair snaked through the air, fired expertly though uselessly, homing in on the spot where the Seyshen had first stood. *A worthy effort,* the hunter acknowledged, as she tore the black silk from the object in Roth's second case.

Two. The Seyshen became a twisting, coiling rope avoiding contact with Orion. *As if a nightfeeder had a chance,* the hunter thought. Then, incredibly, she saw her brother begin to charge the Seyshen. Preceded by the halfling — whose reflexes, though slower than a full-born's, were faster than her brother's.

Roth — the Seyshen's target — desperately wrenched his arms up the sides of his chair so that he could see his hands, the move flaying the

247

skin from his wrists. Even as the elemental began to draw shapes in the air, the hunter knew that his power would be too little, too late.

Three. The Seyshen rose up, lifting from the floor in a towering arc over Roth's struggling body. Hundreds of glittering diamond-tipped claws and fang-rimmed mouths burst through the creature's slick black surface.

But the Clan Arkady *had* honored its commitment to the hunter and the two cases contained *everything* that she had demanded. The hunter's new windblade sang its freedom and bisected the Seyshen before it could engulf Roth.

Two lesser Seyshen dropped from the air, whole and complete, then scattered in confusion when the hunter called her windblade back.

Diandra split the first lesser Seyshen in two from head end to midsection as she swung her windblade lengthwise down its back. This time, she left her blade in place and let it continue singing until the lesser Seyshen vibrated with the hidden notes of the blade, becoming mist, then dying wind.

The hunter turned to seek the second Seyshen.

But it had been chased off by another warrior.

Coat open, silk shirt torn, deep wounds scourging his chest, the nightfeeder leaned back against a wall of equipment that blinked and flashed with lights. But the hunter knew that Orion could heal himself.

She exhaled.

Ko, Martin, and Sword flew out of the lab after the escaping Seyshen. Shocked at last into action, Ko now brandished a shotgun.

Hunched protectively by Forsyte's overturned chair, ears flat and fangs bared, was the creature her brother had called 'Bub. Though the chair lay on its side, the physicist was still strapped into it, unharmed.

The hunter turned back to Roth, still in his chair. "If you want to live, you must trust me," she told him. "*Will* the Tepesh attack to save you?"

A shotgun blast echoed in the Loft. The halfling bayed.

"They had better, for what I've paid them," Roth growled, then looked at her with some fear. "Who *are* you? I know you're not his sister."

The hunter refused his question. "Can you call off the attack?" she demanded.

Roth shook his head. "I'm not in contact with them."

Swiftly, the hunter chose her strategy. No voice that she could use would affect an elemental with Roth's power. So she chose his and her self-interest. "Remain in your bonds. Wait until I have dealt with the Seyshen."

"What about Orion? You have a contract with Arkady!"

"And I shall deliver him to you as promised. But only if you follow my counsel."

The hunter dropped the green cloak from her shoulders, then touched the silver clansign emblazoned on the shoulder of her shadow-suit.

She saw Roth's eyes widen as the entwined dragon and sword of the sign flared with light.

"*Pendragon!*" Roth whispered in shock. In fear.

But the dark hunter was no longer there.

TWENTY-FIVE

Ko's shotgun blast had no effect on Seyshen.

"Was that silver buckshot?" Sword asked Ko in the lowest-pitched voice he could manage. His heart pounded from the run down the stairs to the floor of the Loft's garage. The half-sized Seyshen now flowed ceaselessly around the edges of the closed garage door, exploring every crack and crevice, looking for escape. At least Sword thought that's what the dark shadow was doing.

Ko gasped for breath. "Yes." She held out the chopped-down Remington. "Here, I can't fire again." Sword shook his head even as Martin presented his reason for refusal.

"Silver no work Seyshen," Martin growled as on all fours he circled off to the right of the garage door.

Somehow, Sword knew, there was a technique for up-close battle with the Seyshen. He just couldn't remember what it was. Or whether it worked all the time.

"How could you let it in, Melody?" Sword whispered to Ko, motioning to her to stay back and leave the Seyshen to him and Martin.

"I don't know."

Ko's words were slurred. "I can't ... I can't even remember opening the package slot, let alone the door."

She's acting disoriented, Sword thought as, without weapons, he began circling to the left. *Just as she did when she was under Brin's enchantment.*

As he moved to back up Martin, Sword tried to keep his eye on the shifting shadow that was the Seyshen. But there was something about its shape that made it difficult to fix on. *Maybe the Seyshen also have the power to confuse,* he reasoned. That would explain the courier's presence on the New York city street-corner when Orion had imprinted on a stranger, and in the Rockefeller Center Plaza courtyard when he had told Kendall Marsh about the Tepesh blood clinic. *Both were mistakes. Major mistakes. And the courier was nearby both times.*

"Don't worry, Melody," he said over his shoulder, attempting to sound positive. "We've faced them before, we can face them again."

But even at the end of her resources, Ko was Ko. "Who're you kidding, Sword? The last time we saw Seyshen, we were running for our lives through a fardoor."

Sword looked to the other member of his team, on the other side of the garage door. "Martin, any suggestions?" he called out softly.

"Open door. Seyshen leave."

Sword was tempted. But there was a problem with Martin's plan. "Could be Tepesh out there."

Martin shook his head vigorously. "Daytime, Galen Sword. Nightfeeders sleep." Then he whuffed in surprise as a voice behind him said, "I think not, halfling."

Orion had joined them.

He stood behind Martin, without coat or shirt, Seyshen clawmarks no longer marring his smooth, muscled chest.

"Nightfeeders can function during daylight hours. It is only the sun we must avoid, not time." Orion moved to a central position facing the garage door. Now the Seyshen was constrained from three directions. "With all respect, Mr. Sword, I suggest you draw back."

The Seyshen stopped its probing instantly, flowed down to the floor, and began shifting back and forth like a great cat preparing to leap. It had oriented itself toward Sword.

Great! Orion's just identified me as the weakest of its three attackers! Sword crouched defensively, bracing for the creature's attack.

JUDITH & GARFIELD REEVES-STEVENS

But suddenly, the Seyshen shadow jerked, thrashing frantically on the end of a long silver thread driven deep into its body. Then the thread pulled taut, reeling in the beast, dragging it from the garage door like a hooked, wriggling worm on the end of a fishline held by invisible hands.

Diandra! Sword turned but saw no one — nothing.

Then the thread snapped free.

In the same instant, the Seyshen righted itself and streaked toward the garage door in a smear of darkness.

The door boomed as the fleeing Seyshen struck it, but the reinforced metal and Kevlar webbing held, unlike the last time when —

"That's it!" Sword rose up and shouted out to Ko who leaned against his Porsche. "Melody! When the garage door burst open and Saul Calder escaped, it was a Seyshen that destroyed the door!"

"You said it was an explosion," Ko's tired voice answered.

Again, the Seyshen smashed against the door, but this time with less energy. *Maybe we can actually catch it,* Sword thought in elation, rapidly working out what they could use to hold a living shadow.

"No, Melody! I *thought* it was an explosion. But you said it was something that had burst through from the *inside!* You — "

The Seyshen abruptly lifted into the air, spun around, and —

Something like a haze hovered around the squirming, squealing creature.

Sword's eyes narrowed, trying to bring the scene into focus but couldn't.

"Orion?" Sword asked. "Can you see my — "

But it was all over.

He blinked as light flared from a familiar clansign.

And then he saw the Seyshen — and his sister — clearly.

The Seyshen was hanging limp as if supported by a rope in mid-section, suspended in the same kind of netting Diandra had used to capture Martin.

His sister was in the bodysuit she'd worn when she'd slaughtered the trolls in the alley near the Tepesh enclave.

"Both lesser Seyshen are diminished," Diandra announced. Then she pulled a long, pipe-shaped implement from the side of her leg —

252

DARK HUNTER

Sword couldn't see if there was some sort of holster there — and jabbed the Seyshen's body with it. The creature became a silver flare, and when the light of it faded, the Seyshen was gone.

"Mr. Sword, did you say that Seyshen were in here earlier?" Orion asked.

Sword nodded, on the point of asking Diandra what she had done with the Seyshen's body, and why various pieces of her equipment seemed to disappear every time she attached them to her suit. But the vampire pressed for more details, so Sword told him about the capture of Saul Calder before the Arkady Ceremony of the Change, and how the shifter had been waiting for them when they had returned to the Loft.

"And then," Sword said, "just as we thought Calder might shift again, the bottom panel of the garage door burst open and Calder escaped."

"So the Seyshen was already *in* here when you returned?" Orion asked as Martin, Ko, and Diandra approached to join him and Sword. "You're certain you don't recall any sense of confusion? Any sense that the Seyshen might have tricked you into letting it in when it was in its open aspect, appearing human?"

Martin was adamant. "No headache Martin. No Seyshen trick." For some reason — which Sword would have liked explained, and which wasn't — Orion accepted Martin's comment as proof that they were dealing with two groups of Seyshen. That the Seyshen who had helped Calder escape had not entered Sword's Loft in the same way as the courier — by simple confusion of human senses.

"Then it is as I feared," Orion said, scanning the garage swiftly. "There is another way into this building than those used by humans."

"Something in the basement?" Sword asked. He could see that even Diandra looked disturbed by Orion's conclusion. At least, he assumed it was Orion's conclusion that made her appear so concerned. "Other streets, other passages?"

"No, no Galen Sword. Martin check. Martin find nothing. Martin keep Galen Sword."

"I know what it is," Ko said slowly, her listless voice a monotone. "When I came back here after the hospital that first time ... when everyone had gone to the blood clinic ... "

253

"Brin was waiting for you here," Sword said. "That's what you told us."

"He wasn't waiting for me, Sword," Ko said crossly. "I said he came in while I was here. I had a yellow crystal. A waiting crystal, Brin called it — "

"So that's what happened to it," Orion said.

"I was looking at it and I saw, I saw a, you know, one of those flickers, like a — "

"Fardoor," Sword said. The adrenaline of the day receded in him, replaced in turn by an arctic chill. Fardoors could lead anywhere, from anywhere. And if there was an operational one in the Loft ...

Orion spoke to Diandra without looking at her. "Hunter, do you have detectors? Viewing planes? Telling threads?"

"I have threads," Diandra said. Her admission sounded reluctant to Sword, sparking his interest.

"And the glass fragments from the pyramid glass," Ko continued as if no one else had spoken. "Brin said it was a type of viewing plane."

Orion nodded. "Good. We can use both methods to detect First World influences in the Second."

He turned to Sword. "I suggest we gather the items together at once. We must examine each surface in the Loft for the signs of a fardoor."

But Sword held the group together a moment longer. "But to set up a fardoor, doesn't that mean that a wizard has to have been in here? Don't you need a wizard at both ends to establish the connection?"

"I should check on Roth," Diandra said suddenly, heading for the staircase that led up to the main lab.

Ko followed her with a halting step. "I'd better check on Adrian."

Sword stayed put. And so did Martin. "What about the wizards, Orion?"

"In most cases, yes, Mr. Sword," the vampire agreed, restless to begin their search. "You need wizards to set the portals and align the doors."

"But not in all cases?" Sword wanted to call Ko back so she could hear this. But she was already halfway up the first flight of stairs.

"Not all," Orion admitted with a sigh. "If a portal is already established at one end and its mate is collapsed, then a wizard need only work on a replacement mate."

DARK HUNTER

"Which is how the Tepesh installation was able to reestablish contact with the fardoor in the Pit of the Change," Sword said as at his side, Martin growled fiercely but softly at the mere mention of the Pit.

"There was already a portal in place on the cave wall," Sword added.

"Exactly, Mr. Sword," Orion said impatiently and turned to follow Ko and Diandra. "Now we *must* hurry before the sun sets and the Tepesh are free to leave their hiding places."

Have wizards been at work in the Loft every time I've been away from it? Sword touched Orion's arm to hold him back another moment longer, then just as quickly pulled his hand away as he saw swift affront flash in the vampire's dark-green eyes. "The fardoors, Orion," he said apologetically, but urgently. "Are there any other cases when wizards aren't needed?"

"Short distances, yes," Orion said stiffly. "To cast a fardoor with only a few feet of separation doesn't even require a wizard. With the proper crystals, almost anyone can do it. Almost any adept, I mean. Now really, we must — "

"A fardoor that only goes a few feet? What good is that?"

The tips of Orion's feeding fangs appeared, then disappeared. "Walls, Mr. Sword. Ceilings, floors, crystal vaults, take your pick!"

"Walls ... " Sword repeated. "We didn't ask where Melody saw the flicker of Brin's fardoor. We — "

Orion wheeled to look at the wall behind him, beyond the staircase. "Who owns the building next to you, Mr. Sword?"

"Some Swiss consortium. Why?" Sword asked, puzzled. "They won't sell it to me. I've tried."

"I suggest you try again. The first time I came here I thought I detected — "

Three flickering openings appeared on the wall the Loft shared with the warehouse next door.

" — oh Isis!"

Movement behind that wall. Then through it.

The Tepesh attacked.

255

TWENTY-SIX

The hunter advanced up the stairs with the swiftness of the forest wind. How could her brother be so witless as to seek battle with First World forces and *not* have his enclave sealed to a visit of doors? Even if the Tepesh were not grouping to attack this moment, it was doubtful Galen could survive more than another cycle, so complete was his ignorance.

Dr. Forsyte still lay powerless on his side on the floor as the hunter reached the lab. Roth remained in the examination chair, though the hunter knew at once the chair's restraints had been reformed. The elemental was free. She looked to the desk. The cases were still there.

Roth stared at her, the question unspoken but communicated to the hunter. The adept knew she was Pendragon, and with that, her true identity within the clan. "Your payment is untouched. Deliver the nightfeeder and you may take it as agreed."

The hunter called the hilt of the windblade to her hand and leaned down to withdraw the weapon from the lab's floor and the dark puddle of evaporating sludge that had been the first of the lesser Seyshen.

"The Tepesh will come through fardoors," the hunter said, to confirm her suspicion.

Roth nodded. "Many clans have been interested in Little Galen's fate. Arkady enlisted the help of the Tepesh. It is likely the Tepesh have enlisted the help of another clan to arrange access to this enclave." Roth

DARK HUNTER

tilted his head as both he and the hunter heard the first faint sound from below. "I smell magic. You should deliver the nightfeeder before the Tepesh do it for you."

The hunter looked to the lab's entry door but saw only Ko, righting Forsyte's chair as if she and the physicist were alone in the room.

"Enchanted by Brin and confused by a Seyshen," Roth said with a sneer. "But the stupid creature'll be even worse than that when the Tepesh are through with her."

Ko wheeled Forstye from the lab without once looking back. The sounds from the garage below were stronger now and the hunter had to counsel herself against the distraction. "That Seyshen," she reminded Roth, "might have been tracking Orion and Galen in past weeks, but not today. Today, it was sent in here to kill you."

Such an assassination attempt spoke to the hunter of something more than just a war between Arkady and the Seyshen. *What other stakes are involved here?* she wondered. *And for what reason?*

Roth shook off his restraints, stood, and stretched. The hunter knew her assessment of the Seyshen's purpose was true. *But why?*

"Your imaginings are so much fairy glamor." Roth touched his hands to the bruises and scratches on his face. The flare of his blue power flashed beneath his palms and when he took his hands away, his skin and features were unmarred.

The hunter heard voices shouting from the garage. Her brother's voice among them.

But Roth did not pay them heed. He was studying Diandra.

"So the girl-child does live. Was it Kostas?" He snapped his fingers. "No! It was Alexander! Before the fire consumed him entirely. Old fool gave you to the gargoyles of the Congress of the Hunt. Pledged you to them for transversion and training. All so the line might continue."

The elemental ran his hands over his other wounds. Both of his hands blazed with blue fire. "Old fool thought you'd be safe there."

"I *am* safe." The hunter held her windblade ready.

"Only as long as you keep to your vows."

Roth's face took on his inner essence — dark, foreboding. "There's one too many Swords in the Worlds already. And you are not your brother."

257

In silence they faced each other, each ready to risk all. For honor. Or revenge.

The hunter broke the confrontation first, knowing this time and place were wrong. She melted the windblade into her shadowsuit.

"I have friends in Deep Forest," the hunter warned Roth.

Roth's eyes flickered. He understood the threat. "As do I," he countered. "Among the Tarls."

The hunter gasped. "You lie! The Tarls are fallen! Destroyed ages ago! Swallowed by the moon!"

"Oh, no, hunter." The elemental mage stood against the lab's backdrop of Second World computers and technology, and that part of the hunter that still remembered the superstitions of childhood felt a momentary thrill of fear. "Your mind's been clouded by the misguided lessons of your rooted friends. No matter what the legends might say, the Tarls did *not* fall. And they were *never* defeated. They simply ... withdrew for a time, to a safer place." Roth ran his hand over the blinking lights of the computer equipment beside him, as if aware how much discomfort such action would cause her. "And now," he said quietly, "that time of withdrawal has passed." For an instant, the adept's eyes seemed to flash red with the ancient madness that the Rings had promised could never exist again, so thoroughly had it been banished from the Worlds.

"The Tarls *are* coming back," the elemental vowed, "and not even those of the forest will be safe when they have returned."

Then, deliberately brushing the hunter on his way past her to the door, Roth turned in the entrance to the lab. "We both know the rules we're playing by now. If you'll excuse me, it's time to watch the carnage." And then he turned his back on her and headed down the staircase to savor the defeat of her unwitting brother.

The hunter stood alone in silence, terrified by the meaning of Roth's revelation for the survival of Deep Forest, Dajara, the Ark, and the Rings.

Until the silence was broken by the first screams of mortal agony.

TWENTY-SEVEN

Twelve Tepesh warriors had breached the Loft's threshold. They'd come through three fardoors linked to the adjacent warehouse, prepared for a degree of First World violence known only in nightmares to the Second. Their faces were hidden by Tepesh battlemasks — intricate helmets of elemental iron, spiked and barbed, each visor set with the Tepesh clan-sign of golden web and blood-black stone. The iron of their chainmail shirts and spiked boots and gloves chimed in perfect unison as the cadre of vampire-adepts spread apart in attack formation.

And then their leader stepped through the fardoor.

"You've gone too far this time," Morgana LaVey hissed at Sword, her yellow reptilian eyes glinting with the appetites of a mind trapped within its primeval inner layer. Her shifterform tongue slithering from her humanform lips, its forked tip tasting the air for the scent of his fear.

But Sword felt none. He waved at the Tepesh warriors with his shotgun. "Tell your mercenaries to get out while they still can."

The Tepesh vampires shifted from foot to foot, preparing for their leader's order to attack. But Morgana beckoned instead to an unseen other to come through the fardoor.

Saul Calder.

JUDITH & GARFIELD REEVES-STEVENS

"Let me have him first, my Victor," the shifter begged. "The monster killed my Simone."

But Morgana ran her fingers along the fringe of scales stippling her neck that became human skin only when they reached her cheek. "No! Little Galen is mine first!" She motioned to the Tepesh cadre to advance with her.

Sword stood shoulder to shoulder beside Orion, with Martin crouched before them.

"I'll give you five seconds to call them off, Morgana," he said, as the Tepesh warriors began to to encircle their position. Sword didn't even bother to raise his shotgun. It wasn't necessary.

"I'll give you five hundred years of hell," the Victor of Arkady promised as she raised her arm to give her signal. "I swear you will writhe on the Lesser Heart of my altar until my shift can be completed."

"Two seconds," Sword said.

Morgana turned to address the Tepesh. "Remember, warriors! I give you the substanceless traitor to the Worlds who destroyed your enclave above the city!"

The silence of the Tepesh cadre was as ferocious as any battle cry.

"Last chance," Sword said, lifting his hand.

Morgana's voice rose higher. "Remember also, warriors — the only child of Isis — the sworn enemy of your Victor!"

The Tepesh warriors broke their silence. *"Tepesh! Arkadych!"*

Sword pressed the call button on his locator band. "Adrian, *now!*"

But nothing happened.

"Adrian? Melody? Anytime ... ."

Though the Tepesh were still ten feet away, Sword imagined he could feel the heat of their breath. *The Seyshen must have done something to Adrian.* It was the only explanation. They had tested the new installations too many times for them to break down now.

Beside him, Orion blurred into fighting stance. "You see, Mr. Sword, this is exactly why I do not trust technology. Give me crystal any day."

"Make it slow," Morgana shrieked at her forces, her arm straining upward. "Give them time to know their punishment for crimes against me!"

260

DARK HUNTER

One by one, in quick succession, the Tepesh raised their visors and the heat this time was real. It came from the fighting eyes of warriors born.

That searing light. The pure fire of combat. Sword knew he had seen it many times before, in many faces ... Uncle Alexander ... the old warrior who had saved him from Seth as a child ... and ... *Who else? Where else? In my father's face? My mother's? My own?*

And then a new sound brought new hope to Sword. The sound of chair treads on metal. He looked up to the second-level walkway. *Forsyte! And Ko!*

"*Now!*" Sword's throat burned with the force of his shout. "*Activate now!*"

Morgana dropped her arm.

The Tepesh vampires sprang.

And then in the shadows of the Loft's garage —

— the sun came up.

JUDITH & GARFIELD REEVES-STEVENS

TWENTY-EIGHT

It *was* a massacre but the hunter had never seen its like before.

From each ceiling and the top of each wall in the Loft, in the garage and on the levels above, blinding blue-white light blazed forth from hundreds of mundane, Second World electrical fixtures.

The irises of the hunter's eyes compressed to pinpoints as all color and shadow disappeared in the onslaught of light.

Behind her, she saw Roth throw up his arms to cover his face.

In front of her, Ko squeezed her own eyes shut, using both her hands to cover Forsyte's.

Diandra listened carefully as the whole Loft buzzed with the sudden load of electricity that coursed through its circuitry to power the lights, the low, pervasive hum overlaid by the anguished screams of Tepesh drowning in a flood of ultraviolet radiation.

From her second-level vantage point, the hunter made her calculations. *Fifteen seconds at most.* It was doubtful the warriors could hold their somatic integrity for much longer than that. *So much for Orion,* she thought, then remembered what Dajara had told her: *Orion continues.* She had never known her parent to be wrong before. She hoped that meant Dajara had been wrong about both Worlds being finished, too.

262

DARK HUNTER

The hunter heard a dull, mechanical *thunk* from somewhere deep in the basements of the Loft. The blazing lights faded. The killing field stilled.

She saw twelve empty suits of Tepesh battle armor in the center of the concrete floor, dull-white dust visible through the links of crumpled chainmail. A few helmets still rocked back and forth.

The hunter contemplated the loss of thousands of years of First World battle experience and the final loss of the thousands of lives the Tepesh warriors had consumed and prolonged within them. All gone in seconds because of her brother and his Second World technology.

In front of her, Ko leaned over the railing. "Again?"

And then the hunter saw her brother and his halfling step back to reveal —

The nightfeeder! Alive! Within the shadow of Galen and *Myrchn'tin*. His beautiful back blistered, scarlet, streaked with blood from deep fissures, but still he lived. *Orion continues.*

"How?" The hunter started, surprised that she had spoken her question aloud.

"It's a ritual he has," Ko answered. "He insists on facing the sun every day. Sword had us test him. He can last up to a minute under those lights."

"Aren't you going to do something about him?" Ko asked, indicating Roth who stood rigid, stunned at the scene below the catwalk, muttering something in a hidden tongue unfamiliar to the hunter.

"Don't worry," the hunter said. "I'm going to do something." She held out her catapult tube and sent her climbing wire out to an overhanging bar that appeared to be reinforced. Then she swung out over the railing, down to the garage floor, where she landed softly beside her brother. And Orion.

As she called her wire to return to the tube, her eyes were drawn to the sight of the nightfeeder's body restoration, the process proceeding more rapidly than any blue power or wizard's crystal could work. She felt the sudden impulse to reach out and stroke Orion's smooth golden skin as it regained its impossible perfection. But even as she firmly suppressed the thought, she became aware of a savage keening cry.

263

It issued from the Victor of Arkady who stood in the pile of Tepesh dust and chainmail.

Morgana LaVey turned on her attendant shifter. "You've *been* here! You've *fought* here! You told me it was safe!" she cried accusingly.

The hunter recognized the shifter who had approached her in the Hong Kong alley — Saul Calder, he'd said, was his open name.

Calder stepped back, trembling. "Victor, the lights weren't here before. Next time — "

The shifter's words and heartbeats ended in an instant as his victor's taloned hands converged on his throat and swung away with gobbets of flesh speared upon them.

His decomposition began mere seconds later.

Shaking her hands free of shifterdust, Morgana looked up at Roth on the catwalk and hissed, "You're gaping like a gilled one — *do* something!"

Roth found his voice again. He stared down at the hunter. "It is not up to me."

The hunter knew what the elemental wanted. The moment had come to seal the bargain. "Will you leave without further violence?" she called up to Roth.

Naturally, her brother did not understand what he was witnessing. "Diandra, what do you mean 'leave'? We've got them — "

The hunter held out her hand to silence him. "Will you leave?" she repeated formally to Roth.

She saw Roth eye both Ko and Forsyte beside him on the catwalk, before calling back down to her again. "If you will do the same," he said.

The hunter nodded. She had no intention of doing anything else. She did not plan to return to her brother's enclave. Ever.

"No one's leaving," her brother insisted. But no one of First World was listening to him. Their eyes were on the hunter as — with the forest deep within her, hiding her intentions — she reached into the pouch on her equipment harness and brought out a fully-charged red crystal — a 120 whole.

And before anyone — even the nightfeeder — had time to see her move, the hunter slapped the crystal against Orion's bare chest.

DARK HUNTER

Instantly, a shimmering nimbus of pale blue fire engulfed the night-feeder's body to render it perfectly immobile.

The hunter heard the Victor of Arkady's hiss of pleasure.

Galen's halfling reached out to slap Orion's leg experimentally. When nothing moved, he snorted, "Stupid nightfeeder."

Both reactions were predictable to the hunter, but her brother's was not. He ripped the crystal from Orion's chest, then stared at the stone as if expecting something more to happen. What, the hunter did not know, since the crystal's charge had been completely transferred to the nightfeeder. What she did know was that unless her brother knew more about himself than she guessed he did, it would take a more gifted counter to reverse the chant she'd placed on Orion.

"You coldblasted him," Sword exclaimed, outraged, as if the hunter had tried to do the same to him. "Why?"

The hunter called up to Roth again. "Bring the cases with you." Then spoke to her brother. "Do not interfere. This has nothing to do with you."

On the second-level catwalk, Roth rushed back to the main lab and reappeared almost instantly with the two cases. He carried one case by its handle, the other under the same arm. In his free hand, he held something out.

"Melody!" Sword shouted to his associate. "Do something! Stop him!"

But Roth had already unleashed a blast of seething red energy that sent Ko stumbling back against Forsyte's chair.

The hunter looked into the barrel of her brother's shotgun. "Diandra, what is this?" he demanded. "Are you working with — "

The hunter's snare leapt from her harness, snicked the weapon from her brother's hands, and returned it to her own as Roth ran down the stairs and toward her. In his free hand, the elemental held a fist-sized red crystal. It was the weapon he had used on Ko.

The hunter pulled out a packet of burning resin from her bodysuit and poured it on the shotgun, then she tossed the gun away. Flames engulfed her brother's weapon before it hit the ground.

265

Roth placed the two cases at the hunter's feet, then held the single crystal out to her. "This one is a bit less than a full charge. I trust you will not complain."

The hunter took the crystal and placed it with the others.

"Are those *payment?*" her brother asked.

"That's right, you clever boy," Roth said mockingly. "I'm paying your sister six thousand whole, six thousand in three, and six hundred thousand in American currency. An auspicious number of sixes, I'd say. Especially considering that little white number that you have upstairs in a clear crystal bond. Oh, and don't forget the new windblade. Clan Skye. The best that glitter can buy."

"But payment for what? For leading you to *me?*"

Roth put his arm tenderly around Morgana's shoulders. The Victor had moved to stand beside Orion's coldblasted form. "You?" the adept said scornfully. "We've known where you've been since you brought *Sulcadr'tin* here. And believe me, others have known even longer. Oh no, Little Galen, your sister earned her generous payment for bringing us Orion — in a form suitable for shipment — as a little something for Manes Hel. Thanks to your meddling, Arkady has a great many fences to mend and even more favors to repay."

The hunter forestalled her brother's abrupt move toward her by drawing her windblade from her side.

"You wouldn't," Sword said hotly. The hunter saw the halfling move, resolute, to her brother's side.

"An arm, a leg, I would," the hunter said, with a stern glance at the halfling. "And on this side of the layer you wouldn't have a wizard to help you grow them back, either."

"By betraying me, by helping Roth, you're betraying Pendragon," her brother protested in disbelief. "You're betraying our family."

The hunter picked up the cases as Roth had done, using one arm, leaving the other free. "I am a hunter. I have no family. I choose no sides but my own. I advise you to give up."

"Never," Sword said and the defiance in his voice was almost worthy of the forest.

The hunter took pity on him. He could not be expected to behave as she had learned to. "You cannot succeed and you cannot survive," the

DARK HUNTER

hunter said. "Give up and in fifty cycles I will return and tell you all that I know about our family."

"A better offer than you'd get from us, clanless one," Roth taunted.

But Sword drew himself up, in a warrior's stance, as if not all his First World instincts had been erased along with his memories. "It appears I know more about our family than you do, Diandra. I will never give up."

The hunter nodded, knowing it was useless. The forest and the Ark called to her. She started toward the entry alcove leading to the streets.

"Hunter!" Roth called out. "Why not come with us, through the layer?" Morgana tugged at her consort's arm, frowning.

The hunter paused. "Those fardoors extend only through the wall. The layer is nowhere near here."

"No, no," Roth said. "Watch this." He pushed Orion over so the nightfeeder fell on his back, still frozen in a standing posture. Then with his fingers he drew a sign of lightness in the air — much to the hunter's disgust — and Orion's body began to levitate beside Morgana. "You may follow us, if you prefer," the adept said, as he and Morgana, with Orion between them, headed for the three glowing fardoors on the Loft's common wall.

A moment later, the hunter moved past her brother and the halfling, while up on the walkway she saw Ko on her feet again, though dazed, and Forsyte, already propelling his mechanical chair toward the elevator.

Roth approached the three flickering fardoors through which the hunter saw the empty warehouse that shared a wall with her brother's Loft. The elemental leaned forward to two of the fardoors, dragging his finger through their shadowline perimeters, collapsing their openings like soap bubbles.

"You've left one-way fardoors on the other side of the wall," the hunter said coldly. There was no worse death in either world than stepping into a one-sided fardoor. It took one everywhere, forever, all at once.

But the adept was unconcerned. "They will dissipate in minutes. But here, watch this one." Roth used his fingers to describe the figures of the moon before the third fardoor's opening. The hunter watched his actions disapprovingly. *It is unnatural for an elemental to do this.* She wondered who had dared to teach him. But whoever had, had taught him well.

The warehouse beyond the third fardoor flickered once, then shimmered away. For an instant, the fardoor's perimeter circled only the bare wall of the garage. Then it cleared again and opened onto a small area backed by a distant wall formed of large stone blocks. And as the air pressures adjusted with puffs of First World wind, the hunter caught the scent of oil-soaked torches and old magic. "You opened a door through the layer," she said, not even trying to hide her amazement. As far as she had known, only wizards possessed such skill.

"A simple matter really," Roth said airily. Then he guided Orion's floating body to the center of the fardoor's perimeter and pushed until the nightfeeder floated from one world to the next.

"Shall we?" Roth asked, bowing to the hunter, holding his consort back with one hand.

But the hunter recognized the look in Morgana's wild yellow eyes. In her half-fixed state, the Victor of Arkady would think nothing of collapsing the fardoor. And the hunter had no wish to be cut in half. *Still,* she thought, *it would be simpler to cross through the layer — then travel to the Folded Islands for the transfer back to Africa.*

"Please," the hunter gestured graciously, "let your Victor pass through first. Then you and I shall pass through together."

Roth glanced at his consort. Morgana had turned to stare in blind fury back at Sword. "A wise decision, hunter. Morgana? Shall you?"

Morgana half-growled, half-hissed, "I told you I wanted to punish the substanceless traitor."

The hunter tightened her grip on the hilt of her windblade.

"Soon, my dear. But we have made a pact that takes precedence and for the good of our clan we should keep it." Roth placed a hand on his consort's scaled back and eased her through the fardoor.

"Soon then," Morgana warned, but made no further protest as she left the Second World to return to the First. The hunter saw her on the other side, beside Orion's still-suspended body.

"Perhaps we should hold hands, hunter? To prevent an unfortunate separation?"

DARK HUNTER

The hunter knew Roth distrusted her as much as she distrusted him. She looked behind her, saw that her brother and the halfling had made no move toward the fardoor, and that Ko and Forsyte were still in the elevator cage, halfway between levels. There would be no more trouble here.

She turned back to Roth and let her windblade melt into her shadowsuit. She took his outstretched hand.

With his other, Roth saluted Sword. "Farewell, Little Galen. The last time I took my leave of you, I said that we would not meet again. This time, I guarantee that we *will*. And you will regret that, I promise." He paused on the edge of the fardoor. "Oh, and feel free to step through this perimeter once we've gone through. Just because we'll collapse it on the other side is no reason for you not to try this side out. Who knows? Perhaps you'll find what you left of Dmitri."

The hunter gripped Roth's hand firmly and hugged her cases close to her side. Once through the layer, she knew she could place most of the contents in her compression pockets, but the cases would do for now. She took one last look at her brother.

He stood, silent, one hand resting on the halfling's shoulder. The hunter found she could almost imagine how he'd look with the fighting fire in his eyes even though she knew that option was not his to claim because he had not trained from birth. *Still,* she thought, *he looks so much like the pictures I've seen of ... our mother.*

The hunter turned her back on her brother. She was no longer his sister. She was a hunter. And the Ark awaited her. Whatever she needed — wanted — was, as it had been forever — in Deep Forest.

Your paths are the same, Dajara had told her. But the hunter could not see how her path and Galen's would ever join again.

She was not her brother's keeper.

She stepped through the layer, free of Little Galen forever.

JUDITH & GARFIELD REEVES-STEVENS

TWENTY-NINE

Failure. It was all that Forsyte thought about now. All he could feel. The sum total of his abilities.

He emerged from the elevator, just as Morgana and Orion vanished through the fardoor. Ko stood silent beside his chair, as drained as she had been after the explosion in the MIT lab — his own lab, not Sword's.

What did we just see? Forsyte wondered resentfully. *Teleportation? Anti-gravity? Temporal stasis? All three at once? Is there not enough in the universe to be understood that we have to see these things as well, and know we may never have the chance to understand them?*

He nudged his chair's joystick to the side and back again to skirt a small mound of white powder on the garage floor. *And we have no name for that, either,* he thought crossly, knowing he had been witness to the destruction and creation of huge amounts of mass and energy, against all the tenets of his understanding of science. *No conception whatsoever of the powers at work in the death of ... of vampires.*

Sword and Martin were standing well back from the fardoor on the garage's common wall. Beside that fardoor Forsyte saw Sword's sister, hand in hand with Roth. Roth was speaking to her, though Forsyte could hear nothing of what he was saying.

Feeling that he would never understand anything anymore — except failure — Forsyte and the rest of Sword's team watched Roth and

Diandra disappear as they passed through the fardoor.

The background of the fardoor appeared to change in both color and lighting. Then its perimeter shivered and the bare garage wall returned. Only a flickering shadowline still remained.

Sword sprang toward it, with Martin right behind him.

Forsyte set his chair in action. A moment later, he heard Ko follow.

"Galen Sword not go through!" Martin clutched at Sword's shirt, pleading. "One-way! No other side! Galen Sword not come back!"

Sword stood facing the last remnant of the fardoor, his face dark with conflicting emotions.

The emotions of failure, Forsyte thought. *No wonder we're all still together. We're the same. All of us. Failures.*

He felt his chair shift slightly as Ko rested her damaged arm-cast on his chairback.

"Let it go, Sword," Ko said. "They got away again. Same as the last time. Same as the first time. Nothing to do but wait for them to come back a — "

Ko broke off as Sword reached out a hand to the flickering shadowline and a shimmer of blue sparks shot out, crackling, as if to ensnare him. Martin whimpered.

Forsyte pressed playback keys on his computer. "FARDOOR. ONE-SIDED. BE CAREFUL, GALEN."

"It's *closed,* Adrian," Sword said. "And that means it can be *opened.*" He turned to look at Martin.

The halfling cringed, crouched down, hiding his head in his arms. "No, no. Martin not wizard. Martin fall through door."

Sword knelt down in front of the halfling. "There's no more hiding, Martin. No more losing. The fardoor is closed and you can open it!"

"No," Martin mumbled through his arms, one anxious eye peeking out at Sword. "Not wizard. Not wizard."

"You don't have to be a wizard. You're *Myrchn'tin Pendragych.* You are the son of Astar. You have his blue power in your hands." Sword squeezed Martin's huge hands in his. "Remember in the glass pyramid — on top of the building. We *saw* your father. We saw Astar. And he opened a fardoor *bigger* than this."

"But where fardoor go?"

"Not far at all. Just through the layer. And you've taken us through the layer before." Sword got to his feet. "You are Astar's son. You *can* do it." He stepped back, leaving Martin in front of the fardoor. The halfling stared at the wall as if enchanted.

Forsyte had estimated the halfling's social development as that of a seven-year-old's. From the results of the tests he and Ko had run on Sword's orders, he suspected the halfling's brain lacked anything like a true speech center. But there was a different type of intellect at work in Martin. A First World intellect. *And who could know,* Forsyte thought, *how an intellect such as Martin's actually functions or what thoughts — inexpressible to us — the halfling's mind can hold?*

But Martin's being was loyal to his leader — Galen Sword. Forsyte envied that far-from-simple trust and sureness of belief that Sword had engendered in the halfling. The physicist knew that Ko's feelings of loyalty for himself were not the same. He had not earned that loyalty fairly.

He watched Martin hold up trembling hands to the fardoor. The instant blue fire danced across the halfling's fingers, an answering flurry of blue sparks cascaded around the fardoor's shadowline. *Contact,* Forsyte thought, *but how can that be exploited? What are the probabilities that* — the word flared in his mind like a supernova. Forsyte's two fingers reached for his keyboard.

"No," Ko protested, her attention on Martin, not Forsyte. "Don't make him do it, Sword. This is how we lost Ja'Nette. Doing things we don't understand. Don't do it, Martin."

"I know what I'm asking, Melody. A one-sided fardoor can be linked to another. Orion told me that's what Roth did — in the World Plaza tower."

"But he's an elemental adept!"

"So am I!"

The force of that statement made Forsyte look up from his keyboard to see Sword make a fist, raise it, hold it out, just as the Tepesh warriors had raised theirs. "This is *not* like the last time," Sword said urgently. "Or the first time. This is *now.* And we won't give up this time. We can't! We're going after them. And we're going to *keep* going after them until we've freed Orion. Until they have no place left to run."

DARK HUNTER

"Then *you* bloody well open it!" Ko yelled at Sword. "But don't make Martin risk his life because of something Orion said! Don't open the door, Martin! Don't even try!"

Forsyte saw Martin look from Sword to Ko, from Ko to Sword, unable to understand all that they'd said, knowing only that he was torn by the demands both made.

Then the fardoor's shadowline flickered more strongly than before, like a candle flame sputtering, going out. Forsyte continued typing rapidly.

"Open the door, Martin!" Sword commanded. "It's going to dissipate in minutes! Do it now!"

"Martin, no!" Ko stretched out her one good hand to pull the halfling back to her and to safety.

"Let him go, Melody! He can do it!"

"When you've got proof of that, Sword, then we can chance it. But not now. Not without proof."

Forsyte clicked his finger on the keypad of his synthesizer. "THERE IS PROOF," his voder said.

Martin froze before the fardoor as Sword and Ko stared back at Forsyte.

"THE FARDOORS ARE TTE DEVICES. DO YOU REMEMBER?" the voder asked.

"Your work at MIT?" Sword said. "I remember. But that was science, Adrian. This is ... is magic."

Forsyte was already prepared for the argument. He pressed the playback key. "BOTH EXIST IN THIS UNIVERSE. THEREFORE MUST BE COMMON UNDERLYING PRINCIPLE AT WORK. YOU SAID YOU COULD WRITE THE EQUATIONS FOR THEM, MELODY."

Sword looked from Forsyte to Ko. "I agree that's not proof," Sword said. "But it is confirmation that I might be right. And it's a damned sight better than a guess."

"No," Ko said to Forsyte. "How could this be the same as what you made?"

"WE DID SCIENCE THEN. DO SCIENCE NOW," the voder said. "TRY IT."

Ko kept her grip on Martin's shoulder. "On what grounds?"

273

Forsyte pressed the playback key again. "DOOR COLLAPSED ONLY MINUTES AGO. PROBABILITY PATHS REMAIN. JUST LIKE AT MIT. REMEMBER?"

Ko held his gaze for long moments. "You used the waiting crystal, didn't you? To remember what happened in your lab."

Forsyte blinked once. "DID YOU?" his voder asked.

Ko nodded slowly.

"REMEMBER?" the voder asked.

"Everything," Ko whispered.

The keyboard clicked. "SO DID I. I AM SORRY."

For the first time Forsyte's eyes met Ko's without deception. And then Sword interrupted, urgent. "Whatever this is, you two will have to talk about it later. The shadowline — it's almost gone."

"FOR EVERYTHING," the voder said.

But Ko had already turned her back to him, to face the fading fardoor. And Martin.

"Do it, Martin."

Alone in his thoughts, Forsyte remembered what it was to feel.

DARK HUNTER

THIRTY

"You ready?" Sword stood with Martin before the fardoor, unsure how much longer the connection the halfling had restored would last. Less than five minutes had passed since Diandra and the others had used the doorway to the First World from the Second.

Martin pointed to his locator band. He tugged on his equipment harness, double-sized to stretch across his broad chest and shoulders. He held up his fist, tightly bound. "*Pendragych*," he growled. He was ready.

"Ko?" Sword asked as he checked the breech of his Remington, then pumped a shell into place.

Ko came up to stand beside him and Martin, and Sword heard her pull back on the slide of her dart gun. Ko's broken arm was now wrapped in a sling of black silk taken from Orion's discarded shirt. She held the dart gun in her free hand and Sword could see she had rigged the weapon for killing shifters — silver-halide solution this time, not tranquilizer. Ko wore a sleeveless shirt beneath her black overalls and equipment harness so she had draped one of his black-leather jackets over her shoulders. It was cold in the Second World tonight. No one knew what it would be like in the First.

Sword swung his Remington into the firing holster on the side of his harness, hidden beneath his long black-leather coat. It was the same

275

coat he had worn atop the World Plaza and it carried the scars of that encounter like war medals. "Adrian?" he asked.

Forsyte's chair rolled up beside him. "READY," his voder said. And he was. Extra straps of canvas tied him firmly to his chair so he couldn't easily fall out. Tape held his left hand to the arm of his chair so his two operative fingers couldn't fall away from his keypad. And tape also bound his heavy-framed glasses to the fiber-optic laser guide that ran up his back from the computer housing between his chair's treads. With the equipment upgrades the chair carried, this time Forsyte would be even more formidable.

Sword looked to each of his team as he gave them his promise. "Now it's our turn," he said.

Then he stepped through the layer.

Sword and Ko steadied Forsyte's chair as it climbed up through the fardoor perimeter like a tank, then dropped forward onto the polished stone floor of wherever it was they had arrived in the First World. As far as Sword could tell, it was a long, high-ceilinged corridor, at least fifteen feet wide, constructed from enormous square blocks of light gray stone, each stone four feet on a side. It was lit by sputtering torches angled out from the walls at twenty-foot intervals. The air was hot, enervatingly humid, and acridly smoke-filled.

"THAT'S IT?" the voder asked.

Sword touched the physicist's left hand, remembering his own first experience with a fardoor, when he and Martin had passed into Softwind. "Odd feeling, isn't it? The lack of sensation. As if nothing's really changed."

A few feet back, Martin crouched by the wall in which the fardoor had appeared, intently studying the portal's flickering shadowline. Gingerly, he placed a thick index finger against the stone, six inches from the fardoor's perimeter. After a few moments, he curled his lips in worry.

Sword moved quickly to his side. "What is it?"

Martin tapped his finger against his brow. "Fardoor drifting. Could be unbound."

DARK HUNTER

Sword looked through the fardoor and could see the Loft's garage, just as they had left it. "Could it close behind us?" That might be awkward but wouldn't necessarily mean they'd be stranded here. There seemed to be many ways to pass from one world to the next.

Martin shook his head. "Unbound doors not close for long time. Hard to close."

In the time they'd been talking, Sword judged that the perimeter had drifted an inch closer to Martin's finger. At an inch a minute, it would travel along the wall no more than five feet in an hour. And the corridor walls were hundreds of feet long.

"We'll be okay for a while, then," he said.

"Hope so," Martin said dubiously, but he stood up and moved back from the fardoor to stand beside Ko.

She looked up and down the corridor. "Any idea what this place is?" she asked.

Martin sniffed the damp air deeply, then nodded thoughtfully. "Many elementals. Lots other adepts. Could be core."

"The core of what, Martin?" Sword wiped his forehead. He could feel more sweat trickle down his ribs beneath his long-sleeved shirt and heavy coat.

Martin shrugged. "Lots of cores. Go there find out." He pointed to the left branch of the corridor where it curved away without revealing an end.

Sword checked with his team. Ko nodded. Forsyte blinked once. Sword led the way.

They moved a hundred feet along the corridor in silence, except for the low hum of Forsyte's chair. Ahead of them the curve of the walls remained constant, as if the passageway described an enormous circle. Sword was puzzled and disturbed by the implications of what he saw and stopped briefly by a torch to examine the seam between two of the stone blocks that made up the wall. Martin halted by his side. Forsyte's chair also paused, while Ko continued walking forward.

The blocks appeared to be some form of granite, light gray where soot from the torches hadn't settled, and uniformly flecked with silicates to create an almost sparkling effect where the flickering light was bright enough. Additionally, the size and shape of each wall block was

277

identical to the blocks that made up the floor. Except that the wall stones were smooth while the floor stones were deeply worn in long, irregular grooves, as if something heavy had been dragged along this corridor for ... centuries. Sword frowned.

Ko turned back to Sword. "Something wrong? Other than you're crazy to be wearing that coat in here?" She no longer had his black-leather jacket on her shoulders. She had left it by the fardoor.

With Martin still close by his side and Forsyte behind him, Sword began walking forward again. His leather coat held more equipment than his vest. There was nothing he could do except keep it open and endure the rising temperature as best he could.

"NO TOOL MARKS," Forsyte's voder said.

Sword caught up to Ko. "That means it's old construction, Melody. Hundreds of years at least. Any stone construction that old should show telltale quarry and working marks, especially where the blocks have been fitted together so closely."

"Maybe it's not as old as you think," she suggested, her manner that of an emotionless computer, in great contrast to the way she'd been behaving just a few minutes ago in Sword's lab. She ran a finger along a soot-coated seam, inspecting the moist debris that came off the wall. "Maybe the soot from the torches makes it look older."

Sword shook his head, disagreeing. "I used to study this kind of thing. There's no mortar between the wall stones. And look at the way the floor's been worn. Takes a long time to do that to granite."

"HAVE YOU SEEN THIS KIND OF WALL BEFORE?"

Sword had already been trying to answer that question for himself. "Not exactly, Adrian. The proportions of the stones are wrong for British or European construction. The design is clean enough to be Asian, maybe Japanese. Or if we go back a couple of thousand years, perhaps even early Egyptian."

"A couple of thousand ... ?" Ko shifted her cast as if trying to find a more comfortable position for it. Sweat beaded on her smooth, unlined face. "Could it really be that old?"

That Sword didn't know. "It would help if there were some kind of decoration carved on any of these stones." He peered up to the ceiling, fifteen feet high and so blackened by the torches as to be almost imperceptible. "Or if I could see what kind of arch was holding up the ceiling."

Sword's team continued down the corridor, Ko taking up the lead again. "Sword, there's something coming up around the bend," she called out softly. "A pillar or something like that."

Just as Ko's words floated back to him, Sword glimpsed a light-colored column stretching from floor to ceiling of the curving inner wall of the corridor. The torches near it flickered more rapidly than the others they had passed and Sword felt the sudden force of a strong gust of heavy moisture-laden wind blow his coat wide open.

"Almost there," Martin said excitedly. His large hands brushed the grooved floor as he loped forward. Alone among them, the halfling seemed completely unaffected by the stifling heat and moisture, even though his body fur was plastered flat against him.

"Bloody hell," Ko said.

Up close, the column consisted of three insulated pipes, each eight inches in diameter, originating in a rough hole in a floor block and running up the wall to an equally rough hole in the ceiling.

Ko pulled away the outer layer of insulation on each pipe. The outer layer was merely painted fabric beneath which was a matted mass of crumbling, pale yellow fibers. Two of the metal pipes hidden within the fibrous wrappings were scalding hot. The third was icy cold and slick with condensation.

"Thousands of years old?" Ko said skeptically.

Sword squatted down and traced the rough edges of the hole hacked out of the floor.

Martin tugged on Sword's coat and pointed farther along the corridor. "Hurry hurry almost there," he urged.

"Hang on, Martin." Sword looked up and met Forsyte's gaze.

"RETRO FIT?"

"More than likely," Sword said. "Whatever this structure is, someone's definitely added steam heat to it in the past couple of decades." He slipped a small flashlight from his equipment harness and shone its beam down the pipes into the hole, but he could see nothing.

The anticipation became too much for Martin and he bounded off ahead on his own.

JUDITH & GARFIELD REEVES-STEVENS

Sword told Ko to stick with Forsyte, then sprinted after Martin. He didn't know why, but he felt it would not be a good idea to shout at Martin to stop. He had no idea how far sound might travel in this corridor, nor who or what might be listening.

Sword caught sight of Martin within seconds. The halfling was crouched in the center of the corridor, staring up at another section of the inner wall in rapt attention. It took Sword a moment to realize that the lighting in this part of the corridor had changed. There were no more torches along the walls. Martin was waiting in a patch of what could only be daylight. And it poured down the broad steps of a plain wooden staircase whose age-darkened beams led upward some forty feet or so. To a sky streaked with high, thin clouds and reddened by a setting sun. From somewhere far off came the long, slow crash of waves.

"Do you know what's up there?" Sword asked in a low voice.

Martin shook his head but took Sword's hand in his and promised softly. "Galen Sword not worry. Martin keep Galen Sword."

Then Martin and Sword ascended the staircase together and stepped out on a stone parapet that thrust exhilaratingly into open space.

Immediately, they were assailed by a hot, but welcome, dry wind. Sword leaned into the wind and pushed forward to look over the parapet's low stone railing. Martin hunched quietly beside him.

The parapet jutted from a mountainside whose base was lost in a mist-filled chasm, but on whose sheer cliffs zigzagged stone pathways far below the parapet that linked three enormous hexagonal structures set fast into the craggy rockface. Each was formed of blocks of granite, like the corridor, and each was marked by the same indefinable weight of age and austere design.

The central structure below Sword's parapet, perhaps three hundred feet to each of its six sides, and rising up six stories. Those sides facing the sunset glowed orange, while others were tessellated with small, hexagonal openings, some of which flickered with torches, while others shone with a more constant source of light. One of the terraced pathways joining the three outcroppings to each other was in shadow and each of its steeply-angled steps was lit with a steady pinpoint of what could only be electric light.

280

DARK HUNTER

Spreading out and around the three, huge hexagons, punctuated by wide stone terraces and several vividly green gardens, Sword saw a score of much smaller hexagonal structures of varying ages and materials other than stone, also linked by additional pathways, lit and unlit.

One structure was different, however, its covering luminous, translucent, lit from within by some type of floodlight. And its shape was not hexagonal, more like an air-inflated plastic dome, similar to what might be put in place over a Second World tennis court or greenhouse. Sword leaned over the parapet railing but could not see the full outline of the dome-shaped structure. It remained partially hidden by a fold in the mountain.

Except for the dome, Sword recognized that there was a common aesthetic uniting the mountainside complex. He also knew that that aesthetic unity had no origin or counterpart in the Second World.

But then, he realized, neither did the landscape beyond the parapet.

It wasn't that the sunset, clouds, and crimson sky were in any way remarkable. Nor the craggy mountainscape beneath them. It was the exceptional dryness of the exterior air that seemed to bring everything into sharper focus, as if there was no atmospheric haze here at all.

It was that clarity of vision that enabled him to finally see what was so unexpected, so wrong, about this place.

The sea.

It spread across more than half the western horizon, as if this rough-hewn mountain were some island or promontory thrust up from an ocean, but an ocean unlike any Sword had ever seen or even heard of.

It had no water.

Only sand.

At first, he thought it was a trick of light, some odd atmospheric refraction that made the moving, wave-carved surface of the sea pale wheat in color, and oddly non-reflective.

Then, he decided, the perplexing surface of the sea was a coating of some kind, a layer of buoyant material only similar to sand in color and texture, floating like an oil slick or sawdust, or even powder on the water that surely lay beneath it.

But then he tracked an enormous, slow-moving swell as it pulsed across the ocean's vast expanse, coming closer to the mountain. First peaking, then rising, the crest of the wave began to smear out not in the froth of white water, but in a long trail of dust. Then as it collided with the base of the cliff, the wave erupted, not with the speed and fluidity of liquid, but with the majestic upward billow of earth driven skyward by an underground explosion.

Seconds later, the sound of that impact hit the parapet and Sword held on tightly to the railing. Beside him, Martin shifted his weight from foot to foot but kept his balance unassisted, as if from practice.

The sound of the First World sandwave was indistinguishable from that of Second World water.

Sword had no explanation for what he'd seen or heard. He didn't even know how to ask Martin about the impossibility of the phenomenon. But as he stared out over the parapet's wall at what he had no name for, Sword dimly became aware of the whine of Forsyte's chair behind him as its treads crawled up the wooden stairs. He heard the scrape of Ko's footsteps as she walked up to stand beside him. He heard her gasp, watched as she took in the view, her eyes widening as she saw the ocean. Her mouth opened. But, like him, it was as if she had no words to ask the other questions that almost certainly tumbled through her as well.

"WHAT IS IT?" Forsyte's voder asked.

Martin gave an answer for half the question. "Core Pendragon."

Sword's attention veered away from the dry ocean. His scalp tightened, his muscles bunched. He knew that name.

"YOUR HOME, SWORD?"

Sword struggled to concentrate on what he did know, not on what he couldn't. Somewhere within his half-recovered memories he carried an internal map of the compound which he remembered as his childhood home. But that map contained no granite towers, no cliffs thrust from a sea of sand, no winding pathways carved from living stone.

"No," Sword said. "Not this place." Martin brushed his hand consolingly against Sword's.

"I don't understand," Ko protested, her eyes locked once more on the crashing waves of sand below. "You are a Pendragon, aren't you?"

At the horizon, the sun had almost set against the thunderous swells of shifting dunes. Sword stared fixedly at its final burning arc of fire, feeling a long hidden truth arise within him. "No," he said slowly as the sun flared, then vanished, leaving the sand sea in shadow, though now eerily marked by a faint glowing blue pattern of phosphorescent hexagons at least half-a-mile on each side. "My *clan* is Pendragon, but my *line* is Sword." He repeated words he knew he had heard a thousand times as a child. "I am a warrior in the cause of Pendragon." He held his hand before him, making a fist tightly bound, offering fealty to something, someone he didn't know. "I *am* a warrior and ... and ... " There was something more to that statement, that vow, something that he couldn't quite piece together. Something important.

Ko pressed him. "But you're always saying you're heir to the Victor of Pendragon. How can that be if you're not a Pendragon yourself?"

Sword opened his fist and the answer came as easily as that. "My mother!" He turned to face Ko and Forsyte as his excitement returned, as another fragment of his memory reassembled itself within the influence of the First World. "My father was a Sword. My mother a Pendragon. *She* was the Victor of all the family lines that formed the clan." He looked at the symbol carved into the golden ring he wore. "See, here on my mother's ring? The dragon and the sword entwined. The answer's been here all along." Sword wanted to shout. He wanted to hear his voice echo in triumph against the walls of Core Pendragon.

But Forsyte's next words stopped him cold. "DIFFERENT SYMBOL ON FLAG TOWER."

For the first time, Sword noticed the design of the large banner fluttering above the central hexagon in the dying wind of dusk. Forsyte was right. The symbol, even in the rapidly fading light, was clearly not the sword and dragon of Sword's clansign. Instead it carried four other figures whose metallic outlines gleamed in the last rays of sunlight: two figures in silver, two figures in gold. Two in humanform. And two in shifterform.

Sword gave voice to the name of that clan like a curse. "*Arkady.*"

Martin growled.

"It's Roth," Sword exclaimed. "He's trying to take over Pendragon by allying himself with Arkady."

"Why?" Ko asked.

"Power? Control?" Sword could only speculate.

"Power to do what?" Ko persisted. "Control over what?"

Sword stepped back from the parapet wall. There would be time enough for reflection later. "Maybe greed's the same in all the Worlds. Maybe it's just as simple as that."

Forsyte's voder clicked on again. "DOUBTFUL. WITH HIS KNOWL-EDGE OF MAGIC, ROTH COULD EASILY HAVE GREAT WEALTH."

Though he would not admit it aloud, Sword knew the scientist was correct. Without understanding why he could be so certain, Sword was convinced that whatever Roth's true motive was for exiling him from his clan and his world, it was much more than just a simple desire for riches or domination. Roth needed the power and influence of Clan Pendragon. But what the purpose of that need was, Sword still had no idea.

He drove the maddening distraction from his mind. This time, he and his team were present in the First World for only one reason.

"None of that matters, Adrian." Sword looked to Martin. "Which way now?"

The halfling scented the hot, dry air, its temperature undiminished by the onset of evening or the lessening of the wind. Then he pointed down the side of the parapet to the nearest of the wide, downward-sloping terraced pathways that cut into the side of the mountain.

"Through there," Martin said.

Sword acknowledged the unasked questions in Ko's eyes as she glanced back at the sand sea. But this wasn't the time. "We're here for Orion," Sword said firmly. "All the rest of it can wait. For now."

No one in his team objected. United, they turned their backs on the unceasing crash and sweep of sandwaves. Then, together, with Martin leading, they descended to the Core.

DARK HUNTER

THIRTY-ONE

The terraced pathway descended the mountain in a switchback that eventually led Sword and his team fifty feet down across the mountain's face, almost directly beneath the stone parapet where they had first emerged. There, the path ended in a second parapet from which another wooden staircase led back within the mountain. Hot, moist air gushed from that opening as if forced out by industrial blowers.

"THE MOUNTAIN COULD BE HONEYCOMBED WITH PASSAGES." Forsyte's chair was poised at the top of the stairway. The four of them looked down into the new entranceway. The corridor beyond was lit by a light source steadier than torches.

Martin waited for Sword to give the word, but Sword ran his hand along the smoothly sculpted edge of the opening, large enough for the four of them to stand abreast within it. "I don't get it at all," he said. "The blocks in the first corridor had no tool scrapes or scratches, and this opening is unmarked, too."

Ko studied the entranceway's arch. "It's too symmetrical to be natural, like a cave or underground stream outlet. It's got to be a construction of some kind."

But Sword didn't like what that implied — the death of a culture and the resulting loss of tradition, technology, and history. The hole that those pipes came out of in the first corridor had been rough and

285

JUDITH & GARFIELD REEVES-STEVENS

ragged. If the builders had had a good technique for carving stones a few centuries back when the corridor was made, they'd lost it by the time they had come to put in those pipes.

"DO WE GO IN?" Forsyte's voder asked.

Sword turned to their First World guide. "How about it, Martin? Are we anywhere near where Roth came through with Orion?"

The halfling leaned out over the first wooden step and sniffed the outrushing air.

"Are they down there?" Sword asked.

"Something is," Martin said, then took a first brave step.

The second passageway was almost a duplicate of the first, except for the absence of torches. Instead, a narrow metal pipe ran along each wall and every ten feet a utility light fixture was attached alternately to one pipe, then the other. Each fixture contained what appeared to be a standard lightbulb protected by a wire cover. Sword gestured to Ko, who nodded her head. She also remembered seeing the same type of installation in the other passages they had encountered beneath New York. Sword cupped his hands and boosted Ko up to look more closely at one of them.

"It's an ordinary lightbulb, all right," she said. She jumped down from Sword's hands, holding her arm with the cast carefully to one side. "It even has a GE logo on top."

"MANY LIGHT FIXTURES IN A PLACE THIS SIZE," Forsyte's voder said. "SUGGESTS CONSIDERABLE TRADE BETWEEN THE WORLDS."

That conclusion troubled Sword as well. "But if we're selling them lightbulbs" — he recalled the sophisticated electronic equipment that had been controlling the immense fardoor on top of the World Plaza building — "and computers and who knows what else, what the hell are they buying from us in return?"

Ko gave Sword a wry glance. "Hey, don't forget, *you're* supposed to be one of *them*."

Sword glanced at the ring he wore. She was right. However powerless — *substanceless* — he appeared to be, he wasn't human by birth. This was his world they were in as much as it was Martin's, and Core Pendragon had been built by his kind. He looked for the halfling. By

286

DARK HUNTER

this time, he was almost around the new corridor's curve. "We'd better keep up with Martin."

After a few more minutes, the distant rumble of crashing sand-waves had been left far behind, and the corridor led them to a vast, vaulted chamber, larger even than the Loft's garage, which appeared to be the intersection of at least a dozen other passages. Here, the heat was once again crushing and the air was still, magnifying the effect of the dense and suffocating humidity, but it was not silent.

Through the solid stones of the floor, Sword could feel deep thrum-mings, as if power generators were at work somewhere beneath them, hidden deep within the mountain. *That makes some sort of sense,* he thought. *Something has to be providing the current for the electric lights.*

He moved his arms to let a little air circulate under his coat, and continued to check the chamber ahead. Scattered throughout it were random piles of the four-foot-high building stones of which the floor and the walls were made. There were no more than three or four to a stack, most of them crumbled or cracked, as if this had been a dumping ground for defective building material.

Sword had his team spread out so they could see if anyone or anything were concealed behind the nearest stacks of stones. The closest stacks of building blocks proved free of surprises. The team reassem-bled beside Sword.

"What about *those* arches, Sword? Their design tell you anything about who built this place?" Ko gestured with her cast to the sweep of the ceiling fifty feet above their heads.

As he threw his head back and blinked away sweat to more closely inspect the ceiling arches, Sword wished again that he had something with which to make a sweatband. He was close to abandoning his coat, as well, and was already thinking of the equipment he'd be willing to leave behind. But, in fact, there wasn't much. Since he had no idea what to expect here, he wasn't comfortable ruling out the necessity of anything he carried.

From the highest point of the ceiling, a broad black tube extended down about twenty feet, ending in two smaller, right-angled pieces from which roared and blazed what appeared to be natural gas jets. Other than what little light spilled in from some of the corridors, the gas pipe and burners appeared to be the stone chamber's only source of illumination, and perhaps some of its oppressive heat.

To Sword, the unfinished appearance of the pipe's installation made it seem to be another artless, retro-fitted afterthought to the Core. He counted the stones that formed the overhead vault and tried to make out the shape of the keystone that was punctured by the gas pipe. Unlike the corridors' construction, this room was built with an even more primitive simplicity. But this time, at least, the rough-edged style was vaguely familiar.

"It's a lot bigger than anything like it I've seen before, but I'd say it's similar to early Estrucan burial vaults in northern Italy."

Ko frowned at him. Martin lost interest in their discussion and moved off to explore the room on his own.

"I'm serious," Sword said, raising his voice so that that Forsyte could also hear him. "Core Pendragon seems to be like a ... a Second World city, with elements added throughout its history. Except instead of adding over hundreds of years, we're looking at thousands of years here."

A shadow moved in a darkened corridor entrance on the far side of the chamber.

Sword tensed, signalled Martin with a sharp hand gesture to draw the halfling's attention to the corridor. Martin crouched, his eyes on Sword. Ko saw the signal and automatically checked her weapons. More shadows flowed within the darkened entrance.

But Forsyte was intent only on his keypad and display screen. "CONTINUOUS HABITATION FOR THAT SPAN OF TIME COULD IMPLY EXTREMELY STABLE SOCIOLOGICAL POLITICAL ENVIRONMENT," his voder said.

"Or an extremely powerful clan," Sword muttered and swung his Remington up from beneath his coat. "*Over there, Adrian!*"

Instantly, Forsyte's chair spun in place as Sword feinted to the left and Ko to the right. Martin remembered his lessons in tactics as well and after only a moment's hesitation rushed back to take his assigned position a few feet to the front and side of Forsyte's chair.

Sword saw Ko flick her VOX mike down from her earpiece so she could keep in contact with the team without shouting. He reached inside his leather coat to turn on his own transceiver, then gestured to Martin and Forsyte to do the same.

Ko's voice was low and controlled over the surprisingly static-free connection. "Five. Just inside the passageway."

Sword pulled out his StarBrite viewer and switched it on. The deeply shadowed corridor entrance across the chamber suddenly came to detailed life on the light intensifier's incandescent green screen.

"Martin, any idea what they are?" Ko asked.

But Martin was busy. Throwing back his head to howl in challenge.

"Save it, Martin. You know what to do." Like Martin, he'd just realized he knew the shadows, too. "Close trolls, Melody. Like in New York." After the incident near the World Plaza, Orion had been very forthcoming about trolls. "There will be eight of them."

Close trolls, according to Orion, were non-sentient fighters selectively propagated from the ancient lines of intelligent troll adepts who still served most greater clans. Bipedal in form, though oddly jointed, the small but deadly creatures possessed disconcertingly large and long-lashed eyes set in squashed-up childlike faces. Whatever intelligence they appeared to manifest came solely from a single Far troll, an independent cadre leader who directed their every move like a puppeteer. Even vampires avoided Far trolls.

Sword used the StarBrite to rapidly scan the chamber's other corridor entrances and the outlines of the stacks of stones on the far side of the room. "Yes ... there's a sixth one ... in the corridor entranceway, second to the left."

He took a moment to note his team's positions. "Martin, move out of Adrian's line of fire." The halfling shook his head as if trying to clear a buzzing from his ear — Martin still wasn't used to his transceiver — but dutifully shifted a few steps to the side of Forsyte's chair. Although constrained by her cast, Ko had already holstered her dart gun and brought out a short-barrelled shotgun. The stock had been altered so she could handle it like a pistol and Sword was counting that the recoil wouldn't blast it out of her one good hand at the first shot. They had had time to develop some First World combat strategies, but had not yet been able to test all their equipment and plans. If the Close trolls did attack, it would be his team's first trial by the First World's fire.

JUDITH & GARFIELD REEVES-STEVENS

Devoid of all but the most rudimentary sense of self-preservation, Close trolls were deliberately bred to battle to the death, without sense of pain or injury, retreating only when their Far troll reclaimed them from a hopeless confrontation. Each member of the Close troll cadre was encased in segmented suits of glittering blue-green armor — suggestive of armadillo shell blended into beetle carapace — and that armor was alive and capable of almost instant regeneration when injured.

"Why don't they make their move?" Ko asked.

"Best case: Their instructions are to just guard the entrances," Sword said. "Worst case: The Far troll who runs them doesn't know that we're here yet." Orion had described the apparently telepathic link that joined a Far troll to its mindless fighting cadre.

Across the chamber, a small scuttling shape abruptly scrambled from the first entranceway to another, then ducked behind a single stone. "One of them's on the move," Sword said.

"Thank you, Mr. Obvious," Ko answered. "Do we sit here all night or take one of the other passages?"

Another shadowy troll figure rushed from one corridor to another. That made seven. "What do you bet the corridor they're guarding is probably the one we want to go through?" Sword said.

Ko sighed over the radio link. "How'd I know you'd say that."

Forsyte's synthesized voice came online. "SHALL I BEGIN THE OPERATION?"

"Not yet," Sword said. "Number eight's a no-show."

"Should be no trolls," Martin growled quietly but savagely.

The vibrations under the stone floor suddenly increased in intensity, then stopped, then resumed again, but hesitatingly, as if a vast machine were breaking down, losing its momentum. Dust from the lofty ceiling fell to the floor.

Ko's voice sounded in Sword's ear. "What the hell was that? Earthquake?"

Sword didn't answer. If it was, then this world must have them all the time. It was too much of a coincidence for one to occur just as his team had arrived.

290

DARK HUNTER

"TAKING UP ATTACK FORMATION," Forsyte's voder said. "WE ARE LOSING ELEMENT OF SURPRISE."

"Right," Sword said, swinging the StarBrite to scan the room again. The eighth troll still was missing. "Just as we've planned it then. Adrian, draw them out. Martin, stay in position. Don't move until Melody tells you to."

Martin grunted something unintelligible that Sword took for agreement. As always, the nearer the time for physical action, the greater the decline in Martin's verbal abilities.

Forsyte's chair jerked forward, heading for the largest clear area, almost directly in the stone chamber's center. Martin, though keyed up, obediently held his position as the chair rolled past him, Ko and Sword both flanking Forsyte. The instant they reached the chamber center, Sword leapt to the top of a stack of stone blocks just as Forsyte toggled on his chair's headlights. Forsyte's chair swung back and forth on its treads so that its headlights swept the walls like searchlights. So instinctive, said Orion, was troll hatred for the Light clans from which they were descended, that all trolls, Close or Far, always attacked anything bright and glittery, first.

But the trolls had vanished.

"Get ready," Sword commanded urgently. "They're — "

High-pitched, earsplitting squeals sliced through the thrumming from the floor and the roar of the ceiling gas jets as the Close trolls launched their first assault.

"Stay back, Martin. Stay back." Even as he yelled out his reminder, Sword heard Forsyte's voder.

"FIRE ONE."

The first taser darts flew from the weapons pod on Forsyte's chair. Silvery wires trailed through the air as three of the four darts found their targets. The effect was just as Sword had hoped.

As each of Forsyte's taser darts embedded itself in a segment of troll armor, 60,000 volts of low-amperage current sped from the batteries in the physicist's chair through the trailing wire. A human subjected to the weapon would immediately go into uncontrollable spasms, and Sword saw that as he had hoped, the trolls' armor behaved just as any other living creature might.

Three of the trolls fell to the ground with sharp squeals and snorts of surprise, flailing back and forth in rhythmic jerking, their arms and legs made useless by the sudden rigidity of the shocked armor. And also, as Sword had correctly guessed, the three trolls' abrupt withdrawal from action interrupted the unseen Far troll's control of the other three attackers who slowed in confusion, then wandered off, bereft of orders.

"*Now, Martin! Now!*" Sword shouted.

Yowling full-force, Martin somersaulted through the air above Forsyte, bounding forward the instant his feet touched the ground, skidding to a stop by the first aimless troll. With the swiftness of a cat claiming a mouse, he swept aside the creature's sword and weapon, seized hold of his target, bit down between its helmet and shoulder guard, shook it once and broke its neck. Martin turned to a second directionless troll, which set up a pitiful bleating at his approach.

"FIRE TWO."

The last of the six attacking trolls collapsed as its living armor convulsed.

Ko's response was quick. "Cut the current," she told Forsyte as she beckoned to the halfling to join them. Martin first looked around carefully before opening his jaws to drop his second victim.

Sword knelt to study the still-writhing body of the first Close troll hit by Forsyte's taser just as Ko aimed her shotgun pistol at the creature's still-jerking head and fired. "Just in case Orion was wrong about these things being non-sentient." The creature's head disintegrated.

Sword jerked back, wiping splatters of dark troll blood from his face. "Thanks for the warning."

Unapologetic, Ko checked Forsyte's glasses for blood spots, then she and Martin made sure the remaining fallen trolls were also indisputably dead.

Sword's hand tapped a worried beat on the back of Forsyte's chair. His scheme had succeeded. But had its success come too easily?

"So what's wrong with you?" As she spoke to Sword, Ko awkwardly reloaded her chopped-down shotgun by wedging it against her cast. "We did it just like you told us to and it worked. We did it, Sword. As a team. That's what you wanted, right?"

DARK HUNTER

Sword's restless gaze swept the chamber. Ko *was* right, but he couldn't help feeling it was too soon to claim victory. "Orion told me there're always eight Close trolls in a cadre. We got six here. That leaves two. And I'm sure I saw the seventh just before the attack."

Ko flipped her pistol shut with a snap of her wrist. She turned to Martin who was crouched down, dragging a fingernail through what was left of one of the trolls' head. "Hey, Martin," she said. The halfling looked up with a glassy expression. Ko holstered the pistol and held out her open hand. Martin hesitated as if confused, then lifted his hand and began to make a fist.

But Ko stopped him before he could give her a First World salute, her voice rough with feeling. "No, not like that. That's for Sword." She held out her hand, palm up. "This one's for Ja'Nette."

Martin bared his teeth. His teeth were red. Thick masses of dark, coagulated blood were caught between them. He stood up, leaned forward, brought his huge hand down to slap Ko's, then held it open for her to slap in return.

Then Martin turned, held out his hand to Sword.

Sword brought his hand down on Martin's. *Why not?* he told himself. Why not acknowledge the team's first successful battle in the First World? *First successful* planned *battle,* he amended.

The seventh troll attacked.

It launched itself from a nearby pile of cracked stones and hurtled through the air like an enormous jumping bug, its five-foot-long twisted spear held before it like an immense stinger, directly aimed at Martin's back.

Ko fired wildly, winging the creature and changing its trajectory just as Sword pushed Martin to the side, exposing himself to the troll's attack.

The spear missed his body, cutting instead through the billow of his leather coat. The troll rolled into a ball as it struck the stone floor, the shaft of the spear tugged from its grip by the impact.

Martin whirled, snarling, and kicked at the troll, knocking it toward Ko. Ko shoved the barrel of her shotgun pistol into the troll's balled-up body, wedging it between two segments of the troll's pulsating armor, turned her head, and pulled the trigger. The troll popped like an insect striking a car windshield.

With an approving rumble, Martin helped Sword back to his feet.

"YOU OKAY?" Forsyte's voder asked.

Sword wiggled the spear out of his coat. He examined the Close troll's weapon carefully. "Good excuse for a new coat, Adrian." Rather than metal or wood, the spear appeared to be made of rock, like an exceptionally long stalactite that had been snapped from a cave's ceiling.

Ko wiped the barrel of her gun against her overalls on the back of her leg. "Okay, *that's* the last one. Happy now?"

Sword hefted the rock-like spear in his hand. "That's the last one we saw," he reminded her. "There could still be — "

It came at them from above, a fireball screaming like a thousand birds taking flight at once.

Whether he had noticed something moving or had simply been lucky, Sword didn't know, but he had chosen the moment of the eighth troll's attack to look up just as the troll threw itself from its perch on the gas jet pipes overhead. Though its living armor was encased in flames, Sword had time to see that the troll inside was unaffected as it plunged down for them with a double-edged knife in each hand.

In Sword's mind he saw that the path of the troll's plunge would intersect with Ko's position. He did not question his ability to think so clearly, and analyze so thoroughly, all in the space of the single heartbeat it took him to understand what he must do.

Before the eighth troll had fallen a dozen feet, Sword was at Ko's side, pushing her away even as he twisted around, dropped to one knee, and with both arms outstretched, thrust up his captured spear to aim its razor-edged point directly toward the gap between the eighth troll's helmet and chest segments.

Deafened by the stone-walled chamber's amplification of the troll's high-pitched shriek, Sword roared out his own challenge without conscious thought.

"*Sair Pendragych!*"

The troll fell on the upthrust spearpoint.

DARK HUNTER

Sword shook the spitted troll off the spear shaft. The flaming body hit the stone floor with a liquid thud. Oily black smoke streamed up from the Close troll's crackling, wheezing, living armor.

Breathless, Sword registered the stinging sensation in his palms where the roughness of the stone spear had scraped his flesh. His whole body resonated with ... with ... he had no word for what he felt now.

He became aware that Ko was staring at him with, he sensed, some amount of fear. He saw Forsyte's chair rolling toward the still-burning troll. Sword saw a fire-extinguisher nozzle emerge from the cowling between the chair's treads.

"I've never seen *anyone* move that fast before," Ko said, almost accusingly. "And you called out something."

Sword's throat felt raw as if he'd been screaming.

Behind them, Forsyte blasted the eighth troll's body with a dense white cloud of carbon dioxide.

"Whatever you said had your clan name in it." Ko paused. "The way Martin says it. ... like ... *seer Pendragych.* Or *sore Pendragych.* Something like that."

Forsyte's chair pulled up beside Ko and Martin.

"SAIR PENDRAGYCH."

"That's it, Adrian. What's it mean, Sword?"

Sword was finding it difficult to breathe in the close, humid air of the smoke-filled chamber. Just being in the First World was increasingly engulfing him in jumbled waves of incoherent memories. "I think it's ... something from my childhood," he said. "Something we said when we fought in the old school."

"You were trained to fight like that in school?" Ko asked as Martin whuffed proudly. Forsyte's fingers swung toward his keyboard.

But Sword had had enough of remembering for now. "Aren't you going to thank me for saving your life?" he asked Ko to distract her, knowing she would rise to the bait. Instead, she provoked a new, and even more unsettling flash of recognition in him.

"You got me into this mess, Sword. The way I figure it, saving my life is your job."

Suddenly Sword was struck with the certainty that saving someone's life *was* part of what he was supposed to do. *But how do I*

295

know that? And whose life is it that I'm supposed to save? He rubbed at his temples. Beneath his open coat, his shirt felt drenched with sweat.

"You remember something else we should be worried about?" Ko asked with a quick glance around the stone chamber.

Sword shook his head. "It's just that it's beginning to seem ... as if I belong here."

The gas jets momentarily sputtered and more trails of dust poured down from the ceiling stones as another, stronger tremor shook the stone floor beneath them.

Martin growled, spit noisily, having left his mouth open a moment too long.

"Good," Ko said, brushing the stone dust from Forsyte's face, "because any more of those quakes and we'll be trapped here forever when the ceiling falls in on us. So, what's next?"

"CORRIDOR?" Forsyte angled his chair to point to the darkened entranceway the first Close trolls had huddled in.

Sword nodded. Whatever their answer was, that was where they were going to find it.

With Martin protectively in rear position, Sword and Ko flanked Forsyte as the physicist's chair headlights guided them deeper into the shadows of Sword's past.

DARK HUNTER

THIRTY-TWO

The corridor the Close troll cadre had guarded was different. Its ceiling was oppressively lower; its width narrow enough to force Sword and his team to proceed single file. Forstye had been the first to remark that no stones had been used in the new corridor's construction. From first inspection, it appeared to have been carved through the mountain like a mine tunnel, the surface of its floor, walls, and ceiling that of rough unfinished rock, though, like the previous corridors they had encountered, mysteriously free of any sign of tool use. Only its damp, close breeze was familiar.

"Martin, are you sure we're going the right way?" Ko asked. Her voice sounded oddly muted to Sword who suspected that the tunnel's irregular surfaces were acting to swallow all echoes.

Ahead of the others, Martin turned back to look at Ko, his sweat-covered features gleaming in the pale glow of the trollstone he held between two fingers. Because there was no light source of any world's design in the tunnel, Forsyte had become concerned about how long his chair's batteries would last if he had to use his headlights to show the way. So before they had ventured too far, Sword had sent an eager Martin back to the vaulted stone chamber and the halfling had quickly loped back with a luminescent trollstone.

297

Sword knew where it had come from. He had seen Diandra gut a troll to remove the gemlike organ of influence from its bowels. But, surprisingly, Ko had not peppered Martin with questions about the glowing stone, still warm and sticky from whatever juices had bathed it. Ko's uncharacteristic restraint told Sword she had likely already guessed its origins.

In the eerie yellow light cast by the trollstone, Martin's face was more shifter than human. "Martin sure," he rumbled. "Smell Roth. Nightfeeder stink. Close close close."

As they continued on the path that Martin blazed for them, ignoring certain branchings, taking others, Sword saw that there was something that gave off light in the tunnel after all. If he turned his eyes from the trollstone's glow for a moment, then looked up, in the corners of his vision, he could see almost imperceptible red sparks shining weakly every ten feet or so. He had first noticed them during one of the tremors that were constantly shaking the mountain around the tunnel. Swords had seen the red sparks flicker with brighter light then, as if the earthquake had in some way activated them. Ko and Forsyte had notices the sudden flashes of red light, as well. Obviously, the sparks were the product of some form of red crystal, though it wasn't clear to Sword what function they had — until Forsyte had pointed out that the tunnel had no shoring. Perhaps, the physicist speculated, the small red crystals studding the tunnel's ceiling were its only defense against the force of earthquakes.

Forsyte's theory had not relieved Ko of her concerns about their being trapped by a cave-in, and it had made Sword wonder what other magic might still be functioning within these older sections of the Core. Without knowing why, he had begun to suspect that the rough-hewn tunnel was much older than even the vaulted stone chamber had appeared to be, and that parts of Core Pendragon might have been built before the beginning of recorded history in the world of humans. Then, unbidden, from some deep-buried portion of his consciousness, the half-formed thought arose that some parts of the Core had been built even before the first appearance of humans.

No more than ten minutes after they had left the vaulted stone chamber, Martin slowed his pace. In that same moment, Sword felt the

DARK HUNTER

tunnel's hot and humid breeze quicken to become a searing-hot gale almost powerful enough to block them from continuing. The wind's pulsing nature strongly reminded him of the pressure equalization effect of fardoors. And now, instead of just humidity, Sword was certain he sensed the presence of open water.

Martin gave a warning growl. "Close close Galen Sword."

Sword swung his shotgun up, its stock and barrel slippery in his grip. Behind him, he heard Ko's shotgun click as she primed it.

Abruptly, the tunnel widened.

Martin waved at them to move closer to the wall and Sword saw the first glimmer of a new source of light. Then the tunnel twisted through its final few feet and ended.

They were in an immense natural cavern, larger than the entire city block on which Sword's Loft was sited. *And it's as old as it's large,* Sword thought as he stared out into the vast space before him, expectant, ready. *But for what? This is older than any other part of the Core. Older than ...* Sword swore under his breath as the meaning of what he was looking at him dissipated, continuing to evade him.

His senses at least could tell him that the cavern was not empty. But, once again, like the landscape outside, there was so much to it, both exotic and familiar, that he was almost overcome by a maddening, tantalizing onslaught of impressions: beyond the sweltering heat and humidity; the hivelike humming that permeated the air, blending with the distant rush of water; the pungent scent of decaying vegetation, like that of hay stored in old barns; and, underscoring it all, the chilling certainty that he had visited this place before, many times, when he had been a child. But what its purpose was, remained completely unknown to him.

From the tunnel's entrance to the cavern, Sword saw giant stalagmites rising from the cavern floor, wreathed in diaphanous, low-lying haze, their carved bases intricately detailed with gigantic pictogram panels. In contrast, on the other side, at the farthest reaches of visibility, the natural-rock cavern wall appeared oddly smooth, with not a trace of pattern.

There was further sign of artifice. Two hundred feet away from the low ledge that Sword and the others stood upon, a section of the cavern

299

floor had been raised and levelled with black hexagonal paving stones to support banks of humming electric stadium lights whose pure white illumination was reflected blindingly by the floor's highly-polished surface. The dazzling brilliance obscured further detail of the other objects and figures that Sword glimpsed moving between the light banks on the cavern floor.

The noise of the lights accounted for the thrumming sound Sword's team had heard, and their intense heat had to be, at least partially, Sword reckoned, responsible for the hot wind that had pulsed through the tunnel.

Only one feature was large enough to be seen in any sort of detail. In shape, it was as if part of an immense disk had been thrust up through the cavern floor. Aligned on an angle to Sword's position, it was about ten feet thick, curved up twenty feet, then back down, describing just part of a circle at least one hundred feet in diameter.

The disk segment was highly reflective, but Sword could see no other detail in the harsh white light. And whatever made up the disk's surface seemed to Sword to be shifting, making the reflected light ripple as if from a liquid surface.

Sword squinted, trying to see what was directly beneath the lights around the disk segment. There *were* people there. Or at least, creatures who looked like people, moving purposefully.

Beside him, Ko shielded her eyes with her cast. "Well, the good news is this cavern doesn't appear to be full of shifters like the last time."

Sword turned to Martin. "Are we still on Roth's trail?"

The answer came to him not from the halfling, but through his earphone. "*You're right where you're supposed to be.*"

Ko put her hand to her transceiver in shock. "That's Brin's voice."

But Sword had already identified the voice on their radio link. His eyes sought the adept and located him standing beneath the lights, near the edge of the disk in the center of the paved floor, waving for Sword to join him.

Without a second's hesitation, Sword moved forward, following the path off the ledge. Ko and Martin were with him at once. The whine of Forsyte's chair fluctuated with the physicist's progress across the uneven cavern floor.

DARK HUNTER

With each step closer to his brother, Sword saw more detail emerge from the glowing haze that hung over the paved floor where Brin waited. Whatever had been obscuring their vision in the cavern had obviously been more than just blinding light.

"Bloody ... Sword, look at that wall!" Ko pointed to the cavern's huge smooth vertical surface that Sword had noticed earlier. Now Sword could see that the back wall behind Brin and the disk was made of planks of wood — pale, new wood, not yet stained by age. Scaffolding had been erected around parts of it and Sword could see strange symbols and —

"It's a fardoor installation!" Sword said as they reached the beginning of the paved floor. "Like the one at World Plaza." He moved forward, onto the polished black stones.

"Except this one's five times the size." Ko said as she kept pace with Sword. Martin flanked Foryste's chair whose treads took the physicist easily up from the rough cavern floor to the smooth black paving stones that led to Brin.

Sword was already puzzling out the significance of this new information. "I always wondered how they managed to build something that complex so quickly at World Plaza." He swept his eyes over the distant wooden wall, thankful that whatever the cavern's fardoor's purpose, the structure was clearly incomplete. The fardoor wall in New York had been almost totally inscribed with strange geometrical figures and unfamiliar script. There had also been at least thirty adepts at work on computer terminals and crystals to operate the installation.

Sword tried but failed to count the half-seen shapes moving across the stone floor on the far side of the disk. He turned to Ko. "Maybe the World Plaza installation was already in place, waiting to be used for something else other than rescuing Roth and Morgana."

Ko was not listening to him. Her eyes were fixed on the area in which Brin awaited them. "Orion," she said. "I see Orion."

Sword followed her gaze. They were near enough to Brin that the low-lying haze had almost completely cleared. Next to Brin, Sword saw the vampire adept, frozen in the exact position he had been in when Diandra had coldblasted him in Sword's Loft. Orion's glowing blue form now stood upright by a tower of large wooden crates stacked on

301

JUDITH & GARFIELD REEVES-STEVENS

the far side of the disk. Also piled high, as if being readied for shipment, were huge reels of thick cable, and, inexplicably, an assortment of Second-World office tables and chairs.

Also inexplicable to Sword was the group of three seated facing Brin: Roth. Morgana. And Diandra. The dark hunter's red-gold hair was a nimbus of flame in the reflected banks of light. All three looked unnaturally placid, almost paralyzed, but not quite.

Sword motioned to his team to stop ten feet from Brin. Sword's brother smiled. Roth's face darkened, twisted, contorted with malice. Beyond human speech, Morgana could only flick her bifurcated tongue in and out of her scarlet-lipped mouth. Diandra alone kept her emotions in check, though her strange golden eyes were watchful.

Brin was leaning against a table formed from black stone hexagons that appeared to have arisen like pistons from the smooth-paved floor. Two black attaché cases lay on the raised stone surface. In one hand, Sword's brother held a glowing red crystal the size of a child's skull. Sword guessed it was both the source of the obscuring haze and the explanation for Brin's control of his audience.

Behind Brin, a creature Sword didn't recognize lay sprawled, slumped, against the base of the stone table. On the floor beside the creature lay an almost empty rum bottle and a pile of dented Coca-Cola cans.

But these improbable details could not distract Sword. He looked back at the wooden crates by Orion. Stamped on their sides in foot-high letters was the IBM logo. Clear plastic envelopes were attached to them, too, stuffed with what appeared to be shipping and customs forms.

"This fardoor hasn't been finished," Sword said to his team, not caring if his brother heard him or not. "But if it's like the one we saw at World Plaza, then Arkady and the Tepesh must want to bring someone else back through space and time."

"Someone?" Ko repeated. She stared at Brin in wonder. "Hell, Sword, if that whole wall's supposed to be a fardoor when it's finished, they could fly a 747 through it."

"Not if I have anything to do with it," Sword said. An empty office chair stood between him and his brother and he kicked it aside, making

302

DARK HUNTER

it clatter noisily. He lifted his shotgun and aimed its at his brother's chest. "Hello, Brin," he said.

Brin was almost jovial as he greeted Sword. "Welcome, brother. And dear, dear Melody. And to you, too, plucky halfling. And, of course, the brain without a body. Welcome all." He lifted the red crystal to his lips and spoke into it as if it were a microphone. "*Test, one, two, three.*"

Sword and his team blinked in unison as Brin's voice echoed in their earpieces. Sword exchanged a glance with his team, silently requesting that they follow his lead, and let him do any speaking for them. Ko and Martin nodded. Forsyte blinked his agreement.

Brin took the crystal away from his face. "Such a useful resource. Infinite in capability if not in supply." He raised one eyebrow as he glanced over at Roth. "See? I told you they'd come. Galen is much more resourceful than you give him credit for."

Roth struggled to respond to Brin, his voice strangled as if someone held him by the throat. "Don't be a fool. You've felt the tremors. You know what's at risk."

Brin gestured sharply with his free hand and Roth gagged, then became mute.

Brin admonished Sword as he patted the two black cases on the stone tabletop. "You caused a bit too much confusion at the crystal shop. So when I saw Tomas leaving your enclave with all this glitter, I availed myself of the opportunity to appropriate it again."

Sword wondered how Brin had 'seen' Tomas Roth leaving his Loft. *But then*, Sword thought, *it wasn't the first time that my brother has known where I've been and what I've been doing.* If there were limits to Brin's magic — and Sword knew there must be — he had yet to discover them.

"And since it's been so long since Tomas and I have had a chance to talk," Brin continued, "I took advantage of the situation. But then, that's what I always do, isn't it, Tomas?"

Roth grunted in reply, obviously unable to say anything more. Whatever kind of enchantment Brin had used to subdue and hold such prisoners as Roth, Morgana, and Diandra, it had to be very powerful indeed.

JUDITH & GARFIELD REEVES-STEVENS

Brin's next words suggested mindreading might not be beyond him either. "Tomas is able to talk, Galen. It's just that he knows he is only permitted to talk about certain subjects." He shook a chastising finger at Roth. "Such as why he was planning on joining his line with Morgana's."

Roth noisily gulped in air, then said in a rush, "I was to bind with Morgana to unite Arkady and Pendragon. Think of it! Two greater clans aligned in Council, with — "

Brin cut off Roth with a movement of his finger. "With Morgana's brat as Victor of Pendragon? That would never have done." Brin raised both eyebrows at Sword. "But then, you stopped that plan by cutting little Seth in two in a one-way fardoor, didn't you, brother?"

The floor shook with another tremor. Crates toppled; the stacked tables and chairs slid into disarray. Only Orion's coldblasted form held steady as a deep grinding noise erupted from the surrounding stone walls of the cavern and a metallic squealing poured forth from the disk.

Automatically, Sword's eyes had gone to the disk and discovered that, this close, it was in fact transparent. Ko's quick intake of breath told Sword she was as startled as he by the mysterious artifact. The disk segment itself was like a glass cap set over an underground spring, allowing water to rise within it, only to force the fluid down again. Within the clear depths of that liquid, the currents coiled and twisted tendrils of dark silt and other fine debris caught in their turbulence.

Then Sword's attention turned back to Roth as the elemental moaned and managed to croak out a barely audible plea. " ... we have to stop it, Brin ... in David's name ... "

But Brin was studying Sword. "He's becoming quite boring. Perhaps *we* should talk, brother. I'm sure we can find a subject of mutual interest." He smiled at Ko.

Sword had a thousand questions but he remained silent.

"What, no curiosity at all?" Brin said after a moment. "Nothing more you want, or need, to know?"

"What I want is Orion restored and Roth and Morgana turned over to me," Sword said. "Then I'll let you and Diandra go."

Brin laughed out loud with real pleasure. "We're in the very heart of Core Pendragon and you say *you'll* let *us* go? I love it, Galen. I love it. I see that wearing mother's ring hasn't completely ruined your sense of humor. Even if it has robbed you of a certain spontaneity."

The sudden insight was like a sunrise. Sword let his shotgun swing back under his coat. He ripped the gold clan ring from his finger. Why hadn't he thought of it earlier? The proprietor at the crystal shop had as much as told him the truth. "Light's finest," she had said after tasting the ring. It was *enchanted*. It was how Brin had always seen what was happening. How Brin had always known where to be.

Sword flung the ring to the stone floor and crushed it beneath his heel. A flurry of sparks slipped out from under his boot and sped off toward the distant stalagmite pillars — the escaping Lights of enchantment.

"About time," Brin said. "I was beginning to wonder if you would ever catch on."

Ko swore as she stared accusingly at Brin with what Sword knew had to be her first real understanding of just what role she herself had played in this conflict between the two brothers. *Poor Melody. As if one Sword hadn't been bad enough for her to cope with.*

Sword brought his gun out again. He leveled it at Brin. "You should go now," he ordered. "I'll take care of the rest."

Brin shook his head. "Brother, brother." He nodded his head at the disk. "First, a blast from that thing would damage the wellhead, and I know that somewhere in your memories you understand what that would mean. What could happen to us all if the living waters were released without the proper exclusions and treaties." Sword let his eyes flick back to the transparent disk. He caught his breath. For an instant, the chaotic trails of silt and debris had coalesced into a form that was almost human in shape, only to dissolve again into a froth of random particles.

"And second," Brin went on as if something impossible had not just manifested itself among them, "haven't you asked yourself just how it comes to be that these three are sitting together in such apparent friendship? Even more remarkable, that they haven't yet decided to leave, or to kill me?" He sneered at Morgana. "Because I know you'd like to, wouldn't you?"

JUDITH & GARFIELD REEVES-STEVENS

Sword shifted a step to the side so the edge of the liquid-filled disk was no longer directly behind Brin, then thumbed back the hammer on the right barrel of his gun.

"I said you should go now," Sword repeated.

Brin sighed. He looked down at the creature arranged loosely against the base of the stone table. "Harmonious Ka, it seems it's time to say hello to our guests."

Ko took a step back and raised her own gun. Forsyte reversed his chair to get a better look at this next representative from Sword's world. Martin edged back as well, growling, when the creature slowly raised its enormous head, fluttered its extravagant eyelashes at him, and belched loudly.

It was then that Sword recognized it as a type of troll by its large, and almost human eyes. The rest of the creature, however, was new to him, with shockingly thin limbs beneath an iridescent, partially-feathered, chitinous exoskeleton.

As it swayed to its feet, the troll's body unfolded, revealing the grasping legs found in a praying mantis, which it used to seize and shake the rum bottle. The troll peered morosely at the empty glass bottle. "All gone," it said in a tremulous and sibilant double-chord voice.

"Harmonious Ka's Close trolls were wiped out in battle," Brin explained. "Quite recently in fact. A Far troll without its cadre is rather like your Professor Forsyte. No external limbs. Reduced senses. No reason to live, really. Except to help me make a point."

A bolt of red fire shot from Brin's crystal, penetrated the center of the Far troll's chest and blasted out from its back, the assault knocking the troll to the floor where red flames consumed it rapidly.

Ko dropped to her knees, gun at the ready. Martin assumed fighting stance and Forsyte activated his chair's resources should Sword need his prompt assistance.

"Notice that I didn't even have to aim," Brin said. "Now, I believe you were — "

Sword pulled the trigger. At the same instant, a halo of red energy encircled Brin. Sword's volley of silver buckshot pellets struck and were repelled in a glittering cascade from the energy screen.

306

DARK HUNTER

Brin thrust his red crystal out at Sword. "That was the stupidest thing you could have done."

"I knew you were protected," Sword said, still not taking his shotgun from Brin. His team stayed on alert, though they each seemed to understand that in this situation, he still needed to act alone. "I just wanted to get your attention."

Hesitating only for an instant, Brin shot another bolt of red fire at the spot where the Far troll had fallen.

Why did he blast the troll twice, Sword wondered, *when he clearly wanted to blast* me? He shot a quick glance at Roth, and Morgana, and Diandra but saw no answers in their eyes. So Sword came up with one himself. *Of course!*

"You can't use the power of the red crystal against me, can you," Sword said.

Brin's silence confirmed for Sword that he was right. Elation rose within him.

"Otherwise," he continued in excited discovery, "you would have coldblasted me as soon as I came out of the tunnel, or enchanted me the same way you've got Roth and the others. Hell, Brin, you would have coldblasted me three years ago, instead of making me drive my Testa Rossa up a lamppost so you could get to me in the hospital and bring back just enough of my memories to let me run interference for you."

Brin lunged forward with his crystal. "You don't believe that I — "

Sword fired again. Brin stopped abruptly, a shocked look on his face. Sword shook out the spent cartridges and reloaded before Brin's screen of red energy faded.

Sword leveled his shotgun once more. "What's the charge left in the crystal now, Brin? That's a red shield, not blue like Roth's. You're not the source of its power. Even I know it can't last forever."

Brin's lips thinned. Sword could see he was having an effect on his powerful sibling. *At last.*

"So what do you know?" Brin asked as he brandished the red crystal threateningly, this time making miniature lightning rise from it.

Sword ignored the display as if the threat were meaningless, and hoped it was. "I know that everything you've said to Melody is a lie. I know that you're certainly not trying to help me. And I know that

307

you're not trying to stop me from upsetting the Worlds, either. You've been manipulating me from the beginning — at least since the car crash. If you weren't younger than I am, I'd think you even had something to do with my exile." Once again, Sword saw himself in his family's library, a young child being prepared to be sent away forever. He saw the old wizard with the blue liquid; his father, aged and drained by the fighting fire. His mother, her stomach round with the coming of a new brother, a new sister. Once again, he heard Diandra tell him that she was born just after he was exiled, just before the fall of Pendragon and their father's death.

Sword froze. Brin and his crystal threat forgotten.

Diandra had been the child his mother carried. And their father had died before she was born. Yet here was Brin with eyes just like their mother's.

"You *healed* me," Sword said to his brother as at last he understood. "You used your blue power."

Brin understood as well and did not deny his brother's accusation. "Like father, like son," he said.

Roth. His father's advisor. Pendragon's betrayer. The elemental adept with the metabolism of magic and the one blue power that set the line of Roth apart from all others.

Brin's line.

Brin's father.

Sword swung the shotgun toward Roth. "Where's my mother?"

Brin gestured and Roth's lips parted in a contemptuous sneer. "Your mother breathes with gills, Little Galen."

Brin's firebolt destroyed Sword's gun before he could pull the trigger. But it wasn't enough to stop him. He waved his team back as he flung the charred weapon to the floor and threw himself at Roth.

At the last second, he saw Diandra give the merest signal, the slightest warning. And because she did nothing else, Sword reared back before he impacted Roth. His hand went out to test the apparently empty air between the elemental and himself, then snapped back as a powerful shock singed his fingertips. Some force other than crystal was holding Brin's three captives in place.

Sword wheeled back to his brother "*Everything* you do is a lie. You didn't destroy my shotgun to save Roth. He's already protected by this ... this clear screen, or whatever it is. You did it so I wouldn't shoot at *you* anymore and drain your crystal."

"You're getting tiresome, brother."

"*Half*-brother," Sword corrected. "Who are you doing this for? It's not for Arkady. And never for Pendragon. Is it the Seyshen?" He studied his half brother for a moment. "But then why would that Seyshen have tried to kill Roth in the Loft when you could do it so much more easily? By keeping it in the family."

Brin stared back at him contemptuously. "The Seyshen are beneath consideration. They have no power except confusion. They want nothing more, and expect nothing less."

"Then who are you working for?"

"I work for no one."

"If that were true, Brin, then you'd be Victor of Pendragon, *beholden* to no one. But someone's prevented you from doing that, haven't they?"

Another tremor shook the cavern. The lights overhead swayed. The living water in the wellhead bubbled, frothing. Roth moaned and Morgana hissed. Behind him, Sword heard Martin oohing nervously. Neither Ko nor Forsyte made a sound.

"*You* should go now, brother. While you can."

"And if I don't?"

Brin gripped his crystal with both hands. "Then you will join Harmonious Ka."

But he's lying again, Sword thought. *It's all been lies. Everything he has ever said to me, to Ko, everything. Even this.* He took a step toward Brin.

"No closer," Brin warned. "This crystal is charged to kill."

"Perhaps," Sword said. "But not me." Motioning to his team to keep back, he took another step forward. In the same instant, red fire blasted the floor at his feet, shattering black stone, spraying sparks. Undeterred, Sword advanced on Brin.

"Morgana warned Roth against using red power on me," he told his brother. "At the crystal shop, the same thing happened."

JUDITH & GARFIELD REEVES-STEVENS

Brin stumbled back, struck a chair and knocked it over. A streak of red lightning flew wild but came nowhere near Sword. "I'm warning you, Galen. You can't be so foolish as to think that you're immortal."

"I'm not sure if the crystal won't work against me because it *can't* harm me, or because you are *prevented* from harming me," Sword said.

"You're mad," Brin cried out as he backed up against the smooth, glasslike wall of the wellhead disk whose snakelike curls of silt seemed to press against the inner surface, as if attempting to snare him.

"Prove me wrong," Sword said, reaching out for his brother.

Brin held the crystal over his head and the silt tentacles in the wall of water behind him suddenly pulled back. "This will still work on your companions!" he shouted.

Sword's fist lashed out and caught Brin on the jaw. The adept thudded back against the glass wall of the wellhead, dropping the red crystal. Sword caught it. It flared with red lightning as if it were set to explode in his hands —

And then its fire flickered, ebbed to ember, faded into darkness.

Sword's fingertips tingled, but that was all he felt.

"Maybe so," he said to Brin. "But your timing was off."

Brin sank unconscious to the floor, a thin trickle of blood at the corner of his mouth, the back of his white shirt soaked, as if there had been no barrier between him and the waters coursing through the wellhead.

Sword dropped the dead crystal beside his half-brother, then turned back to free the others.

But his timing was off, too. They were already free.

DARK HUNTER

THIRTY-THREE

The instant Brin lost consciousness, the clear screen holding his captives lost its power. And before Sword could turn to see what kind of disturbance would result from their release, a shimmering coil of silver wire bound Roth to Morgana. *Diandra.*

Sword saw his sister opening the two black cases on the stone table. He gestured to Martin to keep watch over Brin, and set Ko and Forsyte to tearing off the shipping and customs documents from the sides of as many shipping crates as they could in hopes they could begin tracking the complex web of commerce that joined the First and Second Worlds. Then he sought out his sister.

He watched as Diandra methodically and quickly transferred wrapped stacks of hundred-dollar bills from each of the black cases into a thin pocket on the leg of her shadowsuit. The pocket appeared to remain empty no matter how many stacks she put in.

"Your fee," Sword said, glancing pointedly at Orion's rigid, glowing form. "Why?"

Diandra chose not to answer. Suddenly Sword found himself longing to reach out to her, to feel flesh and bone that shared its heritage with his.

As if reading his thoughts, his sister said, "Don't touch me." She closed the empty cases and turned to him. "Nothing has changed. A

311

year ago you had no family and you have no family still. Pendragon is gone. Nothing can be as it was. It's too late."

"Why?" Sword asked again. But any response she might have given him was submerged in deep, pulsating groans as the mountain above them shuddered in the grip of the most powerful tremor yet. Liquid frothed and surged violently in the wellhead disk in time to rhythmic metallic squealing.

"Hunter!" Roth screamed over the roaring din. "You have your vows! You *must* let us go! It's coming closer!" Sword grabbed for the stone table as the floor continued to roll. Unlike the earlier ones, this tremor was continuing to grow in strength and a deafening crack like thunder rumbled through the cavern. "What vows, Diandra?"

"The vows of the hunt." Diandra deftly caught the two cases before they fell from the table, then placed them at her feet. "I can take no sides in matters of the Council."

"Not even for Pendragon?"

"There *is* no Pendragon. Not for any of us. Not anymore."

Far off by the carved stalactites, a huge plume of dust erupted from the ground-covering haze. The living waters of the wellhead disk abruptly clouded with an explosion of silt.

"Now, hunter! Or you'll be lost as well!" Roth thundered.

Diandra raised her arm as she called back, "Agreed!" The silver handle of the wire that bound Roth and Morgana jumped into the catapult tube in Diandra's waiting hand. "But you will take no action against my brother."

"Which one?" Roth growled. The last of the silver wire uncoiled from him and Morgana and returned to the dark hunter.

Sword stared in fascination as the catapult tube seemed to melt into his sister's shadowsuit.

"*Nor* his companions," Diandra warned. "Now call your wizards and do what you must."

With one hand, Roth seized Morgana's arm to keep her from attacking Diandra. With his other hand, he began to trace rapid, complex patterns in the air until a shimmering silver disk appeared and a wizard's face formed in it.

A roiling cloud of dust billowed across the cavern floor.

Sword broke out of his almost mesmerized state, shouted for Martin and Ko and Forsyte, who had been similarly affected and now reacted instantly. Martin was first to reach Sword's side, dragging Brin's inert, limp form behind him.

Sword pointed to the moving dust cloud. "Is that what's causing quakes?" he demanded of Diandra.

Her answer shocked him. "You are the cause, Little Galen."

"Don't be ridiculous," Ko snorted. "No matter where this mountain actually is located, gravity feels the same. That means we can assume your First World has the same approximate mass as our Earth. And that means these tremors are hitting at least six point five on the — "

"Instruct her to be silent," Diandra said as she knelt down to swiftly wrap an impossibly thin black strap around one of the two black cases. "This *is* the Earth. The same world as yours."

In some way he could not explain to himself, and did not challenge, Sword sensed the practiced lie in Diandra's voice. "Then how did I cause all this?" He threw out his hand toward the dust storm that was almost upon them.

"By making the halfling reopen the fardoor!"

Martin bared his teeth and growled bravely at the dark hunter. Sword put a reassuring hand on the halfling's shoulder.

"Creating a fardoor passage is child's play, Galen." Diandra swung the case over her back and it stuck to her as if magnetized. "Keeping the portals in phase is the job of skilled wizards. Crystals must be aligned. Orbits computed and the motions of the worlds corrected for — "

"Hey," Ko interrupted, "I thought you said — "

"She's right, Ko!" Sword stared into the dust cloud, noticing for the first time that its bottommost tip made contact with the cavern floor in an area no more than a few feet across. *An area that was just about the same size as* — "The fardoor opening we came through! Martin said it was unbound but ... I thought that meant it would only drift across the wall ... "

"You thought ... " Diandra said. "Do you see now what happens when one world intrudes upon the other?"

"WHAT HAPPENS HUNTER?" Forsyte's voder asked Diandra. The physicist's keen eyes met Sword's. "WHAT IS GOING ON OUT THERE?"

JUDITH & GARFIELD REEVES-STEVENS

Diandra pulled her hair back and tightly retied it, preparing for action. She gave a respectful nod to Forsyte and honored his question with a full answer. "Fardoor portals must always be the exact same size so that no leakage occurs into the dimensional realm through which the passage is formed. By not using crystal to fix the alignment of the doors, the perimeters of the two portals have become deformed by tidal forces that ... you have no knowledge of. As the portal drifts, mass is pulled into the gaps between the perimeters, and the drift becomes even more energetic."

"Like a black hole," Ko said. "The more mass it swallows, the more powerful it becomes."

"Typical Second-World prattle," the dark hunter said. "It's nothing of the kind."

Sword came to a terrifying conclusion. "Diandra ... is the other side of the door tearing through New York, like that?"

Diandra shook her head. "Of course not. *That* portal was set in crystal by Roth. Only the one that the halfling opened is unbound."

"WHERE IS THE DEBRIS GOING?"

Sword knew what the scientist had noticed. The swiftly moving fardoor portal was leaving a gouged trail of cracked and fractured rock. The volume of rock missing from that gouge was clearly too much to account for the gouts of dust and gravel now spraying up in the fardoor's wake.

But Diandra only shrugged. All her gear was stowed, the money packed, the crystals in their case. "Who knows?" she answered, stepping back from them. "Wherever a one-way fardoor goes."

Ko pushed in front of Sword to confront Diandra. "You know some way out of here! Where?!"

Diandra studied her as if deciding whether or not to speak the truth. "Away from this place, of course."

Before Diandra could turn and disappear, Forsyte's voder spoke. "WAIT. WHAT IS THIS PLACE?"

"An ancient birthing chamber ... for Tomas Roth's superstitions." Diandra's expression told Sword that she knew her response would have no meaning for any of them, nor did she intend to explain further. He saw her send a bitter glance in Roth's direction.

314

DARK HUNTER

The elemental was speaking urgently to the wizard who had appeared in the silver disk that Roth had created from the air, and gesturing frantically at the portal that was sweeping back and forth through the cavern in an almost regular oscillation, like the movement of a Foucault pendulum. With each pass, the unbound fardoor was swinging closer to the level floor of black hexagonal stones.

"Good-bye, Little Galen."

Diandra held her hands together before her and the dark fabric of her shadowsuit poured down her wrists to become gloves.

"No," Sword said. He estimated that there were only minutes remaining until he and his team would have to move back into the tunnels, though he had no idea what that would accomplish, now that there was no way back to the Second World. "I won't let you leave like this. You betrayed me in the Loft. You sold me out to get Orion. You *owe* us ... me ... for that. The whole First World — "

"I owe you nothing. The First World owes you nothing. You don't belong here. You never did." Taking hope as his sister made no move to leave, Sword pressed for more. He pointed to the vampire's blue-glowing body. "Then at least give me back Orion."

Diandra did not turn to look where he pointed. "My part of that bargain has been completed. He is not mine to give."

"He's coldblasted," Sword said accusingly. "And you know you're responsible."

Diandra remained motionless, as if waiting for some other sign from him. A sign he had no knowledge of. "He's coldblasted by crystal, Galen. Surely you know what you can do about that."

Even before his sister could complete her statement, understanding swept through Sword. "Martin! Don't let her go!"

Martin's eyes grew wide in shock at the very thought of preventing a dark hunter from doing anything she wished to do, but Sword couldn't remain to explain anything else. He was already charging across the rolling floor toward Orion.

Taking a deep breath, he placed his hands firmly on the vampire's blue glowing shoulders.

And like an inferno expiring from lack of oxygen, the blue light of the coldblast enchantment faded, flickered, and vanished. Once again,

315

and for a reason still unknown to him, Galen Sword had stolen the power of a red crystal.

Orion gasped deeply, then turned to Sword with resentful eyes. "It took you long enough to surmise what you must do, Mr. Sword." His feeding fangs shifted uneasily behind his other teeth.

"You're welcome," Sword said hotly. "There's an unbound fardoor and —"

"Really, Mr. Sword. True coldblast does not bring unconsciousness. I am fully aware of our situation."

"Then ... do something about it!" Sword raced off to join the others. Martin sighed with relief and edged away from the dark hunter who had not moved in her brother's brief absence. Ko and Forsyte regarded Sword with concern, but let him take the lead. They were in his world now.

Sword wasted no time asking his next question of his sister. "Are Roth's wizards going to be able to stop the door?"

Diandra looked past him and he followed her gaze. Three small fardoor perimeters had opened in the stone floor near Roth's floating silver disk. The top ends of aluminum ladders protruded from each portal. A short, pink-skinned wizard with a mass of curly white hair stepped off one ladder, clad in an apron of robin's egg blue. Another wizard carrying a gunnysack climbed up directly behind him. Roth was calling in reinforcements to deal with the unbound fardoor that was now raging toward the towering wooden wall.

The scaffolding around the wall had already collapsed from the churning of the cavern floor and Sword could hear the creaking and groaning of the wall's wooden planks as they ground against one another. The deep rhythmic clanging of the disk of the wellhead was almost continuous now, as well, reminding Sword in a way of the sound that 'Bub's clear crystal made when it was struck.

Diandra was emotionless. "It would be best if they did not."

"But you didn't stay to tell me that, did you?"

Ko pulled at Sword, uncharacteristically rattled and nervous. Sword realized that both Ko and he had changed while in the realm of the First World, and he hoped he'd have a chance to learn why. "Sword, we've got to get moving."

Sword looked down at Forsyte. "CLOSER WITH EACH PASS," the voder said. At the physicist's side, Martin nodded emphatically.

"Okay," Sword said. "Adrian, start heading for the tunnel we came in by. Martin, you stay with Adrian and — "

"The tunnel will be a deathtrap," Orion's voice said behind them. The vampire appeared to have no trouble keeping his balance as the floor bucked with a near miss of the careening unbound portal. His bare chest was already caked with dust but the nightfeeder did not sweat in the cavern's heat as the others did. "That is the fardoor that you arrived through?" he asked.

"And it's about to take us away again real fast," Ko said.

Orion looked pleased. "Ah, I'm glad to see that you have also concluded what must be done for us to return to your Loft." He turned to Forsyte and with three rapid movements ripped apart the canvas strips and tape that held the physicist in his chair. "I will take care of Dr. Forsyte." The vampire paused a moment to track the movement of the fardoor as it thundered toward the wooden wall. "At the rate at which it is travelling, Mr. Sword, we have fewer than than two hundred seconds until it returns."

"And does what?" Ko demanded.

Orion gathered Forsyte in his arms exactly as Sword remembered holding Ja'Nette's body, like a sleeping child. "And returns us to your home," Orion said, then carried Forsyte toward the edge of the floor.

"He wants us to jump into that thing?" Ko sputtered.

"Will that work?" Sword asked Diandra.

During all of Orion's speech to them, Sword had noticed that his sister had averted her gaze from the vampire. She continued to do so now. "Provided," she warned, "you do not come in contact with the perimeter. Which will be difficult to avoid given the speed at which the portal is moving. Perhaps a nightfeeder's reflexes will be quick enough. Perhaps not."

"Any other way back?"

Diandra looked over to where Roth and Morgana were helping a dozen wizards spread out lengths of uninsulated copper wire studded by gleaming red crystals. "That would be up to Roth and his wizards," she said.

"Then we don't have a choice."

"No, not you," Diandra said as she moved toward Orion, still taking care not to look at him directly.

Suppressing his curiosity with difficulty, Sword directed Martin and Ko to join Orion where he stood at the edge of the stone floor, a few feet up from the cavern's natural floor. "Still take Brin?" Martin asked, holding up the unconscious adept's limp leg.

"You cannot trust him," Diandra said briskly. "Leave him for Roth. They have unfinished business."

Wondering if he would regret the decision, Sword nodded at Martin to leave Brin where he was.

"You two go ahead," Sword said. He hadn't finished with his sister. After a split second's hesitation, Ko and Martin ran off to join Orion and Forsyte.

"Orion said the tunnels are a deathtrap," Sword urged Diandra. "Come with us."

A ten-foot hole suddenly exploded out of the wooden wall as the unbound fardoor made contact with it. Roth cried out as the hole climbed up the wall, splintering it asunder.

Orion shouted to him as the roar of destruction filled the cavern. "Ninety seconds, Mr. Sword!"

"No," Diandra said. "This is my world."

"But not mine?"

Diandra put her hand firmly on his arm. "Perhaps someday it can be. But not as you might think." Then, against his will, she propelled him forward, past the wild eddies of silt and froth that clouded the disk of living water, toward the vampire and his team.

"You must leave with the others, Galen. Once the wizard's constrain the unbound door, not even I will be able to keep Roth from going after you. And when you get back, you *must* have a counter put an exclusion chant on your Loft so that no other fardoors can open within it. An *exclusion* chant. Orion can tell you what must be done."

"Wait," Sword protested. "How can this be my world again? You have to tell me."

Diandra stopped a few feet from Orion and the others. She seemed to come to a decision. She lowered her voice so none but he would hear

DARK HUNTER

what she said. "The Second World is dying, Galen."

"What?" Sword realized he had expected her to speak of First-World mysticism, about the coming of an elemental warrior.

But what Diandra next told him had little to do with mysticism. "The signs are everywhere. Abuse of the biosphere, the ecology collapsing."

"Fifty seconds, Mr. Sword," Orion announced.

"But — "

Diandra interrupted him. "The implications are more far-reaching than anything humans have ever imagined. The interconnections of nature extend far beyond your own single world."

Her voice was low and she spoke quickly. "You don't comprehend how the First and Second Worlds are linked. Do you think it's a coincidence that more than ever the First World intrudes upon the Second? That what you call paranormal events are increasing in frequency and strength? The layer is crumbling as we watch, Galen. The Second World has become an open playground for shifters and nightfeeders without honor, even counters who release Dark Embodiments at will."

"All because the Second World is polluting its — "

"No! You see, you *don't* understand. You can't separate cause from effect, real from imaginary. Both worlds are truly the same world now. *There is no more separation!* The gargoyles have lost control. The layer has become a sieve."

"Thirty seconds, Mr. Sword!" The terrible rumble of the raging fardoor almost drowned out Orion's warning.

"I want no part of your world, Galen. In the years to come, it will disappear. It will be swallowed by the shadows between the Worlds."

Sword accepted the intensity of Diandra's feelings but he had no way to judge the truth of what she was saying. All he felt sure of was that it was important that she, as a member of his family, not give up. And he told her so.

"I have *not* given up," Diandra said. "In the First World, in Deep Forest, I have built an Ark. The animals will be safe. The plants, the insects, as much as I can rescue in the time that remains. There will be a place for you there, when you choose to recognize the inevitable. Forget

319

the errors of the past, Galen. Accept the way things must be now. It is the only way to go ahead, to continue. To save what little can be saved."

"Never," Sword said. What she asked for was impossible for him.

Diandra's only response was to push him to Orion's side. The floor now writhed as if it were alive.

"It is coming, Mr. Sword! Prepare to jump on my signal as it passes."

Sword grabbed his sister's hand. "There has to be another way!"

She leaned close to his ear. "Do you truly want to go home so badly? That you'd risk everything? Even your life?"

For Sword, that wasn't even a choice. "Yes," he cried.

Orion's voice boomed over the avalanche that reached out for them. "Prepare yourselves!"

"Then do it." she said. "Go back to our home. Disturb the bones of the past. Count the headstones. Learn what the cost of the past truly is."

Diandra pulled her hand from his.

Sword felt Martin's strong hand grip his arm as the halfling refused to risk losing his friend. He felt himself drawn closer to the edge of the stones, away from Diandra, only instants from the mad plunge that might take them back to their own world or into forever.

Sword twisted his head to stare back at sister. *But I don't know where home is!*"

With a look of scornful pity, red-gold hair streaming in the whirlwind of the unbound fardoor, surrounded by rising gales of dust and stone, Diandra called out the precious words that at last told her brother where in his world he would find what he had sought so long — the enclave of his birth.

Then, with Forsyte in his arms, Orion leapt into chaos.

Ko and Martin sprang after them.

And, at last, in a halfling's loyal and unshakeable hold, Sword joined his companions in a fall through the maelstrom that raged between the Worlds, overwhelmed by the knowledge that his long search was finally at an end.

He could go home at last.

THIRTY-FOUR

The Caribbean sun blazed down on Sword as if it, too, fought to keep him from this place.

But the sun was only a force of Second World nature and it had no chance against him.

"Is it as you remembered, Mr. Sword?" Orion asked. The vampire stood in the shadow of a crumbling wall, protected by his long coat, broad-brimmed hat, mask, and sunglasses.

Four days ago, Orion and the others had emerged from the fardoor in the Loft to find the garage filled with rubble from the unbound portal's passage through Core Pendragon. One rock had smashed through Sword's beloved Porsche like a missile. But Sword hadn't cared. Even as he and the others continued to be racked by coughs to clear their lungs of dust, and were chilled by the sudden transition from near-tropical heat to an autumn night, Sword had placed his call to the Foundation's travel agency to book passage to what Diandra said had been the Sword enclave. Sword had been surprised when Orion had expressed his desire to join them on their journey.

The vampire kept his hands thrust deeply in his pockets and his eyes averted from the brilliant sky. He was in dark contrast to the sunbleached ancient stones behind him, a crumbling wall overgrown with lush vines and alive with buzzing insects, though Orion had told

JUDITH & GARFIELD REEVES-STEVENS

Sword that neither attribute of Second World life was disguise enough to hide the fading influence of the working crystals that had been employed in the wall's construction. Orion had even detected lingering crystal in the scorched dry rocks and soil that once had been the perfect gardens that Sword had played in as a child.

Sword closed his eyes to better focus on his memories. Where Orion stood now had been, he thought, the library of his family's enclave, lit by floating facets, the last place he had seen his mother and the dying warrior his father had become.

Sword opened his eyes and kicked at the windblown earth that had begun to erase the foundations of this enclave's buildings, hiding what little still remained intact after the ferocious battle that had been fought here.

As he replied to Orion's question, Sword's voice was hushed. "In small ways, it's the same. The shape of the hills to the south. The path the dried-up streambed follows through what used to be the grove." Sword looked away from the ruins, to the beach where Martin splashed, and Ko — protected in the shade of the brightly-colored umbrella attached to Forsyte's chair — took photographs of what she hoped was the layer. It was strong here, Martin told them. It barely moved at all as it stretched to the north-eastern horizon. Martin had also said the east pole was in that direction, though not even Orion knew what he meant by that.

"But there's so much more here than I remember," Sword told the vampire. "The grounds are bigger. More buildings. And fortifications everywhere ... Why were they here in the Second World? Why so many? I remember so little, Orion. So little about my beginnings."

"I remember nothing of mine," Orion replied. He had explained to Sword about the confused mass of lives he contained, the spirits of the prey he had consumed over the centuries, each calling out for recognition, continually assaulting and eroding the boundaries of his own intellect and identity.

"But that is your nature," Sword said. He wiped at his forehead with a handkerchief. The midday heat was intense, almost as bad as in the cavern at Pendragon's Core. He wondered how Orion could survive the weight of his protective clothing.

DARK HUNTER

"Perhaps it is also your nature as well," Orion said.

"I can't accept that. This used to be a paradise."

"To the mind of a child."

Sword gazed out across the vista of his home. A Second World home. Not a First World home. *Why?* Sword thought. *Why did my family not live in the world to which they were born? Why here?*

"They are returning from the beach," Orion said, without looking to verify what his other senses must have told him.

Sword watched Ko and Forsyte making their way back to the ruins. Beside them, Martin loped up the gentle rise, stopping once to shake the water from his fur in a cascade of brilliant droplets.

The image made Sword remember Martin as he had appeared when the Lights in Central Park had surrounded him. He had looked much the same. *Except for his eyes,* Sword thought. *There are more secrets to be uncovered about Martin, as well as about my family's role in both the Worlds.* So many questions stretched out before him, but he felt certain that each would be answered in time.

Ko carried one of the First-World viewers she had constructed with the tiny fragments of viewing planes from the World Plaza pyramid and a modified StarBrite light intensifier. Her first prototype had produced blurry double images of New York's skyline overlaid on the enigmatic structures of the North Shore. Ko hoped that her new version would allow higher resolution under the brighter and more direct sunlight of the Leeward Islands.

But she carried something else in addition to the viewer. Something smaller, held in one hand. Sword went to meet her. Orion remained in the shadows.

Sword met his team halfway between the ruins and the Atlantic ocean, and Ko dropped the object she carried into Sword's hand. "Martin found it on the beach," she said.

It was a translucent, softly rounded triangular shape, no thicker than a dozen sheets of paper, no larger than a folded-in-half dollar bill. It was the dull yellow-white color of discarded skin.

Sword held it to the sky. He thought he had seen others like it, but never so large. "Is it a scale of some sort?" *If it is, then the snake it's from must have been gigantic.*

323

"Martin says it's a Tarl scale," Ko said.

"What's a Tarl?"

"Tarl David first Arkady Victor," Martin said. He stuck a finger in his ear and shook his head. "Long long dead. Wear his scales on robes of Victor now. For Victor's protection."

Sword remembered the iridescent robes that Morgana and Roth had worn in the Pit of the Change. He asked Martin if those were the ones he meant.

"Victor's scale," Martin confirmed. "Tarl scale protect Victor."

Sword examined the scale more closely. "So Arkady *was* here, too," he said. "And from the way this scale is weathered, they must have been here when the enclave was destroyed."

He tried to build a picture in his mind of what might have transpired on this beach, on these grounds, more than two decades earlier. An army of shifters clashing with elemental warriors? Had flames shot out from the roofs of the buildings as they were razed? Had one lone warrior struck out on his own, perhaps hiding among the escaping household trolls, carrying the screaming baby who would grow up to be Diandra to the protection of a mystical forest in another world?

And had his father died that night? Had his mother been captured? Had his line and family truly been obliterated?

And had Tomas Roth stood where Sword stood now and overseen the destruction and the carnage as the fulfillment of his plan? Or of someone else's? Or as just the start of something even more monstrous?

Sword stared at the Tarl scale, struggling to construct some image of what might have been, but he could see nothing. The past remained closed to him. He had gone as far into it as he was able and found only shadows and secrets, treachery and lies. There was nothing left for him here. There was nothing to come home to.

Sword slipped the scale into his pocket and took the heavy viewer from Ko. "Time to get back to the boat," he said.

Even Forsyte looked bewildered.

"That's it?" Ko said. "You don't find exactly what you expect and just like that it's over?"

"It's not over," Sword said. The past might be closed to him but the future remained open and waiting.

He had not found the answers he had sought so long, so there was only one thing left for him to do: Go forward to discover his own answers. Forge his own path. Create his own destiny.

It was not over yet. It couldn't be.

"It's just beginning," Sword said.

AFTERWORD
" ... shadows and secrets, treachery and lies ... "

We know what 'Bub is. We know where a one-way fardoor goes.

Where Galen must go has already been seen; what he must have has already been shown; and what he must do has already been foretold.

In other words, we aren't just making this up as we go along.

As we said in the Introduction, we knew the last line of the last Galen novel when we wrote the first line of the first Galen novel. (By now, observant readers should know it, too.)

Which leads us to The Chronicles of Galen Sword #4, #5, and #6.

True, the manuscripts aren't written. But the very detailed outlines are. How could they not be? Whatever grip Galen has on his fans, trust us, we're in it, too, and have been for a long time — the date on the first Galen material we wrote (a bible for a television series, a story in itself), is October 12, 1988.

That bible covered just about everything, and everyone. Galen's team. Roth and Morgana. The rules and specs for different types of crystals and magic. The clans. A thirty-two-page treatment for the story that became *Shifter*, complete with Seth and the Ceremony of the Change Arkady under the American Museum of Natural History. Orion was there. And so was Diandra. And Askwith and Marjoribanks — oh, that's right, you have yet to meet the reclusive Ms. Marjoribanks. We also created a four-page supplement, which we never included with the

JUDITH & GARFIELD REEVES-STEVENS

bible, which set out exactly what was going on between the First World and our world and ... well, let's just call them the "other" places.

So, to paraphrase a question we heard a few times in the past: When's #4 coming out? Not to mention #5 and #6. And #7, #8, and #9, for that matter.

All we can say right now is that we promise not to make you wait another twelve years.

After all, there's not that much time left.

Or haven't you heard?

The Tarls are coming back ...

J&G

JUDITH & GARFIELD REEVES-STEVENS are the acclaimed authors of more than twenty novels, including the Los Angeles *Times* bestselling thriller, *Icefire*, which Stephen King hailed as "the best suspense novel of its kind since *The Hunt for Red October*," and the New York *Times* bestselling thriller, *Quicksilver*, which *Publishers Weekly* called a "warp-speed technothriller with the most engaging underdog protagonists since *Jurassic Park*." They are also the authors of the groundbreaking *Star Trek* novel, *Federation*, and the epic *Deep Space Nine* trilogy, *Millennium*.

This book was designed by Lydia Marano for Babbage Press using a Macintosh G3 and Adobe FrameMaker. It was printed by LPI on 60 pound, offset cream-white acid-free stock. The text font is Minion, a Garalde Oldstyle typeface designed by Robert Slimbach in 1990 for Adobe Systems. Minion was inspired by the elegant and highly readable type designs of master printers Claude Garamond and Aldus Manutius in the late Renaissance. Created primarily for type-setting, Minion lends an aesthetic quality to the modern versatility of digital technology.

THERE IS ANOTHER WORLD

It is the birthplace of all our nightmares. Vampires, werewolves, demons, deadly creatures that have no name or form ... they are all real.

GALEN SWORD WAS BORN WITHIN THAT WORLD

Destined to be an adept warrior, heir to the Victor of the Greater Clan Pendragon. Yet as a child, his birthright and his memories were stolen from him, and he was exiled to a world without substance, without magic, without hope: Our world.

BUT TWENTY YEARS LATER

A mysterious chain of events restores Galen's memory of who he is, and hints at what he might become. Now Galen will stop at nothing to find the truth —and his home. But with no powers of his own, his only tools are those of science.

Now, for the first time, the complete SF/Fantasy crossover series
THE CHRONICLES OF GALEN SWORD

BOOK I: SHIFTER

After three years of failure, Galen Sword discovers an enclave of shapeshifters in New York City. But when he tries to infiltrate their Ceremony of the Change, the beings who exiled him from his own world exact a hideous price.

BOOK II: NIGHTFEEDER

Galen and his team are caught up in the deadly politics of the First World as the Greater Clan Seyshen provokes a war between vampires and shapeshifters that's ready to explode into the streets of New York.

BOOK III: DARK HUNTER

When Clans Tepesh and Arkady unite to destroy Galen, he must forge a dangerous alliance between the vampire, Orion, and a mysterious dark hunter with a startling secret. With them, Galen at last takes his struggle through the layer to learn the truth of his return from exile, and of an ancient monstrous enemy about to conquer both his worlds.

BABBAGE PRESS

... books you can count on

James P. Blaylock
The Digging Leviathan	1-930235-16-x	18.95
Homonculus	1-930235-13-5	17.95

Ramsey Campbell
The Height of the Scream	1-930235-15-1	18.95

Arthur Byron Cover
Autumn Angels	1-930235-12-7	TBA
The Platypus of Doom	1-930235-22-4	TBA
The Sound of Winter	1-930235-24-0	TBA
An East Wind Coming	1-930235-27-5	TBA

Dennis Etchison
The Dark Country	1-930235-04-6	17.95

Christa Faust
Control Freak	1-930235-14-3	18.95

John Farris
Elvisland	1-930235-21-6	19.95

George R.R. Martin
A Song for Lya	1-930235-11-9	17.95

William F. Nolan
Things Beyond Midnight	1-930235-09-7	17.95

Michael Reaves
The Night People	1-930235-25-9	19.95

Judith & Garfield Reeves-Stevens
Shifter	1-930235-18-6	18.95
Nightfeeder	1-930235-19-4	18.95
Dark Hunter	1-930235-20-8	19.95

David J. Schow
Crypt Orchids	1-930235-26-7	18.95
Lost Angels	1-930235-06-2	17.95
Seeing Red	1-930235-05-4	18.95
The Shaft	1-930235-29-1	TBA
Wild Hairs	1-930235-08-9	19.95

CONTINUED

JOHN SHIRLEY
Eclipse   1-930235-00-3   17.95
Eclipse Penumbra   1-930235-01-1   17.95
Eclipse Corona   1-930235-02-X   17.95
A Splendid Chaos   1-930235-23-2   TBA

JOHN SKIPP & MARC LEVINTHAL
The Emerald Burrito of Oz   1-930235-17-8   19.95

S.P. SOMTOW
Dragon's Fin Soup   1-930235-03-8   17.95
The Fallen Country   1-930235-07-0   17.95

CHELSEA QUINN YARBRO
False Dawn   1-930235-10-0   17.95

Available from your favorite bookstore or order direct. Discounted to the trade.

Babbage Press • 8740 Penfield Avenue • Northridge, CA 91324
www.babbagepress.com • books@babbagepress.com

Distributed by Ingram Book Co. and Baker & Taylor.

Printed in the United States
19988LVS00008B/85-90